ACCLAIM FOR KATHLEEN FULLER

"A warm romance that will tug at the hearts of readers, this is a new favorite."

—THE PARKERSBURG NEWS & SENTINEL
ON THE TEACHER'S BRIDE

"Fuller's appealing Amish romance deals with some serious issues, including depression, yet it also offers funny and endearing moments."

—BOOKLIST ON THE TEACHER'S BRIDE

"Kathleen Fuller's The Teacher's Bride is a heartwarming story of unexpected romance woven with fun and engaging characters who come to life on every page. Once you open the book, you won't put it down until you've reached the end."

—AMY CLIPSTON, BESTSELLING AUTHOR
OF A SEAT BY THE HEARTH

"Kathy Fuller's characters leap off the page with subtle power as she uses both wit and wisdom to entertain! Refreshingly honest and charming, Kathy's writing reflects a master's touch when it comes to intricate plotting and a satisfying and inspirational ending full of good cheer!"

—KELLY LONG, NATIONAL BESTSELLING
AUTHOR, ON THE TEACHER'S BRIDE

"Kathleen Fuller is a master storyteller, and fans will absolutely fall in love with Ruby and Christian in The Teacher's Bride."

—RUTH REID, BESTSELLING AUTHOR OF A MIRACLE OF HOPE

"*The Teacher's Bride* features characters who know what it's like to be different, to not fit in. What they don't know is that's what makes them so loveable. Kathleen Fuller has written a sweet, oftentimes humorous, romance that reminds readers that the perfect match might be right in front of their noses. She handles the difficult topic of depression with a deft touch. Readers of Amish fiction won't want to miss this delightful story."

—KELLY IRVIN, BESTSELLING AUTHOR OF
THE EVERY AMISH SEASON SERIES

"Kathleen Fuller is a talented and a gifted author, and she doesn't disappoint in *The Teacher's Bride*. The story will captivate you from the first page to the last with Ruby, Christian, and engaging characters. You'll laugh, gasp, and wonder what will happen next. You won't want to miss reading this heartwarming Amish story of mishaps, faith, love, forgiveness, and friendship."

—MOLLY JEBBER, SPEAKER AND AWARD-WINNING
AUTHOR OF *GRACE'S FORGIVENESS* AND THE
AMISH KEEPSAKE POCKET QUILT SERIES

"Enthusiasts of Fuller's sweet Amish romances will savor this new anthology."

—*LIBRARY JOURNAL* ON *AN AMISH FAMILY*

"These four sweet stories are full of hope and promise along with misunderstandings and reconciliation. True love does prevail, but not without prayer, introspection, and humility. A must-read for fans of Amish romance."

—*RT BOOK REVIEWS*, 4 STARS, ON *AN AMISH FAMILY*

"Evoking a simpler time, when letters were handwritten and partially narrated in an epistolary style, Fuller's . . . first volume in a new series introduces two charismatic protagonists and an appealing, heartwarming story line. With elegantly clear prose and evocative settings, the author delivers another captivating read fans will relish."

—*LIBRARY JOURNAL* ON *WRITTEN IN LOVE*

"Fuller's inspirational tale portrays complex characters facing real-world problems and finding love where they least expected or wanted it to be."

—*BOOKLIST*, STARRED REVIEW, ON *A RELUCTANT BRIDE*

"Fuller has an amazing capacity for creating damaged characters and giving insights into their brokenness. One of the better voices in the Amish fiction genre."

—*CBA RETAILERS + RESOURCES* ON *A RELUCTANT BRIDE*

"This promising series debut from Fuller is edgier than most Amish novels, dealing with difficult and dark issues and featuring well-drawn characters who are tougher than the usual gentle souls found in this genre. Recommended for Amish fiction fans who might like a different flavor."

—*LIBRARY JOURNAL* ON *A RELUCTANT BRIDE*

"Sadie and Aden's love is both sweet and hard-won, and Aden's patience is touching as he wrestles not only with Sadie's dilemma, but his own abusive past. Birch Creek is weighed down by the Troyer family's dark secrets, and readers will be interested to see how secondary characters' lives unfold as the series continues."

—*RT Book Reviews*, 4 stars, on *A Reluctant Bride*

"Kathleen Fuller's *A Reluctant Bride* tells the story of two Amish families whose lives have collided through tragedy. Sadie Schrock's stoic resolve will touch and inspire Fuller's fans, as will the story's concluding triumph of redemption."

—Suzanne Woods Fisher, bestselling author of *Anna's Crossing*

"Kathleen Fuller's *A Reluctant Bride* is a beautiful story of faith, hope, and second chances. Her characters and descriptions are captivating, bringing the story to life with the turn of every page."

—Amy Clipston, bestselling author of *A Simple Prayer* and the Kauffman Amish Bakery series

"The latest offering in the Middlefield Family series is a sweet love story with perfectly crafted characters. Fuller's Amish novels are written with the utmost respect for their way of living. Readers are given a glimpse of what it is like to live the simple life."

—*RT Book Reviews*, 4 stars, on *Letters to Katie*

"Fuller's second Amish series entry is a sweet romance with a strong sense of place that will attract readers of Wanda Brunstetter and Cindy Woodsmall."

—*Library Journal* on *Faithful to Laura*

"Well-drawn characters and a homespun feel will make this Amish romance a sure bet for fans of Beverly Lewis and Jerry S. Eicher."

—*LIBRARY JOURNAL* ON *TREASURING EMMA*

"*Treasuring Emma* is a heartwarming story filled with real-life situations and well-developed characters. I rooted for Emma and Adam until the very last page. Fans of Amish fiction and those seeking an endearing romance will enjoy this love story. Highly recommended."

—BETH WISEMAN, BESTSELLING AUTHOR OF *HER BROTHER'S KEEPER* AND THE DAUGHTERS OF THE PROMISE SERIES

"*Treasuring Emma* is a charming, emotionally layered story of the value of friendship in love and discovering the truth of the heart. A true treasure of a read!"

—KELLY LONG, AUTHOR OF THE PATCH OF HEAVEN SERIES

WRITTEN IN LOVE

OTHER BOOKS BY KATHLEEN FULLER

THE AMISH BRIDES OF BIRCH CREEK NOVELS

The Teacher's Bride

The Farmer's Bride

The Innkeeper's Bride

THE AMISH LETTERS NOVELS

Written in Love

The Promise of a Letter

Words from the Heart

THE AMISH OF BIRCH CREEK NOVELS

A Reluctant Bride

An Unbroken Heart

A Love Made New

THE MIDDLEFIELD AMISH NOVELS

A Faith of Her Own

THE MIDDLEFIELD FAMILY NOVELS

Treasuring Emma

Faithful to Laura

Letters to Katie

The Hearts of Middlefield Novels

A Man of His Word

An Honest Love

A Hand to Hold

Story Collection

An Amish Family

Amish Generations (available June 2020)

Stories

A Miracle for Miriam included
in *An Amish Christmas*

A Place of His Own included
in *An Amish Gathering*

What the Heart Sees included in *An Amish Love*

A Perfect Match included in *An Amish Wedding*

Flowers for Rachael included
in *An Amish Garden*

A Gift for Anne Marie included in
An Amish Second Christmas

A Heart Full of Love included
in *An Amish Cradle*

A Bid for Love included in *An Amish Market*

A Quiet Love included in *An Amish Harvest*

Building Faith included in *An Amish Home*

Lakeside Love included in *An Amish Summer*

The Treasured Book included
in *An Amish Heirloom*

What Love Built included in
An Amish Homecoming

A Chance to Remember included
in *An Amish Reunion*

Melting Hearts included in *An
Amish Christmas Bakery*

WRITTEN IN LOVE

AN AMISH LETTERS NOVEL

Kathleen Fuller

ZONDERVAN

Written in Love

Copyright © 2017 by Kathleen Fuller

This title is also available as an ebook.

Requests for information should be addressed to:
Zondervan, *3900 Sparks Dr. SE, Grand Rapids, Michigan 49546*

ISBN 978-0-7180-8252-9 (trade paper)
ISBN 978-0-7180-8253-6 (e-book)
ISBN 978-0-310-35992-0 (mass market)

Library of Congress Cataloging-in-Publication Data
CIP data is available upon request.

Printed in the United States of America

20 21 22 23 24   QG   10 9 8 7 6 5 4 3 2 1

To my husband James. I love you.

Glossary

ab im kopp: crazy, crazy in the head
ach: oh
aenti: aunt
appeditlich: delicious
bruder: brother
bu/buwe: boy/boys
daag/daags: day/days
daed: father
danki: thank you
dawdi haus: smaller home, attached to or near the
    main house
Dietsch: Amish language
dochder: daughter
dumm: dumb
dummkopf: idiot
Englisch: non-Amish
familye: family
frau: woman, Mrs.
geh: go
gut: good
gute nacht: good night
haus: house
kaffee: coffee
kapp: white hat worn by Amish women

kinn/kinner: child/children
maedel: girl/young woman
mamm: mom
mann: Amish man
mei: my
mudder/mutter: mother
nee: no
nix: nothing
onkel: uncle
schee: pretty/handsome
schwesters: sisters
seltsam: weird
sohn: son
vatter: father
ya: yes
yer: your
yerself: yourself

CHAPTER 1

November 2

Dear Mr. Chupp,

    Your letter was accidentally sent to my house. I didn't open it but I thought it might be something important and you would want it back.

Sincerely,

Phoebe Bontrager

November 4

Dear Ms. Bontrager,

    Thank you for returning my letter. That was very kind of you. Looks like I accidentally wrote the wrong zip code.

Sincerely,

Jalon Chupp

November 6

Dear Jalon,

    I'm glad you received your letter and I hope you

were able to send it to the right address. Sometimes the mail gets very messed up in this small town.

Sincerely,

Phoebe

P.S. I debated whether to send this to you. Maybe you didn't want to hear from me again. If that's the case, please let me know. Or if you don't write back, I'll know.

P.P.S. I assume by your name you're Amish. I am too. I guess you figured that out, though.

November 8

Dear Phoebe,

I didn't mind hearing from you. Actually, it was kind of nice.

Sincerely,

Jalon

P.S. Yes, I'm Amish.

November 10

Dear Jalon,

Thank you for writing me back. I hope you won't think I'm being too forward in sending you another letter. I'm visiting my aunt in Dover and it's nice to get mail. I'm not sure how long I'll be here. I do miss

my home and my family but my aunt is taking good
care of me.

Sincerely,
Phoebe

November 13

Dear Phoebe,
Are you sick? Is that why you're staying with your
aunt? I hope you are doing well.

Sincerely,
Jalon

November 15

Dear Jalon,
When I said she was taking care of me, I meant we
were helping each other. She's not as young as she used
to be. She's actually my grandmother's sister, so she's
my great-aunt. Have you ever been to Dover? Aunt
Bertha doesn't actually live in Dover, but on the out-
skirts of it, in a very small Amish community. She's
lived here for a long time, as long as I can remember.
She never married, and since she's getting on in years, I
thought I would help her out and keep her company.
Dover is a lovely place, especially in the winter. I
remember visiting here when I was a child and how the
freshly fallen snow sprinkled all over the branches of
the tall oaks and maples. It reminded me of thick layers of sugar. In February they tap the trees for maple
syrup. Aunt Bertha doesn't have many maples on her

property, but if I'm still living here by then, hopefully we can go to the family a few streets down and help them gather the syrup. I used to gather syrup with my brothers. There are eleven of us siblings, so we make quick work of the job. I'm the oldest and I usually spend more time in the kitchen than outside, which I don't mind. We've always been blessed with plenty of syrup for pancakes and waffles through the years.

> Sincerely,
> Phoebe

P.S. It was very nice of you to ask about my health. I hope I didn't worry you. Then again, why would you be worried about me? We don't know each other all that well, although I'm enjoying getting to know you better. Wait, that might sound a little forward, and I don't mean it to be. I'm just glad someone cares, that's all. I should probably end this letter right now before I stick my foot farther into my mouth.

P.P.S. I hope you're doing well.

November 17

Dear Phoebe,

Thank you for your letter. I'm glad you're okay, and don't worry, you aren't sticking your foot in your mouth. It's nice getting to know you too. I've never had a pen pal before. I don't really like writing, to be honest. But I don't mind writing to you.

You have a lot of siblings! I have only one sister. She's a year younger than me. Where do you and your family live?

Pancakes and syrup? One of my favorite breakfasts.

Sincerely,

Jalon

November 19

Dear Jalon,

I used to wish I didn't have so many brothers. I'm twenty-three and they're all a lot younger than me. The oldest brother is Devon, and he's fifteen. I also have two sets of twin brothers. Zeb and Zeke are thirteen and Moses and Mahlon are three. The rest of my brothers fall in between the twins—Owen is fourteen, Ezra is eleven, Nelson is nine, Perry is seven, Jesse is five, and Elam is two months. They can be a pain sometimes. But now that I'm here with my aunt, I miss them. They are all busy with school, except for Devon and the baby, of course. And all the boys help my dad with the farm. We live in a small district outside Fredericktown.

I love pancakes and syrup, too, but my favorite breakfast is eggs Benedict. Have you ever had them? I don't fix them very often because they're kind of fancy, but they're a nice change from a typical breakfast. I enjoy cooking a lot, and try to do it whenever I can. I definitely know how to cook for a crowd!

Sincerely,

Phoebe

November 21

Dear Phoebe,

My father was a farmer, too, but he doesn't farm anymore. When I was a kid I used to help him, just like your brothers help your father. I liked farming when I was younger, but as I got older I didn't enjoy it as much. By the time I was fifteen I wanted a different job, so I've been doing construction ever since. I think I'm more suited to using a hammer and nails than I am a plow and hoe.

No, I've never had eggs Benedict, but they sound interesting. It's nice that you enjoy cooking. I happen to enjoy eating.

Sincerely,

Jalon

November 23

Dear Jalon,

Do you mind if I keep writing to you? I don't want you to feel obligated to write me back.

Sincerely,

Phoebe

November 25

Dear Phoebe,

I don't feel obligated to write to you. Like I said, I like your letters. I like them a lot. I have to be honest, though. Sometimes I don't have a lot to say. I mostly just work, go to church, and keep to myself. Don't get me wrong, I'm not a hermit. I've just been working a lot of overtime lately, so it's made for a pretty dull life. Your letters are a definite bright spot.

I hope you and your aunt have a nice Thanksgiving.

Sincerely,
Jalon

November 29

Dear Jalon,

Whew! I was worried I was being a pest. Can I ask you a few questions? How old are you? Where is your construction job? What size town is Birch Creek? I've never heard of it before. I would look it up on a map but I don't get to the library very much. It's a good thing I brought some of my books from home with me. When you're not working, do you have any hobbies? One of my favorite things to do other than cooking is watching birds. Sometimes I draw them in my sketchbook. I like having the reminder of what they look like. Especially cardinals. I don't see them very often here, so when I do I like to have a picture of them, even though my drawing skills aren't great. I can't let my aunt know— she wouldn't like it if she knew I was drawing. The district here is very strict, and Aunt Bertha is even stricter. But I understand. Breaking rules brings nothing but trouble.

On second thought, maybe I should get rid of my pictures.

Phoebe

December 1

Dear Phoebe,

To answer your questions: I'm twenty-five and I've lived in Birch Creek since I was eleven. Before that I lived in Mesopotamia, which is near Middlefield. Birch Creek is about an hour's taxi ride from Canton. It isn't very big, but we've had a few more families join our district in the past couple of years. I guess you could say we're growing. Our district used to be strict, but we have a new bishop and he's relaxed a few of the rules, which is nice. I'm glad he hasn't done away with all of them, though. I agree with you that rules are important.

Right now I'm working on renovations on a library near Akron. I work six days a week most of the time, since the project is taking longer than expected and we have a deadline. I don't mind, though. I'm happy for the work. That doesn't leave much time for hobbies. I do like to fish. We have a pond near our property that's well stocked.

I really hope you haven't thrown your pictures away. That would be a shame. They're for your own use, so I don't think it's a bad thing for your aunt not to know about them. We all need something that is just our own.

Jalon

December 4

Dear Jalon,

I'm so glad you understand what I meant by keeping my drawings a secret. Growing up with so many siblings, I had to share everything—beds, toys, food. My brothers also share clothes, and at least I didn't have to share my dresses with them! Still, it's nice to have something special that belongs only to me. I hadn't thrown the pictures away yet, so I'll keep them. Maybe I'll put up a couple of birdfeeders in the backyard. That should bring a good variety of birds to visit. Thank you for encouraging me.

Phoebe

P.S. I have to be honest with you, too—I'm glad to find out you're close to my age. I was worried you might be too old or too young, but you're just right.

December 7

Dear Phoebe,

This is a first. I've never been compared to Goldilocks and the Three Bears before.

Jalon

December 9

Dear Jalon,

Very funny. What I meant was that you are the right age for our writing letters to each other. Not that age has anything to do with it. Although it would be weird if you were a lot older or younger than me. Ugh, now that I think about it, I probably shouldn't have mentioned our ages. Let's forget I brought it up. Sometimes I do or say things that are impulsive and

I'm trying to be better about that. I'd get rid of this letter and start all over, but my aunt has work for me to do this afternoon so I need to get it in the mail right away.

Phoebe

December 11

Dear Phoebe,

I'm the opposite of impulsive. My sister tells me I think too much, and that I'm too slow to make a decision. Maybe she's right. But I'm terrified of making a mistake. I've made so many in my life.

You know, I've never admitted that to anyone. Not about making the mistakes—some of those are hard to hide, and people find out about them sooner or later. But I've never told anyone about being afraid. I know God doesn't give us a spirit of fear, but sometimes it's hard to remember that, especially when you're faced with the fallout of the choices you've made. Worrying about making another mistake shouldn't get to me, but sometimes it does. Maybe one day I can throw caution to the wind and not have to rethink things over and over.

I'm glad you're a little spontaneous. We might not be writing to each other if you weren't.

Are you spending Christmas with your family in Fredericktown, or does your aunt still need you to stay with her? It's going to be a quiet Christmas here—just my sister, Leanna, and me. We'll probably go next door the day after Christmas and visit with our neighbors. I'm looking forward to the break from work.

Jalon

December 14

Dear Jalon,

I'm honored you would trust me with such a secret. And I understand about mistakes. I've made more than my fair share. I'm hoping I'm learning from them, through God's grace. He is merciful. Since you trusted me with something so important to you, I'll tell you a secret of mine—I almost didn't join the Amish church. I went through a period of time when I wasn't sure about a lot of things, including whether I wanted to remain Amish. Fortunately, I wised up and realized how much I needed my faith and my family. I love my family so much. I miss them too. I don't have any plans to see them soon, though. My aunt and I will spend Christmas here.

I hope you don't mind if I ask you another personal question. What do you look like? You don't have to tell me if you don't want to. I'm just curious. Not that I think looks matter much. A person can be beautiful on the outside but filled with ugliness, and vice versa.

Phoebe

P.S. I have a feeling you're handsome both inside and out.

December 18

Dear Phoebe,

Thanks for the compliment. I'm nothing special in the looks department. Brown hair, brown eyes, just a regular guy. I am tall, a bit over six feet. I guess that's not exactly average, but it's nothing unusual either. I hope you're not disappointed.

I agree that looks don't matter much in the long run. I've also known some of those pretty people who weren't so nice on the inside. But if I was a betting man, I would say your looks match your personality, which means you must be very pretty.

I went through a time when I wasn't sure if I wanted to join the church. I had friends who joined as soon as they turned sixteen, but I held back and didn't join until I was twenty-two. I love my family, too, but they weren't the reason I stayed. When I realized I didn't need anything but my faith, I joined the church. I don't have any regrets. Although I do miss driving a car.

Jalon

P.S. I wouldn't mind you telling me what you look like. You asked me first, after all.

December 20

Dear Jalon,

What do I look like? Well, I've got dark brown hair. It's almost black. I'm a little on the short side,

I think five foot four but it's been so long since any-one has measured I can't really remember. My eyes are blue, although my mother says they turn gray when I'm angry. I have to take her word for it. It's not like I look in a mirror when I'm mad! But overall I'm pretty plain.

You used to drive a car? I drove a car once, when I was twenty. I felt so free at the time, even though I was breaking the rules and the law. I hope you won't think less of me for that.

Phoebe

P.S. Thank you for saying I must be pretty. That made me smile.

December 22

Dear Phoebe,

I could never think less of you. Remember, I've broken plenty of rules. I promise, you can tell me any-thing and I won't judge you for it. I'm the last person on earth who has the right to judge anyone.

Leanna's decided to go visit our parents for Christmas, so it's just me here holding down the fort. We've got a few pigs along with a pair of old draft horses, plus my buggy horse. Then there's Blue, Leanna's Maine Coon cat. I guess I'll have plenty of company anyway.

Merry Christmas,
Jalon

P.S. I'm glad I made you smile.

December 27

Dear Jalon,

I'm sorry I'm late writing this letter. My aunt and I were busy finishing quilts for the other families in the district. She makes quilts for them every year, and she asked me to help. She's an expert seamstress, unlike me. I can sew a straight line and that's about it. It does take me longer and she lost patience with me a few times, but we got the quilts done and took them to the families the day after Christmas. My hands ache a little from all the sewing, but the families liked the quilts. I didn't know my aunt was so generous. She's full of surprises.

I did have some time to bake a few Christmas cookies like the ones with this letter. I hope you enjoy them.

How is work going? Are you still putting in lots of overtime? I know how important work is, but make sure you're getting plenty of rest. Also, find some time to do something fun! Obviously you can't go fishing in the winter, but surely there's something else you like to do that makes you happy.

Phoebe

P.S. I wasn't going to write this, but I changed my mind. I didn't like hearing that you were alone for Christmas. Animals are great, but they aren't Christmas company. I hope you weren't lonely. That's one of the worst feelings in the world.

January 1

Dear Phoebe,

These cookies are the best I've ever had. Seriously. You should go into the cookie baking business. My favorite ones were the candy cane sugar cookies. I was surprised they tasted a little like peppermint. I shared them with Leanna. Actually, I let her have only one, mostly so she'd stop pestering me. I wanted to savor the rest. She called me greedy, but I'm all business when it comes to food. Especially delicious food.

Anytime you want to send me cookies, go right ahead. I won't mind at all. I can pay you for them. They would be worth every penny.

I'm still working overtime, but we've had to call off a few days over the past month because of bad weather. I usually spent that time working around here. There's always something that needs to be done. My father started on a *dawdi haus* right before they moved away, so whenever I get a chance I work on that. I don't like the idea of leaving something unfinished, although my dad obviously doesn't have a problem doing that.

I did spend the day after Christmas with my neighbors, the Yoders. They have lots of kids. Not as many as your parents have, though. I had a good time.

I am doing something that makes me happy. I'm writing to you.

Jalon

P.S. I know what you mean about being lonely. Sometimes you can be surrounded by people and still feel alone.

P.P.S. If you ever get lonely, think about me.

January 3

Dear Jalon,

I'm glad you liked the cookies, but I don't think people would want to buy them. I'll bake some more and send them to you, but you don't have to pay me. They will be my gift to you. Who knows, maybe someday I could make pancakes with maple syrup for you. And don't forget eggs Benedict. I also make a delicious pizza. It's my brothers' favorite meal. They never complain when they have pizza.

Writing to you makes me happy too. I wish the mail delivered faster. I'd write to you every day if it did.

I do think about you, Jalon, and not just when I'm lonely.

Phoebe

January 5

Dear Phoebe,

I love pizza and pancakes with maple syrup. I'm sure I'd love eggs Benedict, whatever that is. If you're cooking them for me, I'm positive I'll enjoy it.

I also think about you, Phoebe. A lot. There's something else that's been on my mind too. I need to stop

rolling it around in my head and just tell you. You
know how much I like getting your letters. We've been
writing to each other for a while, and I think it's time
we met face-to-face.

I'd like to come see you in Dover, Phoebe. Let me
know when I can, and I'll be there.
                                        Jalon

January 10

Dear Jalon,

I want to meet you in person, too, but we should
wait until spring. The weather is so unpredictable in
the winter, and I wouldn't want you to get stuck . . .

· · ·

Phoebe sat back in the kitchen chair and stared at the
unfinished letter. She put her hand to her chest and felt
the pounding beneath her palm. When Jalon told her
to think about him during her lonely times, her heart
melted. Now knowing he wanted to see her, she could
barely breathe. He had no idea how badly she wanted to
meet him in person. She'd tried to keep her true feelings
from him, making sure her letters sounded casual and
friendly. Still, she'd thought—okay, she'd hoped—there
was something between them. Was this confirmation?
She wasn't sure, but that didn't dim her excitement.

Yet his asking to see her also tied her stomach in
knots. They couldn't meet in person, not yet. She had to
find a valid reason to put him off, and the unpredictable

weather seemed logical enough. Except now that she reread her response, she realized that excuse sounded thin. It wasn't as if it would snow every day. In fact, there would be plenty of clear days when Jalon could easily get to her aunt's house from Birch Creek. She already knew where Canton was, and from what he'd told her, Birch Creek was only a couple of hours away, one taxi ride away—although up until now she hadn't dared to entertain the idea of him coming to visit.

Up until now, she'd refused to think about the reason he couldn't.

The wind-up timer rang and she stood, folding the letter and putting it into the pocket of her apron to finish later. Her pulse still thrummed with thoughts of Jalon as she pulled two loaves of freshly baked bread from the woodstove and set them on top of the burners. She'd never met anyone like Jalon. Over the past couple of months they'd been writing to each other, she had fallen for him. How could she not? He was nice, something she'd known the moment she saw he had written her back, which he didn't have to do. He had a sense of humor, something she appreciated, and from the way he confessed his fear of making mistakes, she knew he was honest. *Far more honest than I am.*

She looked at the golden tops of the bread loaves, tempted to sprinkle some sesame seeds on the top, or at least a few shakes of dried parsley. But Aunt Bertha liked plain white bread. One small pat of butter, no jelly, and definitely no honey. Phoebe sniffed. At least the loaves smelled good, yeasty and fresh. She set the oven mitts on the counter and glanced at the empty wood box. She'd have to replenish the stove's wood supply so she could finish making supper.

She peeked around the edge of the kitchen doorway and saw her aunt sitting at her sewing machine in the living room, working on the mending she took in from both the Amish in her district and a few local English. With her broad shoulders, stiff posture, steel-gray hair, harsh middle part, and flinty blue eyes, there was nothing soft about Aunt Bertha. Even her mouth was little more than a slash above her chin. And if the woman ever smiled, Phoebe hadn't seen it. "Maybe you can soften her up a little while you're visiting," *Mamm* said when Phoebe announced her intention to stay with her great-aunt for a while. "Smooth out her edges, so to speak."

"Has she always been that way?" Phoebe had asked. She'd only met Aunt Bertha once before, when she and her mother visited her grandparents in Dover. Both grandparents were gone now, and *Mamm* didn't have any brothers or sisters. Bertha was the last attachment to her mother's family, except for a few distant cousins.

"As long as I can remember." *Mamm* smiled, but her smile quickly faded. The boys were outside, the older ones working with *Daed* and the younger ones playing in the backyard, which left her and her mother with a rare moment alone in the kitchen as her newest brother slept in his crib. "I wish you weren't going so far away." Her smile reappeared, a little weaker this time. "But I know it's crowded here. Of course, that's nothing new. I guess I understand that you need some time away from all the chaos."

At one time Phoebe would have agreed. Being part

of a large family meant a lot of sacrifices, something she'd resented in the past. But the size of her family wasn't the reason she had to leave home—at least not the main one, and she couldn't tell her mother what that reason was. So she let *Mamm* think she wanted to escape the pandemonium of her large family. It was easier than admitting the truth.

"You'll be back soon, *ya*?" *Mamm*'s eyes had filled with hope.

"As soon as I can." That was all she could say, and it wasn't enough. Her mother's hopeful look faded, which piled on Phoebe's guilt. But there was nothing she could do about it.

Now she was stuck here with a woman whose edges were impossibly sharp. Phoebe would know—she'd been cut by them more than once since she arrived. There was no softening Aunt Bertha. If anything, the woman was more spiteful than she'd been when Phoebe got there. Phoebe had to keep reminding herself that, despite her aunt's attitude, the woman was providing a place for Phoebe to stay. Phoebe owed it to her to follow the rules—even the ones she didn't agree with.

"I'm heading out to get some more wood," Phoebe said, forcing a cheerful tone. One requirement of her staying here was letting Aunt Bertha know her every move. Which didn't make much sense to Phoebe, since under her aunt's restrictions there weren't too many places she could go.

Aunt Bertha pushed on the pedals of her manual sewing machine and continued her task as if Phoebe hadn't spoken.

After waiting in vain for a response, Phoebe sighed, put on her coat and boots, hurried out the mudroom's back door, and went down the porch steps. Puffs of cold air blew out of her mouth as she turned and looked up at one of the bedroom windows on the top floor of the house. What was Malachi doing in his room right now? Aunt Bertha had sent him there an hour ago, after she found him peeling the white paint off one of the slats of wood siding. That had earned him two hours of confinement. Phoebe shook her head. She couldn't deny that he deserved it. He should have known better than to damage her aunt's house like that. But she didn't blame him either. He was four years old, and a precocious four-year-old at that. He was curious. And lively. And trouble, according to Aunt Bertha.

Phoebe's temples throbbed as she turned away, the snow crunching under her boots as she headed toward the woodpile. Her aunt wasn't wrong about Malachi needing more discipline. But Phoebe didn't think the constant groundings were doing him any good. There had to be a middle ground. For the life of her, she couldn't find it.

She gathered up several large pieces of cold wood and stacked them in her arms, then headed back to the house. Once she put up the wood, she'd check on Malachi, despite her aunt's dictate that he be left alone. That was one dictate she was willing to circumvent. She'd have to be careful not to get caught, though. Her aunt seemed to discover everything.

Except for one thing. So far Aunt Bertha hadn't found out about Jalon. Phoebe thought about the letter in her pocket. A postal error had ended up being a lifeline for her. When Jalon's first letter arrived by mistake, she never imagined returning the letter would start their pen pal relationship. She'd been at Aunt Bertha's for less than two weeks, and she had felt the judgment and oppression shortly after her arrival. When Jalon sent his short thank-you note in return, she'd replied on impulse. She hadn't seriously expected him to write her again, but when he did, she'd been thrilled. Having something to look forward to had kept her from being so homesick and lonely. His letters were the bright spot of her life right now.

Naturally, she had built up a mental picture of him, imagining the kindness in his eyes, the gentleness in his voice, and the way her hand would fit perfectly in his—if they ever actually met face-to-face. Seeing him in person was something she'd only dared to dream about. And now that her daydreams about him were on the cusp of coming true, she didn't know what to do. Her heart was ready to meet him, but her mind knew better. Aunt Bertha would have a conniption for sure. And how was she supposed to explain about Malachi? She hadn't mentioned him at all in any of her letters. With each new one she wrote, she thought about telling Jalon about him. How smart he was, how cute he could be when he was trying to get out of trouble, how much she loved him.

But she couldn't bring herself to do it, because if she told him about Malachi, she'd have to tell him about her past. She couldn't risk ruining what they had between them. Their relationship, as distant as it was, meant everything to her.

She opened the back door and went inside, placed the wood in the wood box, then slipped off her coat and boots. A few minutes later the stove was hot, and after washing her hands she started preparations for supper. Again, like everything in Aunt Bertha's life, the meal was both scheduled and planned. Each Monday her aunt pinned up the week's menu, which was to be followed to the letter. It didn't matter if Malachi didn't like beets or Phoebe would rather drink four-day-old coffee than buttermilk. There was no room for negotiation or compromise. Phoebe peered at today's evening meal—cabbage rolls with horseradish. She shook her head. Malachi wouldn't eat either of those. He'd always been a picky eater, but since living with Aunt Bertha he ate like a sparrow. At least he would eat the bread she'd made. She wished he'd eat more. He needed more meat on his bones.

"Make sure you roll those cabbage leaves up tight." Aunt Bertha had come into the kitchen, her silver glasses perched on the end of her nose. It was a miracle they stayed on her face.

"I will."

"I hope you didn't overwork the dough." She poked at the top of one of the bread loaves. "If you did, the bread will be tough."

Phoebe didn't respond. If there was one thing she knew how to bake it was bread. Her white bread was so light it practically floated off the plate. Still, she was sure Aunt Bertha would find something about it to criticize.

When her aunt finally left the kitchen, Phoebe let out a deep sigh and focused on making the cabbage rolls. At precisely 5:45 Aunt Bertha came back into the kitchen. "*Geh* get the *bu*," she said. "And be quick about it."

Phoebe placed the platter of lightly browned cabbage rolls and another plate with sliced bread on the table, then went upstairs. She opened the door to Malachi's bedroom, expecting to see him looking out the window or pouting on his bed. She pushed the door open a little more and smiled. He was asleep on the floor. He rarely took naps even though Phoebe often prayed he would. He hadn't slept well at night since arriving at her aunt's. At first he'd cried every night to go back home. He missed his grandmother and grandfather, and all his uncles. He missed the animals, especially Devon's horse. After a few days he'd stopped crying, but he still didn't sleep enough.

He looked so peaceful lying on the floor on his back, his cheek resting against the frayed rag rug, his arms straight on each side of his slender body. His room was empty save for his single bed and the rag rug. Aunt Bertha's house was surprisingly large for a single woman with no children—three bedrooms and an extra bathroom. Yet all the space seemed claustrophobic. Aunt Bertha insisted on keeping all the upstairs windows locked.

She also refused to let Malachi have anything interesting in his bedroom, so there was nothing for him to do there. No toys. No books. *No escape.* Although Phoebe thought it was unfair, she didn't challenge her aunt's decision.

Knowing her aunt would fuss if she dawdled too long, Phoebe knelt beside Malachi and patted his shoulder. "Malachi. Time for supper."

He moaned and turned his face away from her. That made her smile again. He had a rebellious streak a mile wide. *The apple doesn't fall far from the tree.* She patted his shoulder again a bit more firmly. "Malachi, we have to get downstairs. *Aenti* Bertha is waiting."

"Don't wanna." He didn't look at her.

"You'll like tonight's supper." A lie, but it got his attention.

He sat up. "You made pizza?"

She shook her head. Now she had a craving for pepperoni. They hadn't had pizza in so long, because Aunt Bertha didn't like pizza. "Cabbage rolls," she said, forcing a light tone.

"Ew." He crossed his arms over his narrow chest. "I don't want that."

"Phoebe! You two get down here!"

She winced at Aunt Bertha's voice. "Malachi, don't argue with me."

He pressed his lips together and shook his head. "I'm not hungry."

"But you hardly ate any of *yer* lunch." She tried to speak in a calm voice, the way her mother always did. Sometimes *Mamm* yelled, too, but only when she was furious, which wasn't often. Now that Phoebe was an adult she respected her mother's kind, firm parenting.

"I will give *yer* suppers to the pigs if you are not seated at the table in one minute," Aunt Bertha yelled.

Phoebe tried not to wilt. All that effort to make a perfect dinner and now her aunt was going to throw it away out of spite. "Coming!" she called, then turned to Malachi. "Please. Let's *geh* downstairs and eat." She didn't want to say the next words, but they came out anyway. "If you do, I'll give you two of the cookies I made yesterday."

His blond brows lifted. "We have cookies?"

Phoebe nodded. Like her sketches, cookies were also something she could have for herself. She thought about the Christmas cookies she made a few weeks ago. She'd set a few aside to send to Jalon, but she hadn't anticipated her aunt taking the rest and giving them away to the bishop's family. Not that Phoebe begrudged her aunt's generosity, but Malachi hadn't had a single cookie, even though he helped her make them. To make up for it, she'd baked a batch of Malachi's favorite sugar cookies while Aunt Bertha was out getting groceries. "*Aenti* Bertha doesn't know about them." She leaned forward. "It's our little secret, *ya*?"

"*Ya*. I like secrets." He shot up from the floor and bounded out of the room.

Phoebe said a quick, thankful prayer that he had stopped arguing with her, then followed him downstairs. When they arrived at the kitchen doorway, they both halted. Aunt Bertha was seated at the table, her eyes closed as she prayed.

Phoebe put her hands on Malachi's shoulders to keep him still. She glanced at the clock. Six on the dot. Supper always started at 6:00 p.m. Not 5:55 or 6:05. Nothing short of a natural catastrophe would knock her aunt off schedule.

Aunt Bertha opened her eyes. She turned her head slightly and glared at Malachi, then at Phoebe. They both went to the table in silence and sat down. Phoebe had just started to pick up Malachi's plate to serve him a cabbage roll when Aunt Bertha spoke.

"Do not give him too much food. It's wasted on him."

Phoebe nodded, biting the inside of her cheek to keep from saying anything. This from the woman who less than two minutes ago was ready to feed the feast to the pigs. Phoebe wanted the pigs to eat well, but not at Malachi's expense. She selected the smallest cabbage roll, placed it on the plate, and put the dish in front of Malachi. Then she picked up a slice of bread and reached for the butter.

"Cut that piece in half. And *nee* butter." Aunt Bertha narrowed her gaze at Malachi. "Butter is for *gut* little *buwe*."

"I'm a *gut bu*," Malachi said with a lift of his chin.

"Malachi," Phoebe whispered. "Don't talk back."

"I'm not talking back." He raised his voice. "I'm talking *to* her." He poked a stubby finger at Aunt Bertha. "And I want some butter." He picked up his fork and started banging it on the table.

Before Phoebe could say anything, Aunt Bertha shot up from her chair, grabbed Malachi by the ear, and yanked him off his seat. "You *will* learn manners," she hissed.

"*Aenti* Bertha, *nee!*" Phoebe cried.

Malachi wriggled, then yelled as Aunt Bertha twisted his ear harder. "Upstairs to *yer* room, and you are not to come down until breakfast."

"But I'm hungry—ow!"

Phoebe moved to stand. Aunt Bertha held up her hand, her glare forcing Phoebe to sit back down.

Aunt Bertha marched Malachi out of the kitchen and up the stairs. Phoebe heard her aunt's heavy footsteps, then the slamming of Malachi's door. She closed her eyes and could almost hear the turn of the key as Aunt Bertha locked the door.

When Aunt Bertha returned, she sat down in her seat and placed the key to Malachi's bedroom beside her plate. Upstairs Malachi wailed and pounded his fists against the door.

Phoebe's heart wrenched. "Please, *Aenti*. Can I *geh* upstairs and help him calm down?"

Her aunt placed her napkin in her lap. "*Nee*. You indulge him too much, which is why he won't listen to you."

Phoebe started to protest but closed her mouth. Despite not having any children of her own, her aunt seemed to think she was an expert. Phoebe looked down at her plate, the food she'd spent so much time preparing growing cold. She didn't care. If Malachi couldn't eat, Phoebe wasn't going to either.

She expected her aunt to force the issue, but Aunt Bertha didn't say anything. As she finished her food, Malachi's yelling ceased. She wiped her mouth on the napkin, then picked up the key and put it in the pocket of her apron. She walked out of the kitchen, leaving Phoebe to clean up and do the rest of the evening chores.

Phoebe picked up the plates, her heart hurting for Malachi. Through tears, she scraped the uneaten food into a bowl. The pigs would eat well tonight after all.

Her thoughts turned to the guilt she always carried with her. Malachi wouldn't be suffering like this if they weren't here. She wanted to see her parents, to give her brothers hugs even though the older ones wouldn't want something so mushy and sentimental. But because of her bad decisions she couldn't go back.

She touched the letter in her pocket, wondering if she was making another bad decision by not being up-front with Jalon. She could write him back and give him the real reason she was hesitant to see him. He would understand . . . wouldn't he? By his own admission he also had a past, although she was sure it was nothing compared to hers.

The more she thought about it, the more she warmed to the idea. She could tell Jalon about Malachi. He would come and visit, and she would deal with Aunt Bertha when that happened. She could finally meet the man she was falling in love with face-to-face. Wasn't that worth exposing her shame to him?

She gripped the back of a chair and shook her head. There were so many things wrong with that plan. She couldn't risk inciting Aunt Bertha's wrath for such a selfish reason. More importantly, she didn't want to lose Jalon. Not yet. *Not ever.*

She had to find a way to make peace—in this house, and with herself. She couldn't let Malachi continue to suffer.

"Lord, forgive me," she whispered, swallowing her tears. "Forgive me for being such a terrible mother."

CHAPTER 2

"You sure you don't want to come with me?"

Jalon tapped his fingers against the wood banister. He was standing next to the staircase in the living room, waiting for Leanna to leave. Keeping his gaze on his feet as if he were studying them, he said, "*Nee*. Like I said, I have lots of work to do around here."

"You could at least take a short vacation." Leanna set her suitcase near the front door, then adjusted the tie on her black bonnet. "A couple of days won't hurt. You finally got a Saturday off today."

He could use a vacation, that was true. But even if he would take one, Mesopotamia—or Mespo, as it was sometimes called—was the last place he would go. "Maybe next time." A blatant lie, one he hoped God would forgive.

"You always say that. You know *Mamm* and *Daed* would like to see you."

That statement worked to make him feel guilty, but not enough to change his mind. His fingers drummed faster. He did miss his parents, who had moved to Mespo back in May. He missed his mother especially . . . his father to a lesser extent. Harsh, but true. When they left, his father kicked the dust from Birch Creek off his feet.

"I'm tired of trying to make something of this place," *Daed* had said, stretching his arm toward the ten acres of land he had struggled to farm for almost thirteen years. "It's time *yer mamm* and I moved back to Mespo. You and Leanna are welcome to come with us."

They had both refused. Leanna told her parents Birch Creek was her home, and Jalon agreed. It was his home, too, and had been since he was eleven. But there was a stronger reason he was staying in Birch Creek, and it had nothing to do with the small town being his home. No, he wasn't going back to Mespo. Not to visit, and especially not to live.

"Jalon?" Leanna snapped her fingers in front of him. "You in there somewhere?"

He shook his head to clear his thoughts as he brushed Leanna's hand away from his face. He gave her an irritated look, able to look her straight in the eyes because of her unusual height, which was a hair over six feet. "Stop annoying me."

"Always with the witty comebacks." She laughed, and he couldn't help but chuckle because she was right. He wasn't witty. He spoke plainly and there was nothing wrong with that. Leanna, however, was quick with her tongue, sometimes a little too sharp. A quality that seemed to keep the single men in Birch Creek away. But if his sister was meant to get married, God would make it happen. As for him, he'd never had plans to find a bride.

Until now.

His mind switched gears as he thought of Phoebe. Sweet Phoebe, with her friendly letters he eagerly looked forward to. He hadn't expected for them to become pen pals, but after she responded to his note thanking her for returning his letter, he'd decided to write her back. An impulse choice that had surprised him, but ended up being one of the best decisions of his life.

Initially he thought the relationship was perfect as pen pals. She gave him the companionship he needed, but without strings attached. There had been a time when he didn't mind strings with women, mostly because he hadn't respected them. That tended to happen when alcohol was involved.

But this past year had been one of changes, all for the better. Which meant he kept his distance from the women in his district. Some of them knew of his past problem with liquor, others had heard rumors. In the end it didn't matter much, since he wasn't interested in anyone.

Then he and Phoebe started writing to each other, and his world changed. He wasn't sure exactly when that shift in their letter writing had occurred in his heart, but once it happened he couldn't turn back. He hadn't realized how lonely he'd been, and not because he stopped drinking. Sure, he had Leanna and his neighbors, the Yoders, to keep him company. He'd also recently renewed his friendship with Solomon Troyer, a former drinking buddy who was working through his own problems, fighting his own battle for sobriety.

No, his loneliness didn't stem from a lack of friends. Something was missing in his life, an emptiness Phoebe had unknowingly exposed. Maybe it had been there all along, shrouded in alcohol and guilt.

"There you *geh* again, getting lost in *yer* own thoughts." Leanna huffed and crossed her gangly arms. "You've been acting weird lately."

Jalon grabbed her suitcase and opened the door. "You don't want to miss *yer* taxi."

"It's not here yet."

He pointed outside with his thumb. She peeked around the doorjamb as a silver sedan pulled into the driveway.

"Oh. Well, that was *gut* timing."

"How long will you be in Mespo?"

She shrugged, then clipped a black shawl around her shoulders and took her suitcase from Jalon. "Since Daniel doesn't have much work for me right now, *mei* stay is open-ended."

Jalon nodded. His sister often helped out Daniel Raber, who had moved to Birch Creek the previous year and started a small engine repair business. She had nearly tripped over herself trying to convince Daniel to hire her as extra help. Leanna might not be able to make toast without burning it, but she could take apart any size engine and put it back together blindfolded. She'd offered to do just that when, finally, Daniel agreed to hire her on. "Business is slow during the winter, *ya*?"

"I guess." Her face pinched. "We don't have the yard machine repairs like we do the rest of the year. But I think it has more to do with Daniel's brother taking on the extra work." She wrinkled her nose further. "He's an odd duck."

"Pot, meet kettle."

"Ha-ha. I mean a really odd duck. First off, he's a

terrible mechanic. And he's always writing down stuff in notebooks and journals."

"*Nix* wrong with that."

"Lots of notebooks and journals. Piles of them. That's not normal."

"Then you two should get along great."

"He doesn't like to get his hands dirty, either." She looked at her own hands, which were callused but clean. "He's kind of a wimp, if you ask me." Before Jalon could chastise her for being unkind, or better yet, tease her for knowing so many details about a man she claimed not to like, she waved him off. "I know, I know. That's not nice of me. I can't help it, though. He gets on *mei* nerves."

Jalon knew she'd continue talking about Roman Raber for the next ten minutes if he didn't shift her attention. He opened the door wider. "*Yer* taxi is going to take off without you."

"I'm going, I'm going." She stepped through the doorway, then spun around. "Oh, I almost forgot." She pulled a letter from her purse and grinned. "From *yer girlfriend.*"

Trying to keep himself from snatching the letter out of Leanna's hand, he slowed his movements and took the envelope from her. He folded it and put it in his pocket as if it were no more important than a piece of junk mail.

"Don't you want to know what *yer* sweetums has to say?"

He didn't know what a sweetums was. Probably some stupid word Leanna made up to bug him. "*Mei* mail is none of *yer* business."

"*Ya*, it is. I'm *yer* sister and I care about you."

"You're *mei* sister and you're nosy. Maybe you should keep *yer* mind on finding someone for *yerself*."

"As I've told *Mamm*, I'm a confirmed female version of a bachelor. I have *nee* intentions of marrying."

"So you intend to live here and torture me?"

She tilted her head. "Now that you're behaving *yerself*, yes." Her expression turned serious. "I'm glad you're behaving, by the way. Can I finally stop worrying about you?"

"*Ya*. I'm done with drinking, Leanna."

"*Gut*. That leaves me free to be a burr under *yer* saddle for the rest of *yer* life. Unless Phoebe has something to say about that."

He grimaced despite the glimmer of hope that maybe one day Phoebe would have a say about a lot of things in his life. "Bye, Leanna."

She rolled her brown eyes. "Bye, Jalon. Try not to be so boring while I'm gone."

He gave her a half-grin, trying to decide if he should be insulted. Boring? He was quiet. Practical. Serious-minded, especially since he was off the bottle for good. But not boring. At least Phoebe didn't think so or she would have stopped writing to him.

After Leanna left he pulled out the letter and sat down in the hickory rocker near the woodstove.

January 10

Dear Jalon,

I want to meet you in person, too . . .

He blew out a breath. He'd hemmed and hawed over telling her he wanted to meet, wondering if it was too soon to bring it up. They'd only been writing for about two months, but he felt as though he'd known Phoebe all his life. But if he did put the question out there, he'd considered, what if she refused? He'd feel like a fool. He'd also be heartbroken, which bothered him more than the possibility of a dented ego. In the end he gave in and told her how he felt. Now that he had her answer, he was relieved she hadn't put him off. He smiled and continued to read. Before long his smile slid away.

> . . . but we should wait until spring. The weather is so unpredictable in the winter, and I wouldn't want you to get stuck in the snow. Or have an accident on the ice. I would feel terrible if something happened to you while you were trying to get to Dover.

He leaned back in the rocker, dejected. It had been too soon after all.

She was being practical. He had to give her that. Practicality was something he normally appreciated. Ohio winters were unpredictable, although a little—or a lot—of snow wouldn't keep him from getting to Dover. He kept reading the letter, which like her other letters lately, was at least two pages long. His letters to her had gotten longer too. Sometimes they were filled with mundane happenings, but other times he bared his soul, like the time he'd admitted his fear. When he revealed that to her and she responded with kindness and not judgment, he knew she was special.

Yet while he'd been able to tell her in general about the mistakes he'd made, he couldn't bring himself to be specific. There didn't seem to be a right time to admit he was an alcoholic—albeit a functioning one, not that the distinction mattered. Or to explain what drove him to drink in the first place. Admitting the catalyst for his drinking was more terrifying than telling her he was an alcoholic.

He'd have to tell her, though, if things got any more serious between them. He'd put it off as long as possible, since there was an excellent chance that once she knew his darkest secrets, she would bolt. He wouldn't blame her if she did. But he wasn't ready to lose her. Not yet.

Shoving that thought away, he kept reading. She told him about her most recent drawings, which he hoped to also see someday. While she liked to draw, she was downright passionate about food and cooking. That was something he could appreciate. He hadn't fallen for Phoebe because she enjoyed food and could cook, but in his mind that was a bonus.

She could also make him laugh, and in this letter she talked about the time she made no-bake chocolate cookies for her brothers and they refused to eat them because they looked like fresh cow patties. He chuckled. Then he reached the end of the letter.

I hope you're not upset with me. I do want to meet. I really do. I care about you, Jalon. I care about you very much.

Phoebe

He folded the letter and stilled for a moment, letting the last line sink in. So he hadn't been wrong about her feelings for him. He had no clue how he'd been able to read between the lines, but there it was. He'd wait until she invited him to come see her. Until then he'd be satisfied with letters.

Jalon put the letter back in his pocket. He had started to get up when his gaze landed on the top drawer of the end table beside him. The lightness in his chest disappeared as he pulled the drawer open and took out another letter, one that wasn't from Phoebe. Jalon gripped the paper. His father could have told him his plans in any number of ways. A letter didn't have to be one of them. A few days ago, when he first read it, he'd been so angry he could barely process the news. But he couldn't sit on it any longer.

Dear Jalon,

Here are the mortgage papers to the house. I know I said you and Leanna could stay there as long as you wanted, but things have changed. Your mother and I need a place to stay here in Mespo. Things aren't working out staying with your aunt like we planned and we need our own home. I don't make enough money working with your uncle Jeremy to afford two houses. I have to let the one in Birch Creek go.

I'm giving you the opportunity to take over the payments on the house and farm. I'll need to know in a week what your decision is. I'd make the same offer to Leanna if you weren't interested, but we both know she can't afford it. If you decide to not buy it, let me know within the week so I can put it on the market. I can't wait on this, Jalon. If you don't want the farm, I'll sell it to someone who does.

If you do decide to take over the payments, just know that I'm a couple of payments behind. You'll have to make those payments too.

Dad

Angry all over again, Jalon left the letter on the table and went to the mudroom. He put on his coat and a wool cap and went outside. Winter had been brutal this year, and he needed to split and stack more firewood. He also needed to think. He had to give his father an answer by Monday.

He went to the shed and grabbed an ax, then started splitting the wood, his thoughts racing. He didn't like being cornered. A week wasn't enough time to make this kind of decision. Jalon split a log, then tossed the two pieces to the side. He still didn't know what to do, and he suspected Leanna had no idea about their father's plans. If she had, she would have said something to Jalon about it. Now he was left with the task of saving the house and the farm, or letting them go. Why would his *daed* leave the decision to him? And if Jalon did decide to buy the place, what would he do with the farm?

He'd told Phoebe the truth when he said he wasn't cut out for farming. When he was a kid, he had liked it, and there were a couple of years when the farm had made his father a small profit. But about the time Jalon turned fourteen, things changed. His father struggled, and because of that he was hard to be around, specifically when they were working together. He could never seem to get the land to produce more than what the family needed to eat. There was nothing extra to sell other than pigs, which weren't profitable, and they didn't have the space or facilities to raise more than a few at a time, plus an extra cow or two. *Daed* once called farming similar to a dog chasing its tail—pointless and fruitless. Eventually Jalon had felt the same way.

His father took his frustration out on Jalon mostly with harsh, cutting words, although there were a few times he had given him a smack or two for moving too slowly . . . or simply because he was mad. As soon as Jalon was old enough, fifteen and finished with school, he started working construction. It was something he was capable of. Better yet, he was able to add to the family bank account. As he financially contributed more and his father contributed less, that led to sour feelings between the two, feelings that weren't fully addressed before his father moved away.

Jalon stopped chopping and looked at the field, which had laid fallow this past spring. The acreage was covered by a thin layer of snow, but Jalon imagined it in the summer, when the crops were growing, the timothy grass was almost knee-deep, and everything smelled rich and earthy and full of life. His neighbor, Freemont Yoder, was also a farmer, and while he'd had some lean years, he'd been able to make his farm work. Why couldn't *Daed*?

Why can't I?

It was more than a random question, or wondering about his father's ability as a farmer. Jalon needed a new start. He'd left drinking behind, but it was an everyday struggle. While he made good money at his construction job, it felt as though he was just cashing a paycheck. He wasn't doing anything fulfilling, just drifting through the days like a hot air balloon without an anchor. Construction didn't keep him grounded.

But farming might.

He shook his head, unable to believe he was even thinking this way. His mind turned back to Phoebe. While his vocation lacked purpose, her letters gave him life. During those moments when he was alone and the urge to drink was almost overwhelming, he reread them. He also prayed, and the combination of leaning on God and knowing there was a special woman out there who possibly cared for him kept him from the bottle.

He looked at the land again. Sure, he could purchase the house and let the farmland go to waste. But that didn't sit right. If he was going to do this, he would be all in. That plan would mean hard work and a steep learning curve, but he did know the basics. And if he was stumped, he could always ask Freemont for advice.

The way of fools seems right to them, but the wise listen to advice. He'd heard that proverb a dozen times from Emmanuel Troyer, Sol's father, who had been their bishop for years until he left in disgrace. The bishop had seemed to delight in talking about foolish men. Jalon had always discounted most of his sermons, which usually felt more like guilt trips than actual preaching. Now the words came back to him. Was he being foolish by sinking his savings into property that had been nothing but a bane to his father? There was no guarantee he could recoup the investment. In fact, there was a strong possibility he would lose the farm in foreclosure if he couldn't make a profit. Then he'd have nothing.

Another proverb came to mind, one he'd heard less often in Bishop Troyer's sermons. *Take delight in the Lord, and he will give you the desires of your heart.* He hadn't really thought about what he wanted in life other than peace, something that had been out of his reach for years. Maybe that was changing too. The more he thought about taking a stab at farming, the more he wanted to do it. He would own his own house, taking another step toward a steady future. And now that he knew Phoebe cared about him, maybe a wife and children were in his future too. It seemed God was answering a plea Jalon hadn't been aware he'd been making.

Jalon turned and looked toward the house, this time focusing on the small, half-finished *dawdi haus* set off to the side. The plan had been for his parents to move into it after Jalon married. But as Jalon knew better than anyone, plans changed. He took in the farmland again and thought about Phoebe. Thought about his future. Thought about how he could continue to play life safe, to live in the tight box he'd constructed for himself ever since . . . He shook his head. There was no need for that part of his past to drive his decision. Not this time.

By the time he finished chopping and stacking the firewood, Jalon had made his decision. Now all he could do was pray he was making the right one.

• • •

Monday evening Jalon returned home later than usual. He'd stopped by the bank after work, and after signing more paperwork than he'd ever seen in his life, he now owned his own home and farmland. That should have made him happy, or at least a little satisfied. But before the ink was dry the doubts started to surface again, and not without good reason.

His father hadn't been truthful about how far behind he was on the payments. In fact, the bank was ready to start foreclosure proceedings, and it had taken Jalon his entire savings to pay off the outstanding balance. Which meant his father had left Birch Creek knowing he was already in arrears. Why had his father lied to him? Then again, his father was good at hiding things.

Jalon tried to reassure himself that he'd have a healthy bank balance soon enough. He'd been racking up overtime at work, and their current project would continue for several months, if not all the way until the end of summer. But he'd have to cut back on his hours once spring came. He would need that time to prepare the fields and put in the crops.

Still, he could even be optimistic about that. Leanna would help, and not only with the farmwork. She could also help out a little financially from her job with Daniel Raber. If he had to, Jalon could ask Freemont to spare a couple of his sons to make sure all the planting was finished in time. God willing, he'd have a decent harvest in the fall.

Yes, he had to let go and trust God completely. That was the only way he could bypass his misgivings about all this and focus on the positive. Maybe even in a couple of years he could quit construction completely and run the farm full-time.

He was heading for the barn to feed his horse when he heard a buggy come up the driveway. He turned and recognized it right away—Solomon Troyer's. He walked toward the buggy. He'd stopped by Sol's last week and ordered a birdhouse for Phoebe. Another impulsive decision, but it served two purposes. One had to do with giving Sol a little business in his new woodworking venture. Sol had worked as a carpenter for years, only to lose his job when his drinking got out of control. Now that he was also setting his life right, Jalon wanted to show his support.

The second reason was that he wanted to make Phoebe smile.

When Sol pulled to a stop, Jalon came alongside him. "Hey Sol. What brings you by?"

"I've got some paint chips. I wanted to show them to you, to make sure they're the colors you want."

"You didn't have to *geh* to so much trouble," Jalon said as Sol got out of the buggy.

"I want to do this right, considering it's a special gift."

Jalon hid a smile. Sol had asked if the birdhouse was for someone special, since Jalon had requested the house be painted delicate, feminine colors that made him think of Phoebe—light blue, yellow, and pink. Her letters were always upbeat, but he had a sense that she wasn't completely happy at her aunt's house.

Sol showed him the paint chips and Jalon nodded. "Those are fine." A few years ago, if someone had told him he'd be buying a pretty birdhouse Sol Troyer made to give to a girl he hadn't formally met, Jalon would have scoffed. Not just at the idea that he would make a frivolous purchase, but because up until recently, Sol had been undependable. But like Jalon, Sol had made a lot of positive changes in his life. Quitting drinking was a huge one. Sol could drink Jalon under the table, and at his worst point he had pushed everyone away, including Jalon.

Then the day came last year when he confessed his drinking in front of the church. That had been a turning point for Jalon too. While Jalon had tried to quit drinking over the years, he'd never fully succeeded until he saw Sol courageously admit his drinking and ask for forgiveness. Jalon hadn't had a drink since.

"Want to come inside for a bit?" Jalon asked. "I don't have much to offer food-wise, other than some sandwich fixings."

Sol shook his head. "*Danki*, but I've got to get back home. *Mamm*'s got supper waiting for me." He paused. "How are things going?"

Jalon understood his meaning. They'd briefly talked about their battle with sobriety last week, and Jalon was surprised Sol was bringing it up again. "*Gut*," he said. "You?"

"Staying at it. Seems easy sometimes. Then at other times . . ."

"I know." Again he thought of Phoebe, how her letters had helped keep him from temptation. That and a lot of prayer. "I bought this place," he said, suddenly needing to change the subject. He gestured to the house.

"Really? The farm too?"

"*Ya*. Thought I'd try to make a *geh* of it."

Sol rubbed his chin. "Huh. Never thought you'd work on a farm again."

Jalon brushed his hand along the flank of Sol's horse. The animal twitched. Sol didn't know the reason why Jalon had chosen construction over farming, and Jalon didn't want to get into it right now. "Plans change."

"That they do." He tilted back his straw hat. "I wish you luck. If you need any help, let me know. I don't know much about farming, but I'll help out any way I can."

"I will." Jalon appreciated the offer, knowing it wasn't made lightly. He also knew Sol could now be counted on to follow through on his word.

After Sol left, Jalon went inside, slipped off his boots, and went upstairs to his bedroom. Supper could wait. He took a pad of paper and a pen and started to write.

Dear Phoebe,

It's okay if you want to wait until spring to meet. But I'll admit that if I had my way I'd be in Dover tomorrow.

He paused. Too much? It was the honest truth. He left it in and continued his letter, writing two full pages and leaving out two important things—purchasing the house and farm, and his past. He could have told her about both, but he held back. He'd been forthright about enough, at least for now.

He signed the letter, folded it, then took his checkbook and went downstairs to the kitchen where his mother had kept envelopes and stamps. He pulled out two envelopes—one for Phoebe, the other for his cousin Adam. He actually had Adam to thank for meeting Phoebe, since it was Jalon's mail to him that had accidentally arrived at Phoebe's house.

He wrote a check and slipped it into Adam's envelope, something he'd done every month since he had his first job and bank account at age fifteen. He'd lost track of how much money he'd sent over the years. The amount wasn't important. The checks signified so much more than financial support, most importantly letting Adam know that Jalon never forgot about him . . . or about what happened. *Or that it was my fault.*

Guilt slammed into him. Guilt over what he'd done, over Adam's situation, and now even a little extra guilt for planning his own future. Did he deserve all this happiness, knowing that because of him, Adam's life had changed forever?

Jalon smoothed the envelope. Money wasn't enough. He knew that. However, it was all he could offer. Even if the farm was a success, even if he and Phoebe were to marry, he would always carry the knowledge that he was responsible for what happened. He couldn't take it back. He could only pay his penance, something he intended to do for the rest of his life.

CHAPTER 3

Adam Chupp looked at the return address on the envelope and sighed. Another month, another check. He added the envelope to the stack of mail in his lap, then turned his wheelchair and headed for the house. A fine layer of powdery snow covered the gravel driveway, but it didn't hinder his progress. His chair was small, light, compact, and without armrests, which he preferred. But on days when the snow was heavier and thicker, he couldn't manage his chair by himself. He made sure to take advantage of the winter days he could spend outdoors.

He rolled his chair up the back porch ramp and through the back door and put the mail on the kitchen counter, keeping the one from Jalon. Then he went to his bedroom on the first floor of the house and tossed the letter, unopened, into the top drawer of his bureau. He already knew the contents of the envelope. His cousin had been sending him money for years. Later this week he'd cash it at the bank. He didn't want to, but Jalon gave him no choice. A check every month, without fail, and without any other type of correspondence. Not even a note saying, "Hi" or, "How are you?" Just a check. As if that made up for the loss.

Adam stared at the drawer. He'd tried to convince Jalon he didn't need his money. He also didn't want it. When he received the first check, he sent it back, along with a scathing letter—at least as scathing as a fourteen-year-old boy could write. Jalon promptly sent the check back. Adam tore it up. The next month, he got another one, double the amount, since Jalon knew Adam hadn't cashed the first one. So Adam called him. The conversation was short on words, but long on guilt. Jalon's guilt, which was thick in his voice as they talked. After Adam hung up, he realized Jalon hadn't agreed to stop sending the checks.

At that point Adam gave up and accepted the money. What other choice did he have? If it made Jalon feel better about what happened, then why stop him?

He figured his cousin would eventually stop on his own, once enough time had passed. He hadn't. His checks arrived exactly the same time each month, year after year, for the last ten years. That was Jalon, though. Precise and thoughtful, even as a kid. Except for one time, and that had changed everything.

Adam left his bedroom, refusing to let his mind go too far into the past. Looking at the future was what had helped him cope with his disability. That and living in the present, something he never took for granted.

He glanced at the clock on the wall in the living room. He had a couple of hours before he had to go to work in his uncle's hat shop. His *aenti* Tabitha and *onkel* Jeremy lived next door, which was convenient. The job was part-time, though, and he needed to find something full-time. More to the point, he needed a career, something he could do with his limited mobility. Being Amish definitely narrowed his options. Still, he wasn't about to give up his faith for the sake of a job. He trusted that God would lead him to find work that paid enough for him to live on his own. That was his goal and, at twenty-four, it was past time he'd attained it.

He went to the set of bookcases against the wall. They were custom made, half the height of regular ones, and placed next to each other. Dozens of books lined the shelves, all his. If he could make a living reading, he would be rich by now. But it wasn't about being rich. It was about independence.

Scanning the bookshelves, he spied a book on investing, one he'd purchased a few months ago but hadn't gotten around to reading. He put the book in his lap, wheeled himself near the woodstove, and began to read.

"What's today's topic?" his mother said as she entered the room, carrying a laundry basket. She set it on the couch.

Adam held up the book, *Investing Made Easy.* "Riveting stuff."

Mamm chuckled. "I'm sure. It's a change from those farming books you've been reading."

Placing the book in his lap, he nodded. "Kind of got burned out on that." Especially since the more he read about farming and animal husbandry, the more he wanted to do it. His father had always worked in a factory in Middlefield. Other than gardening, which Adam enjoyed doing, he'd never had the opportunity to farm. It was unlikely he ever would, not here in Mespo. Farmland was scarce and expensive.

Then there was the issue with the wheelchair. Adam knew he was capable of a lot, but managing a farm and animals wasn't one of them, not on his own. That hadn't stopped him from making a few sketches, though. He'd designed an accessible barn, a grid for crops, and a one-level house complete with an accessible kitchen and bathrooms. Yes, more than one bathroom. Being independent wasn't his only desire. A wife and family were also on the table. Another goal that seemed far away, but one he had faith in. God had gotten him through years of pain and disappointment. His faithfulness wasn't going to change, and Adam's faith wasn't going to waver.

"You've always had a variety of interests." *Mamm* sat down on the edge of the couch.

Adam moved closer and looked inside the clothes basket. These were his clothes, stiff from being outside on the porch drying in the cold air. Shortly after the accident, once he'd accepted that he'd be in a wheelchair for the rest of his life, he'd insisted on doing his own laundry, and sharing in the cooking and cleaning too. His mother had balked at first, then let him have his way. Now they split the chores, but Adam still folded his own laundry. He picked up a pair of socks. "Maybe I've got too many interests. I'm having trouble narrowing things down."

"You'll figure it out. God has a plan for you."

"I think I might have heard that before." He winked. "A dozen times or so."

"And it's true every time." *Mamm* stood. "Have you seen Leanna since she arrived?"

Nodding, Adam said, "Once. While I was at *Onkel* Jeremy's. She stopped by. Said she wanted to get together soon."

"*Gut*. She's like a breath of fresh air, isn't she?"

"She's a breath of something." He rolled the socks together. He liked his cousin, but she could be overwhelming sometimes. It was amazing she and Jalon were even related. Leanna was outspoken, energetic, a whirlwind. The opposite of the reserved steadiness he remembered in Jalon.

"I wish Jalon would visit." *Mamm* sighed. "I miss that *bu*."

Adam did too. Before the accident they were close. Adam had always looked up to Jalon, who was not only serious-minded most of the time, but also faster and stronger. That spurred Adam to try to keep up with him. He knew how to have fun too. When they were kids, they used to fish, hunt, play volleyball, climb trees . . .

He threw the socks on the couch. Now their relationship consisted of a monthly check.

"Leanna told me she tried to convince him to come this time," his mother added, "but he said he was busy working."

"So I've heard." Adam didn't doubt Jalon worked a lot. But he also knew the real reason his cousin avoided Mespo.

"Anyway, maybe we'll visit them soon."

"Maybe." Adam quickly folded a pair of pants. The

visit wouldn't happen. Jalon's family used to visit Mespo often, before the accident. The one time his family went to Birch Creek, everything had changed. His parents hadn't been back since, and Jalon's family didn't return to Mespo for a long time. The accident hadn't affected only Adam.

"When are you heading over to *Onkel* Jeremy's?" *Mamm* asked, picking up the empty clothes basket.

"In an hour or so."

"All right. I'll see you at supper, then. We're having fried chicken tonight."

One of his favorites. He smiled and watched his mother leave. When she was gone, his smile disappeared. Another thing he rarely let himself do was think about the impact of his disability on his parents. He was their only child. He was sure they'd had hopes and dreams for him before the accident—ones they'd had to adjust and, possibly, change altogether. They were always encouraging, but more than a few times over the years he'd seen the worry they'd tried so hard to hide.

He piled his clothes on his lap, covering the investing book. He went to his room and put them away, then put the book on his bed. He'd read it later, after supper. Although he didn't have a firm plan for his future, he had to educate himself until he did.

God has a plan. Adam believed that with all his heart and soul. He just wished God would reveal what it was.

• • •

On Wednesday afternoon, Phoebe ran to the mailbox at the end of the driveway and opened the front lid. She frowned at the empty space. Was the mail late? She was expecting a letter from Jalon today. He was always on the spot with sending his letters. For the dozenth time she wondered if she'd made a mistake by putting him off for a visit. What if he saw through her flimsy excuse? What if he decided he didn't want to see her anymore? Or worse—he'd decided not to write her back?

She closed the mailbox and another, sharper thread of panic wound through her. What if her aunt had picked up the mail already? Phoebe made it a point to get it before her aunt did, and so far Aunt Bertha seemed fine with that. It wasn't as if her aunt received a lot of mail, anyway. Still, if she discovered any of Jalon's letters . . .

Phoebe drew in a sharp breath, trying to settle her nerves. She was being ridiculous, not only about Aunt Bertha but her fears about Jalon. It had been only three days since she'd written to him. There was no need to panic. Not yet, anyway. And what was the worst that could happen if Aunt Bertha found the letter? Her aunt didn't know Jalon, and there wasn't a house rule that she couldn't write to a *friend*. Okay, so he was more than a friend, at least in her heart, but her aunt didn't have to know that. Surely she wouldn't keep her from writing to Jalon. Her aunt wasn't that cruel, was she?

The sound of a vehicle came down the street, and she let out a relieved breath as she saw the mail truck approach. She waited by the mailbox, her breath coming out in frosty puffs, unable to keep her toes from tapping the ground. "Please let there be a letter from Jalon," she whispered.

"Morning," the mailman said, then handed Phoebe two envelopes. "Have a good day."

"You too!" she said, waving. Then she looked at the envelopes. The first one was an advertisement from a car dealership. Well, that was a waste of postage. She looked at the second letter. It was from Jalon. She ripped it open, fumbling with the envelope in her gloved hands. As she read, she leaned against the mailbox post. He wasn't angry with her. He said he understood, and then said he would be in Dover right away if he could. The cold surrounding her seemed to disappear as Jalon's letter warmed her through. She continued to read.

Sounds like you're really busy with all the cooking you do. I wasn't sure what to say when you asked me what my favorite meal was, because I like almost everything. I'd have to say the one thing I won't touch is buttermilk. Never had a taste for the stuff.

Phoebe sighed. A man after her own heart.

I guess if I had to pick something, and this is going to sound weird, it would be Hunan beef, which is Chinese stir-fry. There's a Chinese place near the construction site and I go there for lunch at least twice a week. I like my food hot. The spicier the better. It's not something I could make for myself, though. I definitely wouldn't trust Leanna to make it. She can barely boil water.

What Phoebe wouldn't do to be able to make him a Chinese meal. She didn't know how and had never eaten Chinese food in her life, but she could learn. For him, she would do anything. *Except tell him the truth.*

"*Mamm!*"

She turned at the sound of Malachi's voice. He was running toward her, his small boots making light imprints on the thin layer of snow covering the driveway and yard. He'd been bouncing a small rubber ball on the front porch while she got the mail, but the activity hadn't kept him occupied for long. She folded the letter and put it back in the envelope, then tucked it into the pocket of her apron. She'd read the rest later. The few lines she had read would keep her going for the rest of the day.

She squatted down in front of Malachi, then smoothed back a lock of his blond hair. He had his father's hair color and bright blue eyes, along with her round face and the identical dimple in his left cheek. "I love you," she said. "So very much."

He grinned, revealing a gap where his front tooth had fallen out the week before. "Love you too. Can I have another cookie?"

"Later," she said, unable to resist his adorable smile. "Right now we have to stack firewood for *Aenti* Bertha."

The cherubic smile disappeared, his face scrunching. "I don't want to help her. I hate her."

"Malachi! You can't hate anyone."

"*Ya*, I can and I hate her. She's mean and she smells weird."

Her aunt did smell weird, like the homemade arthritis cream she slathered all over herself every morning. "Malachi," Phoebe said, trying to maintain a stern tone. "That isn't nice."

"*She* isn't nice."

"She's letting us live here. That's what's important."

"But I wanna *geh* home. Can we please *geh* home? I miss Devon and Zeb and Zeke and Owen and Ezra and Nelson and Perry and Jesse and Moses and Mahlon and *Grossdaadi* and *Grossmammi* and baby Elam and Crackers—"

She put her finger over his lips. "I get it, Malachi. You miss everyone at home."

"Everyone and Crackers," Malachi corrected, referring to Devon's horse.

She frowned. She wanted to go home too. The idea of being stuck at her aunt's for much longer made her wilt inside, as did the letters she received from her family. Her parents wanted her home. They said her brothers did, too, even though Ezra, who was eleven, was the only one who had written to her. "I kind of miss you," he'd said. That nearly brought her to tears.

With each letter she received from her family, the urge to return became stronger. But she had to resist until she could figure out how to return. Right now that seemed impossible.

She hugged her son, then leaned back so she could face him again. "Now, don't pout. It makes you look like a duck."

He beamed. "I like looking like a duck. Quack, quack." He turned away from her and started to waddle.

Standing, she followed her son to the backyard. He was quacking full force, having a great time and forgetting that less than a minute ago he'd been missing his family. She loved to see him smile and laugh. There was so little to be happy about lately, aside from Jalon's letters.

"Phoebe!" Aunt Bertha poked her head out the back door. "Get *yer sohn* under control."

Her aunt never called him Malachi. She rarely acknowledged him at all, unless he was doing something that bothered her, which was basically everything he did. How had she heard him from inside, anyway? The doors and windows were closed. Letting out a huff of frustration, Phoebe went to Malachi and put her hand on his shoulder. "That's enough."

"Quack, quack!" He looked up at her, then glared at Aunt Bertha. "Quaaaaaaaaaack!"

Aunt Bertha's face turned red as she stormed out of the house. "Get him under control or I will!"

Her words stopped Malachi. He stood up and stopped quacking, but the anger on his face remained. When he stomped over to another part of the yard, Phoebe said a quick prayer of thankfulness. For once he did as he was told.

"The things I put up with from you two." Aunt Bertha adjusted her glasses.

"He's a little *bu*, *Aenti*. He was just playing."

"He was acting a fool. Train up a child in the way he should *geh* and he won't depart from it. Too bad *yer mudder* didn't heed that wise, biblical advice when it came to *yer* upbringing."

Phoebe flinched. Was Aunt Bertha's scorn part of her punishment too?

"Finish sweeping that snow off the walk," Aunt Bertha ordered.

"I thought you wanted us to stack the firewood."

"You can do that after you finish sweeping. I don't want to see a flake left behind. Do you understand?"

"*Ya.*" Phoebe fisted her hands at her sides. "I understand."

After her aunt shut the door, Phoebe rushed to Malachi, who was picking up snow and grass and throwing it. "Please," Phoebe said, taking his cold hands and turning him toward her. "You must behave. *Aenti* Bertha is upset with both of us." He tried to pull from her grip but she held on. "Malachi, listen to me. It's important that you obey while we're here."

"I don't want to obey. I want to *geh* home."

Back to that again. So many times since they arrived here she'd felt out of her depth as a mother. At home she'd had better control over Malachi. She'd also had her parents' help, and even her eldest brothers pitched in when they could. However, he was better behaved at her parents' home. Here, he was stubborn, argumentative, and disrespectful. Yet regardless of where they lived, she was his mother and she should be able to discipline him. "Malachi," she said, giving him her most patient tone. "One day we'll *geh* home."

"Why not today?"

"Because."

"Because why?"

"Because we can't."

"Why can't we?" He bit his bottom lip. "You don't like it here either."

She sighed. "It doesn't matter what I like. What matters is that we do what she tells us to do. That means you can't throw dirt or refuse to eat *yer* supper."

He tilted his head, as if he were considering her words. "Can I quack like a duck?"

"Only around me. But as soon as you see her, you'll be a little *bu* again. Got it?"

He nodded. Then he whispered, "Quack."

"Quack," she whispered back, then kissed his cheek. Another crisis averted, for the meantime. "Now, let's finish sweeping the snow. After that, I'll get you that cookie."

. . .

Jalon opened the back door and, despite the mail in his pocket, dragged himself inside. It had been a long, hard week at work, even with the welcome respite of having lunch at his favorite Chinese restaurant and the excitement of becoming a property owner. The temperatures had dropped and the added cold made working outside harder, despite the extra layers he wore. He took off his boots and outerwear in the mudroom, then walked into the kitchen. Blue, Leanna's Coon cat, swirled around his legs. "*Ya, ya.* You want food, you big ball of fur." He fed the cat, his own stomach growling. But he wouldn't eat until he read Phoebe's latest letter.

Dear Jalon,

I took your suggestion and started drawing things other than birds, which is good because I haven't seen many birds since winter started. It's been great fun trying to draw snow on trees and blowing drifts, but I'm not very good. In the spring there will be more birds to draw, along with other animals like squirrels and rabbits and chipmunks, although Aunt Bertha mentioned that she usually puts poison around the edges of the garden to keep the chipmunks and other critters at bay. I always thought it was nice to leave the edges of the garden for the deer and other animals, but she disagrees. It's her garden, so she can do what she wants.

One day I hope to have a huge garden of my own. I want to plant everything, not just tomatoes, peppers, and onions. I'd like to have an herb garden too. And flowers—definitely flowers. There will be birdfeeders and hummingbird feeders everywhere. And a small pond nearby, where I can skip rocks and take off my shoes and dip my feet in the cool water. You don't think skipping rocks is too childish, do you?

Jalon shook his head, smiling. He didn't think that was childish at all. He hadn't skipped rocks in years, but he used to love doing it as a kid. He finished reading the letter, imagining how great a huge garden would be in addition to his farm crops. He liked that she had an appreciation of the land and nature. He was also glad his instincts had been right about the birdhouse. He dashed off a quick letter of response of his own and mailed it the next morning.

• • •

After work the following day, Jalon was in the kitchen washing dishes. He had two days' worth, and Leanna would have had a fit if she were there. She was a terrible cook but a cleaning fiend, almost to the point of driving him crazy. As he finished scrubbing the last pot, he went to let out Blue, who was meowing at the door. As the cat dashed outside, he heard the distant ring of the phone from the shanty at the end of the driveway. For an absurd moment he thought maybe Phoebe was calling him—but she wouldn't. He hadn't given her his phone number, although maybe that would have been a better step than suggesting they meet face-to-face. But from the way she described living with her aunt Bertha, he wondered if she even had access to a phone.

Jalon jogged out of the house to the shanty, opened the door, and picked up the receiver as the phone rang for a fourth time. "Hello?"

"You sound out of breath."

Leanna. "Of course I'm out of breath. I ran from the *haus*. Is something wrong?"

"You always assume something is wrong."

"Because it usually is when the phone rings." His family rarely used it when he was growing up, mostly if they needed to call a vet or a doctor. In other words, an emergency, and from Leanna's casual tone this definitely wasn't one. Something else made his chest tense. She was visiting family, and family included Adam. When he heard her voice. he immediately thought something had happened to him.

"How else am I supposed to let you know I'm staying in Mespo for a couple more weeks?" she said.

Letting out a relieved breath, he replied, "Why are you telling me at all? I thought you said *yer* visit was open-ended."

"I made it more open-ended than before."

He scratched his head, then shrugged. Sometimes it wasn't worth trying to figure out his sister. "Have you talked to *Daed* lately?"

"I had supper with him and *Mamm* the other day. The tension in *Onkel* Marvin's *haus* is thick as peanut butter, by the way."

"So he didn't say anything about the *haus*?"

"What *haus*? Our *haus*?"

The windows in the shanty started to fog up. He blew on his hand, wishing he'd thrown on a coat. He explained to Leanna about buying the house and farm, leaving out the part about their father being in arrears.

"Seriously?" she said. "You're going to be a farmer?"

"I'm going to try."

"I'm sure you'll succeed." She paused. "You know, with *yer* help I'm sure *Daed* could have made a success of the farm."

"Is that what he said?"

"Of course not. *Daed* wouldn't admit that. Just like you couldn't forgive him for being such a jerk to you."

"I forgave him." Jalon wiped the window with the heel of his hand.

"Sure you did." Before he could respond to that little dig, she added, "Anyway, I'm glad you bought the *haus*. It's *gut* to keep it in the *familye*. It must have taken you a long time to make *yer* decision."

"Not as long as you think."

She chuckled. "Could that be because of Phoebe?"

"I'm hanging up now."

"Beat you to it." *Click.*

He opened the shanty door and stepped out into the cold evening air. The sun had set an hour ago, but streaks of pale gray and lavender crossed the winter sky. His gaze drifted upward. What was Phoebe doing right now? Was she relaxing with a book? Or maybe she was drawing the night sky. He hoped whatever she was doing, she was thinking about him. Lord knew he couldn't get his mind off her.

He heard the snorting of the pigs in the barn. It was suppertime for them too. He went into the barn and the pigs came running from the outside pen to their stall. Two old draft horses whinnied, and his buggy horse lifted his head above his stall. They were all hungry. Blue must have dashed out of the house when he left for the shanty, because he was rubbing his side against Jalon's ankles.

After he fed the horses, he watched the pigs finish their meal. They were still piglets, and greedy. Soon the barn was filled with the munching of animals eating their grain, along with the occasional whinny and whine punctuating the air. That wasn't the only thing filling the air. He sniffed. The barn needed a good cleaning. Tomorrow was Sunday, and he had to work on Monday, so he might as well clean it tonight.

A couple of hours later, after a quick snack and a hot shower, he fell into bed. Having a clean barn wasn't the only benefit of his labor—he'd thought about plans for the farm. And Phoebe, of course. His body was exhausted from a full day's work and cleaning the barn, but his mind continued to whirr. He tossed and turned, punched his pillow twice, then booted Blue out of his bed. The cat never slept with him, but for some reason since Leanna left, Blue had staked out Jalon's bed as his own.

He turned on the battery-powered lamp on his bedside table, sat up, and ran both hands through his hair. Two words repeated in his mind. *Tell her. Tell her.* "Tell her what, God? About *mei* past?" No, that wasn't something he could share in a letter.

Deep down he knew what the nudge meant. He took out a sheet of paper from his nightstand. Stationery wasn't something he'd kept nearby before writing Phoebe. Now he made sure to have plenty of paper, stamps, and envelopes handy.

He stared at the paper, then took a deep breath. This was the most important letter he would ever write. It might scare her off. It might ruin their relationship. But he had to let her know the truth about his feelings, the dreams and plans he had for both of them.

His palms grew damp. He'd never risked his heart before, always keeping himself and his emotions at a safe distance. It was easier that way, less painful. Yet knowing what he felt for Phoebe and having to keep it locked up tight was worse than being detached.

When it came to Phoebe, he didn't want to play it safe.

Dear Phoebe,

I know I wrote you a letter yesterday, but it's the middle of the night and I can't sleep. I can't sleep because you're on my mind and in my heart. I know I said it would be all right to wait to meet, but it's not. I want to see you, and knowing I can't is driving me crazy.

I care about you. No, that's not the complete truth. It might sound irrational because we've only known each other a short time, and we've never met in person, but I love you. I love you, Phoebe. I want to speak those words, not write them down on paper. I want you to hear them. I want you to see my face and know they're the truth. And when I say those words, I want to see your face. Your beautiful face that haunts my dreams.

Please say yes, Phoebe.

Love,

Jalon

He went downstairs, put the letter in an envelope, and addressed and stamped it. Then he took it to the mailbox and put it inside, even though he knew it wouldn't be picked up until Monday. As he lifted the red flag on the box, his teeth chattered. He was out here in the cold night air, barefoot and wearing the pants and shirt he threw on before leaving his bedroom, mailing the one and only love letter he'd ever written. He was probably making the most foolish mistake of his life . . . or the best decision.

He went back inside, undressed, and lay down on his bed, ready to sleep like a baby.

CHAPTER 4

A dam, you don't have to stay out here with me."

He glanced up at his cousin Leanna, who had skidded to a stop in front of him on the ice-covered pond near his house. When she stopped by earlier with her ice skates, he'd offered to go to the pond with her. She'd been in Mespo a week now, and this was the first opportunity they had to spend some time together. The winter air was cold, but the sun beamed in the cloudless sky. He welcomed the warmth. Most of the time he'd rather be outside than indoors anyway. Besides, he liked seeing her have fun on the ice, even though he couldn't participate. Seeing her happy was reward enough.

She stepped off the ice and onto the snow-covered grass. Another layer had fallen overnight, but it wasn't enough to impede his wheelchair. "Can you pass me a sandwich?" she asked, taking off one of her gloves.

He craned his neck to look up at her. She was the tallest woman he knew, even without the ice skates. With a nod he reached around to the back of his wheelchair for the insulated lunch cooler. He pulled it off the hook on the back of his chair, opened it, then handed Leanna a wrapped ham-and-cheese sandwich.

"*Danki.* Oh wait, I don't have to thank you, since I

made these." She grinned before facing the pond and taking a big bite of the sandwich.

He smiled. Her quirky outspokenness was one reason she was one of his favorite cousins. That and her loyalty. Whenever she visited Mespo, she made sure to spend time with him. No matter what they did together, they always enjoyed themselves.

"Aren't you going to eat?" she asked, turning to look at him again.

"Maybe later." He rested his hands on his lap. He was never without his fingerless leather gloves when he went outside. They protected his palms as he pushed the wheels on his chair, but they did little to keep his fingers warm. That didn't bother him too much. He was used to it.

Leanna polished off her sandwich. "*Yer mamm* said we're having fish tonight for supper. Did you catch them at this pond?"

"*Ya*. Back in the fall, right before the first freeze." He'd spent that Saturday morning and afternoon fishing with his father, something they did often when the weather cooperated and *Daed* had the day off. The fish were biting, and they had hauled in more than they could eat at once. *Mamm* had put up the rest in their gas-powered freezer. "I'm not having any. I'll eat some of the leftover roast beef from last night."

Her brow raised in surprise. "You still don't like fish? I thought you would have outgrown that by now."

"It's personal taste, not a pair of pants."

Leanna chuckled. "Then why bother to fish?"

"Because I enjoy catching them. I just don't like eating them." Fishing was also something he could do independently, whether from his chair or on the grassy bank of the pond. He had to make sure he didn't catch the line on anything, but even if he did, he could cut the fishing line and start over.

"I like both," Leanna said. "We've got a lot of fish in our pond back home."

Adam said, "I remember."

She went to him, her gait clunky from the ice skates as she walked the few steps on frozen ground. When she was directly in front of him, she crouched down so they were eye level. He'd never asked her to do that. She just always had. "I'm going to Kentucky with Maria next week. When I get back, I want you to come home with me for a visit."

Her idea surprised him. When he didn't immediately respond, she added, "At least think about it, okay? It's been so long since you've visited us." She sprang up and went back to the pond.

He watched her step onto the ice, then glide gracefully over the surface. But he wasn't paying attention to her skating. It was one thing to contemplate a visit to Birch Creek, another to seriously consider it. His complicated relationship with Jalon aside, it took planning for him to go anywhere. Not because he was homebound. Far from it. He traveled whenever he could, even going to Sarasota two years ago with extended family. He'd fished on an ocean charter, and had even gone swimming in the ocean with the help of his cousin Mose.

But going to Birch Creek . . . That was a different story.

Leanna skated back to the edge of the pond and came to a stop. "So? What's *yer* answer?"

"That's all the time I get to make *mei* decision?"

"I'm an impatient woman."

"Impatience isn't a virtue, you know."

"I'm not worried about it," she said with a wave of her hand.

He rubbed his cold fingers across his chin. "Don't you think you should let Jalon know first?"

"Nah. It will be a surprise."

Adam grimaced. "I don't think Jalon would appreciate this particular surprise."

But Leanna skated off again, as if what he said wasn't important. Then again, to her it might not be. If she ever wondered why he and Jalon didn't talk since the accident, she'd never asked Adam. Part of him was glad. How could he explain to her how their relationship had devolved, when he wasn't sure he understood why himself?

He felt a twinge in his leg. The accident had broken his back and robbed him of the use of his legs, but he still had some sensation in them.

"It's settled then?" Leanna said, as she skated by.

"I don't"—she was nearly on the other side of the pond by the time he got the two words out—"know." He glanced up at the sun, which was almost directly overhead. It was nearing noon. "I have to be at work by two," he yelled as she skated by again.

"We'll leave soon." Then she came to a stop and skated toward him, her hazel eyes twinkling. "You should skate with me."

Adam scoffed. "If you haven't noticed, I hung up *mei* skates a long time ago."

"*Yer* sarcasm is noted. I mean skate in *yer* chair."

His brow lifted. "Are you serious?"

"Of course I am. This pond is frozen straight through. But we don't have to *geh* to the middle. We'll just stay at the edge."

He eyed the pond again. A few strong pushes would get him on the ice, so logistics wasn't a question. Wisdom, however, was. He wasn't sure how smart it would be to put his chair on the pond. The ice could crack, or break completely, and he would fall into the frigid water. Worse yet, Leanna could fall in too. It wouldn't take any time for them to get hypothermia, and they weren't close enough to the house to yell for help.

Yet the ice beckoned to him, as did Leanna's pleading look. She would be the only one brave enough—or foolish enough—to suggest this. Finally, he shrugged. Why not? Life wasn't worth living without taking risks.

Grinning, he shoved the chair over the bank easily due to the cold, hard ground and sparse snow. Immediately he started to slide on the ice. "Whoa!" he said, as his chair coasted forward, farther than he expected. He started to yank on his brakes, wondering if they would even work on ice. *Probably should have taken that into consideration.*

Then he felt Leanna grab the handles of his chair and pull back, slowing him down. "Maybe this wasn't a good idea," she said, sounding uncharacteristically unsure.

He turned his head and looked up at her. "Are you kidding? This is great! I haven't been on the ice in years." And he'd never thought he'd be on the ice again.

"Then let's *geh*." With her guiding his chair, they

made a turn around the pond, staying close to the side but not too close so his wheels wouldn't catch on the bank.

Exhilarated, he couldn't stop smiling. Freedom. Anytime he got a taste of it, like when he was swimming in the ocean, he could forget about his disability and his limitations. His face and fingers were freezing and there was the possibility that at any moment the ice would break under his chair, but he felt too good, too *free*, to care.

After several spins around the pond, Leanna pushed him back onto the bank. Once his wheels were able to grip the grass, he took over and shoved himself farther along the snow-dusted ground. He spun his chair and faced her, still grinning like a fool. "*Danki*, Leanna. That was the most fun I've had in a long time."

"You're welcome." She wiped her gloved hand under her red nose, her expression growing serious. "I really want you to come back to Birch Creek with me."

Back to that again.

"Can you get the time off work?"

He thought for a long moment. "I might—"

"*Gut*. Then that means you're going."

"I never said—"

"You implied, which is the same as saying yes."

"*Nee*, Leanna, it isn't."

Her left eyebrow lifted, disappointment entering her eyes.

Adam paused, curious about the full-court press she was giving him over this visit. She'd been to Mespo many times since the accident, and this was the first time she'd pestered him about going to Birch Creek. "Why is it so important I *geh*?"

She leveled her gaze at him. "Because it is."

A non-answer, but clearly the only one she was going to give him. He still didn't think it was a good idea to surprise Jalon, but it was past time the two of them talked face-to-face. "All right. I'll *geh*."

She clapped her hands together, her eyes shining with delight. "You've got a few weeks while I'm in Kentucky to work it out with *Onkel* Jeremy."

It wouldn't be a conversation with Leanna without a little bossiness thrown in. He didn't need a few weeks. His uncle was pretty lenient about time off, and the winter months were always slow. "Okay."

Leanna smiled again, her cheeks rosy from the cold. "Let's celebrate with another skate around the pond." She started to move toward his wheelchair, but he shook his head.

"You *geh* ahead." While the skating had been invigorating, reality had set in. He didn't want her to spend the rest of her time pushing him around the pond. He knew she wouldn't mind, but he would. "I'll watch."

"Are you sure?"

"Positive. *Geh* on, have fun."

As Leanna did figure eights on the ice, Adam thought about his decision. Despite his unease, he was oddly looking forward to seeing Jalon, not only because he missed him, but because he needed to confront him about the money, once and for all.

There was also something else he had to confront—his past. By going back to Birch Creek, he'd be surrounded with reminders of what happened to him. He could block most of that out while he was here in Mespo. He wouldn't have that luxury once he got to Jalon's.

He tensed at the thought, but it didn't cause him to change his mind. If putting those memories to a final rest was the key to moving forward with his life, he was ready to do it.

. . .

Four days after Phoebe sent her last letter to Jalon, she received one from him. When she read the contents, she was a little disappointed. The letter was shorter than his previous ones, as if writing it had been an afterthought. He told her about work and about eating at the Chinese restaurant. That was it.

Was he losing interest in her? Did he think she was boring? Worst of all, was he writing to her out of obligation because she put off meeting him in person? He said he understood, but did he really, or was he just being polite? She wrung her hands as she walked back to the house, barely aware of the thick, heavy flakes of snow coming down.

There was a time when she hadn't been so racked with doubt and worry. Now she questioned every little thing, especially since living with Aunt Bertha. She drew in a deep breath and tried to relax. *Don't borrow trouble. Tomorrow has enough trouble of its own.* She'd heard that all her life, knew the concept was from the Bible, but had often dismissed it as a stale cliché. Now she saw the wisdom in those words.

She tucked the letter in the pocket of her coat and put the rest of the mail on her aunt's bureau in her spotless, boring bedroom. Everything was so dull in this house—from the grayish-white paint on the walls to the off-white blanket on Aunt Bertha's twin-size bed. She didn't have a single bit of color anywhere—everything was gray, off-white, and lifeless brown. There was nothing on the walls, not even a clock. It struck Phoebe how the stark interior of the house matched the bleak, wintry surroundings outside.

Fortunately that would change in the spring, at least outside. Once the snow went away, there would be plenty of green grass carpeting the yard. Verdant leaves would appear on the trees, and by June there would be yellow flowers on the squash and zucchini plants in the garden. Her aunt hadn't mentioned anything about planting flowers, though. *God forbid the yard have too much color.* Somehow she'd have to sneak in a few flower seeds here and there. *If we're still here . . . and, Lord, I hope we won't be.*

She felt a little bad thinking that way, but she couldn't help it. To ease her conscience, she helped her aunt iron fabric while keeping her eye on Malachi through the window as he played in the backyard. Her son enjoyed being outside regardless of the weather. Today was frigid, but he dashed around the yard, catching the few snowflakes that fell here and there on his tongue. She had enjoyed doing the same thing as a child. Even now she wished she could join him. *Aenti Bertha would have plenty to say if I did.*

For supper she made a plain meal of stewed chicken,

noodles, and bread. Malachi had behaved himself during the day and she'd served supper on time, so Aunt Bertha had nothing to complain about. But having a relatively peaceful day didn't help Phoebe fall asleep that night, as her mind, and her worry, turned to Jalon again.

By morning she realized she was being silly about Jalon's letter. So what if it was shorter than his usual ones? After supper she would write him back, just as she always did. She smiled and got dressed. Everything between her and Jalon was fine.

Later, after she'd mopped the kitchen floor, washed clothes, and then hung the laundry on the back porch to dry, she prepared lunch. Aunt Bertha ate the meal in her usual stern silence, then left the kitchen. Phoebe glanced at Malachi, who seemed to visibly relax now that Aunt Bertha was gone. "Help me wash these dishes, Malachi," Phoebe said. "When we're done, we can play a game of checkers."

He nodded and scrambled off his chair. "Okay."

Thankful and a little surprised he hadn't refused her request, she pulled a small stool over to the sink. Her aunt's diminutive height meant she couldn't reach the top shelf of the cabinets, so she used the stool often. Malachi played with the soap bubbles as they filled the sink. Phoebe smiled at him. He was having another good day.

She slid her hands into the warm, soapy water, mentally composing her letter to Jalon. She peeked at Malachi again. He was intensely focused on drying his plastic drinking cup. Should she tell Jalon about him tonight? Her anxiety rose again, as it always did when she contemplated telling Jalon she had a child. She didn't like hiding Malachi from him—and not only because she was afraid of Jalon's reaction. She loved her son. He wasn't the reason for her shame. That was all on her.

"Phoebe!"

Her aunt's shrill voice made Phoebe jump. Whirling around, she saw Aunt Bertha marching toward her. Great, what was she upset about now? "Malachi, get down," Phoebe whispered through clenched teeth, in case that was the source of her aunt's ire. She wouldn't put it past her to be proprietary about the stool.

Once again Malachi didn't argue, and he stepped off the stool. She didn't have time to ponder his sudden decision to start minding her because her aunt started waving a piece of paper in the air.

"Who is Jalon?" her aunt demanded.

Phoebe's blood turned to ice. She hadn't made it a point to check the mail this morning because she hadn't expected another letter from Jalon until she responded to his last one. Usually she collected the mail every day, sooner or later, and her aunt had never said a word about it. Why had she changed her routine today? Then again, did the answer really matter? "He's a friend," she said as Malachi leaned against her.

"A young woman does *not* have male *friends*." She shook the letter at Phoebe. "A young woman of godly character, that is. I did not take you and the *bu* into *mei* home so you could conduct an affair behind *mei* back."

Her jaw dropped. "We're not having an affair. I wouldn't do that."

"Wouldn't you?" Aunt Bertha sneered. She cast a scathing look at Malachi, then back at Phoebe. "Haven't you before?"

She couldn't respond to that, not without explaining the details of Malachi's conception, and she wasn't going to say a word about that in front of her son. "I promise," she said, keeping her tone as even as possible, "Jalon is just a friend." Again, no need to explain to her aunt anything different. "A letter he sent to someone else was accidently—"

"Do you expect me to believe *yer* lies after the way you have conducted *yerself* in the past?" Somehow she managed to shake her head and, as short as she was, look down on Phoebe at the same time. "I should have known you could never be trusted."

"*Aenti*, please listen—"

"I don't want to hear another word." She took the letter and tore it in half.

"*Nee*," Phoebe said, instinctively reaching for the letter.

"You will not write to him again," she said, tearing the halves into fourths with slow, agonizing movements. "Or any other man."

She might as well be ripping Phoebe's heart. "There is *nee* other man."

"Then you admit you are conducting an affair while under *mei* roof?"

"How can I do anything when you control *mei* every move?" At her aunt's arched brow she added, "Please, *Aenti*. I'm lonely. I don't have any friends here. I'm not allowed to *geh* to singings or have a job or even meet with the ladies to quilt."

"And whose fault is that?" Aunt Bertha ripped the letter into even smaller pieces. "You flout God's rules as if they don't apply to you. You think highly of *yerself*, even though you can't control that *bu* of *yers*. You have shamed *yer familye*." She leaned forward, a fine sheen of perspiration on her upper lip. "You will not shame me. You are forbidden to write another letter, including to *yer* parents. I'll write them myself, explaining *yer* transgression."

"But—"

"And because I can't trust you, I will collect the mail. You will not *geh* near it." She turned around, taking Jalon's destroyed letter with her.

No more writing to Jalon? No more letters from him? She couldn't allow that to happen.

"What if he wants to marry me?" Phoebe blurted, desperate not to let her aunt take away the one thing other than Malachi that made her happy.

Aunt Bertha faced her again, narrowing her eyes. "So he *is* more than a friend."

Now she was in a pickle. She was tempted to tell her what she wished in her heart, that Jalon was not only more than a friend, but that he might possibly, someday, love her. Not only was it a lie, but when he found out about Malachi, it was an almost sure thing he would run the other way—and she wouldn't blame him. "*Nee*," she admitted. "He's only a friend."

Aunt Bertha tossed a cold glance at Malachi again, causing him to grip the skirt of Phoebe's dress. Her eyes shifted back to Phoebe's. "It would be a miracle if any decent Amish man *ever* married you." With that, she left, taking the remnants of Jalon's letter with her.

Phoebe couldn't hold it together anymore. She sank to the floor, tears spilling without her making a sound. She should be angry, but all she felt was defeat because what her aunt said was true. She had flaunted God's rules—not with Jalon, but in the past. She had thought highly of herself, believing the freedom the world had to offer was better than her Amish faith and way of life. And she had brought shame to her family.

But how could she survive living with Aunt Bertha without Jalon's letters?

"*Mamm?*"

She looked at Malachi. At the sight of his pale face and fearful eyes she quickly wiped her tears away and scooted closer to him. Her lips formed an empty smile. "Well," she said, unable to stop herself from sniffing, "that was quite a show, wasn't it?"

"Why is *Aenti* mad? Why did she make you cry?"

Phoebe didn't know how to answer that. While her aunt's words held a ring of truth, she was being cruel and unreasonable. If she didn't want Phoebe and Malachi here anymore, why was she still allowing them to stay?

Appearances. That's all it is. Her aunt was acutely aware of what others thought. Phoebe had noticed it at church. When they were in public together, there was little trace of the hard woman Phoebe saw behind these closed doors. If word had gotten out that she had refused to give her and Malachi a place to live, it would have made her look less devout. "Because she believes she's doing the right thing," Phoebe finally said. Maybe deep inside she thought she was. At this point Phoebe didn't care.

"Can we *geh* home now? Please?"

His question almost made her cry again. "*Nee*, sweetheart. Not yet." She pulled his slim body into her arms. "It's going to be okay."

He moved back enough so he could look into her eyes again. "*Aenti* Bertha doesn't like you very much."

Phoebe smoothed back a lock of his hair. "*Nee*. She doesn't. But I'm trying to change that. *Yer mamm* is trying to be a better person."

"You're already the best person I know," Malachi said as he hugged her neck.

The most important person in her life thought she was worth something, and that would be enough to get her through. "*Danki, sohn*." She squeezed him tight before pulling away. "But there's always room for improvement," she couldn't resist adding, because it was absolutely true. "Now, why don't we finish these dishes?"

"Then can we play checkers?"

"*Ya*."

They made quick work of the dishes, then played two games of checkers before she tucked Malachi into bed. For once, he seemed ready to take an afternoon nap. Then she went to her own room and sat on the edge of her bed.

The dishes and game had been a distraction, but now that she was alone, staring at the plain white wall of a bedroom she was never completely comfortable in, the pain returned. She was trapped in a cage of her own making. But at least here Malachi had food to eat and a roof over his head. By herself, Phoebe couldn't give him even that. No, she had to stay here, and that meant following her aunt's rules, despite how unfair they were. Which also meant she couldn't write to Jalon anymore.

Her throat constricted around the lump forming there. Was her aunt right? Would any decent Amish man ever be willing to marry her? Not out of force or obligation, but because he loved her? Maybe Jalon would have been the one man who could overlook everything and love her anyway. Now she'd never know.

CHAPTER 5

Three weeks had passed since Jalon had sent Phoebe his last letter. The first week he didn't panic. Phoebe had sent him a letter on the late side once before, around Christmastime when she'd been helping her aunt make quilts. There had to be a good reason why she was late again.

During the second week, however, doubt set in. By the third, he was kicking himself. Her lack of response to his letter told him he'd made a huge mistake by being so frank about his feelings and intentions. He'd taken a risk, and look where it ended up. *I pushed her away.*

Still, he hadn't completely lost hope. When he'd arrived home from work that evening, he checked the mailbox. Nothing except a couple of pieces of junk mail. He shoved them back into the box and shut the lid. He went inside and sat down at the kitchen table, not bothering to take off his coat, pausing only to yank off his hat and throw it on the table as his thoughts warred within him.

Should he write her another letter and explain that he hadn't meant what he said? Or should he try to make his feelings into a joke? But he couldn't do either of those things. His feelings weren't a joke and he meant what he said to her in the letter. Backtracking was not only unwise, it was disingenuous. In the end he figured whatever he'd write would make things worse, so he decided to not do anything.

A minute later he was drumming his fingers on the table. Inaction didn't sit well with him either.

Maybe he had to face the truth—he'd scared her off and she didn't want anything to do with him. He balled his hand into a fist and thumped it on the table. If only he'd thought that letter through. *Stupid, stupid . . .*

A knock sounded at the front door and he hauled himself up from the chair, his body sore from working in frigid air and snow. The temperature had steadily dropped over the past week, which made working outside difficult and tiring. He opened the door to see Karen Yoder standing there. "Hey," he said, opening the door so she could come in.

Karen stepped inside, her hands tucked inside the sleeves of her navy blue coat, her nose bright red from the cold. "You're invited for supper," she said. "We're having Salisbury steak, mashed potatoes, and canned corn."

His stomach turned at the mention of food, making him pause. He rarely lost his appetite. Now food was the last thing he wanted, even though he knew from experience the meal, while simple, would be delicious. "*Danki* for the offer, but I'm not hungry."

Karen lifted her eyebrow. "What's wrong?"

"*Nix.*" His gaze flicked to the side, then back to her.

"You're always ready to eat, Jalon." She gave him a knowing look. "Something is obviously wrong."

"I'm . . . tired." Which was true. He was tired from

working, and even more exhausted from stressing over Phoebe.

"You know if I tell *Mamm* that she'll send me right back over. Probably with reinforcements."

Jalon didn't doubt her words. Once Mary Yoder got an idea in her head, she wouldn't give up. Which meant he had no choice but to give in. "Let me get a quick shower, then I'll be right over."

When he arrived at the Yoders', Mary greeted him with a mug of warm apple cider. "To take the chill off," she said, her round cheeks rosy from the warmth of the woodstove in the living room. "Karen, there's one for you in the kitchen. Please help Ivy with the dessert."

Even the mention of dessert didn't get Jalon's appetite up, but he took a sip of the sweet, tart cider to placate Mary. "Where's Freemont?" he asked, surveying the empty living room.

"Out back with the *buwe* splitting and chopping a load of wood Benuel dropped by earlier today."

Jalon started to hand her his mug. "I'll *geh* help him."

"*Nee*, you won't." Mary pointed to the couch. "You'll sit in front of the fire and warm *yerself*. Supper will be ready shortly."

He nodded, knowing it was useless to argue with her. When she left to go to the kitchen, he made his way to the couch. It was well-worn from serving a family of seven. He took another drink of the cider, then set the mug on the coffee table, Phoebe back on his mind. More accurately, the embarrassment and sting of rejection. This was why he didn't take chances or do impulsive things. When he did, they never turned out well.

"Do you want more cider?"

He looked up at Karen, who was holding a ceramic pitcher. "I'm fine." He picked up his mug and took a big gulp, not wanting to let Mary or Karen think he didn't like or appreciate the drink.

She set the pitcher on the coffee table and sat down next to him on the couch. Not too close, though. They had never been anything but friends, and he had always appreciated her friendship, even though she was five years his junior. She had a steady head on her shoulders. She also had that annoying woman's intuition. "What's got you so out of sorts?"

"*Nix.*"

"I don't believe you," she said.

I don't care. "Really, I'm fine. Everything's fine. Other than this weather."

"Yeah, it's a mess out there." She looked toward the window, then back at him. "That's not what's got you bent out of shape, though."

She was as relentless as her mother. "I'm just . . . deep in thought."

"About what?"

"Karen, it's none of *yer* business."

"True." She folded her hands over her knees, not insulted in the least by his straightforwardness. "But that's not stopping me. The only times I've seen you like this are after you've . . ." She glanced down. "You know."

"Been drinking too much." He flinched, remembering the few times she'd seen him hungover, usually when she was visiting Leanna. Her sister, Ivy, had seen him, too, stumbling down the stairs, bleary-eyed, his sister and his mother pretending he was fine in an attempt to save face. None of them had called him out on it. But if they had, it wouldn't have changed anything. He had to come to the decision to quit drinking on his own. Still, he hated that he'd put his family and friends through such worry.

"*Ya*." She looked up. "Is that what's going on?"

He relaxed his shoulders. "*Nee*. I'm not hungover, and I haven't had a drink in a long time. I'm past that, Karen."

"*Gut*." She smiled. "That's what I wanted to hear." She started to get up. "I better finish up in the kitchen."

"Wait." Something made him stop her from leaving, and despite telling her his problem wasn't any of her business, he was about to make it her business. *Lord, I'm so confused.* "I think I need some advice."

She sat back down. "All right. I'm listening."

He rubbed his palm along the top of his pants leg. "I . . . uh, I . . ."

"Female problems!"

His head shot up. "Maybe." He sighed. "I'm not sure."

She grinned. "I didn't know you were seeing someone."

"I'm not."

"Then you're trying to see someone."

"Not exactly."

"Jalon, if you want to play twenty questions, we can, but wouldn't it be easier if you just told me what's going on?"

"For you, probably." At her annoyed look he explained about Phoebe and the letters, without giving too much detail. "Then I wrote to her three weeks ago, and I said some things I shouldn't have."

"You fought through the mail?"

He shook his head. "The opposite."

"Oh. *Oh.*" She nodded.

"Since then I haven't heard from her. We've been writing for months, and her letters have always arrived like clockwork. The only exception was around Christmas."

"So you're thinking it's not a coincidence that you haven't heard from her yet?"

"Do you?"

Karen shrugged. "I don't know her, Jalon. Maybe she's just late with her letter, like she was before. Or maybe she needed time to think about something so serious. Maybe there's something wrong—"

"Wait." He moved to the edge of the couch. He hadn't thought about that. What if she was in trouble? He knew something was going on at her aunt's house, a subtext in her letters despite her effort to be vaguely complimentary of her aunt every time she wrote. "What if something has happened to her?" He jumped up.

"Jalon, that was only a possibility—"

"I've got to talk to *yer daed.*" Without waiting for her to respond, he left the living room, went out the front door, and walked around the house. Behind the barn was a huge pile of wood, with three of the Yoder boys processing it like a well-oiled machine as Freemont supervised. Seth, the oldest boy at sixteen, was manning the ax, splitting the short, fat logs. Judah, the youngest at seven, was piling the split logs up against the back of the barn. A blue tarp lay on the ground, which they would put over the woodpile to keep the rain and snow from soaking the wood. Ira, who was fourteen, was piling up the unsplit wood within Seth's easy reach.

The cold air burned Jalon's lungs as he walked over to Freemont. He was about to jump out of his skin with impatience, but he didn't want to startle the boys.

"Hi, Jalon," Freemont said, not moving his eyes off his sons. The man must have eyes in the back of his head to have noticed Jalon. "Mary said you were coming over for supper tonight."

"*Ya*, but I can't stay. I also have a favor to ask, if you don't mind."

Freemont looked at him. "What do you need?"

"I'm going to be gone for a couple of days. Could you take care of the animals for me? Or the *buwe* could do it, and I'll pay them when I get back."

"*Nee* need to pay them and we'll take care of it. When are you coming back?"

"I'm not sure."

He arched a brow, and Jalon could see where Karen had inherited the gesture. "A few days? A week?"

"A few days," he said, having no idea if that was accurate. "I'll contact you when I know for sure."

Freemont glanced at his sons, then turned his attention fully to Jalon. "Something wrong?"

Jalon clenched his jaw. He appreciated that the Yoders were caring people, but right now he wasn't thrilled with their nosiness—although his caring did make Freemont a good bishop, and he was a definite improvement over Bishop Troyer. True, he had stumbled at first and was unsure of himself. He also hadn't wanted the job. But he had a relaxed manner about him, which translated into his sermons. They weren't as eloquent, or, thankfully, as long as Emmanuel's had been. But they were heartfelt, and everyone knew he genuinely cared about the people he was serving.

"*Nee*. It's all *gut*," Jalon said, fudging the truth a little. *More like a lot*. "I have to leave Birch Creek for a couple of days, that's all."

Freemont didn't answer right away. He kept his eyes on his sons, flinching slightly when Judah tripped over his feet and nearly fell, only to right himself and place a split log on the growing pile. "Are you drinking again?" he asked as Judah went back to fetch another piece of split wood.

Since Jalon had asked Freemont to help keep him accountable when it came to his drinking, he wasn't offended by the question. "I'm sober," he said. "Have been since I told you I stopped drinking."

Freemont peered into his eyes, as if he was searching for a lie. He could search all he wanted. Jalon was telling the truth.

Seemingly satisfied, Freemont relaxed his expression. "Do you need anything for *yer* trip?"

Prayers. Luck. And a guarantee that Phoebe was okay. "I'm *gut*."

"All right. Be safe."

Jalon started for his house. "Tell Mary I'm sorry for missing supper."

"She'll understand. Are you leaving now?"

"If I can get a taxi this late. If not, first thing in the morning. I'll take care of the animals tonight regardless."

"Godspeed." Freemont tipped his head toward Jalon.

Jalon rushed home, stopping by the shanty and calling Max, one of the English drivers his family had hired over the years. Max answered on the second ring and was willing to drive him to Dover, despite the fact that he would get home late since it was almost a four-hour round trip. "You don't need me to stick around in Dover?" Max asked.

Jalon paused. He didn't know what he would find when he got to Phoebe's aunt's house and he didn't want to put Max out anymore than he already was. "*Nee.* I'll get a taxi there to bring me home. "

"All right, then. I'll see you in a bit."

Jalon hung up the phone, made a call to his boss to tell him he wouldn't be at work for a couple of days, quickly settled the animals in for the night, then washed up. He couldn't meet Phoebe smelling like a barnyard. Then again, if something was wrong, she wouldn't care what he smelled like. *Please let her be okay, Lord. Please.*

He threw some clothes into his duffle bag and waited for Max to pick him up. It would be a long, uncertain ride to Dover, but when it was over, for better or worse, he would finally see the woman he loved.

An hour into the trip, the snow and wind started to pick up. Visibility was low, and Max's car moved at a crawl. "I've got to pull over," he said. "There's an exit close by. It's got a truck stop. We can find out there how long this storm is going to last."

Impatient, Jalon nodded. He couldn't blame Max for the weather, and the man had been generous enough with his time.

Slowly Max pulled into the parking lot, his back tires fishtailing. He got out of the van and Jalon followed. A blast of wind hit Jalon head-on, nearly knocking him off his feet. He tucked his chin into his coat, glad he'd left his hat in the car or he wouldn't have it anymore.

The truck stop swarmed with people escaping the storm. The attached restaurant was also full of customers, but Max suggested they find someplace to sit and have a cup of coffee to warm up and kill time until the storm let up.

The wind outside shook the windows of the restaurant. Not wanting to give up their seats once they found them, Max said, "Stay here. I'll see what the weather report says."

When he came back, his face was solemn. "Going to storm straight through the night. We're not going anywhere."

. . .

Midmorning the next day, Max pulled into the driveway of a very plain residence, even plain by Amish standards. A thick blanket of snow layered the yard, the driveway, the roof. Dover had felt the brunt of the storm, too, but he could see the snow on the porch and steps had already been shoveled and swept away.

"Here you go." Max yawned. "Sure you don't want me to stick around? Or I can come back and pick you up."

Shaking his head, Jalon said, "Thank you, but you've done more than enough. Go home and get some sleep." To show his appreciation he paid Max double his usual rate. "Stay safe."

Jalon stepped out of the van, the cold air enveloping him. Each breath felt like razor blades slicing through his lungs and every nerve in him danced on edge, and had since the moment they drove across the Tuscarawas County line. He was running on caffeine and adrenaline. Max had been able to nap in the booth seat at the restaurant, but Jalon hadn't, and he'd spent the night drinking cup after cup of coffee until his eyes crossed, the entire time questioning if he'd lost his mind. He fought with himself, going back and forth on whether to have Max take him right back to Birch Creek. Yet he couldn't turn back.

Even if nothing was wrong with Phoebe—and he prayed there wasn't—he had to meet her face-to-face. And he had to know how she felt about his letter.

The driveway led to the small white house with a front porch devoid of any sign of life—not a single rocking chair, end table, or even empty flowerpot to be seen. He slung his duffle bag over his shoulder, took a deep gulp of air, immediately regretted it as his lungs rebelled from the cold, and started toward the house. *Here goes nothing.*

As he approached, a small boy bounded out the front door and down the porch steps. He appeared to be around four years old, although Jalon was never good at guessing kids' ages. The boy didn't seem to notice Jalon as he settled in the yard and started digging his mitten-covered hands in the snow.

Jalon frowned. Had Max dropped him off at the wrong place? He had Phoebe's address stamped on his heart, so he knew he'd told Max the right one. Maybe in his fatigue he'd made a mistake. Jalon started for the mailbox at the end of the driveway to check the house number when the little boy looked up and said, "You wanna play?" Then he went back to digging a hole in the snow.

Jalon watched him for a moment. He remembered doing the same thing when he was a kid. His specialty was snow forts. That reminder brought back memories he didn't want to think about. Not wanting to hurt the child's feelings, he walked over and squatted down. "I can stay for a few minutes. What are we playing?"

The boy's eyes grew round, as if he hadn't expected Jalon to agree to his request. Then he went back to digging in the snow as if he'd never asked Jalon to play.

Jalon thought he'd help him out. "Do you have a ball?"

The boy shook his head. "I used to. Not anymore." He tossed a handful of snow over his shoulder. He was dressed for the weather, with several layers of clothes that made moving and digging a challenge, but he was managing. His dark blue wool hat covered his ears, and a similarly colored scarf hung precariously around his neck.

"A Frisbee?" Jalon asked. "A tricycle?" Although that would be pointless in the snow, but at least it was something. "How about a swing?" Each time the boy shook his head. "Do you have any toys?" Jalon asked.

"I've got this." He pulled out another handful of snow. Instead of throwing it, he attempted to make a snowball.

Now Jalon was convinced he somehow had the wrong address. Phoebe had said her aunt was older, so the boy couldn't be Aunt Bertha's son. Her grandson, maybe? Odd that Phoebe never mentioned him.

The boy tossed the pitiful, lopsided snowball, which

was more of a snow nugget. "I can't do it," he said. He wasn't exactly pouting, but he was disappointed.

"Let me show you." Jalon picked up a handful of snow and started to shape it. "You have to keep turning it as you squeeze the snow." He handed the boy the snowball. "See?"

The child nodded and set it carefully next to him. Then he picked up a handful of snow.

"Turn and squeeze." Jalon watched him form an imperfect but decent-size snowball. "You've got the hang of it now—"

The snowball hit him in the face.

Jalon wiped the snow from his eyes with his gloved hand, expecting to see the boy laughing at him. Instead, the child looked shocked. "I'm sorry. I shouldn't have done that."

"Then why did you?"

"I don't know." Then he added, "I thought it would be fun."

With a chuckle Jalon wiped the rest of the snow from his face. If he wasn't cold before, he was now. But he wasn't upset. Resisting the urge to throw a snowball wasn't easy, after all.

The boy had gone back to digging in the snow, the lure of snowballs abandoned. Jalon needed to figure out where Phoebe was, but for some reason he couldn't leave this little boy just yet. "Did you lose something in the snow?" he asked.

"*Nee.*" He continued to dig.

"Are you hoping to find something, then?"

The child's eyes lit up. "*Ya!* I'm trying to find treasure."

"What kind of treasure?" At the boy's confused expression, Jalon said, "Is the treasure money?"

He shook his head. "*Nee.* Not money."

"Is it jewelry?"

"What's that?"

"Necklaces, rings, bracelets."

"Never heard of that stuff before."

"I guess you wouldn't have." Jalon tapped his finger on his chin as if in deep thought. "Is the treasure books?"

"Books?" The boy huffed. "Books aren't treasure."

"You might think they are someday." He lifted his hands. "I give up. What's the treasure?"

He leaned forward and cupped his hand around his mouth. "Cookies. *Mei mamm* makes the best cookies ever. I don't get to have them very often, though."

Jalon frowned at his nonsensical answer. Cookies wouldn't be buried in the snow, but to this kid, they were treasure. His frown deepened. What kind of child didn't have toys? And cookies were a rare treat? He looked at the boy a little more closely. He appeared well cared for, although Jalon could tell even through the thick layers of clothes that the child was on the thin side. Unable to linger any longer, he said, "Good luck finding *yer* cookies, pirate."

"What's a pirate?"

"Pirates sailed on the ocean a long time ago. They would steal coins and jewelry and put them in treasure chests. Then they would bury the chests and dig them up later."

"Stealing is wrong."

"*Ya*, it is."

"I don't steal. So I'm not a pirate."

"True, you're not," Jalon said, checking himself. "That was probably the wrong word to use."

"How do you know about pirates?"

"I read about them," Jalon said, getting to his feet. "In books."

The boy looked up at him, his blue eyes wide. "I'm sorry I threw the snowball in *yer* face."

Jalon hid a grin. "So you said. And I forgive you. Now it's *mei* turn to be sorry because I have to *geh*."

"Where are you going?"

"I need to find someone. I thought she might be here, but I think I'm at the wrong *haus*."

The boy looked up at him, his eyes twice the size they'd been a few minutes ago. "I wish you could stay."

For some reason Jalon did too. He shook his head, clearing the thought. He hadn't come here to entertain a child. He needed to find Phoebe and make sure she was all right. "Hope you find *yer* cookies," he told him almost absently as he glanced around at his surroundings again.

"I won't." He stuck out his bottom lip. "*Mei aenti* is mean."

The words drew him back to the child. "*Yer aenti?*"

Before he could respond, a young woman came out on the front porch. "Malachi, that's enough time outside. I've got hot chocolate for you—" She stopped at the bottom of the steps, her gaze locking on Jalon.

Jalon couldn't move. He couldn't even breathe. The woman had a round face with high, round cheekbones and full lips. Her blue eyes were the color of cornflowers.

Beautiful. Then something shifted inside him that transcended his appreciation of her beauty. He wasn't at the wrong house after all.

"*Mamm?*" The boy ran up to her, then pointed at Jalon. "That man is lost. And I'm sorry I threw a snowball at his face."

Jalon *was* lost—lost in the feelings ramming into him. He barely recognized his own voice as he said, "Phoebe?"

Her eyes grew wide and she slowly nodded, a spark of recognition entering them. "Jalon?"

Even her voice was perfect, a sweet, lilting sound that propelled him to her. But he'd only taken two steps when he realized what the child had said to her.

He called her *Mamm*. He was Phoebe's son. At that moment she glanced down at Malachi, then back at Jalon, color draining from her face as if silently telling him his assumption was correct.

His body turned to stone. Phoebe had a son. One she'd never mentioned in any of her letters. One she had kept hidden from Jalon.

CHAPTER 6

I'm hungry, *Mamm*." Malachi tugged at the skirt of Phoebe's dress. "Is it lunchtime yet?"

She needed to answer him, but the words wouldn't come. She couldn't keep her eyes off Jalon, and she couldn't stem the dread filling her. She'd known it was him the moment she saw him. It was the kindness in his brown eyes. For a moment she thought she saw something else flicker across his expression, tugging at an emotion deep inside her.

Then he froze. Glanced at her and Malachi again. The emotion disappeared, along with the kindness. Now the handsome man who stood in front of her looked completely expressionless.

The dread churned like the ocean during a storm. This was the worst possible way for him to find out about Malachi.

"*Mamm?* I'm hungry. I want hot chocolate *and* food." Malachi tugged on her skirt again.

"*Geh* inside and take off *yer* coat and boots, then wash up," she said, her gaze remaining locked with Jalon's, willing him not to leave, not until she had the chance to explain. Malachi scampered into the house, but Jalon didn't move, to her great relief.

She also couldn't stop looking at him. He'd said he was average, and he'd been wrong. *So very, very wrong.* Handsome didn't begin to describe him. He was tall—he'd been right about that—and even from this distance she could see the freckles dotting his face, which gave him a bit of a boyish look, making him appear a little younger than twenty-five. His curly brown hair stuck out from beneath his straw hat, and his mouth . . . She had to rein in her thoughts about that part of him. She met his eyes again, and the confusion she saw there brought her to her senses. At least he hadn't bolted.

She heard a crash inside the house. Forgetting about Jalon, she ran inside to the kitchen. Malachi was on the floor, still in his outdoor clothing, one of the chairs toppled over. "Are you all right?" she asked, kneeling next to him. She checked him over, saw that he was fine, then frowned. "What were you doing?" Realizing she sounded snappish, she softened her tone. "I told you to take off *yer* things and wash up."

"I was trying to get that," he said, pointing to the top of the fridge.

Surprised, she said, "How did you know I had cookies up there?"

"I didn't. But you always hide them up there."

She'd have to come up with a better hiding place, because if Malachi knew where her secret cookie stash was, Aunt Bertha would soon find out. "Next time, ask, don't guess. And don't use a chair to climb up without permission. Now do as I say and wash up."

"Then can I have hot chocolate and a cookie?"

"Since you're so hungry, we'll have an early lunch

first." She could tell he was about to talk back. He was eroding her patience, which was nothing new—except now she didn't want Jalon witnessing it. "Malachi, don't argue."

"Fine." Malachi pulled off his coat, scarf, hat, and boots, then slunk off, leaving them all on the floor. She'd have him pick them up later, but now she had to face Jalon. She turned around and jumped. He was right behind her, standing in the doorway of the kitchen. Not only did she realize she hadn't invited him in, but she also hadn't heard him come inside.

"I'm sorry," she said. "I didn't mean to be rude. Do you want some cookies?" Her babbling sounded ridiculous, but she couldn't stop herself. She took down a plate covered with foil from the top of the fridge. "They're only sugar cookies. I can't keep chocolate chips here. Well, I could, but I'd have to hide them."

"Another secret, then?"

She cringed. His words were calm, his expression unreadable. "*Ya*." It was all she could think to say.

Another drawn-out pause stretched between them. "Should I leave?" he finally said.

The words hung in the air. The fact that he was still here spoke volumes. She'd lied by omission—and it was a huge lie. He had every right to leave, and she didn't have the right to ask him not to. But she didn't want him to go. Not when he was finally here. "Stay," she said, barely hearing herself say the word. "Please, stay."

Malachi came bounding back into the kitchen, full of energy and hunger. She turned to him, setting the plate of cookies on the counter. "Malachi, put your things in the mudroom, then be seated and wait until I make lunch for you and our friend Jalon."

"Friend?" Malachi asked, his blond brows lifting in awed surprise as he stared at their guest.

"*Ya*," she said, turning back to Jalon. "Will you join us for lunch?"

He delayed his response, looking at her with the same blank expression he'd had almost from the moment they recognized each other. Then he set his duffle bag on the floor near the table and sat down.

She spun around, took what she needed from the fridge and cabinets, poured glasses of milk, and quickly prepared their food. She was relieved Jalon had decided to stay, and annoyed that she didn't have anything tastier to serve than peanut butter and jelly sandwiches, celery sticks, and milk. At least Malachi would eat the sandwich, and maybe a celery stick with a little coaxing.

"Tell me more about the pirates," Malachi piped up.

Phoebe glanced over her shoulder. "Pirates?" The topic was so random she couldn't help but ask.

"We were digging for treasure outside," Malachi said, as if that explained everything. "Do you know about pirates, *Mamm*?"

"Only from books I've read."

"So you and Jalon read the same books?"

"I'm not sure." She put a sandwich in front of Jalon. "Sorry. This is all I have right now. *Mei aenti* went to the grocery store."

"She never lets *Mamm geh* shopping," Malachi said.

"Malachi, hush." Phoebe sat down, ignoring Jalon's

questioning glance. "Close *yer* eyes and pray." Instantly Phoebe put her hand on Malachi's, knowing that his idea of praying was to blink his eyes and either attack the food or, more often, push it away. After a few seconds and not nearly long enough to praise God, Phoebe opened her eyes. Malachi was willing to eat for once, and she didn't want to make him wait any longer.

Jalon picked up the sandwich, took a small bite, then set it down.

He was being polite. Of course, that didn't surprise her. He remained silent as he glanced at Malachi, then at her, then back at the uneaten sandwich.

She wanted to fade away right there, and not just because Jalon now knew her secret. All her talk in her letters about cooking, and his first meal from her was a child's sandwich. He probably doubted every word she'd ever written.

"*Aenti* Bertha never lets *Mamm* do anything," Malachi said, his mouth full of peanut butter and bread. "She's meanth."

"Malachi, I said be quiet."

Malachi took a drink of milk. "You said not to tell lies, and I'm not telling lies."

"Don't talk about our business in front of strangers."

Malachi looked confused. "But you said Jalon is a friend. If you know him, he can't be a stranger."

Phoebe drew in a breath. Normally she appreciated his precociousness, but not right now. "I know him, but he doesn't know *Aenti* Bertha. Besides, it's not nice to talk behind someone's back. That's called gossip."

"*Aenti* Bertha gossips all the time. She and Bessie

Eicher were talking about you the other day. They didn't know I was listening."

Jalon took a sip of his milk, staying silent.

"They said you were foolish. What does foolish mean, *Mamm*?"

"Finish *yer* sandwich, Malachi," Jalon suddenly interjected. "Now."

His authoritative tone had an effect, because Malachi finished the rest of his sandwich without saying another word.

Phoebe wasn't sure what was worse—the revelation that she was being gossiped about, the silence that filled the kitchen, or the fact that her son would listen to Jalon but not to her.

Malachi gulped the last of his milk and turned to Jalon. "May I be excused?"

Phoebe gaped. Aunt Bertha had been trying to get him to say that since they arrived.

"That's up to *yer* . . . *mamm*." Jalon looked at her again. The confusion wasn't as strong as before, and now suspicion entered his eyes.

"Can I, *Mamm*?"

"*Ya*." Pulling her gaze away from Jalon, she forced a smile at her son. "You may be excused."

"Can I *geh* outside again?"

"It's too cold out."

"Not for me." He looked up at her with eyes she could never resist. "I want to dig for more treasure. Like a pirate."

Unable to dim his optimism and tell him there was no such thing as Amish pirates, and still stunned at his sudden use of good manners, Phoebe nodded. As he dashed out of the room, she stood, giving Jalon a wavering glance. "I have to help him get dressed for the snow," she explained, twisting her fingers together. "Or else he'll *geh* out there barefoot."

He nodded, his eyes not leaving hers, his body completely still.

In the mudroom, she made sure Malachi was dressed warmly for treasure hunting and sent him outside. "Twenty minutes," she said, opening the back door. A blast of frigid air hit her, chilling her to her bones. "Then you have to come inside."

Malachi ignored her and ran out into the snow. She shut the door and leaned her forehead against it. Jalon was waiting for her and she had no idea what to say. *Coward.* That's what she was, plain and simple. She prayed for courage, then went back to the kitchen.

Jalon stood near the table, his back to her and his food and drink barely touched. As she neared, he turned around. There was no confusion in his eyes now. Only betrayal edged with anger. "Why didn't you tell me?" he demanded.

Unable to meet the accusation in his gaze, she stared at her feet. "I was going to—"

"When?" Her head flew up, and before she could answer he added, "Was this why you didn't want me to come here?" His jaw jerked. "I never would have kept writing to you if I'd known you were married."

"What?" She stilled, her brows pinching together. "I'm not married." It hadn't dawned on her that he would think she was married, but now it made perfect sense. It also gave her a tiny bit of relief. "Jalon, I'm not married. I never have been. Malachi is *mei sohn*, but his father isn't in his life." A chaotic place in her heart suddenly calmed enough that she could ask the question, "Why are you here?"

"It's been three weeks since *yer* last letter. When I didn't hear from you . . ." He averted his gaze. "I wanted to make sure you were okay."

She had to force herself not to swoon. "I'm okay." She almost whispered the words, so touched that he would check on her because he hadn't heard from her in a few weeks.

He took a step back, then ran one hand over his face. Dark, russet-colored whiskers covered his chin and upper lip, and she saw strain at the corners of his brown eyes. "Phoebe, if you didn't want to write to me anymore, you could have let me know. I would have accepted *yer* answer."

"*Mei* answer? To what?"

"The question I asked in the last letter I sent you." He frowned. "The one where I . . . oh, forget it." He picked up his duffle bag. "I see that you're fine now. I'll head back to Birch Creek."

"Jalon, I couldn't write back."

"Couldn't?" His eyes narrowed slightly. "Or wouldn't?"

She took a step toward him. "Whatever you wrote in *yer* last letter, I never read it. *Mei aenti* tore it up. She found out we were writing to each other."

"She didn't know?" His expression dulled. "You're full of secrets, aren't you?"

His words were harsh, and she deserved them. "I—"

The back door opened. "Phoebe!"

Phoebe froze. "Oh *nee. Mei aenti*'s home."

"Tell the *bu* to get the rest of the shopping bags," Aunt Bertha yelled from the mudroom.

But Phoebe couldn't move. She couldn't speak. If her aunt had been upset over Phoebe writing to Jalon, she was going to be furious when she found him here.

"Phoebe!" Her aunt walked into the kitchen. "Why didn't you answer me? I said tell the *bu*—" She stilled, her lips pinching as her darkening gaze landed on Jalon. "*Who* is this?"

Struggling to compose herself, Phoebe flinched at the icy glare in Aunt Bertha's eyes. By some miracle she found the strength to smile. "*Aenti* Bertha, this is Jalon. He's the *friend* I was writing to." She held on to the thin hope that reminding her aunt she and Jalon were only friends might help calm her reaction.

But Aunt Bertha's glasses did nothing to veil the aversion in her eyes. As Phoebe gestured to Jalon, she forced a wider smile that painfully stretched the corners of her mouth. "Jalon, this is *mei aenti* Bertha." She sounded as though she was strangling on a feather.

"Hello." He seemed relaxed, almost casual. Except for the muscle still twitching in his jaw. "It's nice to meet you," he said. "Phoebe's mentioned you in her letters."

Aunt Bertha set the bags of groceries she was carrying on the counter. "Phoebe, you should have told me you were having company."

Phoebe opened her mouth to speak, but Jalon beat her to it. "She didn't know I was coming for a visit." He hooked his duffle bag over his shoulder.

"You were planning to stay *here*?" Aunt Bertha said as her eyes took in Jalon's bag. Her eyes grew hot-looking. "Because despite what Phoebe led you to believe, I do not approve of unmarried men and women sleeping under the same roof."

"*Nee*," he said, his expression a little bewildered. "I was going to get a room close by."

"*And*," Aunt Bertha said, narrowing her gaze at Jalon, "it's basic good manners to make sure whomever you're visiting knows of *yer* arrival ahead of time, so *appropriate* plans can be made."

Phoebe cringed as Jalon looked chastised. "You're right. I should have let Phoebe—and you—know I was coming. It's just that when I didn't hear from her I thought something might be wrong."

Aunt Bertha crossed her arms, looking down her nose at Jalon even though he was more than half a foot taller than her. "As you can see, everything is fine."

Jalon looked at her. Then he turned to Phoebe. "Is everything fine?"

Phoebe hesitated. She should just say yes. It's what Aunt Bertha would expect and it would defuse the situation. Then Jalon would be on his way . . . and out of her life forever.

But she couldn't lie to Jalon. Not again, and not after he traveled all the way here because he was worried about her. *Because he cared.* And even if he walked out that door and she never saw him again, she wouldn't let the last thing she said to him be a falsehood.

"*Nee*," she whispered, then swallowed. "Everything isn't fine." She looked up at Jalon. "It hasn't been fine for a long time."

Jalon pressed his lips together and nodded.

"And whose fault is that?" Aunt Bertha snapped. "You made *yer* bed. Don't whine because you don't want to lie in it. The shame you brought on *yerself* and *yer familye* is *yer* fault."

"I'm not ashamed of Malachi." She lifted her chin. Regardless of her decisions, she would not allow her son to be maligned. He didn't deserve that.

Aunt Bertha leveled her gaze at Phoebe. "You should be."

"That's enough," Jalon said, surprising both women. "You can't talk to Phoebe that way. I won't allow it."

Aunt Bertha clammed up, which didn't surprise Phoebe. Above everything else, her aunt was a rule follower, and she took the traditional roles of men and women to heart. Jalon had spoken and he had made his position clear.

Yet while Aunt Bertha's voice was silent, her furious expression wasn't. She shot a look at Jalon, then at Phoebe before leaving the kitchen. A few moments later footsteps sounded on the stairs.

Phoebe wrung her hands. She also breathed an inward sigh of relief. No doubt her aunt was going upstairs to cool off. Then she would come back, pretend nothing had happened, and be the perfect hostess. Rules and propriety came before everything in her world, and for once Phoebe was glad for it. "She's having, uh, a bad morning." The excuse sounded lame to her own ears, and she could see Jalon wasn't buying it.

"Does she talk to you like that all the time?" He faced her squarely. "Tell me the truth."

She was surprised by the protective tone of his voice. "*Ya*," she whispered, telling him the truth again. "She does."

His jaw muscle practically pulsed. "She has *nee* right to say those things."

That was where Jalon was wrong. If he knew about her past, he would know Aunt Bertha had every right to say the things she did about Phoebe. But *not* about Malachi.

"If she's that cruel to you, why don't you and Malachi leave?"

She swallowed, which was difficult since her mouth felt like it was coated with cotton. "I don't have a choice," she admitted.

"Everyone has a choice."

"Not me."

His lips thinned before he spoke. "I don't believe that." He moved closer to her. "You deserve better, Phoebe."

Her eyes started to burn with unshed tears. Oh, she wanted to believe him. Yet how could she? She surely didn't deserve a man who would come to her defense even after she lied to him. Swallowing again, she said, "*Danki* for saying that, but I don't think so."

"You're wrong." His voice lowered, his brown eyes growing warm and soft, touching her deeply. "You absolutely deserve better." She shuddered, and his hands covered her shoulders. Then they moved up and down her arms. The intimate gesture was natural, as if they'd known each other for years instead of meeting in person for the first time under less than ideal circumstances. "Cold?" he asked.

She shook her head, soaking in the concern in his low voice. How long had it been since someone showed her simple, true kindness? It meant everything to her.

Her aunt burst into the room, and they broke apart. She dropped a large suitcase at Phoebe's feet, the one Phoebe brought when she and Malachi had arrived. "*Yer* things."

Phoebe's eyes widened in shock. Her aunt wasn't even bothering to hide her anger now. "*Aenti—*"

"I take you and the *bu* in out of the kindness of *mei* heart, and this is how you repay me? By bringing men into *mei* home while I'm gone? By choosing sin and pleasure over godliness?"

Phoebe glanced at Jalon. He looked just as taken aback as Phoebe felt. "I promise, that's not what I'm doing!" she insisted.

"Stop *yer* lies! You pulled the wool over *yer* parents' eyes, but you won't do it to me."

"*Mamm!*" Malachi bounded into the kitchen, covered in snow, his nose and cheeks crimson from the cold. "Can I have some hot chocolate and a cookie now?"

Aunt Bertha looked at him. Water dripped from the snow clumps on his boots, sullying her pristine kitchen floor. She turned her cold gaze to Phoebe. "The proof of *yer* sin."

Phoebe started to shake. Jalon moved to stand beside her, but she hardly noticed. This was the last straw. She would not subject Malachi to this woman anymore. She took the suitcase in her hand. From the weight of it she could tell her aunt had packed up all her and Malachi's belongings—more likely thrown them into the case and slammed it shut. "Malachi," she said, unable to keep the shocked fury out of her voice, "let's *geh*."

"But I want hot chocolate."

She grabbed his hand, got a better grip on the heavy suitcase, and without looking at her aunt or Jalon she went through the mudroom and outside. It didn't dawn on her until she'd walked halfway down the driveway that she'd left her coat, bonnet, and boots in the house. She halted her steps, knowing she'd have to go back and get them. She was already shaking from the cold as well as anger.

"Why is *Aenti* so mad?" Malachi asked. "Are we going somewhere? Why aren't you wearing a coat? You're always telling me I have to wear *mei* coat."

Her temples throbbed and her teeth tapped together as she ignored Malachi's questions and set down the suitcase. What was she going to do? Where would they go? Before she had few options, but now she had none. She couldn't look at Malachi, couldn't let him see the failure and despair she carried. *God, what am I going to do?*

Then she felt her coat slip over her shoulders, and Jalon's large hands lightly touching her arms before letting go. She turned and he handed her purse to her. "Can't let you freeze," he said, handing her a bonnet as well.

She looked up at him, shame flooding her. "You shouldn't have had to see that."

"You shouldn't have had to *geh* through it."

"*Mamm?*" Malachi said in a tiny voice. His fearful voice.

Phoebe crouched down in front of him. "It's going to be okay, sweetheart. God will take care of us. He always does." She truly believed that. But right now she was fighting her doubts. She had a little money in her purse, and there was a small inn a few miles away. They could walk there, spend the night, and then she'd figure out what to do. At least she could get her son out of the cold for a little while, and away from the cruelty of her aunt.

"Where's the nearest phone?" Jalon asked, interrupting her thoughts.

"Just down the street. Why?"

"You're coming with me." Not a question or a suggestion. A statement of fact.

"But—"

He held up his hand. "I'll call a taxi."

She shook her head. "I couldn't—"

"You can." He met her gaze with an intensity that nearly took away her breath. "You're coming with me to Birch Creek."

"*Mamm?*"

When she looked at her son, she saw he was trembling, probably more from fear and confusion than the temperature. Either way, they couldn't stand here in the driveway much longer. Her body was growing numb and she had to make a decision. "All right," she said to Jalon. "We'll *geh* with you."

He shifted his duffle bag strap so it crossed his body, then took her suitcase. She put her arms in her coat sleeves, tied her bonnet on her head, and fastened her coat buttons before slinging her purse strap over her shoulder. Then she scooped up her son, wishing she had her boots as well.

"Where are we going?" Malachi asked as they headed for the neighbor's phone shanty.

"We're taking a trip." She held him close, unsure how much to explain to him.

"Where?"

"*Mei haus*." Jalon grinned, but there were lines of strain around his mouth.

"Really?" Malachi looked at Phoebe. Unlike her and Jalon, he seemed excited at the news. "We're leaving here?"

Phoebe nodded, steeling herself for more questions.

"Yay!" Malachi gripped her around the neck. "Let's *geh*!" he said to Jalon.

As they walked, Phoebe felt like she was moving in slow motion. Despite Malachi's positive reaction, her doubts grew. What was she doing, leaving with Jalon? Anywhere was better than Aunt Bertha's right now, but that didn't mean she was being wise by leaving with a man she didn't know.

Wrong. I do know him. The problem is he doesn't know me. Not the real me, anyway. Although he was getting a pretty good glimpse of her right now. Which made what he was doing for her—more importantly, for her son—even more amazing.

Lord, what do I do now?

CHAPTER 7

L *ord, what am I doing?*
        Jalon sat in the front seat of the car, trying to sort out his jumbled thoughts and emotions. He wasn't having much success. He glanced over his shoulder. Malachi was leaning on Phoebe's shoulder, asleep, while she looked out the window, her hands twisting in her lap. Seemed he wasn't the only one wrestling with his thoughts.

He faced front, everything passing by in a blur even though their driver was going slow over the still-icy roads. Jalon barely noticed the shoveled driveways, the heaping piles of soft snow, the starkness of a landscape that come spring would be vibrant and bustling. It all hardly registered as he tried to figure out if he was doing the right thing.

No, that wasn't the problem. He knew he was doing the right thing. He'd gotten the sense from Phoebe's letters that living with Aunt Bertha wasn't easy, but he'd had no idea the woman was downright abusive. Her glare alone could cut through stone. This was what Phoebe had been living with all these months? From what he could tell she was a loving mother, and it was clear she and Malachi were close. Why had she subjected herself to abusive treatment, then? Why had she subjected her son?

Which led him to the real issue that made his head ache. Phoebe had a son. He was relieved when she said she'd never been married, or at least his jealousy had been relieved. But there was still the question of why she hadn't told him about Malachi. Why would she neglect to reveal something so important?

At the moment the answer didn't matter. He'd taken on the responsibility of Phoebe and her child, for now anyway. Not that he understood what that meant. Her aunt had torn up his letter, which meant Phoebe hadn't read it. She didn't know how he felt about her, and considering the circumstances, that might be a good thing.

She hadn't said a word since they got in the car, other than to tell Malachi to be quiet. He complied and soon fell asleep. Since then she'd been staring out the window.

He looked over his shoulder again and studied her profile. Right now he wasn't sure about anything when it came to her . . . other than the deep attraction he still felt. It was hard to keep his eyes off her. She was so pretty, but that wasn't the only thing that drew him. He'd seen the pain and defeat in her eyes when her aunt berated her. But he'd also witnessed her inner strength as she stood up to the harsh woman. And he could see Phoebe deeply loved her son. Her heart was in her eyes when she looked at the boy.

Suddenly she turned away from the window, and he quickly faced front. He shifted in his seat, his confusion growing. How could he have these tender feelings about her when he really didn't know her? How could he still care about her when she had kept such a huge secret from him?

Almost two hours later, the taxi driver pulled into Jalon's driveway. Jalon turned to Phoebe. "I'll get *yer* suitcase," he said.

"I can get it." She scrambled out of the car before Jalon could stop her, Malachi remaining behind. He was awake now and looking at Jalon with wide, expectant eyes. Jalon had never felt so out of his depth.

"I'll pop the trunk," the driver said, pushing up his black, square-rimmed glasses as he opened the car door.

Jalon paid him. "Thanks for the ride."

"No problem." He took the cash, then gestured with his thumb to the backseat. "Cute kid you got there."

"He's not—" Jalon clammed up as he spied Malachi sitting on the seat with his feet barely reaching the edge, still looking at Jalon. "Thanks," he said to the driver, then got out of the car.

Malachi scooted from his seat and climbed out of the vehicle. Jalon walked around to the back of the car as Phoebe tugged her heavy suitcase out of the trunk.

"Malachi," she called out.

Jalon turned to see him barreling through the snow. At least eight inches were on the ground.

"Stay close," Phoebe instructed.

He nodded and ran up to Blue, who was meowing indignantly in the middle of the driveway. Malachi squatted down in front of the cat and started petting his head. "Good kitty."

"I'll take this," Jalon said, reaching for the suitcase.

"I've got it."

He wasn't about to let her carry her own bag. He knew how heavy it was too. His hand touched hers as she held on to the handle with both hands. A jolt went through him, and he couldn't keep himself from meeting her gaze. *This could be a problem.* He composed himself and said more firmly, "Let me do it." He took the suitcase and grabbed his duffle bag. He paused, then said, "We should *geh* inside. Get out of this cold." Once they were in the house he would figure out what to do next.

She walked a few paces behind him. Malachi was still enamored with Blue, and the cat was rubbing the side of its face against the boy's fingers.

When they were in the living room, he set down the suitcase. "*Mei* sister isn't here right now. She's in Mesopotamia, visiting *familye*."

"So you're alone?"

He turned to her. "*Ya.*" Remembering her aunt's assumptions about both his and Phoebe's character, he added, "We've got a *dawdi haus* in the back. I'll sleep out there."

She shook her head. "Malachi and I will be fine in the *dawdi haus*."

They wouldn't, since it was only half-finished. As it was, he'd have to fix it up so he could stay there more than a few nights. "You and Malachi can have *mei* room. Or he can sleep in *mei* room and you can have *mei* parents' old room here on the first floor. Either way, you're both spending the night in this *haus*, so make *yourself* at home." He set his duffle bag near the base of the stairs. "I have to *geh* next door and let *mei* neighbor know I'm back." He paused. "I won't be gone long."

Her brow knit tightly above her pretty eyes as she nodded. "All right."

Jalon looked at her for a long moment, feeling the pull of attraction once again. Yep, this was going to be a huge problem if he didn't rein it in. He couldn't focus on feelings right now. He had to think logically, which had never been a problem for him before, except when he was drinking. Now that he was sober he was completely levelheaded . . . except when it came to Phoebe. *Get a grip already.*

As he went back down the front porch steps, Jalon glanced at Malachi, who was digging in the snow again. Blue was nearby, resting on the snow as if he didn't feel the cold, licking a paw. Malachi paused in his digging to look at Blue, patted him on the head, then resumed his mission. Maybe he was looking for pirate treasure again. Despite everything, Jalon smiled. He definitely was a cute kid.

That didn't mean he wanted instant responsibility for him.

He walked across the field, even less sure about what to do than when he'd been in the taxi. He saw Freemont and Ira outside. Ira was on the roof of their house brushing off the heavy snow. Before Jalon got to them, Ira shimmied down the ladder, his job done. He waved at Jalon, which made Freemont turn around. He patted Ira on the back, and the boy went into the house.

"That was a quick trip." Freemont pushed his hands into his coat pockets. "Everything *geh* okay?"

"Could have gone better." He looked at Freemont,

knowing he had to tell him what was going on. "I've got a problem. A big one."

"What happened?"

Jalon explained about Phoebe and Malachi, leaving out the parts about her keeping her son a secret. He also didn't mention falling in love with her through the mail. Love. That was in question now that he realized she was practically a stranger to him. "She doesn't have any place else to *geh*, and I couldn't leave her in that situation."

Freemont nodded. "I understand. I would have done the same thing."

"Leanna's not home yet. I'm not sure when she's coming back. She left her stay open-ended."

"And you don't want anyone gossiping about you and . . . Phoebe. Is that her name?"

"Exactly." He wouldn't submit Phoebe to that kind of scrutiny. Hearing it from her aunt was enough.

Freemont tugged his beard. He wasn't wearing any gloves and his hands were red from the cold and leathery from years of hard farmwork. "I'll send Karen over. She can stay tonight. It should be all right as long as you stay in the *dawdi haus*."

Jalon was relieved. "I'll call Leanna and ask her to come back early. If she can arrange a ride yet today, Karen might not have to stay."

"Sounds *gut*." He clapped Jalon on the shoulder. "Don't worry, Jalon. You did the right thing. I'm sure God will work all this out."

Jalon nodded, glad the bishop had that kind of faith and trust when Jalon's own was wavering. He was doing the right thing for Phoebe and Malachi. He didn't have a doubt about that. But was he doing the right thing for himself?

. . .

"I don't want to *geh* inside." Malachi crossed his arms and pouted, his breath coming out in tiny white puffs. "I want to stay out here and play."

Phoebe ground her teeth. Her nerves were frayed and the last thing she needed was Malachi throwing a fit. She wasn't familiar with this house and property, and she couldn't leave him unsupervised. "Malachi, you have to come inside. It's too cold out here anyway."

"Is not." But his teeth were chattering and his lips were turning blue. She glanced down at the ground and saw the cat sitting at Malachi's feet, staring at her with as much defiance as Malachi. *Traitor.*

She and Malachi shouldn't have come here. The more hospitable Jalon was to them, the more guilt piled on her conscience. He'd paid for the taxi ride, and now he was giving up his house for her and Malachi's benefit. He was giving her more than she deserved.

Malachi, on the other hand, seemed to have no qualms about staying at Jalon's. In fact, he appeared the most content she'd seen him since they left Fredericktown.

Malachi took advantage of the pause in the conversation to make a break for it. However, one thing he consistently underestimated was Phoebe's reflexes. She was fast—always had been. As a kid, she'd won every footrace against her brothers, and against the boys at school, both older and younger. So it wasn't difficult for her to catch Malachi by the back collar of his coat and yank him in place. "You will *geh* inside. And you will stop arguing with me."

He went with her, but complained the entire way until she thought she would grind her teeth to dust. Why couldn't she get him to behave? He'd minded Jalon just fine. Then again, Jalon had a commanding air about him. Not forceful or condescending. Only that he clearly wasn't a man to be crossed. Which gave her an idea.

She stopped at the bottom of the front porch steps and crossed her arms. "Jalon's not going to like how you're behaving. Not one little bit."

Malachi paled, which made his red, cold cheeks look like buggy taillights at a stop sign.

"Do you want to disappoint him? After he's been so kind to us?"

He shook his head. "*Nee.* I'll *geh* inside."

Phoebe couldn't help a small smile of satisfaction. Yes, she'd have to learn how to get him under control herself, but at least right now he was listening.

She directed him around the house to the mudroom she was certain was there. Once inside she could see it was larger than Aunt Bertha's and about the size of the one back home, which was still too small for a family of fourteen. She helped him take off his wet outer clothes and hung them on empty pegs, then placed his boots on the floor underneath. Fortunately, he'd been wearing his boots when Aunt Bertha had kicked them out. Since she'd had to leave hers behind, she was wearing only black sneakers, and her toes were stinging as they warmed up. At least her gloves had been in her coat pockets.

"Where's Jalon's cat?" Malachi asked as Phoebe took his small, cold hands in hers and started rubbing them.

"He came inside with us."

"Can I *geh* find him?"

She paused. Could Malachi be trusted in Jalon's house? Not that he would intentionally do anything bad, but in his zeal to find the cat he might knock something over or make a mess.

"I promise I won't do anything wrong."

"Oh, Malachi." She hugged him, then held him at arm's length. "*Ya*, you can find the cat. But please be mindful that we don't live here. We need to treat Jalon's *haus* like it's our own."

The irony of her words struck her. Over the past few months she'd allowed herself the fantasy of being married to Jalon. It was a pleasant daydream and a welcome distraction at Aunt Bertha's. Now she had to set that dream aside. Actually, she should probably destroy it. There was no time for fantastical dreams when she didn't even know what she was going to do about tomorrow.

"Oh, so I can pretend I live here?" Malachi smiled. "I like that!"

"That's not what I meant—"

He darted off, calling, "Kitty! Kitty!"

Phoebe leaned against her heels and let out a long sigh. Malachi was already getting attached to the cat. That wasn't good. Neither of them needed to be attached to anything, especially Jalon. *Too late for that.*

She went into the kitchen, eager to focus on supper and not on her still-strong feelings for Jalon or her predicament. The kitchen was simple, but much larger than the one at Aunt Bertha's. Unlike her aunt's it had a few personal touches—a wooden calendar on the wall, a battery-operated clock over the window, and, oh wow, an actual cookie jar on the counter in plain sight. A normal kitchen, which made her smile and allowed her to forget her problems for a moment.

It didn't take much time to find the ingredients to prepare a meal. She found some ground beef in the gas-operated refrigerator. A jar of canned green beans, a few potatoes, an onion, some cheese, butter, and a jar of tomato sauce and she had the makings for shepherd's pie. Too bad there wasn't time to make fresh rolls. But she would make do with what she had.

Before long the scent of chopped onions sautéing in butter filled the kitchen. By the time the potatoes were boiling on the stove she heard footsteps on the kitchen floor. Assuming it was Malachi coming from elsewhere in the house, she didn't turn around. "Did you find the cat?" she asked.

"Is he lost?"

Surprised, Phoebe turned at the feminine voice. The woman, who appeared to be Phoebe's age, walked over to her, carrying a cake container in her hands. She'd apparently shed her outer clothing at the front door. Auburn hair peeked out from her white *kapp*. Phoebe assumed she was Leanna come home early until she said, "Hi. I'm Karen." She set the cake container on the counter. "I live next door. Jalon told us you and *yer sohn* are staying here. *Daed* thought it would be a good idea if I stayed here too."

Phoebe nearly sank against the counter with relief.

Even with Jalon in the *dawdi haus*, she'd been afraid people in his community would gossip about him. Having a chaperone here would help dispel that temptation. She smiled and held out her hand to Karen. "Nice to meet you. Is Jalon still at *yer haus*?"

"He was still talking with *Daed* when I left." She sniffed. "Something smells delicious. What are you making?"

"Shepherd's pie."

"Can I help?"

"*Danki*, but there's really not much left to do."

"I can whip up some cornbread." She walked over to the pantry and opened the door. Phoebe noticed how familiar Karen seemed to be with Jalon's kitchen.

Phoebe tested the potatoes with a fork. They needed to cook a little longer before she drained and mashed them with butter and milk. She set the fork down on the counter and turned to Karen. "I'll be back in a minute. I need to check on *mei sohn*."

Karen glanced over her shoulder. "I'm assuming he's the little *bu* fast asleep on the couch?"

He was asleep again? "He must be tired," she murmured.

"I'm surprised to see Blue snuggled next to him."

"They've kind of taken to each other."

"*Gut.* That cat needs to expand his social horizons. He usually only likes being around Leanna. Unless you have food. Then suddenly he's *yer* best friend." Karen found the cornmeal, flour, and baking powder she needed. "Can you hand me one of the mixing bowls?" she asked Phoebe.

"Where are they?"

"Lower cabinet on the right."

Phoebe found the bowl exactly where Karen said.

Karen took it as Phoebe lifted it out. "I know this kitchen almost as well as *mei mamm*'s. I've known the Chupps for a long time. Almost fourteen years, I think, since they moved to Birch Creek." Karen went to the fridge and opened the door. "My older sister, Ivy, is best friends with Leanna, and since Ivy and I are the only daughters in *mei familye*, we used to come here all the time. We always helped Jalon's *mamm*, Rose, with the cooking." She pulled out eggs and a carton of milk, then shut the fridge door. "Rose makes the best lemon chiffon pie you've ever tasted. Leanna makes . . . boiled eggs."

"Really?" Phoebe said, relaxing enough to smile a little.

"*Ya*, she's a great friend, and she can throw a baseball and spike a volleyball like nobody's business. But she's an awful cook. Ivy's not much better, but at least you don't have to worry about her burning down the *haus*."

"I love to cook," she said, feeling at ease for the first time since she arrived here. Karen was easy to talk to.

"So do I. With four siblings, it's a good skill to have."

"I agree." She glanced over her shoulder and saw Karen measuring out the cornmeal. "I have ten. All boys."

Karen's eyes widened. Like Jalon, she also had freckles, but hers were more prominent. "And I thought our *familye* was big."

As they continued to cook, they fell into easy conversation. Phoebe was pleased to find someone who was as adventurous in the kitchen as she was. "You're lucky *yer familye* is open to experimentation," Phoebe said as she mashed the hot potatoes in the pan.

"They just like food. Especially *mei* brothers and *mei daed. Nee* one's very picky."

She thought about her aunt, who would never have had cornbread with shepherd's pie. Rolls only. And no putting cheese on top of the potatoes, which Phoebe planned on doing because it added a tasty richness. "Can't say the same for *mei familye.* Some of them, anyway."

"Where are you from?"

"Originally Fredericktown, but I was staying with *mei aenti* in Dover."

"And you and Jalon met through letters?"

She turned and looked at her. "How did you know that?"

Karen's face turned red. "He, um, said something. Right before he left yesterday."

Phoebe put down the potato masher. "He talked about me with you?"

"I shouldn't have said anything." Karen sighed. "I'm sorry. He was worried about you, and wondering whether he should *geh* see you."

The warm feeling she'd had knowing Jalon cared enough to check on her faded. "Then it was *yer* idea for him to *geh* see me?"

"Well, kind of. As soon as I suggested you might be in trouble, he left right away."

"Oh." He hadn't come to see her without prodding from Karen. That disappointed her. Would he have checked on her if Karen hadn't thought of it? Or would he have let their relationship fade away?

"Me and *mei* big mouth," Karen muttered.

Phoebe lifted the corners of her lips, wanting to put Karen at ease. "You didn't say anything wrong." But she did wonder what kind of friendship the two of them had, since Jalon felt comfortable talking about her with Karen. A close friendship, obviously.

"I don't want you to think Jalon talks about his private business with me. He doesn't. He wouldn't have said anything if he hadn't been so worried about you." Karen scooped the cornbread batter into a muffin tin. "I also had to drag it out of him. He's not a big talker, not about personal stuff."

"I wasn't worried." At least not much. She sighed. She didn't have the right to be concerned about who Jalon was friends with. She turned back to the potatoes, defeat overwhelming her once more. She mashed them a few more times, then set the masher to the side again. "I'll take a peek at Malachi," she said, needing to remind herself of the main reason they were here.

Karen nodded and carried the muffin tin to the oven. "I'll keep an eye on everything here."

Phoebe left the kitchen and went to the living room. Blue was lying on the back of the sofa, but when he saw Phoebe approach, he jumped down and curled himself against Malachi's small belly. Her son shifted at the movement but remained asleep. His lips twitched into a half-smile. He looked so peaceful, so content. Seeing him this way meant everything to her. If only the happiness could last.

How could it, though? She was in the same position she had been in right before she left home. She had to find a place for her and Malachi to live. She couldn't take advantage of Jalon's hospitality for long. She had very little money and no job. How was she going to take care of her son now?

God, what am I supposed to do?

CHAPTER 8

L eanna didn't tell you she was going to Kentucky?"
Jalon leaned back against the wall of the phone
shanty. "*Nee.* She didn't."

"She and *yer* cousin Maria decided to visit some friends
for a few weeks," his aunt Tabitha said. "They're not supposed to be back until February twentieth, if then. They
like to keep things open-ended, and they said something
about maybe going to Horse Cave too."

Another one of Leanna's open-ended trips. Jalon
sometimes wished he had his sister's freedom to do whatever she pleased. "Is there a number where I can reach
her?"

"Not until they come back here or go to Horse Cave.
The friends they're staying with right now don't have a
phone."

That was a week away. Great.

"Is it an emergency? I can try to get a message to them
somehow."

He paused. This wasn't a true emergency. Karen was
going to stay in the house, and even though he didn't want
to ask her to stay with Phoebe a whole week, he knew
she would. He also didn't like the idea of staying in the

unfinished *dawdi haus*, but it was better than staying in the barn, which is where he would have slept tonight if he'd had to. Then again, maybe he was making this complicated for no reason. He didn't know Phoebe's plans. There was so little he knew about her, and that frustrated him more than anything.

"Jalon?" Aunt Tabitha said.

"It's not an emergency," he said, coming out of his thoughts. "But can you let her know she needs to call me as soon as she's near a phone?"

"Sure." Aunt Tabitha didn't say anything for a moment. Then she asked, "How are you doing, Jalon?"

"*Gut.*" He cringed, knowing what was coming next.

"The *familye* misses seeing you," Aunt Tabitha said. "It's nice having *yer* parents nearby again. Maybe you'll come for a visit soon?"

"I don't know." He rubbed the back of his neck. "*Mei* job keeps me busy."

"That's what Leanna said."

"I've got to *geh*, *Aenti*. *Danki* for passing along the message to Leanna." He hung up the phone, the breath in his chest speeding up. He pushed open the shanty door and trudged through the snow to the house. Now wasn't the time to think about his family. He had Phoebe and Malachi to worry about.

He stripped off his boots, coat, and hat in the mudroom, then went into the kitchen. Phoebe and Karen were scurrying around in a smooth rhythm, as if they had been cooking together for years instead of an hour. "I see you two have met," he said.

Phoebe turned around, a small smile playing on her

lips. He stilled. There it was again. A trip of the heart, but much different than the anxiety he'd felt after his phone call with his aunt. Her eyes flitted shyly downward, her long black lashes resting against her cheeks. *Quit noticing stuff like that.* He had to keep a level head. *She doesn't exactly make it easy.*

"Supper will be ready in a little while." Karen glanced at him as she set the table.

Jalon watched Phoebe spread mashed potatoes on top of some sort of casserole, then slide it into the oven. He spied a bowl on the counter covered with a kitchen towel. The scent of onions, butter, and cornbread made his stomach growl. For the first time that day he had a real appetite, and if Phoebe's cooking was anything like her baking, he was in for a delicious meal.

As usual, he felt helpless in the kitchen, despite being a marginally better cook than Leanna. "I'll leave you to it, then." He stopped when he saw the cake container on the counter. "Is that what I think it is?"

Karen smiled. "If you think it's an Orange Bliss cake, then you're right."

His mouth literally watered. "I haven't had that in a long time."

"I've been meaning to make one and bring it over. I thought you'd want a treat while Leanna was gone."

"Because you know she'd eat the whole thing if she was here."

"Not the whole thing." Karen laughed. "But most of it."

Jalon chuckled, then glanced at Phoebe. She wasn't laughing. She stood in front of the stove, staring at the empty pot that had held the mashed potatoes. She didn't look at him as she took the pot to the sink and rinsed it out.

"We've got everything under control here," Karen said to him, making a shooing motion with her hands. "*Geh* find something to do and let us finish."

Freemont had been right in sending Karen here. Jalon liked Ivy well enough, but Karen had a way of making everyone around her feel at ease. She was more than a chaperone; she was a buffer between him and Phoebe.

He went to her, lowering his voice so Phoebe couldn't hear. "Can I talk to you a minute? In private?"

Karen nodded, then set her dish towel on the table. She and Jalon walked out of the kitchen and stood just inside the living room. "Do you think you can stay a few extra days?" he asked. "I just found out Leanna's in Kentucky."

"Phoebe's going to be here that long?"

"I'm not sure."

She paused as if she were going to say something. Then she nodded. "I have to work most of this week, but I'm usually home by three. Tomorrow I'm off, though."

Jalon nodded. Karen and Ivy had been apprenticing for the last couple of years at Thomas and Judith Miller's bookbinding business. "I'm at work until five or six. Sometimes seven if we're working overtime. As long as you're here in the evenings, it will be fine." Of course, it was all contingent on whether Phoebe was going to be here beyond tonight. They would have to talk about that soon.

"That sounds *gut*. It will be nice to get away from home for a bit. I love *mei familye*, but sometimes the chaos drives me crazy."

He knew from experience that the Yoder household was chaotic, especially when Karen's three brothers had been younger. They were a rambunctious group. "*Danki* for staying, Karen. I really appreciate it."

"Phoebe is nice." She lowered her voice. "I can see why you like her."

"Oh," Jalon said. "One more thing. Do you have a pair of boots Phoebe could borrow? We were in a hurry when we left her aunt's."

"Sure. I'll bring them over later."

Jalon leaned against the doorjamb as Karen walked back into the kitchen. One issue solved for the moment. Or two, if he counted the boots. He'd noted that Phoebe was wearing only tennis shoes when they left her aunt's house, but he hadn't wanted to go back for her boots. Now her feet would be warm and dry when she went outside.

He went into the living room and found Malachi sitting on the couch, his hair a tousled mess, his eyes drowsy and groggy as if he'd been sleeping. Blue was draped over Malachi's small lap, his front paws and back feet resting on the couch cushions on either side of the boy's legs.

"I think this cat likes me," Malachi said, running his hand over Blue's back. "What's his name?"

"Blue." Jalon sat down on the edge of the couch and reached to scratch Blue's face, but the cat pulled away and leaned against Malachi. "He belongs to *mei* sister,

Leanna. I think he likes you too. Which is something, because he's a picky cat."

Malachi continued petting Blue, who was purring so loudly Jalon was sure the women could hear him in the kitchen. "I wish he was mine," Malachi said, stroking the cat with more gentleness than Jalon thought a child his young age possessed.

Jalon's heart went out to him. He seemed lonely. *So does Phoebe.*

"Can I sleep with him tonight?" Malachi asked, looking at Jalon.

"That depends on Blue. And *yer mamm*. Does she let you sleep with pets?"

"I've never had a pet. *Aenti* Bertha doesn't like animals. And *Grossdaadi* says animals are for work and food, not for pets."

"So you used to live with *yer* grandparents?"

He nodded. "I miss them. And *mei* cousins. Crackers too."

"You miss crackers?" Jalon asked, thinking it was an odd thing for a child to miss. Then again, he knew next to nothing about little kids.

"*Ya*. He's the best horse."

Ah. That made more sense.

"Sometimes I got to ride him as long as Devon said it was okay. He would lead Crackers around while I hung on to his mane." Malachi hugged Blue.

Once again the situation made little sense to Jalon. If Malachi missed home so much, why couldn't they go back? Why had Phoebe been so insistent she and Malachi had no place else to go? Jalon wanted answers, but he wasn't going to take advantage of Malachi's youth and trusting nature to find out. He'd have to ask Phoebe. *If she'll tell me the truth.* The bitter thought came unbidden and he frowned.

"What's wrong, Jalon?"

At Malachi's worried question, Jalon shook his head. He tousled the boy's hair. "*Nix.* Just waiting on supper. *Mei* stomach's growling."

"Mine too. I hope *Mamm* made pizza. She makes the best pizza."

"Better than her cookies?"

Malachi tilted his head, deep in thought. "Her cookies are better."

Jalon laughed. "Cookies are always better than pizza."

Blue continued to purr away. Remembering the lack of toys Malachi seemed to have at his aunt Bertha's, Jalon thought of something. "Stay here. I'll be right back." He ran upstairs to his room, opened the bottom drawer of his dresser, and found what he was looking for. A few seconds later he was sitting next to Malachi again. "Have you ever used a yo-yo?" He handed the toy to Malachi.

Malachi nodded. "*Mei grossdaadi* had one. Really old and made of wood."

"Those are the best ones. But this green plastic one isn't too bad. I played with it when I was a *kin.* Do you want to see a trick?"

"*Ya.*" Malachi sat up straighter on the couch. Blue adjusted, then went back to purring while looking bored.

Jalon stood, hoping he remembered how to do his favorite trick from childhood. "The important thing is to make sure you have a clear space. I learned that the hard way and broke one of *mei mamm*'s glass flower vases."

"Did you get in trouble?"

"*Ya.*"

"Lots of trouble?"

"Um, *ya.*" Admitting his childhood mishaps to a four-year-old was a lesson in humility. "Anyway, the best place to do this is outside, not in the *haus*. But just this once I'll show it to you inside." He put the looped string around his middle finger, then gripped the yo-yo in his palm. It was amazing how quickly everything came back to him.

He moved away from the couch and stood in the middle of the living room. "First thing you do is warm up a little." He threw the yo-yo straight down, then caught it when it rolled back up. Malachi and Blue watched, their heads moving up and down in sync.

After a couple of practice throws, he threw out the yo-yo again, but this time instead of throwing it downward, he propelled it forward. Then he placed the index finger of his free hand three quarters down the end of the string, then looped the yo-yo back toward his other hand. He flipped the yo-yo up the string two more times, then dropped the yo-yo and let it roll back up.

"Wow," Malachi said. "Do it again!"

Bolstered by the boy's enthusiasm, Jalon performed the trick two more times. It was one of the easier ones he knew. At one time he could swing two yo-yo's at once, one in each hand. The more he yo-yo-ed, the more he realized he missed it. But he'd stopped playing with it years ago. The same time he stopped doing a lot of things . . . and started doing other, less innocent things.

He removed the yo-yo and handed it to Malachi. "It's *yers*, on one condition."

"What's a condition?"

He started to define the word, then realized he didn't have to in order to make his point. "I need you to promise me you'll follow the three rules of yo-yo's."

"I will." Malachi reached for the yo-yo.

Jalon pulled back. "You don't know what they are yet."

"Oh." He put his hand on Blue's back.

"Number one, *nee* yo-yo'ing in the *haus*."

"Okay."

"Number two, always make sure you have plenty of room to yo-yo. Look all around you so you won't hit anyone or anything."

"Like a vase?"

"*Ya*. Like a vase."

When Malachi nodded with absolute seriousness, Jalon had to fight to maintain a strict face. "Number three"—he put the yo-yo in Malachi's hand—"have fun."

Malachi turned it over in his palm, running his fingers over the bright green plastic. He looked up at Jalon and grinned with thankful awe.

Jalon felt a tug in his heart, altogether different from anything he'd felt before. Without thinking, he tousled the boy's already messy hair again. "*Geh* wash up. The bathroom's near the downstairs bedroom. It's almost time for supper."

Malachi scrambled off the couch, ran a few feet away, came back to pat Blue on the head, then dashed away. Jalon grinned. What a ball of energy.

"I wish he'd listen to me the way he listens to you."

Jalon turned around to see Phoebe behind him. "What?"

"He went to wash his hands without complaint." She sighed. "Usually I have to argue with him to do it. You didn't notice how he minded you back at *mei aenti*'s *haus*?"

Jalon shook his head, not sure what she was referring to. Then he remembered lunch. "Oh, that. I just told him to finish his sandwich."

"And he finished his sandwich." Her lips curled into a smile, but it didn't reach her eyes. "Supper's ready," she said, then turned around and went back to the kitchen.

Before Jalon could say anything else, Malachi flew past Jalon. Jalon followed and saw Malachi go straight to Phoebe, who settled him at the table. Jalon couldn't stop watching as she whispered in his ear, then brushed the top of his shoulder with her hand before she seated herself. She'd sounded so full of doubt a moment ago, and Jalon didn't understand why. Anyone could see how much these two loved each other.

After they prayed over the meal, Karen passed the casserole dish to Jalon first. Shepherd's pie. He should have known what it was when he saw Phoebe spreading potatoes on the casserole. He'd had this dish dozens of times growing up. His *mamm* never put cheese on it, though. He took a bite—and was amazed. "Wow," he said. "This is really good."

Phoebe put a cornbread muffin on her plate, her small smile letting him know she was pleased. He didn't expect her to acknowledge the compliment, as that might seem prideful. But food this good deserved recognition. He took another bite, savoring the creamy potatoes and perfectly seasoned ground beef.

"I agree," Karen said after finishing her first bite. "This is the best shepherd's pie I ever tasted."

"Corn muffins are good too." Jalon didn't want to leave Karen out because she was a great cook in her own right. But he'd had her corn muffins before, which was why he'd guessed she made these. They were good, but nothing special. Now, her Orange Bliss cake was a different story. He couldn't wait to tear into that.

They finished the meal in near silence—Malachi kept wanting to be excused, even though he ate only a third of his meal. Several times Phoebe told him to finish his food, only to be met with various excuses. Now Jalon could see what she was talking about. "Malachi," he said, sternly enough to get his attention.

The boy looked at him, a defiant spark in his eyes. "What?"

"Finish *yer* supper."

"I did."

"There's still food on *yer* plate."

"I'm full."

"Jalon, it's okay—"

"Phoebe, it's not okay." Jalon looked at Malachi again. "Malachi, I won't tell you again. Finish *yer* supper. Then you'll help me with the chores in the barn."

The tension at the table thickened. Karen kept her head down and continued eating, wisely staying out of it. Jalon could sense Phoebe's eyes watching to see what Malachi would do. Jalon wasn't a hundred percent sure the boy would do as he was told, but he continued to look at him sternly.

Then, without another word, Malachi picked up his fork and started eating.

CHAPTER 9

While Jalon and Malachi were out in the barn doing chores, Phoebe started washing dishes and Karen cut the delicious-looking cake she'd brought. "He's a cute little *bu*," Karen said, running a serrated knife through the bundt cake.

"He's a handful." She was stating the obvious, but there was no reason to deny it. After Malachi's defiance at the table, Phoebe thought it was a wonder Jalon still wanted Malachi to help him.

"Aren't all *kinner* handfuls at that age?"

"Some more than others." Phoebe thought about her siblings. They were well-behaved for the most part. Her father commanded respect, but not in an authoritarian way, and her mother had a gentle, firm method of discipline. When she was younger and had so much responsibility for her siblings, life was frustrating. Still, her brothers didn't give her as hard a time as Malachi had lately.

"They are in *mei familye*. I remember watching Ira when he was a few years older than Malachi. He decided to play hide-and-seek." Karen carried two small plates with slices of cake to the table. "I looked everywhere for him, and I thought I lost him. I was crying when *mei* parents came home from visiting friends. Turns out he was asleep under their bed. He kept moving around so I couldn't find him, and then he got bored and conked out."

"Sounds like something Malachi would do." Phoebe paused, water pouring from the tap into the right side of the sink. Karen had explained that Jalon asked her to stay for a week, until Leanna came back. Phoebe almost told her she wouldn't have to stay that long, then thought better of it. She had no intention of being here for a week, but she would let both Karen and Jalon know that later.

"I'm surprised Jalon didn't mention Malachi before," Karen said.

Phoebe rinsed off the casserole dish. "I didn't tell Jalon about him," she said, tired of lying.

"Oh." After a long pause she added, "I'm sure Jalon understands why." Karen placed two more plates on the table.

Phoebe could only hope he would when she told him her reason. But her aunt's words weighed heavily on her mind. *Why* would *any decent Amish man want to marry me?* Jalon had proved he was far more than decent. He was special. And he deserved more than a woman who not only couldn't tell him the truth, but also had a shameful past. She leaned against the sink and closed her eyes.

"You're exhausted."

Opening her eyes, Phoebe saw Karen looking at her. Shaking her head, she went back to washing the dishes. "I'm fine."

"I'll finish here. Why don't you *geh* upstairs for a little while? You could take a hot shower if you'd like. I'll watch Malachi when he and Jalon get back."

"I couldn't let you do that."

"Why not?"

"I don't want to impose."

"You're not. I'm offering. Besides, I don't lose little ones anymore." She took the dishcloth from her. "*Geh* on. You need to relax a little bit."

She finally gave in, thanked Karen, and went upstairs. She peeked into the first room at the top of the stairs and saw her suitcase sitting on the floor. When she walked inside, she realized she was in Jalon's room. She looked in the closet. He'd already removed his clothes.

Overwhelmed, she sat down on the edge of his bed. In the past several hours she had felt more cared for and accepted than she had in months at her aunt's house. Not just from Jalon, but Karen too. But Jalon . . . she could hardly fathom what he'd done for her and Malachi. And what had she given him in return? Deception. Obligation, at least for tonight.

She hung her head. Karen was right. She was exhausted. But as soon as possible, she would set everything right with Jalon . . . and pray that she wouldn't ruin things with him forever.

· · ·

Malachi turned out to be a good helper in the barn. He was also a chatterbox, something Jalon wasn't used to. The child talked about his grandfather's farm, his cousins, digging for pirate treasure, Blue, yo-yo's, pizza, and how much he hated taking a bath. The rapid-fire switch of topics gave Jalon auditory whiplash. It also amused him.

After he shut the latch on the pigs' pen, he turned to Malachi, who was picking up a stray piece of hay from the barn floor. "They're all tucked in for the night," Jalon told him. "Ready to *geh* inside and have dessert?"

"Dessert?" Malachi dropped the hay. It floated to the floor. "What's for dessert?"

"Karen made a cake—"

"Cake!" He tried to dart out the barn, but Jalon stopped him. "Not yet. We need to have a little talk first."

Malachi grimaced. "I don't like talks."

"It doesn't matter if you like them or not." He hunkered down in front of the boy so they were face-to-face. "We're going to have one." He drew in a breath, unsure if this was a good idea. He'd been thinking about having this discussion with Malachi while they were doing the chores, but he wanted to make sure he had his undivided attention. "You need to mind *yer mamm*."

"I do mind her—"

"Not all the time." At Malachi's pout Jalon wondered if he should have kept his mouth shut. But he'd had a good reason to start this conversation, and he was going to finish it. "You also have to stop arguing with her."

Malachi's pout turned into a look of confusion.

Jalon regrouped, giving Malachi a stern look. "Bottom line—mind *yer mamm*. If she tells you to eat *yer* supper, you eat *yer* supper. When it's bath time, you don't fuss."

"Why?"

"Because *yer mamm* loves you, and she deserves respect."

"What's respect?"

Yeah, he was terrible at this. Time to wrap it up. "Just mind *yer mamm*, okay?"

Malachi hesitated, then nodded. "I will."

Good enough. Grinning, he stood. "Now, let's get that cake."

By the time he reached the kitchen Malachi was already at the table. "Cake!" Malachi exclaimed, his eyes filled with anticipation.

Jalon was pretty eager to dive into the cake himself. Karen gave Malachi a pointed look. "Wash *yer* hands first," she said.

Malachi nodded and went to the sink. When he struggled to reach it, Jalon picked him up. After Malachi finished washing his hands, Jalon set him down. As soon as his feet touched the floor, Malachi bolted toward the table. Did the kid ever slow down?

"Where's *Mamm*?" Malachi asked, plopping into the chair, then getting up on his knees.

"Upstairs. She was tired."

"*Mamm*'s always tired. Can I eat this cake now?"

"*Ya*, you may," Karen said.

Jalon scrubbed his hands, frowning at Malachi's words. He'd seen the lines of strain and fatigue at the corners of Phoebe's eyes and he could only imagine how tiring it was chasing after Malachi all the time, to say nothing of living with her aunt's abuse. But he had a feeling those weren't the only reasons for her weariness. He sat down at the table and picked up his fork.

"After you're finished," Karen said to Malachi, "would you like me to tell you a story before you *geh* to bed?"

"I like stories." Malachi took a big bite of the cake and smiled, crumbs tumbling out of his mouth.

While Malachi and Karen ate their cake, Jalon poked at his, unable to get Phoebe off his mind.

"Something wrong with the cake?" Karen asked.

Jalon shook his head. "It's fine." He pushed away from the table. "I'll be right back."

He went upstairs, pausing when he neared his room. He'd put Phoebe's suitcase inside, hoping she didn't mind that he'd decided where she and Malachi would sleep. Karen planned to sleep in Leanna's room, where she and Ivy had stayed many times while growing up. Over the years he'd heard the girls giggling, and he never hesitated to yell at them to shut up so he could get some sleep.

He moved to his doorway, stopping just outside in the hall. The door was partly open. Tilting his head, he listened. Silence. Before he could stop himself, he peeked in. Phoebe was curled up on his bed, still wearing her dress and white *kapp*, asleep on top of the covers. The tension that had been on her face all day had disappeared and, as it had been since he first laid eyes on her that morning, he couldn't stop staring when she wasn't looking. Her long, dark eyelashes rested on her cheeks, and a strand of nearly black hair had somehow escaped the *kapp* and lay against her ear. Her palms were pressed together underneath her head, and her lips were slightly parted.

Pulling himself away, he leaned against the hallway wall and blew out a breath. He'd been so sure of his feelings when he wrote that last letter, completely positive that he was in love and that she was the one for him. That should have changed when he found out about Malachi. In some ways it did. He didn't trust her. He couldn't, not yet anyway. He also didn't know how she felt about him. But these feelings . . . They were still in his heart. He had no idea what to do with them anymore.

When he went downstairs, he found Karen and Malachi on the couch. Blue was beside them, and Karen was telling the story about David and Goliath. Malachi listened with rapt attention. Not wanting to interrupt, Jalon quietly went into the kitchen. His piece of cake was still on the table. He grabbed it, then took his hat and coat from the pegs on the wall in the mudroom, slipped on his boots, and left for the *dawdi haus*.

When he walked inside the small house, he frowned. His father worked on the structure off and on for the last three years he was there. From the looks of it, mostly off.

Of course, it wasn't as though there had been any hurry to get it built, since neither he nor Leanna had had any marriage prospects. Fortunately, at least the frame of the house was finished and the drywall was in place. But right now the three rooms—a bedroom, a combination living room and kitchen, and a bathroom, with enough space for his parents to live comfortably once it was finished—were little more than a shell.

Jalon turned on the gas lamp in the kitchen and yellow light filled the living room. In the corner was a small woodstove. Jalon had forgotten his father installed it a few months before his parents moved back to Mespo. At least he'd have heat tonight. There wasn't a stick of furniture in the house, and he didn't bother walking into the bedroom, where he knew the closet wasn't even finished. That was all right. When he took his clothes from his room earlier, he put them in a hall closet near the upstairs bathroom in the main house. He'd have to shower and change there.

He'd get his sleeping bag and park it in front of the stove. It wouldn't be as comfortable as a bed, but he'd get a decent night's sleep.

Once he could get his mind off Phoebe and Malachi. That, obviously, was easier said than done.

• • •

Phoebe felt a tickle on her nose. She wiped it away with her hand. Then she felt it again, this time not just on her nose but also her cheeks. "What on earth?" She opened her eyes, still thick with sleep, to find a furry tail directly in her face.

"Morning, *Mamm*!" Malachi brushed her face with Blue's tail again.

The cat, for his part, didn't seem to care that Malachi was using his tail as a wake-up assistant. Phoebe opened her eyes more fully. "I'm up, Malachi. I'm up."

"Karen's already made breakfast. I ate mine. It was good. She made blueberry pancakes."

Those did sound good. Then what Malachi said registered. "She's already made breakfast?" And had Karen also brought Malachi to bed for her last night?

"*Ya.* When I woke up and went downstairs this morning, Jalon said to keep letting you sleep and not wake you up. So I ate *mei* pancakes. Jalon said I had to eat them all and I did. Now I can play with Blue. Doesn't he have a fuzzy tail?" He shoved the cat's tail in Phoebe's face again, apparently not realizing that he had indeed just awakened her. But she was glad he had.

"Malachi, that's enough." She gently pushed both Blue and Malachi away from her. "I've got to get up. I shouldn't have slept so long."

"Jalon said you must've needed it."

Phoebe got up from bed, glanced down, and saw she was still wearing her dress from yesterday. She touched her head, felt her *kapp*, and frowned. She went to her suitcase, still on the floor, and dug for fresh clothes. She found them, and was about to stand when she saw a flash of green underneath one of Malachi's shirts. She picked up the yo-yo. "Where did you get this?"

"Jalon gave it to me." Malachi climbed off the bed and took the yo-yo from her.

Worried he would start flinging the toy around, Phoebe reached for it. "*Nee*, Malachi. You can't play with that in the *haus*."

"I know. Jalon told me. He also said I have to watch for people and to have fun." He examined the yo-yo before tucking it back into the suitcase. Then he picked up Blue and left the room.

Phoebe sat back on her heels, marveling at the effect Jalon had on her son in such a short period of time . . . and also worried about it. Malachi was already attached to Blue, and it would be difficult enough on him when they left. But if he formed an attachment to Jalon . . . Wait. What was she thinking? He already had.

Sighing, she got up and went to the bathroom. She

hurriedly washed her face and changed into the fresh clothes. What a great impression she was making on Jalon and Karen. She should have made everyone breakfast instead of Karen. She brushed out and pinned up her hair, fixed her *kapp* to her head, took her belongings back to the bedroom, and headed downstairs.

"I'm sorry I fell asleep last night and then overslept," she said as she rushed into the kitchen. "It won't happen again."

Karen smiled. "*Nee* worries. You were tired, and it's okay to sleep in every once in a while."

"I'll make lunch," Phoebe said, not feeling any better despite Karen's kind words. If she'd overslept at her aunt's house, the woman would have shot through the roof.

"Deal." Karen placed a fresh plate of pancakes on the table, then surveyed the spread, frowning. "Guess I made too much. I'm so used to cooking for *mei* whole *familye*."

"Everything looks delicious," Phoebe said. "Have you seen Malachi?"

"He and Blue are playing outside. It's cold, but with all the sunshine this morning, it's not too bad. I told him to stay close to the *haus*. I've been checking on him, and he's doing exactly what he was told."

It seemed that Jalon wasn't the only one having a positive effect on Malachi.

Phoebe sat down, fully taking in the food for the first time. Karen was right. There was far too much food for two people to eat. She had pancakes, a blueberry topping, bacon, boiled eggs, sliced bread, and orange juice and milk, plus the leftover corn muffins from last night.

"Jalon made a pretty good dent on all this food, though." Karen sat down across from her. "I thought I'd wait to eat with you."

"That's nice of you."

Both women bowed their heads and said grace. When Phoebe opened her eyes, Karen handed her the plate of pancakes. "I already buttered them. I hope you don't mind."

"Not at all."

"I really enjoy cooking when we have frolics and barn raisings." Karen took a sip of her coffee. "Now that the community is growing, there's more of that going on. *Daed*'s a little more relaxed than our previous bishop."

Phoebe dropped her fork, then quickly picked it up. "*Yer daed* is the bishop?" Then she remembered Jalon had gone over there and talked to him when they arrived the day before. *What he must think of me . . .*

"*Ya.* He has been for almost a year. It's a long story. He was nervous about it at first, but almost everyone has been welcoming of him. A couple of families moved away."

"Including Jalon's parents?"

"I think they had other reasons." Karen shrugged. "I never asked Jalon about it. It's not really *mei* business. I'm just glad Jalon and Leanna decided to stay."

Malachi came in, carrying Blue. "I took *mei* boots off in the mudroom," he said.

Phoebe blinked. How many times had she told him to take his boots off before coming in the house at Aunt Bertha's? Too many to count. "*Danki*, Malachi."

He grinned, his face flushed with cold. Little balls of

snow stuck to Blue's long fur. "Jalon said I had to mind you, because you deserve . . ." He frowned, his lower lip sticking out a bit as he was deep in thought. "Respeck. You deserve respeck."

"Respect," she said softly.

"I'm sorry I didn't mind you before," Malachi added.

Phoebe touched his cheek. She wanted to tell him it was okay. She didn't, because it wasn't okay for him to ignore her wishes the way he had been. She reminded herself to thank Jalon for talking to him.

Karen got up and went to the sink. She opened a lower cabinet door and searched for something. "Found it." She stood, holding a comb with thin silver teeth. "Leanna always keeps a few of these around the *haus*." She handed the comb to Malachi. "I think Blue is overdue for a combing. Would you mind doing it?"

He took the tool from her. "*Ya!* I'll be careful too." He left the kitchen, still carrying Blue and filled with enthusiasm.

"Poor Blue." Phoebe smiled. "That cat doesn't know what he's in for." When Karen sat back down, she added, "*Danki* for helping me with Malachi."

"Anytime. And speaking of boots, I have a spare pair to lend you. Jalon said you left *yers* at *yer aenti*'s."

"*Ya*, I did. *Danki*."

Phoebe pulled in a breath and tried to sound nonchalant, asking the question that had been on her mind since she'd walked into the kitchen. "Is Jalon around?"

"His taxi came to take him to work right after breakfast." Karen placed her fork and knife on her empty plate.

"Oh." They needed to talk, not just about the past but also about what she and Malachi were going to do next. She'd meant to do that last night, despite cowardice. Instead she'd fallen asleep. She couldn't do that again, not before they talked.

She also had to write to her parents and tell them she wasn't at Aunt Bertha's anymore. She should have written them last night, but she'd been busy with supper and clean-up, then had fallen asleep. But she didn't see the sense in telling them anything until she figured out something definitive. And she couldn't do that until she talked to Jalon.

Karen stood and picked up their plates. "He said he comes home from work around five or six, later if they're busy."

That gave her time to plan and cook him a fantastic meal tonight. She owed him at least that much. "Is there a grocery store nearby?"

As she put the dishes in the sink, Karen said, "Schrock Grocery. It's about twenty minutes away by buggy."

"I'd like to get a few things." While the little bit of money she'd saved up wasn't enough for her and Malachi to live on for any length of time, she could afford groceries for a meal or two and still have some money left over.

"I noticed the kitchen needs restocking too." Karen turned around. "We can *geh* after we do the dishes."

A short while later, Karen had fetched the boots for Phoebe and hitched up Jalon's horse and buggy. Then she, Phoebe, and Malachi were on their way. Cold air bit into Phoebe's cheeks, but the sun made up for the temperature. Malachi had wanted to bring Blue, but

Phoebe put her foot down. "We are not taking the cat to the grocery store."

"Why not?"

"Because he might run off."

"He wouldn't run away from me."

"Malachi, the answer is *nee*."

As they pulled away from the barn, both she and Malachi looked out the back of the buggy. Blue sat in the driveway, watching them leave. Phoebe had to admit the cat looked a little forlorn.

They arrived at the grocery store, which was a small building across from a fairly large Amish house. They pulled into the driveway and Karen guided the buggy to the designated parking spaces. As Phoebe helped Malachi jump out, he exclaimed, "What's that?"

She turned to see a man wearing all white, including a helmet with a screen in front of it. He almost looked like a walking snowman. She'd never seen anything like it before.

"That's Aden Troyer," Karen said, waving at the man as he approached the house. He took off his helmet, his red hair sticking out at different angles, and waved back, then went inside.

"What's he wearing that stuff for?" Malachi asked.

"He's a beekeeper," Karen said.

Malachi's eyes grew big. "He has bees?"

"*Ya*. And they make the most delicious honey."

"Can I see the bees, *Mamm*?"

Phoebe crouched low in front of him. "That's not a good idea. You might get stung."

"Not if I wear some of those white clothes."

"Malachi, *nee*—"

"I don't think Aden would mind showing him the bees. Besides, they probably won't be doing much buzzing around since it's so cold." Karen smiled. "We can ask Sadie when we get inside. That's Aden's wife."

Phoebe didn't like the idea of Malachi being around bees, but if Karen thought it was safe, Phoebe would trust her judgment. Malachi bounded after Karen and they went inside the store, Phoebe close behind.

The inside of the store was surprisingly spacious with plenty of neatly organized shelves laden with food and supplies. "There's a pretty extensive tool section in the back," Karen said. "And over there," she added, pointing to a separate section, "are items made by our very own Birch Creek residents. You'll find Aden's honey there—but not very much. He has new hives now, and it takes time to produce. Also, his brother's beautiful birdhouses are for sale."

"I can see that." She walked over to the display of finely made birdhouses. She touched one of them. How she would have enjoyed having a couple of these in Aunt Bertha's yard. They would certainly draw in a variety of birds for her to sketch. She hadn't thought about her sketches since they got here. She shifted her gaze from the birdhouses to some simple but perfectly made rag rugs.

"Those are Abigail's, Sadie's sister. She also works here. The baked goods were made by their younger sister, Joanna, who's a good friend of mine. She used to work here until she married Andrew Beiler."

Phoebe nodded politely, knowing she would never

remember all the names. Why was Karen telling her this, anyway? She almost sounded as if she thought Phoebe would be staying for a long time. Well, Karen would find out soon enough that she wouldn't.

She was about to leave the handmade goods section to start shopping when she spied a few jars of jam. She picked up a jar of apricot jam, which was her favorite. "Have you tried any of these?" she said, turning to Karen.

Karen's cheeks pinked. "*Ya.*"

"What did you think?"

"Considering I made them, I think they're all right."

Phoebe grinned. "I'm sure they're more than all right."

"I don't plan on making any more, though. I don't really have time since I started working with the Millers." Karen had mentioned her work for the bookbinding business as they finished preparing supper the night before.

"When can I see the bees?" Malachi piped up, clearly bored with the conversation.

"Malachi," Phoebe said, putting the apricot jam back on the shelf. "Hush. Don't be rude. We're here to shop, not play."

"I don't want to *play* with the bees. I want to see them."

"Here comes Sadie," Karen said, gesturing to a slim Amish woman coming toward them. "We can ask her."

Phoebe shook her head. "Karen, Malachi doesn't need to see the bees. He's fine with us in the store. Malachi, don't touch that."

Malachi withdrew his hand from one of the birdhouses.

"Hi, Karen." Sadie smiled. "Sorry it took me so long.

I was working back in the office, and Aden is out with the bees."

"Sadie," Karen said, "this is Phoebe and Malachi Bontrager. They're here visiting Jalon."

Sadie's smile widened. "Nice to meet you both."

"We stopped by to pick up some groceries. Leanna's gone and there's slim pickings in Jalon's pantry."

Sadie nodded and looked at Phoebe. "Let me know if I can help you find anything."

"Can I see the bees?" Malachi asked.

Phoebe grimaced at him, then looked at Sadie. "I'm sorry. He saw *yer* husband outside in his beekeeping clothes and got excited."

"That's all right. A curious mind is a *gut* thing." She bent down in front of him. "Have you ever seen a beehive before?"

"*Nee.*" Malachi grinned. "But I want to."

She stood. "Why don't you two do some shopping, and I'll take Malachi to talk to Aden. He's recently set up the hives and it might not be a good idea to disturb them. But I'll let him decide."

Phoebe was about to protest, but Malachi looked so excited, and Sadie seemed happy to take him. "*Danki.* Malachi, you listen to Sadie and Aden, okay?"

"I will."

After Sadie slipped on her coat, she and Malachi left and Karen brought over a small shopping cart. "We'll start with the baking staples first."

They shopped for a few minutes, then the bell above the door rang. Sadie walked inside without Malachi. "Aden saw us out there looking at the hives. Now he's telling Malachi every little thing about bees. They'll be out there for a while."

Phoebe relaxed a little bit. It wasn't that she didn't trust Sadie, but now that Aden was with him, he would make sure Malachi understood not to upset the bees. Malachi would learn something too.

Two English customers came through the door, and Sadie started toward them. "Let me know when you're ready to check out," she said to Karen and Phoebe.

"Will do," Karen said.

When they finished shopping, Phoebe checked her selections and realized she didn't have enough money to pay for what was in the cart. "I've got to put some back," she whispered to Karen, annoyed that she hadn't paid close attention to the prices.

"Why?"

"I can't afford all of it." She felt her cheeks heat with embarrassment.

"Don't worry about it. Jalon's got an account here. And before you say you can't accept his generosity, trust me that he'd want you to get whatever you wanted. You and Malachi are his guests and he'd want you to be comfortable. Besides, you're cooking for him."

Phoebe nodded, knowing Karen was right but not feeling any better about being so dependent on Jalon. She had to figure out a way to pay him back.

They were heading to the front counter to check out when Malachi and Aden came into the store. "I saw the bees, *Mamm*!" Malachi bounced on his toes.

"You did?" She smiled, relieved he hadn't been stung.

"Only a couple. Aden said they were hiber . . . hiberan—"

"Hibernating," Aden supplied.

"*Ya*. And I got to taste some honeycomb too."

"I had a jar in the kitchen at the *haus*," Aden explained. "There isn't enough honeycomb in the hives yet."

She looked at Aden. "I appreciate you taking the time to show him."

"Glad to. It's nice to show the hives to someone who's actually interested."

"I'm interested," Sadie said, coming alongside him. She gave him a knowing look, then started for the counter to check out one of the other customers.

"You're interested in the honey. And the money we make from the honey."

She looked over her shoulder. "If it will make you feel any better, you can show me *yer* bees later." She gave him a small grin before turning her head, then switched to English as she answered her English customer's question about one of the items she was about to purchase.

"Can I come back sometime and see the bees again?" Malachi asked.

Aden nodded. "If it's okay with *yer mamm*."

"Maybe." It was as close to the truth as she could muster. She didn't like seeing the disappointed look on Malachi's face, but he also couldn't always get his way. And she couldn't lie to him and say yes when in all likelihood they weren't coming back.

"Wait a minute." Karen took off for the back of the store.

Phoebe looked at Sadie, who shrugged, then started ringing up their groceries.

Karen returned with a box of wood blocks for children

and put it on the counter. Phoebe started to protest, but Karen put her hand on her arm. "I want to buy these for Malachi," she said quietly. "Please let me."

Nodding, Phoebe watched as Sadie rang up the blocks, then handed them to Malachi. He looked up at Karen. "*Danki*," he said softly, his eyes shining with gratitude.

After saying good-bye to the Troyers, Malachi was quiet on the way home, content to watch the passing landscape as they made their way back to Jalon's. Phoebe and Karen discussed the meals they planned to prepare for the next few days, even though Phoebe doubted either of them would be staying at Jalon's house that long. She knew when she and Malachi did leave she would miss Karen. She'd never had a sister, and she and her childhood friends were no longer close. It was nice to have another female her age to talk to.

Malachi sprang into action as soon as they pulled into the driveway. He started to run off when Phoebe called, "Malachi, you can play after you help us with the groceries."

He stopped in his tracks, snow puffing up around his feet. She could see him battling within himself, deciding if he would mind her. Then he went to her, short arms outstretched.

With a smile she handed him the lightest grocery bag, pleased he was still taking Jalon's words to heart. "Come on, Blue," he said to the cat, who was rubbing his face against Malachi's leg. The two of them headed toward the house.

Phoebe collected the rest of the bags, leaving Karen to put up Jalon's horse and buggy. "I'll be in soon to help you put the groceries away," Karen said, then guided the horse to the barn.

When Phoebe walked inside the mudroom, Malachi was waiting at the door, holding Blue. "Can I *geh* play now?"

At her nod, he and Blue dashed out the door.

Phoebe set the groceries on the counter, then picked up the bag Malachi had set on the floor since he was too short to reach the counter. She started to hum as she unpacked the groceries, tension escaping her shoulders. Tonight they would have chicken cordon bleu, a recipe she found at the library a few years ago and had always wanted to try. She was going by memory, but between her and Karen they could figure out the preparation details. They would also have fresh cabbage and carrot salad, freshly baked bread, canned peaches, and for dessert, the rest of the Orange Bliss cake, which Phoebe was eager to try.

By the time she started grating carrots for the salad, she was able to smile a little. Jalon would eat well tonight. It wasn't close to what she owed him, but for now it would have to be enough.

CHAPTER 10

I'm sorry, Jalon. That's how it's got to be."

Jalon gaped at his boss, feeling like he'd been sucker punched. He was clocking out for the day when Gary—a thin, overly energetic guy in his late forties who smoked too many cigarettes and drank too much caffeine—called him into the trailer that also served as his office while they were working on this construction project. Jalon fought for composure. He should nod, thank the man for the work he'd been given, and go home. Instead he said, "You're *firing* me?"

"Letting you go. Big difference." Gary tapped a pencil against this desk. "You do excellent work. All you Amish do. I hate to lose you, but"—the tapping speeded up—"family is family. You get that, don't you?"

Now he did. When Gary said today was Jalon's last day, Jalon thought he'd done something wrong, even though he couldn't figure out what it was. He was always on time, never hesitated to work overtime, and made sure his work was as close to perfect as he could get it. He even apologized for taking yesterday off, although he hadn't explained why he had. He thought maybe that was the reason for the firing, but once Gary mentioned family, Jalon knew he wasn't simply being let go. He was being replaced.

The door to the trailer opened and a skinny, wiry guy who looked like a twenty-years-younger version of Gary walked inside. He had on a brown leather jacket and wore a baseball cap that said CAVS on the front. He came in and plopped down beside Jalon. "Hey dude," he said, nodding his head at Jalon. "How's it going?"

"Gary," Boss Gary said, the pencil hitting the desk at breakneck speed now. "I'm in a meeting."

"Oh. My bad." Younger Gary held up his hands. "Just wanted to know if we were still cool for Monday."

"Yeah. Eight sharp."

"That early?"

"Yes, that early."

Younger Gary let out a small sigh. "All right. I'll be here." He stood, nodded at Jalon again, and left.

Boss Gary tossed the pencil on the desk. "Sorry about that. He needs a job. College has been a challenge for him. School always has been, ever since his mother and I . . ." He shook his head. "Don't want to drag you into the family drama. If something opens up, I'll let you know." He drummed his fingers against the desk. "I'm really sorry."

Jalon nodded, keeping his expression blank despite the panic inside. He walked out of the trailer, got in the van with four other Amish guys who worked with him and shared the same taxi ride, and kept his mouth shut on the way home. His coworkers would find out he'd been let go soon enough. No need to discuss it here.

His hands clenched and unclenched. He'd worked for

this particular construction company for three years, and it had paid well. What was he going to do now? He needed this job. He had a mortgage to pay as well as meeting regular living expenses. Leanna contributed to those, but her job didn't provide steady work. He'd depleted his savings making up his father's back payments on the farm, and he had nothing to put *into* the farm he now owned. Being laid off was never in his plan. It never even crossed his mind.

On top of everything else, there was Phoebe and Malachi to think about. Two extra mouths to feed for who knew how long. His gut tightened. He'd have to find a new job, in the middle of winter, when jobs were scarce to begin with.

By the time he got home, his stomach was in knots. He walked into the kitchen, still thinking about his job prospects. Lack of job prospects, to be more accurate.

"Supper will be ready soon." Phoebe stayed near the stove, as if she didn't want to get too close to him.

For some reason that irritated him too. If he was wondering how she felt about him, she'd done a good job of showing him yesterday, keeping her distance, barely looking at him, then falling asleep so early. Good thing she hadn't read his last letter or he'd be dealing with embarrassment too. "Okay," he said curtly and left to shower and scrub off the dirt and disappointment from work.

He passed Malachi in the living room. He was on the floor in front of the woodstove, playing with a set of wood blocks that looked brand-new.

"Can you show me another yo-yo trick?" Malachi asked, abandoning the blocks and rushing toward him.

"Not right now."

"Please?"

"Maybe later."

"But I want to learn now."

Jalon took a deep breath, keeping an even tone so he wouldn't upset Malachi. "Later, okay?"

Malachi nodded, then went back to playing with the blocks.

The shower washed him clean, but did nothing to make him feel better. He dressed and, although he wasn't hungry, headed for the kitchen. He'd go through the motions. Fewer questions that way.

They said grace, then Karen passed Jalon a bowl of shredded carrots and cabbage that glistened with some type of dressing. "We went shopping today," she said. "Charged it to *yer* account at Schrock. I didn't think you'd mind."

"That's fine." What else was he supposed to say? Take back the food because he lost his job and he was broke?

"We were careful with *yer* money."

Jalon looked at Phoebe, seeing the sincerity and trepidation in her eyes. Was she afraid he was going to be mad at her for buying food? He took a breath and tried to smile. "I'm sure you were."

Her focus shifted back to her plate and she continued to eat.

He took a serving of what looked to be baked chicken. He cut it open, and white cheese oozed out, revealing thin slices of ham in the center. "What's this?"

"Chicken cordon bleu." Phoebe bit her lower lip.

"Sounds fancy." And it looked interesting. Curiosity

overriding his lack of appetite, he took a bite. This was even better than the shepherd's pie. "Wow. This is really *gut*."

Phoebe lowered her head, but he could see a small smile form on her face. Suddenly he wasn't so despondent. Nothing had changed, except he was eating some of the best food he'd ever tasted, prepared by a beautiful woman he seemed powerless to resist. *Definitely a healing combination.*

He finished his supper. So did Malachi for the most part, which was a surprise considering the meal wasn't exactly kid friendly, although he ate approximately one piece of shredded carrot from his salad. When they finished, Jalon said, "How about I show you that yo-yo trick after we do the chores?"

Malachi grinned, which brought a genuine smile to Jalon's face. He still had to find a job, and he and Phoebe couldn't put off talking about the future for much longer. But for the moment he wasn't tied up in knots, and he'd take it.

. . .

"Can I help you, Jalon?" Malachi asked.

Jalon looked up from the floor joists he was positioning on the concrete floor of the *dawdi haus*. He'd spent the morning looking for a job and, as he suspected would be the case, he hadn't had much luck. He could have continued to look, but decided to renew his efforts tomorrow. In the meantime he could work on the *dawdi haus*. His father had already purchased the plywood and stored it in the barn. All Jalon had to do was lay it down. Once he figured out the layout of the joists, he would hammer them in place. "Sure. You can hold this for me."

For the next ten minutes, Malachi was an attentive assistant. However, he soon became bored, and when Jalon caught him playing with the hammer, he took it away. "Why don't you see if Blue needs some company?" he said. He didn't have to make that suggestion twice. The boy shot out of the *dawdi haus*.

After he was finished with the joists, he stood and stretched his back, then went into the house. He was in the kitchen getting a drink when Phoebe walked in. "You're home early," she said.

A strange feeling came over him as he turned to face her. The comment had been so natural sounding, as if she wasn't a guest in his home . . . or in his life. His eyes latched onto hers and held. She didn't look away this time, and the spark of attraction he saw pulled at him. He had to jerk his gaze away. "I took the afternoon off," he said, facing the sink again, trying to collect himself.

"Malachi said something about you working in the *dawdi haus*, but I thought he was being imaginative. He does that sometimes."

He gulped down the water and faced her again. "He was helping me, until he got bored."

"It doesn't take long for him to lose interest in things. That's pretty normal for his age." She threaded her fingers together. "Jalon, I appreciate everything you've done for me and Malachi. I don't know how to repay you."

"You don't have to repay me," he said. And if she tried, he wouldn't take a dime from her. "I'm just glad you and Malachi aren't living with *yer aenti* anymore." He paused. "Has anything changed at home?"

"Are you asking if I can *geh* back?" She shook her head. "*Nee. Nix* has changed."

"You called *yer* parents, then?"

Again, she shook her head. "They don't have a phone."

"Then how do you know *nix* has changed?"

Karen came into the kitchen carrying her purse and two partially bound books. "Sorry I'm late. Judith asked Ivy and me to stay an extra hour. I brought some of the work home with me." She looked at Jalon. "I thought you'd still be at work."

"Took the afternoon off," he said quickly.

"I better get started on supper." Phoebe headed for the pantry.

"I'll be back in a minute to help," Karen said. "I need to put this stuff away upstairs."

Once he and Phoebe were alone again, he expected her to answer his question. How did she know nothing had changed at home? Instead she kept her back to him, but she didn't move farther. He moved until he was a few inches behind her. He noticed that the top of her head reached his chin, and he was tempted to put his hands on her shoulders, remembering how much he enjoyed the brief contact in her aunt's kitchen, even though he was only comforting her.

He kept his hands at his sides instead, leaning forward and saying in a low voice, "I'm trusting that you'll eventually explain what's going on. Until then, you and Malachi can stay here as long as you want." Before she could face him, he left and went back to the *dawdi haus*.

He didn't want to hear her protests—or, worse, the news that she was leaving. He wasn't ready for that, despite his worries about his job and their relationship, whatever that was at this point. They needed to talk. He knew that, and she did too. Yet he wasn't sure he was ready to hear what she had to say. While they were in limbo, she was still here. And he'd take that over her leaving.

. . .

Two more days had passed since Jalon told her she and Malachi could stay as long as they needed to, two days since he told her he trusted her to eventually explain things. And she had planned to, yet the timing had never seemed right. Either he was at work, or she was busy with Malachi, or Karen was around. She didn't resent Karen's presence, but it had kept her and Jalon from spending any time alone. Which was the point, after all. But if Phoebe was honest with herself, she could have found a time to talk to him. He seemed to be letting her take the lead on this, and she kept putting it off. Because as much as she told herself she and Malachi had to leave . . . she didn't want to.

She and Malachi were happy here. Safe too. Jalon gave her security she hadn't known she wanted until she experienced it. She didn't have to worry about him flying off the handle or being cruel. He had a good job, so she didn't feel as though she and her son were that much of an imposition, and Jalon never remotely hinted they were. She enjoyed spending time with Karen. Most of all, she looked forward to the evenings when Jalon came home. He ate her cooking with enthusiasm, which made her happy. And the way he looked at her sometimes . . . it made her knees wobble.

Still, that didn't excuse her taking advantage of her situation, and that had to stop. Last night she promised herself she would talk to him, but after she and Karen finished the dishes, she found Jalon in the living room showing Malachi how to use the yo-yo again. She watched from a distance as he looped the string over Malachi's small finger, then helped him with the throwing motion. Malachi had tried to do it himself several times since Jalon had given him the yo-yo, but he still struggled to make it go back and forth smoothly. He practiced a couple of times, then handed the yo-yo to Jalon. "I like watching you do it."

Jalon took the yo-yo, adjusted the finger loop, and started to throw it. Phoebe marveled at the tricks he could do, and like Malachi she was mesmerized. Jalon grinned as he did a trick called walking the dog. He'd been a little sullen when he'd come home from work earlier, but Phoebe chalked that up to him being tired after a long day. His mood had lightened considerably since then, and now he was chuckling as he threw the yo-yo back and forth in front of Blue, who vacillated between disinterest and trying to catch the yo-yo.

Not wanting to spoil the moment for her son, Jalon, and even the cat, Phoebe went back into the kitchen. Her purse was hanging on a peg in the mudroom, and she went to get the small pad of paper and a pen she kept in there. She sat down at the table and started to write a letter that was long overdue.

Dear Mom and Dad,

I'm sorry I haven't written to you sooner. I'm sure
you've heard from Aunt Bertha by now. I don't know
what she told you, but I'm also sure it wasn't good. I'm
sorry about that too. I keep making mistakes. But leaving Aunt Bertha's wasn't one of them.

She paused, tempted to list Aunt Bertha's crimes
against her and Malachi. But that wouldn't serve a purpose, other than to tear down her aunt. Having been
torn down enough by her, Phoebe didn't want to imitate
that behavior.

Malachi and I are all right. We're staying with a friend
in Birch Creek. His name is Jalon, and he's a good friend,
despite what Aunt Bertha might have said about him.

Phoebe paused. Oh well, she wasn't perfect. She
continued.

Jalon and I have been pen pals for the past few months.
He has a sister named Leanna, and I'm becoming friends
with his neighbor, Karen. I've met some very nice people
here. Malachi has already made a friend. His name is
Blue and he's a beautiful Coon cat. Please don't worry
about us. We're doing fine. I'll write soon.
                              Love,
                              Phoebe

P.S. Please don't write back or try to come after me. I
can't come home right now. I'm sorry.

Her parents wouldn't be happy with such little information. They definitely wouldn't be happy to learn she was staying with someone they didn't know, although she hoped mentioning Leanna and Karen would put them at ease a bit. They deserved to know exactly what was going on, but she couldn't tell them. When Jalon asked her if anything had changed at home, she had been one hundred percent honest. The reason she couldn't go back home still loomed, and the situation was impossible.

She folded the letter and put it in her purse, planning to mail it on Monday, deciding at the last minute to include the return address. It didn't feel right not to let them know where she was. She just hoped that they would honor her wishes and not contact her until she and Malachi were settled somewhere. The possibility of that happening occurred to her last night. She had a cousin in Ashtabula. A third cousin, one she hadn't seen since she was eight years old. It was a long shot, but Sylvia was listed in Phoebe's address book, and maybe she and her family would be willing to take her and Malachi in until she could figure something else out. It would be worth a try.

The next morning was Sunday. Phoebe put the hairpin in her *kapp* and fastened it to her hair. Her stomach lurched and she put her hand over it. *Stop being so nervous.* But she couldn't help it. Soon she would be attending Jalon's church, and while she craved worship, her knees were knocking together.

"I'm ready, *Mamm.*"

She turned and saw Malachi standing in the middle of Jalon's bedroom, wearing his Sunday clothes. Her mother had made him the small church outfit last year, and it still fit him, although the pants were nearly too short. "You're almost ready," she said, picking up her hairbrush and sitting on the end of Jalon's bed. "Let's take care of that hair."

Malachi put his hands on his head. "I don't want to brush *mei* hair."

"You're not. I am."

"Ow!" Malachi yelped. "That hurt."

"Sorry." She gentled her movements with the brush, focusing her mind back on her task. When she finally got his thick hair into some kind of decent shape, she set the brush on the bed. "Okay, that's the best I can do. Time to *geh* downstairs. We can't keep Jalon waiting." Karen had left a few minutes earlier, choosing to ride to church with her sister.

Malachi didn't say anything. He also didn't move away from her.

Uh-oh. It was a rare moment when her son's mouth and body were both still. She peered over his small shoulder so she could look him in the eye. "What's wrong, Malachi?"

"I don't want to *geh* to church." He looked up at Phoebe. "That makes me bad, doesn't it?"

Phoebe curled her arm around him and hugged him close. "*Nee.* Not wanting to *geh* to church doesn't make you bad. But I am wondering why you don't want to *geh*."

"People are mean at church."

She stiffened. "Sometimes," she said, unwilling to deny what he'd already experienced at her aunt's church. The congregation was small, and everyone knew everyone else. That meant everyone knew everyone's business, and while people had been friendly enough to Phoebe and Malachi while they were at church, she hadn't received too many invitations and no visitors. Part of it, she was sure, was Aunt Bertha's doing—quashing Phoebe's social life seemed high on her agenda. But she also never had the feeling that she was part of the community, or would even be allowed to. She could see behind the friendly faces and polite small talk that they didn't approve of her. They didn't know the circumstances of Malachi's birth, and they didn't ask. Not that she would have told anyone. Still, it hurt to know that they simply weren't interested, in either her or her son.

She turned Malachi in her lap so she could continue to face him. "But people aren't like that all the time. Remember *Grossmammi*'s church? They were nice, weren't they?"

"*Ya.*" He squirmed a little in her lap. "I wanna *geh* back home." Phoebe was about to say something when he added, "But I want to stay here too. I'd miss Blue and Jalon. And Karen. She's nice."

"*Ya,* she is. But you know we can't stay here much longer."

"Because we're going home?"

She shook her head. "Not yet. But the next place we live will be just as nice as this one." *God willing.*

"Will Jalon and Blue come with us?"

Her heart squeezed. "This is their home, remember?" Before he could ask any more questions, she set him on the floor. She ruffled his hair, not caring that she ruined all her work with the hairbrush. "*Geh* on downstairs and find Jalon. I'll be there in a minute."

Malachi smiled and flew out the door as if they hadn't just had a serious conversation. Children were so resilient. *Thank you, God, for creating them that way.*

Phoebe stood, her nerves ratcheting up again. If only she could be calmed with a few words the way her son had. So far everyone she'd met in Birch Creek had been nice. Then again, they didn't know her. Didn't know her past. Would they be as friendly if they did? She didn't have good experiences with strict, unyielding people. Right now her feelings were more tender than Malachi's.

Yet she couldn't dwell on that. She had to get through the next couple of hours, and the best way to do that was to focus on worship. She went downstairs, determined to put God first in her mind and everything else in the background.

Then she saw Jalon, and her plan flew right out the window.

He stood in the kitchen looking out the window, clearly deep in thought. She didn't move. She barely breathed. She'd known from first sight, and because of his profession in construction, that he had a good physique. It was hard not to notice. But the black pants, crisp white shirt, and black vest he was wearing drove that point home. His profile was thoughtful, and his curly hair almost as messy as Malachi's. She wanted to tame it, not with a brush but with her fingers. Great. These were *not* the worshipful thoughts she wanted to have before going to church.

"Where's Malachi?" she asked, forcing herself to focus on her son and not the gorgeous man in front of her.

"He's in the buggy. With Blue." He turned and grinned,

which sabotaged her efforts to focus on worship and not on him. "I think he's expecting to take him to church."

That made Phoebe chuckle and relax a bit. "I wouldn't be surprised. He wanted to take him to the grocery store the other day." She steadied herself, trying not to lose her senses in Jalon's smile. She was failing, so she changed to a subject that would somber them both. "Jalon, I know we need to talk. About . . . the future." *About us.*

His smile faded, and while talking was what she wanted, she was sorry to see it go. "I know. This afternoon, okay?" She agreed, and he picked up his black hat from the table and put it on. Her thoughts immediately derailed again. She gave her head a quick shake. They moved to the mudroom for their coats, then went outside.

After convincing Malachi that Blue didn't need to attend church, they were off. The weather had slowly warmed up over the past few days, and while there was still some snow on the ground, the air wasn't as sharp as it had been. Malachi sat between her and Jalon, and she welcomed the buffer. She was used to the tight confines of Amish buggies, but this one felt smaller than most. It didn't help that she could smell the fresh, clean scent of Jalon's soap, or that all she had to do was reach across Malachi and she could touch Jalon's shoulder. Or his hand. *Stop!*

Soon they arrived where a family was hosting the church service in their barn, and Karen greeted them. She smiled at Malachi, but the smile faded as he uncharacteristically shrank away. Karen looked at Phoebe, concern in her eyes. Phoebe put her hand on Malachi's back as he tried to melt into the skirt of her dress.

Jalon came up beside them. He didn't say anything, just took Malachi's hand. Then he walked away, hand in hand with Malachi as if the child were . . . his.

"I've saved us seats next to Ivy," Karen said as they walked into the barn where the benches were set up for church. Karen scanned the space, then waved. "She's over there."

Phoebe saw a tiny woman who resembled Karen sitting on one of the benches. They walked over to her, and instead of the curious stares Phoebe expected to feel, she realized everyone else was busy talking to each other, the comfortable murmurs of pleasant conversation filtering around her. She didn't feel the same tension she'd experienced at her aunt's church, nor the uncertainty present at her parents'. Instead there was friendship. Community. Things she'd been missing in her life for a long time.

"Hi." Ivy patted the seat next to her and Phoebe sat down. "I'm Ivy Yoder. I've been excited to meet you. Karen's told me all about you."

Phoebe smiled, fully relaxing for the first time that morning. Karen was petite, but Ivy was tiny. Her feet dangled above the barn floor, and her small hands were folded in her lap. She was lovely, with the same freckles as her sister, but her hair was pale blond rather than red. Phoebe turned to Karen, who smiled, then squeezed her hand.

At that point Phoebe knew she would be okay. Released from worry, she was able to worship freely, to pray, to ask God for direction, and above all, to give thanks.

• • •

Jalon tried to focus on worship. He needed to focus. He was lost, not only when it came to his lack of employment and his future, but he'd been lost in Phoebe when she came into the kitchen before they left for church. That was becoming a normal thing for him, but this time it was clear she returned the attraction, and that had thrown him for a loop. He'd been glad Malachi was sandwiched between them in the buggy. If he hadn't been, Jalon might have done something stupid, like reached for her hand or put his arm around her.

What was it about her that made him lose every bit of his common sense? *Everything. It's everything about her.*

That wasn't exactly the thing to be thinking about in church, or while he was sitting next to her son. Malachi, to his credit, was being as quiet and still as he could during the service, only whispering to Jalon a couple of times, then swinging his legs a little too hard while sitting on the bench. When he saw Malachi clinging to Phoebe when they arrived, he knew he had to do something to put the boy at ease. As he walked into the church, the men glanced at the two of them but didn't say anything. Sol had given him a particularly pointed look, but Jalon only nodded in return.

By now everyone knew Phoebe and Malachi were staying with him. The grapevine worked fast in Birch Creek. Yet folks in his community weren't quick to judge, especially since Freemont had become the bishop. The man's open frankness in his preaching and in showing his doubt about being a bishop had affected the congregation. The atmosphere was more relaxed. More friendly. And definitely more accepting. And since he had allowed Phoebe and Malachi to stay with Jalon, and Karen was their chaperone, the rest of the community, while curious, were also accepting.

Not that that helped him get his mind off Phoebe. A few days ago he'd been fairly sure she didn't think of him as anything but a pen pal who happened to have good timing. But lately he'd been catching her looking at him, quickly shifting her gaze before he could see the expression in her eyes. Yet every once in a while he did see the spark of attraction there, and it had been in full force in the kitchen earlier. The thought forced him to suppress a smile.

When the service was over, Sadie Troyer invited them to lunch with her family. Jalon declined, and he could tell Phoebe agreed with his decision. They couldn't put off talking any longer. Karen was going to have lunch with her family and then she'd be back at Jalon's later that afternoon.

Malachi fell asleep on the way home, his head leaning against Jalon's arm. Phoebe tried to reposition him to lean on her, but he kept shifting closer to Jalon, and eventually she gave up. "He really likes you," she said as Malachi snuggled his cheek against Jalon's shirtsleeve.

"I'm *nee* competition for Blue."

Her smile, coupled with the twinkling blue of her eyes, made him almost drop the reins.

When they arrived home, Malachi stirred, but didn't waken. Phoebe scooped him up and took him inside while Jalon put up the horse. When he entered the kitchen, he found Phoebe had made him a plate of boiled eggs, cheese, bread and butter, pickles, and a sliced apple. She set it on the table. "Sorry about the boring lunch."

He glanced at it. "Looks like a regular Sunday lunch to me."

She sat down across from him. "*Ya*. Boring."

Noticing she didn't have a plate of her own, he said, "Aren't you eating?"

Phoebe shook her head. "I'm not hungry. Malachi is asleep on the couch, so I'll fix him something to eat later. If I'm hungry then, I'll eat."

Jalon nodded. Although he was starving, it didn't feel right to eat in front of her. He pushed the plate to the side.

She frowned. "Is there something wrong with the food?"

"*Nee*." He took in a deep breath. Karen was gone, Malachi was asleep, and they were alone. They had run out of excuses and diversions. "It's time we had that talk."

CHAPTER 11

Phoebe wasn't prepared. She should have been, since she was the one who had brought the topic up that morning. She also had the whole silent ride home to think about what she was going to say. Yet now that she was face-to-face with Jalon—which was enough to keep her off-kilter—her brain short-circuited.

"We can talk later," she said, sliding his plate closer to him. "You need to eat *yer* lunch." She was clucking like a worried mother hen, but she was desperate.

"Lunch will keep." He folded his hands together on the table, and her gaze went to them. They were large hands, strong-looking and callused from construction work. Those same hands that built things, that spun a yo-yo with ease, had also held her son's small hand with gentleness.

"*Danki*," she said, unable to keep the words from spilling out.

"For what?"

"For . . . everything. Giving us a place to live for a little while. Being so nice to Malachi."

"I did what anyone else would do."

Of course he had. He was nice, and nice guys didn't

abandon women and children. It was also biblical. She wasn't a widow, but she was a single mother and it was part of their faith and beliefs to help those who needed assistance. She needed to get that straight in her head, and not jump to the wrong conclusion that he was doing anything other than his Christian duty.

He tilted his head and gazed at her, his brown eyes darkening in a way that appeared to have nothing to do with duty and everything to do with attraction. How could she think straight when he was looking at her like that? As though he felt something more than obligation, and that his conscience wasn't anywhere in sight right now.

She picked at a tiny divot in the wood table, realized what she was doing, and put her hands in her lap. She glanced at him again. The attraction had disappeared, replaced with confusion, which proved that she had no clue how to read him. Of course he was confused. She had kept him in the dark and taken advantage of his kindness long enough. "Malachi and I have stayed here longer than we should have."

Jalon looked stunned. "I never said that."

"Because you're nice."

"Because it's not true. Phoebe, I meant it when I told you I wanted you and Malachi to stay."

"But not indefinitely. That wouldn't be right." She drew in a breath. "I've got a cousin who lives in Ashtabula. Malachi and I will be leaving for her *haus* in the morning."

Jalon frowned. "Have you contacted her?"

Phoebe shook her head. "I only have her address. I don't think she has a phone."

"So you're just going to show up on her doorstep?" His words were edged with uncharacteristic sarcasm.

Lifting her chin, she said, "*Ya*. That's exactly what I'm going to do."

"That's ridiculous."

She frowned at him, mostly because he was right. Arriving unannounced at a distant cousin's and imposing on her and her family was not only impulsive, it was foolish. But what other choice did she have?

"It's past time you tell me what's going on, don't you think?"

She nodded, then clasped her hands together and rested them on her lap. "*Mei* parents are poor." Oh, her father wouldn't appreciate this. But Jalon deserved the truth. "I told you about *Daed* being a farmer. He barely makes enough to support *mei familye*. Sometimes . . . sometimes he doesn't even make that. They never planned to have as many *kinner* as they do. After they had me, eight years passed before they had Devon. They always said the number of *kinner* a couple has is up to God, whether it's one or twenty. They're well on their way to twenty.

"I had a job, but I was laid off last year." She thought she saw a muscle jerk in his cheek. Or maybe she'd imagined it. "*Mei mamm* has her hands full with *mei* siblings, and Malachi, as you know, can be a double handful sometimes."

"He's a *gut kin*."

"He's . . . busy. It seemed best that we leave and strike out on our own."

"So *yer* parents don't have two extra mouths to feed."

She nodded. That wasn't the only reason . . . and not

even the most important one. But it was the easiest one to explain. "I don't want to saddle you with us either."

"Phoebe." He leveled his gaze. "I'm not saddled with anything."

"What about Karen? She has to stay here, and we're keeping her from her own *familye*."

"Trust me, she doesn't mind the break." He leaned forward. "What do I have to do to convince you I want you here?"

. . .

The words left Jalon's mouth before he could stop them. Not because they weren't true. They were. And that was the problem. She wanted to leave. That much was clear. But despite everything, he wanted her to stay.

"I appreciate that, Jalon. But it's better if we leave."

He tried to hide his disappointment and ignore the pinch in his heart. While his feelings for her were still strong, other than those few and far between glimpses of seeing his attraction to her returned, her own feelings were a mystery to him. If her eagerness to leave was any indication, she didn't feel as strongly for him as he did for her. And that was a whole other problem.

He should let her go without argument. She had a place to stay, although she sounded about as sure of that as the wisdom of walking a tightrope across Lake Erie. If she and Malachi left, it would be good for him too. He wouldn't have to admit to her that he'd lost his job, or that he'd sunk everything he had into this farm. From the sound of it, she knew very well how difficult farming could be. He could get his life back on track, the way it was before he received her letter and decided to write her back.

That was what his mind was telling him. His heart was saying something else. "Leanna will be back soon. When she returns from Kentucky, *mei aenti* will have her call me and I'll tell her to come home. Then Karen will *geh* back to her *haus*."

"But—"

"Meanwhile, you can write to *yer* cousin and ask if you can stay there. Until you hear back from her, you and Malachi have a place here, in *mei* home." His home. It felt odd to say the words out loud. Yet it also felt right.

"Jalon . . ." Tears swam in her eyes. "That's more than generous. More than I deserve."

"You keep saying that." Before he could stop himself, he took her hand. "I don't understand why." He fully expected her to pull away. She didn't, and he stared at her hand. It was soft, her fingers on the short side but still elegant. "It's going to be okay, Phoebe." And for some reason, he believed it. He looked into her eyes. "I promise."

She pulled her hand from his, her eyes dry now. "Don't make promises you can't keep."

"I'll keep this one." He put his hands in his lap.

She nodded, but didn't look convinced. "We'll stay out of *yer* way. I'll make sure Malachi doesn't bother you—"

"He's not a bother—"

"And a delicious supper will be on the table every night when you come home from work."

He flinched. Work. He'd have to tackle that problem tomorrow. The past week had proved fruitless as far as finding a job, but he wouldn't give up. He couldn't afford to.

"I can even learn how to make Hunan beef." A hopeful shine entered her blue eyes. "It won't be as good as the restaurant's, but I'd like to try."

She remembered his favorite food. That had to mean something, right? Or was he seeing something that wasn't there? "I'm sure it will be terrific. Everything you've made so far has been."

She looked away, swallowing, her face a cloud of emotion. And although he was at a loss when it came to figuring out her feelings for him, he could plainly see she was fighting some sort of internal battle. "Phoebe," he said softly, "everyone deserves to be treated with kindness and respect. Especially you."

She dipped her head, and while he couldn't see her expression, he saw her shoulders relax. He leaned back in his chair. There was still more he wanted to know about her. What happened between her and Malachi's father, for one thing. And he wasn't completely convinced she was telling him the whole story about why she couldn't go home, although he did believe what she told him was the truth. She didn't like putting people out. She was independent, or at least wanted to be. He appreciated that. Clingy women weren't appealing.

But he didn't want to push her. This conversation was enough of a start. She wasn't fragile, but it was clear she'd been hurt in the past. Definitely by her aunt, and possibly by Malachi's father.

Phoebe looked up and tilted her head. "You look deep in thought."

He wasn't about to admit what he'd been thinking about, so he said, "I'd like to see *yer* drawings." Which was true, even though her sketches had been the furthest thing from his mind.

Her face fell. "I don't have them anymore. I hid *mei* sketchbook underneath *mei* mattress at *Aenti* Bertha's." She shrugged. "I guess she'll be surprised when she finds it. And I can always get another one."

Malachi came into the kitchen rubbing his eyes. He climbed into Phoebe's lap and leaned his head against her shoulder. Jalon's heart tightened at the sight. No, he couldn't let her walk out of his life. Not yet. *Maybe not ever.*

. . .

Phoebe was determined to be the best houseguest in the history of Birch Creek, if not Ohio itself. On Monday she'd mailed off a letter to her cousin Sylvia, along with the one to her parents. Then she and Karen and Malachi went to the library in Langdon to get some books for Malachi and look at some cookbooks.

At the library she looked up a variety of recipes, bolstered by Karen's interest and knowing Jalon liked spicy food. She picked out a few Mexican recipes featuring chilies, a couple of Asian ones, and a Hungarian one that wasn't spicy but looked interesting. She'd have to make sure there was simple food for Malachi to eat, but she couldn't wait to try out these recipes. That evening she made taco soup, something even Malachi enjoyed. Jalon had expressed his appreciation too.

He didn't linger after supper. Instead he went to the *dawdi house* shortly after he finished eating. Phoebe thought that was odd considering their conversation the day before. She'd been hoping they could spend some more time together. Not alone because Malachi and Karen were always there, but at least in the same room. Obviously he had other plans.

On Tuesday Karen had to work, and Phoebe set about cleaning the house, taking a break here and there to read a couple of Malachi's library books to him. Jalon said he expected Leanna would be home later this week, and she wanted the place to be spotless. After being pestered by Malachi to make pizza, she gave in and created two pies—a small plain cheese one for Malachi and a pepperoni, sausage, and mushroom one for her, Karen, and Jalon. Karen pitched in and made a salad when she came home from work. "Did Leanna call?" she asked Phoebe.

"Not yet." She sprinkled a little grated parmesan on the ends of the pizza crust

"Maybe she decided to stay in Kentucky awhile longer." Karen chuckled. "That would be typical Leanna. She's lucky she has a job that gives her so much time off."

"What does she do?"

"Small engine repair." At Phoebe's surprised look, Karen said, "Jalon's sister is one of a kind."

Phoebe took the pizzas to the oven. "I know Jalon's eager for her to come home." She glanced at Karen. "I'm sure you are too."

"I'm fine with her staying away longer."

"You are? I thought you'd be ready to *geh* home by now."

Karen shrugged. "I'm fine either way. It's not like I haven't seen *mei familye* every day."

The pizzas were fresh out of the oven by the time Jalon got home. Once again he had a dour look on his face, and she wondered if he was having trouble at work. He washed his hands as Phoebe sliced the pizza, telling Malachi several times to sit down and be patient. When everyone was at the table, they said grace. Malachi tore into his pizza. "Yum!" he said before cramming a huge bite into his mouth.

"Malachi, don't eat so much at once," Phoebe said. "You'll choke."

He swallowed. "Jalon's taking big bites."

Phoebe looked at Jalon, who was indeed almost inhaling his pizza. He didn't seem to hear Malachi's remark, and once he finished eating, he got up from the table. "Chores," he said, then went outside.

She and Karen exchanged a puzzled glance. They didn't see Jalon for the rest of the evening, and he was gone by the time Phoebe got up the next morning.

On Wednesday Phoebe decided to make Hunan beef, hoping that preparing Jalon's favorite meal would improve his mood. She wished she knew what was going on with him, but he seemed so distant that she didn't feel right asking him outright. Hunan beef was one recipe she was unsure of, and she wanted to make it perfect for him. Not because she owed him, but because she didn't like seeing him out of sorts.

She was stir-frying thinly sliced onions, julienned

carrots, and sweet peppers when Malachi came into the kitchen, Blue on his heels as usual. The kitchen was filled with the spicy scent of ginger and the sweet smell of the cooking vegetables. She'd add the sliced beef to the vegetables, then once it was cooked through supper would be ready. She glanced at the clock. Karen had gone over to her house for a few minutes, and Jalon would be home soon.

Malachi sniffed. "Something smells funny."

"It's the ginger." Phoebe pushed the meat off the cutting board and stirred it around with the vegetables.

"I don't want ginger for supper."

"Ginger is a spice, not a meal." She set down her spoon and knelt in front of her son. "Don't worry. I made you some macaroni and cheese."

The back door opened and Phoebe heard Jalon walk into the mudroom. She could hear him shuffling around as he no doubt removed his boots, coat, and hat, and then he came into the kitchen. This time he didn't even give her a passing glance or a greeting before going upstairs.

Deflated, Phoebe pushed the vegetables and meat around the skillet with a wooden spoon. Yes, something was definitely wrong with Jalon and she had no idea how to help him.

• • •

Water ran down Jalon's face. He'd been showering so long that the water was more lukewarm than hot, and in his mind he could hear his father's voice. *Jalon! Get out of*

*the shower. You're wasting hot water. Money doesn't grow
on trees.*

It didn't grow on his father's farm either.

He shut off the water but didn't get out. He just stood
there, letting the water drip off him. He didn't want to
go downstairs, even though the delicious smells of Asian
food had made his stomach rumble with hunger as soon
as he walked into the house. Hunan beef. She'd said she'd
make it for him and she had, plus a whole slew of other
delicious suppers and breakfasts. What did he give her
in return? A curt nod before tucking tail and running.

Lord, I'm pathetic.

Jalon stepped out of the shower, toweled off, then
put both hands on either side of the sink and leaned
forward. His daily job hunt had produced nothing.
He'd thought he would find work by now. He'd scoured
Barton, Langdon, and even Canton. He'd talked to a
couple of his friends about leads, asking them to keep
his secret so Karen and Phoebe wouldn't find out he was
jobless. He'd never had a difficult time finding work
before, even when he was drinking. Now that he had
straightened his life out and was trying to do the right
thing when it came to Phoebe and Malachi, he kept slamming against walls.

Last night, he'd told Karen he was going to call his
Aunt Tabitha since he still hadn't heard from Leanna,
but Karen stopped him. "Let her enjoy her vacation,"
she said. "I can stay here as long as you need me to." But
then shortly afterward Leanna did call. Jalon explained
about Phoebe, adding that Karen was fine with staying longer. "I'll be back Saturday, then," she said. She

started to quiz him about Phoebe and Malachi, and he ended up almost hanging up on her. He couldn't blame her for being curious, especially about Malachi, but her questions irritated him—not that it took much to irritate him lately.

His sister's curiosity probably would see her back home on Saturday, despite being prone to change her plans at the last minute. But he had decided not to tell Karen and Phoebe he was expecting Leanna. If she followed through, they could just be surprised.

Looking up, he stared at his reflection in the mirror. He looked sullen. Worn. Defeated. He couldn't let them see him like this. He got dressed, brushed his damp hair, tried to press down the curls that had been the bane of his life and would never settle down, and forced a calm, placid expression. But that disappeared quickly as he thought about Phoebe and Malachi leaving for Ashtabula. That would happen soon, he was sure of it.

If Aunt Bertha—the very definition of a piece of work—had been willing to take them in, surely her cousin would. As much as he wanted them to stay, he was starting to think leaving might be the right thing for them. He didn't have much to offer them right now, except for a roof over their heads and food on the table. *And his love.* It was getting harder to ignore his feelings, not just for Phoebe but also for Malachi. The child was ingratiating himself into Jalon's heart, something he hadn't anticipated—and something he wasn't completely ready for. What had seemed so straightforward—falling in love with Phoebe—was now turning into a complicated mess, and he felt powerless to fix it.

When he opened the bathroom door, he could once again smell the Hunan beef, and again his stomach grumbled. He went downstairs and entered the kitchen. The table was set, Malachi was in his seat, and Jalon could see Blue's thick tail sticking out from under the table near Malachi's chair. That cat was just as attached to Malachi as the boy was to it. Leanna would definitely have to share when she came back. Karen was also seated at the table. She gave Malachi a smile.

Phoebe placed a huge platter of Hunan beef surrounded by a circle of white rice on the table. Steam rose from the dish. There was also a plate of bread and butter, which didn't exactly go with Asian food, but Phoebe's bread was so good he didn't care. He glanced at Malachi and saw that his bowl was filled with a child-size portion of creamy macaroni and cheese.

He tried not to look at Phoebe as she sat down, but he couldn't keep his gaze from moving over to her. She met his eyes, and he saw the expectancy in hers. He pulled his gaze away, closed his eyes, and prayed, more for his sanity and equilibrium than for the blessing of the food.

Phoebe handed him the Hunan beef. "The picture in the cookbook showed the rice around the meat like that. Does it look right?"

With a short nod he took the plate from her. "Looks fine."

She outwardly withered a small bit, and he wanted to kick himself. He was being a jerk and he knew it, although Karen's pointed look gave him extra confirmation. Unable to bring himself to say anything else, he took a scoop of beef and rice and put it on his plate. He handed the platter to Karen, then took a bite.

The balance of spices was perfect. The kick of heat he felt seconds after he swallowed his first bite was exactly enough. Somehow without knowing what Asian food tasted like, Phoebe was able to make this the best Hunan beef he'd ever had.

His head jerked as he heard Karen cough. She reached for her glass of water. "Hot!" she said before gulping down the water, her face turning red.

Knowing drinking water wouldn't cancel the spicy heat from the food, he got up from the table and poured a glass of milk, then handed it to her. "Try this."

She gulped down the milk. When she set the glass down, she had a milk mustache, which Malachi immediately pointed out. She wiped her napkin over her mouth. "Phoebe, what did you put in this?" she choked out.

"I followed the recipe." Her voice was small, and she shrank in the chair. "I'm sorry."

"It's okay. I know it's supposed to be spicy. I'm just not used to it." Another coughing fit erased her weak smile.

Jalon slid the plate of bread and butter over to her. "This will help too."

Phoebe started to rise. "I'll make you something else, Karen."

She held up her hand and finished chewing the bite of bread. "It's okay. There's some leftover macaroni and cheese. I'll have that."

Malachi, who'd been oddly restrained during all this, pointed to the Hunan beef and blurted, "*Mamm* shouldn't cook that stuff anymore. It's yucky."

Phoebe stilled. Then she looked at Jalon. "I . . . I'm sorry." Before he could respond she left the kitchen. A few seconds later he heard her running up the stairs.

"This is *yer* fault." Karen took another drink of milk.

"Mine?" Jalon said.

When she swallowed, she added, "She wouldn't have reacted that way if she wasn't already upset before you got here." She set the glass down, her eyes watery. "Something's going on with you, and clearly it's affecting her. You need to straighten this out."

Karen was right. He'd convinced Phoebe that he wanted her and Malachi to stay, only to turn around and practically ignore both of them. But if he went to her, he would take her in his arms and let her know the beef was perfect and Karen was a wimp when it came to spicy food. He'd hold her and remind her that Malachi is four and didn't mean to hurt her feelings. He'd apologize for giving her mixed signals, for being rude and upsetting her. Then he would cup her face in his hands and kiss her until the tears disappeared and a smile appeared in its place, because for the past week kissing her and seeing her smile had been two things he was desperate to do.

Since he couldn't, he didn't go after her. Instead, he left the house, like the coward he was.

. . .

Phoebe sat at the edge of Jalon's bed, her face hot with embarrassment. She should have warned Karen about the spice, even though Phoebe hadn't thought it was all that hot. Actually, she thought it was delicious. No wonder

Jalon liked it. Or at least, someone else's version of it. He didn't look too thrilled with the bite he took. And now she'd wasted a good cut of meat and spices she wouldn't normally buy because she ruined the dish. Her guilt was compounded by knowing it wasn't her money she'd wasted, but Jalon's.

She got up from the bed and walked to the window. She should go downstairs and apologize to Karen and Jalon, and to make sure Malachi was eating his macaroni and cheese, because she didn't want that to go to waste too. Instead she stared out the window. Dusk blanketed the sky, but there was enough gray light that she could see Jalon walking toward the field. Short stalks of old corn stubble poked through the snow over part of the field, and the rest was covered with snow. It reminded her of her father's field right before he and her brothers tilled the soil to prepare for planting in April. While they did that, Phoebe and her mother would plant the garden.

Phoebe pressed her forehead against the cold window glass. This year *Mamm* would have to do it without her.

Jalon leaned against the white wood fencing that surrounded the pasture. The horses were still out, pushing their noses through the snow to reach the stiff, cold grass underneath. He leaned his forearms on the fence. His shoulders slumped, and he hung his head.

Her heart squeezed in her chest. He was unhappy. She'd suspected it the past few days, but seeing it firsthand drove it home.

"Phoebe?" Karen poked her head through the doorway.

Her eyes were a little red-rimmed from the hot-pepper coughing fit, but she looked fine otherwise.

"I'm so sorry." Phoebe opened the door wider to let her in. "I didn't realize it was that hot."

"You tasted it?"

"*Ya*, I thought it was fine."

She chuckled. "You have a fireproof tongue, then."

"I didn't mean to ruin the meal."

Karen shook her head. "You didn't. It was good. Even through the heat I could taste that the flavors were delicious."

"Jalon didn't think so."

Sighing, Karen said, "I don't know what's going on with Jalon. He's definitely not acting like himself."

"Because Malachi and I are here."

Karen paused. "Maybe you should talk to him," she finally said.

"We talked, when he told me he wanted Malachi and me to stay."

"That sounds like him." She put her hand on Phoebe's shoulder. "I know he cares about you."

Phoebe turned and walked back to the window. Jalon was gone. So were the horses, so Jalon must be doing the chores. "He's a nice man."

"*Ya*. He is." Karen came up beside her. "But that's not why he cares about you. When he thought you were in trouble, he dropped everything and went to see you. Then he brought you back here. He wouldn't do that only because he's nice."

No one with half a conscience would have left Phoebe and Malachi there after what Aunt Bertha said and did.

She faced Karen, suddenly needing to ask a question that had been on her mind since she first arrived. "Why haven't you and Jalon gotten together?"

"Because I don't need any more brothers," she said, sounding a bit surprised. "Like I said, Jalon and I are friends."

"*Gut* friends," Phoebe couldn't help but add. Karen didn't have a child or a past she had to continually run from. Karen was pretty, sweet, great with Malachi, and just as good of a cook as Phoebe. She was the perfect woman for Jalon.

"That's because we've been neighbors for so long. Jalon has never been interested in me and the feeling is mutual." She gave her a knowing look. "He is, however, interested in you." The look disappeared, replaced with determination. "I'm going to have a talk with him."

Phoebe stopped her. "Please. Don't."

"He can't keep acting this way. Weird and out of sorts. Something is bothering him, I can tell, and it's not you and Malachi."

Phoebe wanted to believe that. But Jalon didn't act weird and out of sorts around Karen. He acted comfortable. Caring. They made more sense than he and Phoebe did, despite the thought of them being together making her blood pressure spike. "Did Malachi eat his macaroni and cheese?" she asked, resisting the urge to grind her teeth.

"Every bite."

"I'll clean the kitchen, then," she said, moving past Karen.

"Phoebe, hold on—"

Phoebe ignored her and went downstairs. When she got to the kitchen, she saw that everything had been left where it was, except for Malachi's plate, which was probably in the sink. Malachi and Blue were nowhere in sight.

"He's helping Jalon with the chores." Karen came up behind her, answering Phoebe's unspoken question.

Phoebe nodded. Despite Jalon's mood lately, Malachi still helped him feed and put up the animals every night. She scooped up the plate of Hunan beef and dumped it in the trash.

Karen looked inside the trash can, then at Phoebe in disbelief. "What did you do that for?"

"*Nee* one was going to eat it."

"Jalon would have."

She put the platter in the sink next to Malachi's supper dish, her back stiffening. She was being logical. Practical. The beef was cold, the rice glutinous and sticky. It wouldn't taste the same heated up on the stove. It wouldn't taste special like she'd intended it to.

"I'm going upstairs," Karen said, sounding frustrated.

Phoebe busied herself with clearing the table as Karen huffed out of the room. Then she washed the dishes, pots, and pans. Cleaned the table, the counter, the stove top. She was wiping the last crumbs off the stove when Malachi bounded in. Before he opened his mouth she said, "Upstairs. It's time for bed."

"I don't wanna—"

"Now!"

His lower lip trembled and he turned around and dashed out of the kitchen.

Phoebe leaned against the sink, guilt washing over her in a cold wave. She shouldn't take her frustration out on Malachi or Karen. She needed to apologize to Karen and hug her son. And she needed to stop hoping she and Jalon would be together. It was easy to pretend she had a life here in Birch Creek, that the past didn't mean anything and the future was filled with promise, acceptance, and, possibly, the love of a good man. But it was all a fantasy, one that was out of her reach. It was time for her to face reality, and that meant focusing on Malachi—not her selfish desires.

CHAPTER 12

Jalon lingered outside before going back to the house. He stared at the land again, the outlines of the corn stubble barely visible in the shadowed light of dusk. If he didn't get a job soon, he'd miss the planting season because he couldn't afford to buy seeds. He'd also inspected his father's plow, and it needed repair. The two old draft horses might be able to plow one more year, but he'd need to purchase a new pair and break them in by next year. That would cost a lot of money. Money he didn't have.

He turned to go inside, tired of dwelling on his problems. The kitchen was dark. He turned on the lamp and it hissed to life. He opened the oven, expecting to see a foil-covered platter sitting on top of the rack. The Hunan beef should still be good. If not, he'd heat it up on the stove. He was used to leftovers.

The oven was empty.

He walked over to the opposite counter, which was spotlessly clean like the rest of the kitchen. He opened a couple of cabinets, even though it didn't make sense that Phoebe or Karen would put leftovers in the cupboards. When he didn't find anything, he shut the doors, then looked down at the trash can beside the counter and saw clumps of Hunan beef.

Sighing, he walked away, his stomach still hungry but his appetite gone. Yeah, he deserved that. She'd prepared the meal for him and he'd left without eating it.

"You're a jerk, you know."

Jalon looked up to see Karen in the doorway, her arms crossed over her body, clearly recovered from the spicy food. "I know."

"If you know, then why are you acting this way?"

He sank down onto one of the kitchen chairs. "That's something I don't know."

Karen joined him at the table. "Why don't you *geh* talk to her?"

"And say what?"

"That you care about her. That you love her?"

He blinked. "How do you—"

"Know that you're in love?" Karen rolled her eyes. "It's obvious to everyone. I can't believe she hasn't figured it out by now. You two . . ." She shook her head. "I don't know why you're both making this so complicated."

Because it is. Jalon rubbed his hand over his face. "I can't tell her how I feel."

"Why not?" She leaned back in the chair, her arms crossed again. "Jalon, I knew you were thickheaded. I didn't realize your head was as thick as a brick."

"You should mind *yer* own business."

"Right now this situation is *mei* business. The only reason I'm here is to keep an eye on you two, although *Daed* had nothing to worry about. You can't even be in the same room together for more than five minutes without one of you running away from the other."

"She wants to leave. She has a cousin in Ashtabula—"

"I know. Unlike you, I *talk* to her." She got up and headed for the doorway to the living room. "Did you ever think if you were honest with her about how you feel, she wouldn't *want* to leave?"

With that, Karen left, and Jalon stared at the empty doorway. She was right. He was making this complicated. He loved Phoebe . . . He never actually stopped. Simple as that. It was past time he showed her how much. Whatever her response to his feelings were, he'd handle it.

. . .

Thursday afternoon Phoebe sat on the front porch and watched Malachi and Karen's youngest brother, Judah, chase each other around the yard. Blue curled up beside her, and she was glad for once to get the cat's attention. She stroked Blue's back as Judah ran several feet in front of Malachi, then slowed down a bit so he could catch up. Judah was almost eight, but he didn't seem to mind playing with Malachi. As for Malachi, he was screeching, laughing, and having a great time. A part of her enjoyed seeing him having so much fun, while the rest of her knew it would be short-lived.

She hadn't received a reply from her cousin yet, but if she didn't hear from her by Saturday, she would figure out other arrangements. Jalon left before Phoebe and Karen got up, cementing in Phoebe's mind that he was avoiding her.

"Judah! Malachi!" Karen said when she came outside. "Cookies and milk are ready."

Malachi and Judah skidded to a stop on the damp

grass. The snow had melted that morning, but it was still cold enough for Phoebe and the boys to wear coats. They scampered up to the house and slipped off their boots on the front porch. Malachi paused to pet Blue before going inside.

"Are you coming in?" Karen asked.

"In a minute."

"Stay out here as long as you want. I'll keep an eye on the *buwe*."

Phoebe looked over her shoulder. "You don't mind?"

"Not at all." She smiled. "More milk and cookies for us."

Phoebe smiled. She brought her knees up to her chest and watched as a few birds pecked on the grass, now that the boys weren't running all over it. For a minute she thought about getting her sketchbook, then remembered she didn't have one anymore.

She started to get up, pushing Blue to the side a bit, when a car pulled into the driveway. She recognized it as the taxi Jalon took to work every morning. She should have gone inside at that moment. She could play the ignoring game as well as Jalon. Yet as he got out of the car—tall, lanky, and handsome—her breath hitched. Why wouldn't her heart do what her mind had already done—dropped Jalon Chupp like a hot potato? But that wasn't right either. Her mind was also betraying her, because all she could do was sit there and watch him as he leaned through the window of the passenger door and handed the driver his money for the ride.

Not wanting to get caught staring, she stood up and stepped back, only to hear a shriek from Blue that shot straight through her spine. She looked down as the cat dashed off and realized she'd stepped on his tail. "Sorry, Blue." When she looked up, the taxi was pulling away, and Jalon was walking toward her. She turned around, ready to go in the house.

"Phoebe."

She twisted her fingers together. Maybe this was it. He was going to tell them he'd made a mistake and they had to leave.

"Do you have a few minutes to talk?"

Swallowing her nerves, she nodded.

"Not here." He looked around at the empty yard. "I was thinking somewhere more private."

Oh, this wasn't good. Whatever he had to say to her, he wanted it out of Malachi's earshot. "We have privacy here. Karen and the *buwe* are inside," she said.

"*Buwe?*"

"Judah's here."

Jalon nodded. "Karen said he might be coming over. It's good for Malachi to have company, *ya?*"

"*Ya*." She and Jalon were on shaky ground, but he had a soft spot for her son, and that meant everything to her.

He opened the front door. "I'll let Karen know you and I will be gone for a little bit."

Gone? She couldn't even nod as he brushed past her to go inside. Where were they going?

After a minute he came back out, but she didn't move. Forgetting her awkwardness around him, she said, "What's going on, Jalon?"

He pushed his hat back from his head. "*Nix*. And that's the problem."

"What?"

"I'll explain everything in a minute." He walked down

the porch steps. Then he turned around and extended his hand toward her. "Come with me, Phoebe."

She couldn't resist him when he sounded like that. Confident. In command but not pushy or overbearing. Letting her know that he was secure in what he wanted . . . and right now he looked like he wanted her. As tired as she was of these seesawing emotions, she went to him. She stared at his hand, not knowing if he expected her to hold it or if he'd made the gesture just to get her off the porch. Before she could decide what to do he dropped his hand.

Phoebe walked with him past the field. "This is where *mei daed* used to farm," he said. "Last year he stopped."

"Why?"

"He gave up. That's the short answer."

She looked at his profile, saw his jaw clench.

"He was never able to make a real *geh* of things here. He tried. I tried to help him . . ." He didn't finish, and Phoebe didn't pry further.

They were walking past the field, Phoebe noticed, and toward a copse of woods. She wondered where he was taking her, but she didn't dare interrupt him.

"When *mei* parents decided to *geh* back to Mespo, Leanna and I wanted to stay. We've been in Birch Creek most of our lives. This is home to us." He glanced at Phoebe. "There are a lot of great things about Birch Creek."

"Like?"

"Like this." They walked into the woods, which really weren't woods but just some thick trees surrounding a small pond. A wooden bench was positioned near the bank. It was a perfectly hidden little oasis.

"I spent a lot of time here when I was a *kin*." He

moved toward the bench. "Not as much when I started working construction and . . ." He cleared his throat. "I like to come here and think. It's peaceful."

She looked around, listened to the bullfrogs, the chirping birds. The trees were tall and so crowded together that it cut down the sunlight by half.

"It's a great fishing pond. Leanna likes to skate on it during the winter, although the past couple of winters it hasn't frozen over completely." He bent down and picked up a rock, then tossed it on the pond. It bounced off the ice. "I guess it did this year." He went and sat down on the bench.

When he looked up at her, her breath caught. Gone was the sullenness. The awkwardness, the trepidation. The confusion, the betrayal. All that was replaced with an almost searing attraction. He seemed like the man she knew from his letters.

"Sit with me."

She couldn't resist his offer. She sat beside him, and he angled toward her.

"I owe you an apology."

"You don't owe me anything—"

He held up his hand. "I do. I've had a lot on *mei* mind and I've been acting like a jerk. I'm sorry about that."

He stared out at the pond and shoved his hands into the pockets of his jacket. "I've been confused."

"About . . . about us?"

"Yeah." He turned to her again. "When you didn't answer *mei* last letter, I wasn't sure what to think."

"I answered all *yer* letters I could, Jalon."

"Yes, but you couldn't answer the most important one."

The one Aunt Bertha ripped up. "What was in the letter that was so important?"

"It doesn't matter anymore. I shouldn't have written it. I was jumping the gun. Assuming things I shouldn't have assumed."

"Oh." She unclasped her hands and stared at the pond, which didn't seem as magical as it had a moment before.

"It's a *gut* thing you didn't read it," he added.

"Jalon, I wanted to read it. I was devastated when she ripped it up." She might be revealing too much, but at this point what did it matter? "Getting *yer* letters . . . writing to you. Besides Malachi, that was what I lived for."

He turned to her. Tilted his head slightly to the side, which made him look boyishly adorable. "Me too." He took her hand, running his work-roughened thumb over her knuckles. "I want to start over. With us, I mean." He looked at her. "But before I can do that, I have to be honest with you."

She frowned. Had he been keeping secrets too?

"I lost *mei* job. Got laid off, actually. I haven't been going to work every day, just pretending to. I've been trying to find a job, but I haven't had any luck. It's been frustrating."

She looked at their hands clasped together, then up at him again. So that's why he was upset.

"*Mamm!*"

She turned around in time to see Malachi and Judah burst through the woods. Jalon let go of her hand and shot up from the bench. Her son had the worst timing.

"How did you find us?" Jalon asked, his voice tight.

"I guessed." Judah rocked back and forth on his heels. He was a rugged kid, with wild hair and piercing green eyes.

"And he was right." Malachi launched himself into Phoebe's lap. Then as if he remembered Judah was nearby, he scrambled back down. He went near the edge of the pond. "Are there fish in here?"

"*Ya.*" Judah came up close to him. "*Mei* brothers and I fish here a lot when it's warm out."

"Don't get too close to the edge." Phoebe moved closer in case Malachi ignored her and fell in through the ice.

Fortunately, he listened to her and stepped back. He picked up a rock that was nearly the size of his hand and threw it into the pond. It was a larger stone than Jalon had thrown, and it broke through the ice with ease.

"Hey now." Jalon squatted next to him. "You don't want to disturb the fish."

"What does disturb mean?"

"Bother them. They're sleeping."

"Fish sleep?"

"*Ya.*"

"Do they close their eyes? I've never seen a fish with closed eyes."

"You haven't seen that many fish," Phoebe added.

"I have to *geh* back home," Judah interjected. "*Mamm* wants me to help with supper." He made a sour look. "That's girl's work but Ivy's not home tonight."

"Cooking is a good skill to have." Jalon stood, then glanced at Phoebe. "Some people are truly gifted in the kitchen."

"Race you back to the *haus*, Malachi." Judah sprinted off as he said the words, and Malachi bolted after him.

"I remember being that age." Jalon moved to stand next to her. "Not a care in the world."

"Freedom," Phoebe added.

"*Ya*. Plenty of freedom, although at the time I didn't realize it." He turned to her, his expression intense. "I'm serious about what I said before, Phoebe. I know we've had a rocky start since you got here, and I want to change that. I want to take you on a date, without Karen and Malachi looking over our shoulders." He suddenly looked a little uncertain. "But if you don't feel the same way"—he released a long breath—"I'll understand."

She couldn't believe what she was hearing. He was interested in her, not as a friend, not as an obligation. But romantically interested. Her dream of being with Jalon lit up again, warming her heart.

"Phoebe?" More uncertainty clouded his eyes.

Blinking, she realized she hadn't answered him. "Oh! I do. Feel the same way, that is." She beamed, unable to hide her smile.

Relief washed over his expression, and he was grinning too. Which made her swoon a little bit. *Okay, a lot.*

"You don't know how glad I am to hear that. How about tomorrow afternoon? I'll take you for a drive, show you around Birch Creek."

She nodded, her plan to make arrangements to leave forgotten. She and Jalon were going on a date. It took everything she had not to squeal with joy. Forcing her practical side to take over, she said, "We better get back. We don't want Karen to think we're up to something."

"Trust me," he said, his eyebrows wagging a little, "she wouldn't be surprised."

When they were a few feet from the house, Jalon pulled up short.

"Is something wrong?" she asked, looking up at him.

He turned and gazed at her for a long moment, and all the attraction she'd wanted to see in his eyes for so long was there and vulnerable. He brushed his fingertip against the lower part of her cheek, making her smile.

"That's what I like to see." His voice was low and a tiny bit husky. He ran his finger over her dimple before stepping away.

Her toes curled in her shoes, and she savored the private moment. Once they were in the house, he couldn't touch her, or look at her the way he was doing now. This was something special, just between them.

Karen was sitting at the table reading a magazine when they walked into the kitchen. Her gaze went from Jalon to Phoebe, then back to Jalon again. "You two have a good afternoon?" she asked, her voice sweet and innocent but her expression knowing.

"It was . . . nice." Jalon's wink was barely detectable, but Phoebe saw it. "I've got work to do on the *dawdi haus*," he said, looking at Phoebe but talking to both her and Karen. "I'll see you later."

"Oh, Phoebe," Karen said. "There's a letter for you on the counter. It's from Ashtabula."

• • •

Jalon froze halfway out the doorway as Karen pointed to Phoebe's letter on the counter. He'd been elated when Phoebe said she felt the same way he did. Suddenly everything that had been weighing him down became lighter. For a few bright moments he'd felt the clouds begin to lift, and he couldn't wait for their date tomorrow afternoon. Then in one moment his good mood swiftly disintegrated.

Jalon tensed as Phoebe picked up the letter. She looked at the envelope. Then her eyes shifted to Jalon. She was thinking the same thing he was. Whatever was in that letter would change everything.

She sat down at the table and opened the envelope, her expression inscrutable. Then she took out the letter and read out loud:

Dear Phoebe,

It was nice to hear from you. Andy and I went to Pinecraft for the winter. The kids are grown and we like to go there a lot. I didn't get your letter until yesterday. I wrote to you right away because I know you want an answer. You and Malachi are welcome to come here anytime. I'll make up the sparc bedroom for you, and it will be waiting when you get here.

Sylvia

Phoebe put down the letter, and Jalon felt his chest constrict.

Karen closed the magazine. Jalon noticed she didn't look too happy either. "Sounds like *gut* news," she said with little enthusiasm.

"*Ya.*" But Phoebe didn't sound convinced. She also didn't look excited, and he had to admit that made him feel a little better. "I should write her back. Let her know we're coming." She said the words to Karen, but her eyes stayed on Jalon.

"Do you have to leave right away?" Karen asked. "You haven't met Leanna yet. And I know Ivy has been meaning to come over here. She's been busy with some genealogy project of *Daed*'s when she hasn't been working. *Mamm*'s also determined to have you over for supper."

Phoebe nodded, still looking at Jalon. "I suppose we could stay a little while longer."

He nearly sank against the doorjamb in relief. She'd always been in such a hurry to leave, and now that she had the opportunity, she chose to stay. He tempered his excitement in front of Karen and shrugged with a nonchalance he didn't feel. "It's up to you." And it was. It always had been. He'd never force her to stay.

"Then we'll stay." Her lips curved into a small smile, her dimple appearing in her cheek. "After all, I have plans tomorrow afternoon. It would be a shame to cancel them."

It took all he had not to break into a huge grin. "*Ya.* It would."

"Then it's settled." Karen stood back up. "I'll let *Mamm* know we need to make supper plans sooner than later." She put her arm around Phoebe and squeezed. "I'm glad you and Malachi will be in Birch Creek for a little while longer."

Never taking her eyes off Jalon, Phoebe's smile grew. This time he smiled back at her.

Tomorrow couldn't come soon enough.

CHAPTER 13

Phoebe was singing.

She was actually singing. At first it started as a low humming of one of her favorite hymns, but as she hung out the laundry, she burst into full song. The day was sunny, and in spite of the cold temperature it looked to be a beautiful day. But the weather wasn't the only reason for her good mood. In a few hours she was going to go on a buggy ride with Jalon.

She had once sought far more excitement in her life than spending time in the slow pace of a buggy. But now she realized she looked forward to such a simple activity, even though she was sure the topic of Malachi's father and her past would come up. Yet she wasn't dreading it as much as she had before. After their time at the pond yesterday, she had hope that she and Jalon could move beyond her past.

She clipped the last pair of Jalon's pants on the line and smiled. She could see herself doing this on a regular basis. Really see it, imagining that she wasn't doing the work as a favor or as recompense for staying at his house, but as his wife. In the past she would put a stop to such foolish thoughts, but this time she allowed herself the luxury of experiencing the warmth that circled her heart.

Grabbing the empty clothes basket, she headed back to the house. Karen had gone home for the morning to spend time with her family, and Jalon had headed out to find a job. She prayed he was successful. Although he seemed a lot more lighthearted than he was before their talk at the pond, she saw the apprehension in his eyes before he left.

Malachi met her at the kitchen door. "Can I *geh* outside and play?"

"Did you make the bed?"

He nodded.

"Brush *yer* teeth?"

"*Ya.*" He beamed, and she could see a tiny white spot where his tooth was growing in.

"Fed Blue?"

"Uh-huh."

"Hmm." She looked up at the ceiling, pretending to mull over his request.

"Please?" he begged.

Grinning, she nodded. "Stay in the backyard, and don't *geh* near the pond."

He dashed outside, and Phoebe watched him scamper into the yard through the mudroom window. She sighed, pleased that Malachi wasn't just happy here, but was thriving. They both were. *Thank you, Lord.*

Time got away from her as she finished up her chores, her mind not focused on her tasks because she kept getting sidetracked thinking about Jalon and anticipating their date. She was dusting the baseboards in the living room when she heard a car door shut. It had to be Jalon. She glanced at the clock, surprised that he was home after only being gone a few hours. Hopefully that meant he had good news about his job hunt.

She looked at the clock again, realizing that Malachi had been outside longer than she intended. She leaned the dust mop against the wall and headed for the door.

"Malachi!"

Alarm shot through her at the panic and anger she heard in Jalon's voice. She rushed to the backyard, horrific scenarios running through her mind. Had her son done something destructive? Was he hurt, or worse?

When she got outside, she saw Jalon, red-faced and furious, standing under a large oak. He was still yelling at Malachi.

"Get down here, now!"

"I was just getting Blue—"

"I said *now*!" He moved to the base of the tree.

Phoebe recoiled.

Malachi started to cry. "I'm scared."

"I'll give you something to be scared about if you don't come down here."

Phoebe's mouth dropped open in shock. She hurried to stand in front of the oak. "Jalon! Can't you see you're upsetting him?"

"Get. Down!" he yelled again, ignoring Phoebe.

She quailed, but stood her ground. "Stop yelling at him and he will." She whirled around and looked up at Malachi. He wasn't that far up, just a few branches. He also seemed perfectly fine, except for the tears streaming down his little face. "Malachi, sweetheart. It's okay. You can come down now."

He clung to a thick branch. "I'm scared," he repeated.

"But I'm right here. I won't let anything happen to you."

"Jalon's mad."

"I know he's mad." She shot Jalon a black look. He took off his hat and thrust his hands into his hair so hard she thought he would pull some of it out. Why was he so upset? Malachi wasn't in danger. He had climbed trees at home with her younger brothers.

"Am I in trouble?" Malachi asked.

"*Ya*," Jalon snapped.

"*Nee*, you're not in trouble." She reached up her arms. "Please, come down."

He didn't move, and Phoebe thought she'd have to climb up and get him down herself. She used to climb trees when she was younger, and if Malachi needed her to, she would right now. Finally, he shimmied down the oak, landing on the ground with light feet, unharmed.

"Don't you ever climb that tree—or any tree—again." Jalon shoved his hat on his head. He looked at Phoebe. "Why weren't you watching him? What kind of *mamm* lets her *kin* do something so dangerous?"

Phoebe held Malachi close. Why was Jalon attacking her like this? "I'm a *gut mamm*," she said, indignant. But that didn't stop every doubt she'd ever had about being a capable mother from coming to the surface.

"*Mamm*, are you mad too?" Malachi whimpered.

"She should be," Jalon said.

How dare he say how she should feel?

"Is Jalon going to spank me?"

Phoebe wasn't completely sure he wouldn't. "*Nee*." She brushed back his hair. "He won't." *I won't let him.* She glared at Jalon, keeping Malachi by her side, daring him to say another word against her or her son.

He scowled, turned, and stormed into the house.

It was only then that Phoebe realized her hands were shaking. Steadying herself, she said to Malachi, "You should stay out of the trees from now on."

She half expected him to ask her why. Instead, he only nodded.

She tweaked his nose, needing to lighten the mood. "*Gut.* Now, where's Blue?"

"Over there." He pointed to where the cat was, near the back porch, keeping a safe distance, as if he realized he was the catalyst for what had happened. "I should see if he's okay. Then I'll take him around to the front porch."

Phoebe nodded, watching Malachi comfort the cat. Blue seemed to have special intuition where Malachi was concerned, because he leaned into him, looking up into Malachi's eyes as if silently telling him it was going to be okay. Then her son picked him up and walked around the house.

Jalon's words slammed into her. *What kind of* mamm *lets her* kin *do something so dangerous?* Now her hands were shaking again. Is that what he really thought, that she was a terrible mother? Granted, she had trouble disciplining Malachi at times. But she loved her son with every fiber of her being. And she was doing her best.

She wasn't about to be judged by a man who knew nothing about being a parent.

Jalon came out of the house again. He paused at the porch's one step and looked at her. Anger was still ripe in his eyes along with . . . regret? She wasn't sure because he turned and stormed into the backyard.

She put her hand to her chest. This was a side of Jalon she never expected to see. One she didn't want to see.

. . .

Jalon went to the shed and got an ax. He should have done this years ago. But his mother loved that tree, and his father refused to cut it down. Well, his parents weren't here. He owned this house and farm, not them. And he was getting rid of that tree.

A mix of fury and fear churned inside him. Job hunting had been a failure—again. But he hadn't been as upset about it as he had been before, mostly because he had his date with Phoebe to look forward to. But when the taxi driver dropped him off, all thoughts of their date vanished when he saw Malachi in the tree. His blood hadn't run that cold since . . .

He gripped the ax handle, more angry with himself now than he was with Malachi. Or Phoebe. Still, his heart was hammering from the fear, then the fury, at seeing Malachi in that tree.

When he arrived at the tree, he didn't hesitate to plunge the blade of the ax into the thick base of the oak. This was a two-man job, probably three. Maybe four if he was honest, but right now he felt the strength of ten men in his arms as he continued to whack at the dense, un-yielding wood.

Three hits later his arms ached. Nine and he was out of breath. He was in shape, but this was no ordinary tree.

It was huge, lush in the spring and summer, vibrant in the fall, and still majestic in the stark winter. He continued to strike, pouring out years of anger and guilt and remorse. Sweat ran down his back and pooled on his forehead, despite the chilly air.

Finally, he had to stop. He threw his hat on the ground and wiped his palm over his face. His emotions switched gears, and a dull dread gathered in his stomach. He stopped thinking about his own fear and remembered Malachi's terrified expression. Truth be told, Malachi had seemed fine in the tree, and he wasn't scared until Jalon had started yelling at him. Then there was Phoebe. He'd scared her too. He'd also angered her. Two things he'd never wanted to do.

He put the ax back in the shed and walked to the front of the house. Malachi was sitting on the porch, his chin resting on his knees. Jalon took a deep breath and walked over to him. Malachi didn't look up, and Blue snuggled closer to him.

"All right if I sit down?"

Malachi didn't say anything, then shrugged.

Making sure not to sit on Blue—he'd done that a time or two over the years—he sat down and put his forearms on his knees. "I'm sorry for yelling at you." When Malachi didn't say anything, he added, "I shouldn't have gotten so angry. I was worried you would be hurt. That's why I was mad."

The boy's shoulders twitched. At least he was listening to Jalon.

Phoebe came out on the porch. "Malachi," she said, ignoring Jalon. "Come inside."

Jalon looked at her over his shoulder and withered inside. Her face was red with anger, her eyes cold as they finally flitted to him, then back to her son.

"Is it time for lunch?"

Jalon almost laughed, amazed at how easily Malachi had gone from shutting him out to being concerned about food.

"We'll get something to eat later," she said. "*Geh* inside and wait for me on the couch."

"But—"

"Malachi, now." Her voice was low. Calm, but barely controlled. Without a word Malachi went inside.

Jalon rose from the porch step. "Phoebe—"

She blew past him and headed for the driveway. She was halfway down it when he realized she was going to the phone shanty.

"Wait," he called out, hurrying to her. Her steps quickened and she didn't answer him. He jumped in front of her, blocking her way. "Stop. Let's talk about this—"

"There's *nix* to say." She squared her shoulders, but her lower lip trembled slightly. "Please get out of *mei* way. I need to call a taxi."

"For what?"

"We're going to *mei* cousin's."

He blew out an exasperated breath. "Don't you think you're overreacting?"

"Overreacting?" Her eyes widened. "Are you serious? You terrified *mei sohn* because he climbed a tree—"

"I know and I'm—"

"And then you accused me of being a bad *mamm*."

He stilled. "I never said that."

"*Ya.*" Her voice quavered. "You did."

She tried to move past him but he stepped in front of her again. "Phoebe, let's talk about this. I know I shouldn't have lost *mei* temper."

Crossing her arms over her chest, she glowered.

"You have the right to be mad at me. I deserve it. But I don't think you should leave now. Malachi's been upset enough for one day."

She didn't answer, just glared at him. If her eyes had been daggers, they would have shot right to his heart. "We won't leave today," she finally said. "Because of Malachi." Then she whirled around and went back to the house.

She wasn't going to make it easy on him, and she shouldn't. He didn't deserve easy.

At a loss, he walked around the house to the back-yard. He couldn't go inside, not yet. He had to give Phoebe time to cool down. He didn't remember saying she was a bad mother, but he'd been so terrified at see-ing Malachi in the tree he didn't doubt that he had. He couldn't take back those words, or any others he'd said that hurt her, but somehow he had to make it up to her.

He'd convinced her to stay one more night because of Malachi, and his concern for him was genuine. But he wasn't completely selfless in his motives. He couldn't bear the thought of them leaving, remembering him angry and, yes, overreacting. He had to fix this.

He looked at the oak again. What he'd done was the very definition of a hack job, and represented ex-actly how he felt about himself right now—ragged and damaged. He'd let his fear and guilt overcome him, and now he was on the verge of losing two people he cared about deeply.

But he hadn't changed his mind about the tree, and he couldn't cut it down by himself. He'd get Sol and a few other men in the community to help him do it properly. He would get rid of the tree once and for all—along with the painful memories it held.

• • •

Phoebe sat on the edge of Jalon's couch, her teeth grinding together. She'd made Malachi a snack and told him to stay in the kitchen. She needed a moment—more than a moment—to compose herself. Her heart thudded in her chest, and it wasn't only because she was angry with Jalon. She was also mad at herself. He'd been right about Malachi. Her son had been distraught enough, although seeing him and Jalon on the front porch moments ago reminded her once again how irrepressible Malachi could be. Suddenly uprooting him with little explanation and leaving to stay with a family he didn't know wasn't the right thing to do.

The front door opened, and out of the corner of her eye she saw Jalon. He didn't walk inside right away, and despite herself, she looked at him. His expression was contrite and pained and she could see the apology in his eyes. In fact, it was written all over his face. And as much as she wanted to hang on to her anger and hurt, she felt her heart soften a tiny bit.

"Phoebe?"

His voice was gentle and uncertain. Was it just a short time ago that everything had been right between them?

"I'm very sorry." He took off his hat and moved the brim back and forth in his fingers. "I shouldn't have lost *mei* temper with Malachi, or with you."

"You scared us."

"I know that too." He was practically bending the hat brim in half. "I'm glad you're staying."

The ice around her heart cracked a little more, but she wasn't ready to let him off the hook. She rose from the couch and walked past him to the kitchen. He didn't follow her.

Malachi had finished his snack, and she handed him the pad of paper and crayons Karen had brought over the other day. She watched as he started drawing and thought about Jalon. She'd caught his hurt expression as she'd breezed past him. That should have made her feel a little better, knowing he was paying the consequences for scaring Malachi and insulting her.

It didn't. If anything, she felt much, much worse.

. . .

Supper was simple and quiet. Phoebe had helped Karen prepare stewed chicken and dumplings, brussels sprouts, and a Yum Yum cake for dessert. Phoebe had never heard of such a cake, a Yoder family favorite. The combination of yellow cake, pudding, pineapple, and whipped cream looked delicious. Too bad only Karen and Malachi were hungry.

Phoebe nibbled on her meal, trying not to pay attention to Jalon as he pushed his food around his plate. Karen had stopped trying to force conversation. She had asked about the tree, and as far as Phoebe knew Jalon had given her some excuse about trying to cut it down without going into any details.

Malachi did eat most of his food, and by the time he was finished his head started to bob with exhaustion. He'd spent the rest of the afternoon coloring and playing inside, not asking to go out as he usually did. He'd stuck close to Phoebe, even helping her dust the furniture without her asking him to. "Come, Malachi," Phoebe said. "Let's get you to bed."

His head popped up. "I'm not tired," he slurred.

"You're falling asleep at the table." She rose and said to Karen, "I'll help you with the dishes when he's settled."

She waved her hand. "*Nee* worries. I'll take care of them. *Gute nacht*, Malachi."

"I'm not tired." His head lolled to one side.

Phoebe was about to take Malachi's hand when Jalon appeared at her side. "I've got him," he said, scooping Malachi up into his arms.

She was going to protest until she saw Malachi wrap his arms around Jalon's neck. She followed them both upstairs, and Jalon set Malachi on the bed. He stepped out of the way as she took off Malachi's shoes and socks, then moved his legs onto the mattress and pulled the covers over him. His eyes were already closed. "*Gute nacht*," she whispered, touching his cheek. She stood, turned around, and looked at Jalon.

He motioned for her to come into the hallway. When she joined him, he shut the bedroom door.

"Can we talk?" he asked.

"Not if you're going to yell at me again."

His brow shot up. "Why would I do that? Phoebe, I said I was sorry, and I meant it."

She rubbed the middle of her forehead and frowned. She was being rude and hurtful while he was trying to set things right. "I'm sorry too."

"You don't have anything to apologize for."

"*Ya*. I do." She drew in a deep breath. "I should have been paying more attention to Malachi. But I was working in the *haus* and . . ." Her face flushed.

"And what?" he asked, his brow furrowing a bit.

"I was thinking about . . . things." She swallowed, and it was hard to keep looking at him, especially when he leaned against the wall, his brow relaxing slightly, as if he knew exactly what she was referring to.

"What kind of things?"

"I was distracted thinking about you, okay?"

"Then I had to *geh* and ruin it." He pushed off the wall, suddenly looking hopeful. "Or not."

"What?"

"We could still have our date. Tonight. It won't be a ride in the buggy but it will be something."

"Jalon, I don't know . . ."

"I'd like a second chance."

After everything he had done for them, he deserved at least that. "Okay," she said.

"I'll meet you in the living room in a few minutes."

Phoebe nodded, and he disappeared downstairs. She

peeked to check on Malachi, who was fast asleep. At some point Blue had come into the room and snuggled right next to him. The cat usually left the bed once Phoebe got in it for the night, but until that point he was stuck like glue next to Malachi.

She went downstairs and sat in the rocker next to the woodstove. Heat from the fireplace warmed her body, and she leaned back and closed her eyes.

"I'm tired too," Karen said.

Phoebe opened her eyes to see Karen standing at the bottom of the staircase. "Are you going to bed already?"

"*Ya.* I got sleepy all of a sudden. I'll see you in the morning." She paused. "Unless there was something you wanted to talk about?"

Karen didn't miss a thing. Phoebe shook her head. "Everything is fine."

Karen nodded, but didn't look convinced. "*Gut.* Just know that I'm here if you ever need to talk."

"*Danki,*" she said, finally able to muster a smile. "I appreciate that."

A few minutes after Karen went upstairs, Jalon walked in, carrying a mug. He handed it to her.

"Tea?" she said, taking a sniff.

"Also known as a peace offering." He sat down across from her, and she noticed he didn't have a drink.

"Jalon, it's okay." She held the warm mug in her hands. It was the perfect temperature. "I understand losing *yer* temper. I also understand saying things you don't mean when you're angry. You're not the only one who does that." She leaned forward. "What I don't understand is why you were so angry. Malachi was fine. He hadn't climbed that far up in the tree."

Jalon looked away. The firelight from the stove flickered faint shadows along his strong profile. "I know."

She paused, wondering if she should ask the question, then realizing that she had to. If they were going to make this work, they had to be honest with each other. "Why did you try to cut down the tree?"

His legs spread apart, he stared down at the floor. "I can't . . . I can't talk about it. Not now."

"Part of *yer* regrets?" She took a sip of the tea. She wouldn't push, but at least she'd put the question out there. And she could see he was responding as honestly as he could. It was all she could ask for.

Nodding, he turned toward her. "*Ya.*"

Outside, the wind kicked up, rattling the windows. She shivered.

"Are you cold? I can get some more wood for the stove."

"*Nee*, I'm fine." She shuddered again, feeling an unexpected prodding in her heart.

It's time to tell him.

I can't talk to him about that now.

Tell him your story.

She looked at him. His head drooped a bit, and she could see he was tired, and she had a feeling the cause was more than getting upset at Malachi and battling a tree.

Tell him your story.

She took a deep breath, unable to ignore the small nudge any longer. "I have regrets too."

He looked up at her, expectant and wary, as if he knew she was finally going to tell him about Malachi's father. She almost changed her mind, but if admitting her past would help Jalon—would help *them*—she would do it.

"I was eight when *mei* brother Devon was born. After that, I barely remember a time when I wasn't helping *mei mamm* with *mei* siblings, whether it was changing their diapers, feeding them, washing all their clothes, babysitting them when *mei* parents wanted to *geh* out alone or visit friends without little ones grabbing at them."

He nodded. "You basically raised them."

"I felt like I did. By the time I was seventeen I was tired of it. *Mei* girlfriends were talking about getting married and having *kinner*. But I didn't want to be a *mamm*. I didn't want to get married either. I also questioned *mei* faith—whether or not I wanted to be Amish. I felt suffocated by rules, by *mei* siblings. I wanted to be free." She glanced down at her unsteady hands and closed them into fists. "I started sneaking out of the *haus* with one of *mei* friends. She knew a lot of English boys, and those boys knew where all the parties were." She paused, expecting censure from him.

His face held no expression at all.

Shame grew inside her as she kept talking. "For the next two years I rebelled. Eventually I didn't bother sneaking out. I just left. I hadn't joined the church, and there was nothing *mei* parents could do to stop me. They needed me more than I needed them. Or so I thought.

"One night I met this guy at a party. Brody. He was a few years older than me, and in college. I thought he was smart and cute and funny." Her cheeks flushed. Maybe she shouldn't have added that part. But if Jalon was affected by her description of another man, he didn't show it. His blank expression unnerved her, but she continued to explain. "I saw him at a few other parties over the next two months, and one night we started talking. He'd been accepted to medical school in California and was planning to become a cancer doctor. We started drinking, then decided to celebrate . . ." Oh, this was hard. She wanted to jump out of her skin when she admitted the next part. "Malachi was born nine months later."

"I see."

She wished he would show some emotion. She'd even take his anger right now. She'd spent enough time being angry at herself. And guilty, especially after admitting to her parents that she was pregnant and the father wasn't Amish. She closed her eyes at the memory, remembering the shock and disappointment in both their eyes.

"I told Brody I was pregnant," she said, opening her eyes but unable to look at Jalon. "I thought it was only fair that he knew. When he said he didn't want to be a part of the *boppli*'s life, I was relieved. But I was also scared. I felt alone, even though *mei* parents hadn't asked me to leave. They could have, you know. They could have cast me out, but they supported me. Even after all the trouble I gave them . . ." She swallowed the lump in her throat. She hadn't fully appreciated her parents until that moment. She'd spent so much time resenting them for giving her so much responsibility. "I was selfish. I'd lived for myself, hurt *mei* parents, and turned away from God. Even though I had a home and *mei* mother and father's love, because of *mei* choices I felt separated from God. How could he forgive me for all the things I'd done?"

He blinked once. Then twice. "There's always forgiveness," he said in a low voice.

"I know that now. *Mei* parents forgave me, and so did God. I joined the church a short time after, and it became a haven for me." She scratched the back of her hand. "Ironically, the two things I thought were boxing me in ended up giving me the freedom I'd always wanted." She looked at him. "I want to be clear—I don't regret Malachi. He's the best thing that ever happened to me."

His expression was still shuttered. "What about Brody? Are you in contact with him at all?"

"*Nee*. After I told him about the *boppli*, I never saw him again. I'm sure he's in medical school out in California right now. Malachi and I have been living with *mei* parents since he was born. Up until we went to *Aenti* Bertha's."

"Because you didn't want to be a burden to *yer* parents."

She took a deep breath. "That's the excuse I gave everyone. *Mei* parents live in a poor community. We're a small district—only eight families. When *mei mamm* became pregnant with *mei* youngest brother, Elam, the farm was barely supporting us, even though we all pitched in with the work. I also helped out with odd jobs—making baked goods to sell, doing some cleaning for an English *familye* that lived a few miles away. Then I lost the cleaning job, and *mei* bread and pies sales became nonexistent. I wrote to *mei aenti* and asked if Malachi and I could stay with her. She never married and doesn't have any *kinner*. I offered to help her out at home. I also hoped there would be better job opportunities in a new community, so I could work and send money home to *mei* parents. When she said yes, Malachi and I left the next day."

"*Yer* parents didn't ask you to stay?"

"They did, but I insisted on going." Her voice grew thick as she remembered her mother, the strings of her *kapp* frayed at the edges, holding on to her youngest brother, looking confused and sad at the same time. "Things didn't turn out the way I planned."

He rubbed his finger across his chin, and she could hear the soft scraping of his short whiskers against his skin. "You said that was an excuse. What's the real reason you left?"

She bit her bottom lip, averting her gaze. "I left for the same reason I can't *geh* back."

"I'm sure whatever that is, *yer* parents will understand. I'm sure they want you to come home."

"*Mei* parents aren't the problem. The bishop is." She balled her hands again. "He's the one who made me leave."

CHAPTER 14

Jalon struggled to remain impassive as Phoebe spoke, but he was losing the battle. He could see what it cost her to tell him about Malachi's father. The humiliation of admitting her family's poverty. She was telling the truth, he was absolutely sure of it this time. Now he understood why she hadn't told him about any of this in her letters. It wasn't something you casually wrote down and hoped the other person would understand. He felt the same way. Telling her about his alcoholism—which he still needed to do, especially now that she wasn't holding anything back from him—was something he'd also put off. And he'd continue to do so, at least for the time being. Right now this was about her, not him.

More than once he'd wanted to take her hand but held back. He didn't need to make a mistake right now, so he kept his cool and listened, his emotions tightly wound. "Why did he ask you to leave?"

Her cheeks reddened more deeply than before. "The bishop who baptized me passed away early last summer. I'd known him pretty much *mei* whole life, and while he was strict, he was also compassionate. When he found out I was pregnant with Malachi, he didn't judge me. I had to confess *mei* sin, of course, but afterward he didn't say anything else about it. Then a new bishop was chosen . . . and everything changed.

"One afternoon he came to see me. *Mei* parents were out and *mei* brothers and Malachi were busy with chores. I was thankful for that, because Bishop Weaver wasn't there five minutes before he told me I was an embarrassment to the community."

"What?" Jalon said, stunned.

"He said I shamed *mei familye*, I shamed *mei* church, and most of all I shamed myself." She shook her head and let out a bitter chuckle. "If I didn't know any better, I would think he and *Aenti* Bertha had been talking to each other. She told me the same things once I got to her *haus*, more than once."

His hands fisted. "You made a mistake."

"Malachi is not a mistake." She lifted her chin, which made her rosy cheeks even more appealing. "I want to make that clear. Regardless of *mei* choices, *mei sohn* is not a mistake."

"Of course not." He leaned forward. "That's not what I meant."

She sighed, her chin lowering, and the moment of defiance disappeared. "I, on the other hand, have made plenty of mistakes. I'm the only unwed *mamm* in the community. Apparently the bishop isn't happy about that. He told me I needed to get married. If I didn't choose a husband, he would choose one for me."

"He can't do that." But Jalon didn't totally believe the words. Bishops had a lot of sway in a community, even in Birch Creek. Emmanuel Troyer had established the community, was its bishop, and had refused to let the members elect a minister or deacon. He'd had complete control over the community's money, and when it was revealed he'd been hoarding funds community members could have used in lean times—Karen's family was one of them—he left, and no one had heard from him since.

"He could. And he would have." She stood and moved away from the woodstove. "I . . ." Her voice was shaking. "I couldn't marry someone I didn't love and be with him for the rest of *mei* life. That wouldn't be fair to Malachi, or to me." She whirled around and faced Jalon. "I know that sounds selfish."

He popped up from the couch. "It doesn't, not to me." He moved closer to her, but maintained his distance. "Marriage should be based on love. Not coercion."

For the first time since she'd started talking, her features relaxed. "I think so too. I really believe it. I've been with someone when there was *nee* love. It didn't feel right. It *wasn't* right. I promised myself I would never be with a man I didn't love again. A man who wasn't *mei* husband. I want to marry someone because I love him, not because he could be a father to Malachi or a financial support to me. And I intend to keep that promise."

Something inside Jalon stirred, and his attraction to her was deeper than before. "That's a *gut* decision."

"*Danki.* I'm glad I made at least one."

"Phoebe, you make plenty."

"Going to *Aenti* Bertha's was a bad decision. A really bad decision."

"You didn't feel like you had any choice."

"And whose fault is that?"

"Sounds like it's the bishop's fault."

She held up her hand. "I'm not blaming him. *Mei* circumstances are *mei* own. His reaction, and even *mei aenti*'s, are the consequences." She lowered her hand. "I know I've made more mistakes since then, but I hope you can forgive me for not telling you about Malachi."

He went to her, stopping short of being too close. "I understand. And I get why you kept Malachi a secret from me. So there's *nix* to forgive."

Her blue eyes shined with unshed tears. "I was afraid you wouldn't understand," she whispered. "That you would never want to talk to me again once you knew the truth."

"Phoebe." He ran his thumb over her cheek. "I would never do that." Her skin was warm beneath his palm, and it wouldn't take much for him to take her in his arms. But something held him back. There would be time to hold her. To kiss her. To finally tell her how much he loved her. Now wasn't the time. He didn't want her to think his feelings were born out of pity, or for her to doubt his sincerity. He couldn't just tell her he loved her. He had to show her. And he had to do it right.

It took everything he had to step away from her, even though he knew he had to. "I'm glad you told me," he said.

"I should have told you sooner."

"You told me when the time was right. That's all that matters."

They looked at each other for a long moment. Finally she said, "I should get to bed."

"Me too. I've got more job hunting to do in the morning." That statement put a damper on things. He frowned. "I just wish I understood why I haven't found anything yet."

"You will." She put her hand on his arm for the briefest of moments before pulling away. "*Gute nacht*, Jalon." She turned and went upstairs.

He sat down on the couch and watched the flames flickering in the woodstove, marveling at Phoebe, not only for making difficult choices but for taking responsibility for her actions. He hadn't had the same maturity at her age. But the more he thought about the bishop's actions, the angrier he became. Because of one man's righteous pride and strict rules, Phoebe and Malachi were homeless.

His hand gripped the arm of the couch. He refused to allow that. The two of them would always have a home. He would make sure of it.

. . .

The next morning Phoebe reviewed the previous night's conversation in her mind. Jalon had said very little at breakfast before he left to job hunt again. She feared she had revealed too much. But once she had started talking, the words spilled out of her, and while she didn't feel any less shameful about her past, she did feel some relief that he not only knew what had happened, but he hadn't shunned her. He'd understood, and she'd seen the compassion in his eyes, the sweet gentleness when he wiped away her tears. He amazed her. She'd never met a more perfect man in her life.

"We have a change of plans," Karen said as she finished sweeping the kitchen floor. "*Mamm* forgot that she and *Daed* are visiting Rhoda Troyer later on today." Karen paused. "She's the wife of our former bishop. *Mamm* asked if we could come over for lunch instead of supper."

Phoebe crimped a sheet of foil over the platter of left-over French toast. "That would be nice." She was looking forward to meeting Karen's parents. She'd always been social, and spending the last several months being a near hermit was wearing on her.

She and Karen made quick work of the rest of the chores, then headed over to the Yoders'. They crossed a large field that stood between Jalon's house and theirs. "We're not trespassing, are we?" Phoebe asked. She glanced over her shoulder at Malachi, who was dawdling a few feet behind them.

"*Nee*. At least I don't think so. This field belongs to an English man, but *nee* one has ever seen him come around. Years ago *Daed* tried to buy the property, but the guy wouldn't return his calls. It ended up being a good thing because we had some lean years after that, and we probably wouldn't have been able to make the payments on the loan."

Phoebe understood about that. Her parents had had more than their fair share of lean years.

When they arrived at the Yoders', Phoebe found herself thrust into a bustle of activity. Ivy came out of the house, and Phoebe was struck again by how petite she was. She smiled as she approached them. "We need *yer* help in the kitchen," Ivy said. "*Mamm* decided it would be a *gut* idea to make donuts again."

Karen shook her head. "She didn't learn from the last time?"

"*Nee*. Or the time before that, or the time before that." Ivy turned to Phoebe. "Do you know how to make donuts?"

Phoebe nodded. "I used to make them all the time at home."

"Then maybe you can show *Mamm*, because for some reason none of us can get the recipe right."

Judah came up to Malachi. "We're playing tag in the backyard," he said before running off and disappearing behind the large house.

Malachi glanced up at Phoebe, who nodded her head. Then he zipped behind the house too. Phoebe could hear the shouts of the boys as they continued their game.

"*Daed* and Seth, our oldest brother, are helping an English *familye* up the road build a pole barn. It's a small one, so they'll be back in time for lunch." Ivy started for the house, then smiled at Phoebe. "We're glad to have you and Malachi over."

"We're glad to be here." And it was true. Were things finally settling down for her and Malachi? She didn't want to hope—her hope had been dashed too many times— but she couldn't help it. She knew she and Malachi would have to leave at some point, unless . . .

No. She wouldn't let her mind dwell on the possibility of a future with Jalon. They still had so much to learn about each other, although the big obstacle was out of the way. She wouldn't jump in and do anything impulsive like she had in the past. She couldn't afford to, because she wasn't the only person who would be affected.

They walked into a spacious but simple kitchen. Mary Yoder looked up from kneading a glob of dough on the table. "Phoebe, so nice you could come for lunch. Sorry about the change in plans." She lifted her hands, the sticky dough covering her fingers. "Do you like donuts?"

"You might not after you eat these," Karen mumbled.

"What was that?"

"*Nix, Mamm.*"

"I love donuts." Phoebe went to the table, trying to figure out what was wrong with the donut dough. It looked all right to her, except it was too sticky.

"Looks like you need more flour," Ivy said, as if she'd read Phoebe's thoughts.

"I added too much flour the last time and they turned into hockey pucks."

"Maybe you should try a new recipe."

Mary looked at her, indignant. "This is *mei gross-mammi*'s recipe. Her donuts were the best I've ever tasted. I'm determined to get it right."

"How long have you been kneading the dough?" Phoebe asked.

"About ten minutes."

"Do you let it rest for a couple of hours afterward?"

"Not that long. Thirty minutes, then I roll it out."

"I've found that letting donut dough rest for a couple of hours right before rolling it out makes the donuts light and fluffy."

"I never thought about it. I made these once with *mei grossmammi* when I was little, and I didn't pay attention to the rise time. I just assumed it was similar to bread." She looked at a scrap of paper with the recipe scrawled on it. "Doesn't say anything here except 'let dough rise.'" She gave a half smile. "I'll admit to not being a *gut* baker."

"Honesty is the best policy," Ivy said.

Mary shot her a pointed look. "I actually don't bake at all, except for bread. Karen's the baker in the *haus*."

"I offered to make the donuts for you." Karen moved near the table. "Several times."

"I know, I know. But I want to conquer this recipe myself." She looked at the sticky dough. "It needs more flour."

"I believe I said that." Ivy went to the sink and washed her hands.

Without thinking, Phoebe reached into the flour container and took out half a handful. "That should be enough."

Mary started kneading and the dough began to come together. She put it in a bowl and placed a kitchen towel over it. "Two hours?" she asked Phoebe.

"At least. The longer it rests the better. Also, it needs to be in a cool place. That will help the dough firm up."

Nodding, Mary took the bowl and left the kitchen, saying, "The mudroom will be a good spot."

Ivy and Karen were cleaning up the table. "Can I help?" Phoebe asked.

"You've already helped a lot." Karen grinned. "I think the donuts might be saved."

Phoebe smiled, happy she was able to help out. Malachi would be thrilled to have a donut or two.

When Mary came back, the women worked on lunch. Mary and her daughters talked nonstop, mostly Mary, but they brought Phoebe into the conversation enough that she didn't feel neglected. Mary might not have been much of a baker but she was a good cook otherwise, at ease in the kitchen the same way Karen was. Ivy preferred to wash the dishes and set the table. "You don't like to cook?" Phoebe asked.

"Only out of necessity." She stood on tiptoe to reach the dishcloth that was near the back of the sink. "Karen and *Mamm* are the cooks around here."

"You'll have to improve *yer* skills before you get married." Mary added diced green pepper to the potato salad ingredients in a large bowl.

Phoebe didn't miss Ivy's eye roll. She glanced at Karen, who looked equally annoyed. "*Mamm*'s been trying to marry us off for years," she said.

"Feels like decades," Ivy added. "Or an eternity."

"I just want *mei* girls to be happy." Mary stirred the potato salad.

"We are happy." Karen sliced the bone-in ham.

"You'd be happier married. Look at *yer* father and me. Five *kinner* later and we're still like newlyweds."

Phoebe laughed out loud at that, while Karen and Ivy groaned. Then all talk about marriage and newlyweds stopped when Judah, Ira, and Malachi came into the kitchen. After she and Mary sent the boys to wash up, Freemont and Seth walked in. Freemont was a wiry man, not very tall, with a weather-beaten face and huge forearms that looked out of place compared to the rest of his body. He took off his hat and put it on the back of one of the kitchen chairs, then went to the sink to wash his hands.

"You're home a little sooner than I thought you'd be," Mary said.

"We finished early." He peered over his wife's shoulder as she was standing by the stove. "You put plenty of butter in that?"

"Of course," she said, looking at him. "I know how you like it."

Freemont's eyes twinkled, and Phoebe could see Mary was right, even though Karen and Ivy didn't want to discuss it. After so many years and hardship, they were very much in love.

Before long, everyone sat down at the table. After a few words and a sharp look from Freemont, the boys settled down. Phoebe was glad to see Malachi following their lead. She closed her eyes and prayed, thankful for the joy that was breaking free in her heart, for the Yoders' open and welcoming home, and for Jalon. She wished he was here with them.

Phoebe stayed quiet during lunch, which was delicious, and observed the chatter at the table. Although she was happy, there was a small ache in her heart, one that was always there but was magnified by being around the chaos of a large family. She missed her family, never more than right now.

"Everything okay?" Karen asked, touching her arm.

"*Ya*. Everything is fine." She pushed her family out of her mind and engaged in conversation, only having to remind Malachi twice to use his napkin. After they finished eating, the boys went outside to help Freemont with the animals.

"Are you sure you don't mind Malachi tagging along?" Phoebe asked.

"Not at all. More hands make less work."

"I'll be over in a little while," Karen said when Phoebe and Malachi were ready to head home. Phoebe wanted to be there before Jalon arrived. "I think *Mamm*'s going to fry the donuts in a little while. I'll be sure to bring some over."

"If they're edible," Ivy piped up.

"They will be delicious," Mary declared. "You'll see."

They left the Yoders', Phoebe taking Malachi's hand. "Did you have fun?"

"*Ya.* Judah's *familye* has a lot of animals."

"They run a farm."

"I'd like to be a farmer someday."

"Farming is hard work." *That sometimes doesn't pay off.*

"I know." He slipped his hand out of Phoebe's and ran ahead of her. Phoebe crossed her arms against the cold air. When she caught up with Malachi, he was standing in front of the *dawdi haus*. Before she could stop him he opened the door. "Malachi, we shouldn't be in here."

"Jalon says it's okay."

"It is when he's here." But she followed him inside, and for the first time she saw how unfinished the *dawdi haus* really was. She'd known Jalon was using the bathroom in the main house because the one here wasn't yet in working order, but although the plywood subfloor was almost completely laid, he hadn't even had a chance to put in the wood flooring. There wasn't a single piece of furniture anywhere, and there was an empty space where the kitchen sink was supposed to go.

Then she saw the sleeping bag in front of the woodstove. Jalon had slept here every night since she and Malachi arrived. He'd not only given up his room, but given up a bed. Again, he was amazing.

She turned to see Malachi making a game of stepping between the floor joists. "Malachi," she said, not wanting to disturb anything in the house. "We need to *geh*."

He skipped over the last joist, then blew past her out the door. She followed him to the front of the house in time to see a van pull into the driveway. She stilled and watched as a woman stepped out of the passenger side. The first thing she noticed about her was how tall she was, taller than any Amish woman Phoebe had ever seen. The exact opposite of Ivy, actually. She went to the back of the van, where the driver had opened the hatch. Phoebe's view was obscured, but then she saw the woman push a compact wheelchair to the side of the van. The side door opened and an Amish man slid into the wheelchair's seat. They headed for the porch while the driver brought two suitcases to the house.

The woman noticed her and waved as she pushed the wheelchair. Phoebe hesitated, then waved back. This had to be Jalon's sister, Leanna. But who was the man in the wheelchair? And why hadn't Jalon said anything to her about their arrival?

They all reached the house at the same time. Leanna said to the driver, "You can put the suitcases by the door." He did, then she said, "Thanks, Max."

"You're welcome." He extended his hand to the man in the wheelchair. "Good meeting you, Adam."

Adam looked up and shook Max's hand. Leanna gripped the handles on the back of his wheelchair and pushed him toward the house. Phoebe could see he was in his twenties, close to her age. His shoulders were noticeably broad under his dark blue coat. His brows were dark brown and thick, and currently flattening over his eyes in annoyance.

"You don't have to push me, Leanna," he said, looking over his shoulder.

"Of course I don't. But I want to."

He rolled his eyes and put his hands in his lap. They were covered with fingerless gloves.

They reached the bottom of the front porch steps. "Hmm. I didn't think about this," Leanna said. When Adam started to slide out of the chair, she said, "You're not crawling up the steps."

He made a long-suffering face, but didn't look insulted. "I do it all the time."

"You're not doing it here." She took the handles of Adam's wheelchair and pulled him back from the steps.

"Leanna . . ."

But she didn't listen to him. Phoebe watched as she took him toward the back entrance of the house, which had one shallow step. She followed in time to see Leanna tilt Adam's chair and push him onto the porch. "Can you open the door, please?" she asked Phoebe, as if they'd already been introduced.

Phoebe complied, and Leanna pushed Adam into the mudroom. Then she let go of his chair. "The kitchen is through there," Leanna said to Adam, pointing to an interior door.

"I remember," he said. His grayish-blue eyes were now somber instead of annoyed.

"I'll *geh* back and get the suitcases," Leanna said as she sailed out the door.

Phoebe stood there for a moment, confused as she looked at Adam. He gave her a wry grin and glanced at the kitchen door. "Oh," she said, realizing she needed to open it for him. She did, and he rolled his wheels forward, disappearing inside the house.

He wheeled around in the kitchen and faced her, still smiling, and held out his hand. "I'm Adam, Leanna and Jalon's cousin."

She took his hand, feeling the worn, cracked leather of his fingerless gloves. "*Mei* name's Phoebe. I'm Jalon's . . . friend."

"Nice to meet you."

"I have to check on *mei sohn*," she said.

"Don't let me keep you. I know *mei* way around here."

Nodding, Phoebe left and went out the front door. She found Malachi in the front yard with Leanna and Blue.

"Blue is *yer* cat?" Malachi said as Leanna cuddled the big feline.

"*Ya.*" She squatted down and put Blue back on the ground. "I've had him since he was a kitten."

"Oh." Malachi looked forlornly at Blue, who was rubbing his face against the skirt of Leanna's plum-colored dress. Then the cat went back to Malachi, who brightened immediately.

Leanna laughed. "You must be feeding him."

"I do." He looked up at Leanna as she stood. "I also play with him, and comb his hair, and he sleeps with me. He leaves when *Mamm* comes in the room, though."

"Sounds like Blue." Leanna caught Phoebe looking at them. She crouched down again. "Would you mind taking care of him for a little while longer? I'm pretty busy right now. I've got a lot of catching up to do from being gone for so long."

Malachi grinned. "*Ya!*" He sat down on the grass and hugged Blue to him.

Leanna went to Phoebe. "You're Phoebe, right?"

"*Ya.*"

"I'm Leanna, Jalon's sister, and by the look on *yer* face when I got here, I'm guessing *mei* brother didn't tell anyone I was coming home today. Probably because he knows I sometimes change *mei* plans on the spur of the moment. But I wanted to meet you."

She glanced at Malachi. "He looks just like you," she said. Phoebe steeled herself for further questions, but all Leanna said was, "Blue doesn't usually like strangers. Or people in general."

Phoebe breathed a sigh of relief. She wasn't prepared to explain her past to Leanna. "That's what Jalon said."

"So *yer sohn*—his name is Malachi, *ya*?"

Phoebe nodded.

"He must be pretty special."

Her tension lifting a little, Phoebe said, "He is."

Leanna started to move away. "I better check on Adam and make sure he isn't doing backflips in the living room." Phoebe couldn't hide her surprise at Leanna's tasteless joke. Leanna chuckled. "Believe me, *nee* one has a better sense of humor about his situation than Adam. He wouldn't mind me poking a little fun."

They went inside, Leanna carrying both suitcases, and found Adam in the living room. He'd picked up one of the cooking magazines in the wooden magazine rack next to the couch. "Surely this isn't *yers*." He held it up and waved it at Leanna.

"Of course not. *Mamm* left her magazines here, probably hoping I'd glance at them every once in a while and learn how to cook something." She set down the suitcases and plopped onto the couch, her long legs stretching out before her. "Where's Jalon?"

"Uh, working." She wasn't sure if Jalon had told anyone else he'd lost his job, but she didn't think he had since Karen hadn't said anything. She wasn't going to tell his secret.

"Of course he is." She sighed. "He's always working. He doesn't take time to relax, at least not lately." A frown tugged at her lips before she sprang up from the couch. She was like a thin, energetic reed that couldn't keep still. "Is Jalon staying in *Mamm* and *Daed*'s old room?" she asked Phoebe.

"*Nee*. He's in the *dawdi haus*."

"*Gut*." She turned to her cousin. "Adam, you'll take *mei* parents' room."

He shook his head. "I'll be fine on the couch."

She put her hands on her hips. "No, you'll be in a bed, in *Mamm* and *Daed*'s room since it's on the first level."

She picked up one of the suitcases and went down

the hallway Phoebe had barely thought about except to clean. "She's impossible to reason with," Adam said, shrugging.

"I can see that."

Adam angled his chair toward her. "So you're a friend of Jalon's. Do you live in Birch Creek?"

She shook her head. No reason to be coy about the situation, and it was clear Leanna hadn't said anything to him. "Something happened to *mei* living arrangements. Jalon was kind enough to let me and *mei sohn* stay here for a while."

He clasped his fingers together and rested them against his abdomen. "Where are you from?" She told him and he said, "You were living near me, then. I'm from Mesopotamia. Small world."

Right now it felt too small. She had that feeling of discomfort again, of feeling as though she and Malachi didn't belong here.

"You're on *yer* own putting *yer* stuff away." Leanna appeared in the living room again.

"Leanna," Adam said, "I told you I'd sleep on the couch."

"Too late, *yer* suitcase is in the bedroom."

He wheeled around and faced her. "I'll bring it out here, then."

"And I'll just put it back in."

Adam looked at Phoebe. "Told you she was stubborn."

"I should probably start some preparations for supper," Phoebe said, amused by the exchange but not wanting to get involved.

"Do you need some help?" Leanna asked, looking like entering the kitchen was the last thing she wanted to do. "Please say you don't need any help."

"Yes, please tell her that." Adam chuckled. "Otherwise we might risk food poisoning."

"I should dump you out of *yer* wheelchair for that."

"For telling the truth? Nah, that wouldn't be fair."

"I don't need any help." Phoebe smiled, steering the conversation back on track. These two were so entertaining. "I'm used to cooking for a crowd." Besides, Karen would be back soon.

As she walked toward the kitchen, the bickering continued. Phoebe smiled. Now it really felt like she was home.

CHAPTER 15

O ut on the front porch, Adam leaned back in his wheelchair and watched Leanna and Malachi playing with Blue in the front yard. He let out a sigh. He'd missed this place. He hadn't realized how much until right now. Everything was the same as he remembered it, as if time had stood still over the past twelve years. He was glad he gave in to Leanna and came to visit. Although he might not say that when Jalon showed up.

The thought punctured his good mood. He and Jalon would definitely have a talk. It might end up being more of a showdown, but Adam was prepared. He'd spent enough time away from his cousin. Enough time letting him unnecessarily stew in his guilt. Adam would put an end to that, or at least he'd try. Jalon could be as stubborn as Leanna sometimes.

He rubbed his left thigh. Despite putting up an argument for sleeping on the couch, he was glad he'd have the bed. He'd be more comfortable there, not that his comfort was an issue. He was never truly comfortable, not since the accident.

That was the last time he had seen his cousin.

"Hello?"

A sweet female voice pulled him out of his thoughts. He turned and saw a woman who looked to be close to his age standing at the bottom of the porch steps. Leanna, Malachi, and Blue were nowhere in sight. He'd been so caught up in his memories that he hadn't noticed them leaving.

"Hi." He leaned forward in his chair.

"Are you . . . ?" She paused. "Is *yer* name Adam?"

"That's me. Do we know each other?"

"It's been a long time." She came up the porch steps. "*Mei* name's Karen Yoder. I live next door. I've been friends with Jalon and Leanna for years."

Now he remembered her. Although she hadn't looked so . . . grown up back then. Dark, russet-colored hair poked out beneath her white *kapp.* Her fair skin was covered with delicate freckles, her nose sloped and rounded at the end. Her eyes were a silvery gray, and right now they were fixed solely on him.

"I didn't realize you were coming for a visit," she said.

"It's a surprise. Leanna and I arrived a little while ago."

"Oh." She looked a little uncertain.

"Is something wrong?"

"*Nee.* It's just . . . well, I've been staying here until Leanna got back, and now I need to *geh* back home since she's here."

"Well, if I have any say in it, I vote you stay." Did he really just say that?

She chuckled. "At least that's one vote."

"Karen!" Leanna appeared in the front yard, Malachi

and Blue not far behind. She skipped up the steps. "*Danki* for staying here while I was gone."

"You're welcome. It was nice to get to know Phoebe and Malachi."

Adam watched the exchange between the two women. Leanna had left a few things out when she'd invited him here for a visit—like the fact that Jalon had a friend and her son staying here, along with Karen, who was clearly a chaperone. That kind of thing was unusual enough that Leanna should have said something. If he'd known Jalon already had company, he wouldn't have come. Then again, maybe that's why she hadn't said anything.

The women continued to talk as Blue and Malachi came up behind them. Malachi sat on the top step and Blue crawled into his lap.

"That's a fine-looking cat," Adam said.

Malachi ran his fingers over Blue's back. "I need to brush him again. He's got knots."

"I imagine they're hard to get out since his fur is so long."

Leanna must have heard the conversation, because she turned to Malachi and said, "You've done a great job keeping him looking nice. I can show you the best way to get the knots out." She gestured for him to go inside. "I'll be there in a minute."

Malachi picked up Blue and tottered his way to the door. Blue wasn't helping by going limp in the little boy's arms, but Malachi stayed the course. Leanna opened the door and they went inside. She poked her head out and looked at Karen. "You're staying for supper, right?"

Karen nodded. "Right."

With a firm nod, Leanna disappeared inside.

Silence stretched between Karen and Adam. Finally, she said, "I should see if Phoebe needs some help with supper."

Adam gave her a half smile. "Better you than Leanna."

Karen smirked. "For all you know I could be as bad a cook as Leanna."

"*Nee* one is as bad a cook as Leanna."

"True." Karen laughed. "Can I get you anything? A glass of tea, or some water?"

Adam shook his head. "I'm fine. Just going to sit out here a little while."

She didn't say anything for a long moment. Was it his imagination, or was she staring at him? Not out of shock or pity but out of . . . interest? No, that couldn't be possible. They only just met—re-met, to be precise, but still. Instant attraction wasn't something he was used to receiving.

He also wasn't used to feeling it for someone else . . . but he was definitely feeling it now.

"All right," she finally said. "I'll see you in a bit, then."

The cold air was invigorating, and Adam felt an unexpected sense of peace, as though he was meant to be here. Which didn't make any sense. Jalon had been avoiding him all this time . . . but hadn't he done the same thing? He could have returned here, more than once. He hadn't, and now that he thought about it, he didn't have a valid excuse.

Adam had always known he and Jalon had a lot in common. He hadn't realized how much until now.

• • •

Jalon practically dragged himself home late that after-noon. After asking a local farrier if he knew of any jobs available, he'd been sent to an English horse farm a few miles outside Birch Creek. He'd spent hours mucking stables. Not his favorite job by far, but the man seemed pleased when he paid him. "Wish I could hire you on," he'd said, peeling back bills from a thick stack of cash. "The guy who normally does this job will be back next week. Wife just had a baby."

Despite being desperate for a job, Jalon wouldn't take one from someone who had a young family. He paused as he looked out the window of the taxi that drove him home. Didn't he have a young family to support? Phoebe, Malachi . . . and Leanna too. His sister had her own job, but it was only part-time. He'd never worried about that because his income would have supported them both. But now he'd gone from basically being only concerned about himself to having three people de-pending on him, one of them a child.

The pressure he felt, however, wasn't because Phoebe and Malachi depended on him as well as Leanna, who should be back sometime today. In fact, he was getting used to the idea. Too used to it, which could be a problem. Seemed like his problems were lining up lately. Yet there were the bright spots, too, and he saw one of them as the taxi pulled into the driveway.

Malachi was outside playing with the wood-cup game Karen had brought over the day before. Jalon was sur-prised not to see Blue nearby. Maybe the cat had decided he could be without Malachi for a few minutes. Jalon paid the driver and started to walk up the driveway. He slowed his steps and watched Malachi, whose concentration was intense as he tried to capture the ball on a string in the cup. Jalon smiled. He looked exactly like Phoebe did when she was focused on cooking.

Malachi looked up, then ran toward Jalon. There was something about seeing the unabashed joy on his face as he barreled toward Jalon—as if he'd been waiting all day to see him and now that Jalon was here, his day was complete. Without thinking, Jalon crouched down and held out his arms, then scooped Malachi up and hugged him tight. *Yes. Definitely a bright spot.*

"You stink." Malachi pulled away, wrinkling his nose. "Like horse patties."

"Pretty much. Think I need a shower?"

"*Ya!*"

"Malachi!"

They both looked up as Phoebe stepped onto the front porch. The skirt of her light blue dress fluttered a bit around her legs, which made him pull his gaze away. He didn't need to be staring—and appreciating—her legs. He lifted his gaze and met her radiant blue eyes, seeing the welcoming happiness there. And just like that, his problems disappeared.

"Supper's almost ready," she said, her dimple deepening with her soft smile.

"Then I'm home just in time." He set Malachi down and the boy dashed into the house.

Phoebe looked down at her feet. Despite the cold, she was barefoot. Jalon followed her gaze and saw her toes curl under. She even had cute feet. "What's for supper?" he said, steering the conversation and his thoughts to something safer.

"Meat loaf." She looked up at him. "Not as exciting as Hunan beef."

"But just as good, I'm sure."

"I hope so." She wrinkled her nose. "What's that smell?"

He laughed, then explained about the job. "I'll keep looking for something full-time on Monday, but it was nice to have the work." He walked past her. "Don't worry, I'm heading for the shower."

"Jalon—"

But he was already inside when he heard her say his name. He halted his steps, and realized why she was trying to get his attention. The last person he wanted to see was sitting in the living room.

What was Adam doing here?

CHAPTER 16

Every nerve in Jalon's body danced on edge. He gaped at Adam, unable to speak. Adam didn't say anything either, but instead of surprise, there was determination in his cousin's eyes. He'd changed a lot since the last time Jalon had seen him. His upper torso was broad, his biceps and forearms were muscular and strong. Then Jalon saw Adam's legs. Thin. Useless. The guilt slammed into him like a brick to the gut.

Leanna entered the living room. "Whew, something stinks." She eyed Jalon. "Or someone, rather."

That gave Jalon an out, and without saying anything to his sister or cousin, he went upstairs and spent every last second he could in the shower. When he couldn't tarry any longer, he dressed and went to the kitchen. His throat tightened as he sat down at the table. He closed his eyes but couldn't pray. He put a slice of meat loaf on his plate, but couldn't bring himself to eat it. He felt everyone's eyes on him, including Phoebe's, but he kept his head down. He was paralyzed. The thought forced him to glance at Adam. *Bad choice of words.*

"How long are you visiting for?" Karen asked Adam, breaking the thick tension enveloping the room.

"It's open-ended," Leanna said.

"That seems to be *yer* answer to everything," Adam muttered. He turned to Karen. "I'll be here a few days."

"Maybe longer." Leanna scooped up a forkful of mashed potatoes.

What was his sister up to? He shot her a look, but she pretended not to notice. "Jalon should show you around Birch Creek," she said to Adam. "It's changed since you've been here."

"Not much." Jalon gripped his fork.

"Jalon taught me tricks with his yo-yo," Malachi said. He was sitting next to Adam. Had insisted on it, actually. That had annoyed Jalon a bit.

"I remember how *gut* he was when we were *kinner.*" Adam took a bite of his bread.

"Do you know how to yo-yo?"

"I used to. Kind of hard for me to do it now."

"Why?"

"Because it's easier to yo-yo when you're standing up."

"Why don't you stand up?"

The table went silent. "Malachi," Phoebe whispered. "That's not polite."

Adam laughed. "It's okay. He's not the first person to ask." He turned to Malachi. "I had an accident."

"What kind of accident?"

"I have chores to do." Jalon shoved away from the table, aware that he was abandoning yet another one of Phoebe's delicious meals, which would either upset her or tick her off. Still, he couldn't stop himself.

When he got outside, he took in big gulps of air. *Why, Lord? Why is Adam here now? Just when things were going . . . okay.* He couldn't say great. He still didn't have a job, he still didn't know what he was going to do with the farm, and his relationship with Phoebe was like riding a seesaw. But he'd felt a little happiness. A little hope. Now all he felt was the ache of guilt and shame pressing down on his chest.

His cousin used to be his best friend. Now he couldn't stand the sight of him. He couldn't be in the same room with him. Which made Jalon feel like the lowest lifeform on earth.

• • •

"Well," Leanna said, picking up her tea glass. "That was rude."

Phoebe couldn't move. Jalon had looked physically ill from the moment he'd seen Adam in the living room. The pallor of his skin had frightened her. She glanced at Karen, who had her head down but wasn't eating. Adam was still, as if he were carved out of granite, his mouth in a flat, grim line. Only Malachi and Leanna were acting somewhat normal.

"I told you it wasn't a *gut* idea to surprise him." Adam's words were low. Serious. And edged with a sharpness that seemed in direct contrast to the easygoing man he'd been a moment ago.

But Leanna wasn't fazed. "He needs shaking up sometimes."

"So you used me to do it?"

She narrowed her eyes. "You know I'm not using you. Just like you know this has been a long time coming."

"Malachi, would you help me with the dishes?" Karen said, rising and picking up her almost-full plate.

"Judah says that's girls' work."

"Judah doesn't know what he's talking about."

"It's okay." Adam started putting on his gloves. "I'll leave."

"Adam," Leanna said, the first sign of discomfort showing on her angular features.

"I'm talking about leaving the *haus*, not Birch Creek. I'm going to talk to him. That's all." He shoved on his other glove, then wheeled himself into the mudroom.

"Does he need any help?" Karen asked.

Leanna shook her head. "He can manage. Better than most people who walk."

"Why doesn't Adam walk?" Malachi asked.

If there was one thing consistent about Malachi, it was his persistence. Phoebe was about to chastise him again when Leanna said, "He had an accident. A very bad one, and it happened here." There was a slight catch in her voice. "That's why he's in a wheelchair."

"What happened?"

"He climbed a tree . . ."

As Leanna explained Adam's accident in vague detail to Malachi, Phoebe stiffened. Jalon hadn't been over-reacting to Malachi climbing that tree. He'd been thrust back into his past, terrified that the same thing that happened to Adam would happen to Malachi. *Oh, Jalon.*

She glanced at Karen. Saw the sadness in her eyes. And understood that Karen knew about the accident too.

"Why don't you show me some of those yo-yo tricks?" Leanna said to Malachi.

"Okay."

They left, and Phoebe stared at the food on the table. Another meal wasted, but that wasn't her concern right now. She wanted to go to Jalon, to try to comfort him somehow. Regrets. Now she truly understood what he'd meant by that.

"I don't understand why Leanna did this." Karen sat down at the table, suddenly looking weary. "Was she trying to cause a rift between them?"

"Isn't there one already?" Phoebe wondered if she'd misspoken. Who was she to infer anything about Jalon and Adam's relationship? But at Karen's nod she relaxed.

"The two of them have to work this out," Karen said. "I just hope they can."

Phoebe nodded, choosing to remain silent. She prayed they could too.

. . .

Adam entered the barn and looked at his cousin, who was standing by one of the horse's stalls, his back to the barn entrance. "I'm not in the mood," Jalon snapped, keeping his back to him.

Adam's teeth clenched. He wasn't about to let Jalon off the hook that easily. "In the mood for what?" Adam shot back, wheeling his chair closer to Jalon. "In the mood to talk, or are you only interested in sending me money and ignoring me the rest of the time?"

Jalon turned, opened his mouth to speak, then clamped it shut. "I deserve that." He looked away. "That and so much more."

Adam blew out a breath. "I don't know how to get it through *yer* thick head after all these years. I don't want *yer* money and I don't blame you for what happened."

"I egged you on."

"And I climbed the tree. I would have climbed it whether you were there or not. I lost the use of *mei* legs that day. I also lost *mei* cousin . . . who was also a *gut* friend." His throat tightened. "That hurts more than anything."

Jalon coughed, and Adam could see he was struggling with his emotions too. "You're trying to make me feel better."

"I'm trying to make you understand that I'm okay. I've come to terms with this. Do I wish the accident never happened? Of course. I wish I was standing here talking to you, instead of sitting in this chair. But for whatever reason, this is God's plan for me. And I know it's not his plan for you to beat *yerself* up over something that happened when we were *kinner*." He moved closer. "It was an accident, Jalon. *Nee* one was at fault, especially you."

Jalon sat down on a hay bale. He didn't say anything, just stared at his feet. Adam moved again until he was positioned in front of him. *He can't even look at me.* "I'm not leaving, Jalon. You can't run away from me anymore."

"I'm not running away."

"Then why haven't you visited me? Why haven't you given me those checks in person—not that I wanted them."

He finally lifted his head. "I'm trying to help you."

"I don't need that kind of help. I've worked since I was fourteen years old. I've never lived on anyone's handout."

"Not even *yer onkel*'s?"

So Jalon had kept tabs on him. Maybe he did care beyond assuaging his guilt. "I don't mind doing that job."

But his cousin must have seen something else on his face. "You'd rather be doing something else, though."

"You're right. I would. But *mei* disability isn't the main reason I'm not getting work. The job market stinks in Mespo. Not just for the Amish, but for the English too. But that's how it goes, just like in construction. You get work sometimes, then you get laid off. You *geh* with the flow. That's something I've had to learn, not just with work but with life."

"Which is *mei* fault."

"Would you stop saying that?" Adam raised his hands, frustrated. He wasn't getting through to him. Then again, he couldn't expect one conversation to change everything. Still, he couldn't resist a parting shot. "You must be getting something out of this."

Jalon frowned. "What do you mean?"

"Clearly it's easier to hang on to the guilt than to forgive *yerself*." He shook his head and started to turn his wheelchair, only to stop short. "I'd like us to be friends again." An ache appeared in his throat. "I've missed you."

Jalon didn't say anything. Didn't look at him. *Yeah, nothing's changed.* That hurt Adam more than anything.

He rolled out of the barn and looked up at the evening

sky, the clouds barely noticeable in the fading daylight. He'd said everything that was on his heart. He'd been honest, and he'd extended the olive branch, only to have his cousin clam up and retreat. "There's nothing else I can do, God," he whispered. "The rest is up to Jalon . . . and up to you."

CHAPTER 17

You can't run away from me anymore.

Jalon felt like he'd been sucker punched. Adam had put a positive spin on things. Said he'd come to terms with what happened. *Why can't I?*

Then he thought of everything Adam couldn't do. He couldn't stand. Couldn't walk. Couldn't run. Even if he wanted to climb a tree, he couldn't. Jalon could do all that, and much more. How could he not feel guilty about that?

Jalon shot up from the hay bale. Fed the animals. Cleaned up a little bit even though the barn was nearly spotless. Then he went over to the ladder that led to the hayloft. He didn't need any more hay bales, having brought some down last week, but he also couldn't be in here and do nothing. He couldn't leave, either, knowing Adam was inside, that his sister was expecting a miracle to happen between the two of them, and that Phoebe . . .

Phoebe had seen his cowardice. No doubt Leanna had explained what happened. Now she knew he was to blame for Adam's accident. He was the one who put his cousin in that wheelchair. How could she see past that?

He scrambled up the ladder and started hurling bales. They hit the ground and flopped on their sides, stray hay and puffs of dust hovering above the barn floor. He went to the back corner of the loft and started shifting around bales. Physical work had always helped him put his thoughts to rest, but it wasn't working now.

He yanked on an old, dried-up bale in the far corner of the loft. When he dislodged it, an amber-colored bottle rolled toward him, stopping near his feet. He picked it up, recognizing it. The same kind of bottle his father used when he'd made his home beer.

Jalon examined the bottle and the stopper at the top. He didn't know how long it had been there. Maybe a year or two, or even longer. It was probably still decent since it hadn't been opened. Not fresh but at least drinkable.

He rolled the bottle around in his hand, listening to the liquid slosh inside the glass. His mouth started to water, a familiar craving coming over him. A few swigs of this and he could down the whole bottle. It wouldn't take away his pain but it would be a start.

The urge came back, stronger than ever. In the back of his mind, Jalon had always blamed his father for starting him on the road to drink. But his dad hadn't forced him to drink. He hadn't made Jalon an alcoholic. The choice to consume liquor to dull his pain was all on him.

And right now, all he had to do was open the bottle. Take a deep pull. Before long, he'd feel nothing.

. . .

When Phoebe looked through the kitchen window and saw Adam leaving the barn without Jalon, his shoulders slumped, she knew their talk had gone badly. On impulse she set down her dish towel. "I'll be right back."

"You're going to talk to Jalon?" Karen asked, her brow furrowing slightly.

Before she could chicken out, she nodded. "*Ya*. I think he needs me."

"Phoebe, I know he does."

Bolstered by Karen's confidence, she set out for the barn. She paused as she saw Adam wheel himself toward the huge tree Jalon had tried to cut down. She wished there was something she could say to him too. But right now Jalon was her main concern.

She whispered to herself, rehearsing what she would say to him. Nothing sounded helpful as she reached the barn entrance. But that didn't mean she was giving up. Taking a deep breath, she walked inside.

Her gaze jerked as Jalon threw something against the barn wall. Glass shattered into pieces, littering the floor with glittering amber shards. "Jalon!"

He looked at her, his expression haunted.

A familiar smell filled the air, overpowering the scent of hay and animals. She recognized it right away. She should have, since she'd spent enough time drinking at parties to know the liquid dripping down the wall was beer. Her nervousness disappeared as she turned to him, stunned.

"Leave, Phoebe."

His harsh tone made her flinch, but she stood her ground. "I'm not leaving you."

"I want to be left alone."

She marched over to him. "Too bad. I'm staying."

He faced her and scowled, putting his hands on his hips. "I've had enough talking for one day."

"And I think you've had enough escaping for one day."

"Now you sound like Adam."

"Then Adam must be right."

Jalon narrowed his eyes. "How would you know? You don't know him . . . you don't know *me*."

She put her hands on her hips, imitating his stance. He was trying to intimidate her, and while it was working, she wasn't about to budge. "I know you're not the kind of man to put his head in the sand. At least I never thought you would be."

"I don't have *mei* head in the sand."

"Don't you?" She softened her tone. "Leanna told us what happened."

"Figures," he muttered. His shoulders drooped. "She never keeps her mouth shut."

"Malachi asked why Adam can't walk."

"*I'm* the reason he can't walk." He crossed the barn and sat down on a hay bale, his head in his hands.

"You pushed him out of the tree, then?"

His head shot up. "What? *Nee*, of course not. He fell."

"Then how is that *yer* fault?"

"Because he was chasing me. I was older, faster, stronger. I knew I could out-climb him, and I did. I went to the top of the tree. He stopped halfway to catch his breath, and I goaded him on. He climbed a few more feet." Jalon paused. "A branch broke and . . ."

Phoebe didn't know what to say. They were kids, and it was an accident. But Jalon didn't see it that way.

She sat down next to him and took his hand. Words wouldn't comfort him. She knew what it was like to be filled with regret, to have somebody spew scriptures and platitudes that didn't mean anything. Sometimes it was nice to have someone by your side, sitting in the quiet, just being there.

After a few minutes he changed the grip of their hands and entwined their fingers.

She didn't know how long they sat there, holding hands, lost in their own thoughts, her thoughts totally focused on him. Finally he said, "The accident isn't the only regret I have."

She squeezed his hand, silently urging him to continue.

"I'm . . ." He drew in a deep breath and pulled away. "I'm an alcoholic. I had *mei* first drink after Adam's accident, and up until recently, I never stopped. At first it was because I liked the taste, especially beer. Then because I realized that when I drank, I could escape, even for a little while." He scrubbed his hand over his face. "I'm an alcoholic without a job. Oh, and I also sunk all *mei* money into a farm I'm not sure will ever be successful. I'm almost broke, and if I don't find work soon, I'll end up in foreclosure before planting season starts."

He turned to her, and the despair in his eyes nearly brought her to tears. "You once said you didn't deserve what I was offering you. You were wrong. I'm the one who doesn't deserve you."

. . .

Jalon couldn't look at her anymore, couldn't take any of the sweet kindness he saw in her eyes. She knew everything now—how he'd been at fault for Adam's accident, losing his job when he needed the money more than he ever had in his life, and now his alcoholism. Admitting this last thing to her didn't make any difference. He felt the failure, the shame, the helplessness all the way to his bones. He'd been so hard on his father, who had struggled for so long to succeed. Now he understood his father's anger. His frustration. Jalon had always said he would be different. Yet here he was. The circumstances weren't the same but the feelings were.

He waited for Phoebe to say something, to tell him that yes, he was right. He didn't deserve her, because she deserved better. She deserved a man who wasn't filled with scars from the past and a bleak outlook for a future.

But she remained silent and took his hand in hers again. Her touch kept him from falling completely to pieces and gave him another shot of courage to admit yet another failing. "I came so close to taking that drink," he choked out. "I even opened the bottle. I wanted one drink. One last drink to numb everything, even for a little while."

"But you didn't." She covered his hand with her other one.

"I came close—"

"But you *didn't*." She stroked the back of his hand while she held his gaze. Again, she was silent, but her eyes, and the fact that she was staying by his side, said everything he needed to hear.

She loosened her grip but didn't let go as her gaze

wandered around the barn. "I thought this was *yer* parents' place."

"It was." He exhaled, grateful for the change of subject. He explained how he bought the house and spent all his savings. "I wasn't worried about it at the time because I had the construction job. Everything seemed to be going *mei* way."

"You're worried."

He looked at her, dumbfounded. "Of course I am."

"One of the bishop's favorite sermon topics was worry," Phoebe said. "Not Bishop Weaver. Our other bishop. He said over and over that Jesus told us not to worry. Then he explained that worry was about living in the future instead of the present. If we're focused on each day and not fretting about tomorrow, we won't worry."

Jalon let out a bitter laugh. "Easier said than done."

"It is. And it's something I've struggled with too. Ever since Bishop Weaver told me I had to leave, I've been consumed with worry. Where were Malachi and I going to *geh*? How was I going to manage? And when we were at *Aenti* Bertha's, I worried about what I would say, what Malachi would do . . . I worried almost every minute of the day." She paused, smiling slightly. "Except when I got *yer* letters. For a few moments I didn't have to worry. I could focus on you."

He couldn't stop himself from reaching over and brushing his thumb over the dimple in her cheek. His simple letters, which he thought were pretty boring, had been important to her.

"God's taken care of us, Jalon. Despite *mei* worries and doubts and mistakes, he's provided." She leaned into his touch. "He'll take care of you too. The burden isn't all on *yer* shoulders."

Reluctantly he drew away his hand. "*Danki* for the reminder. I do believe God is faithful, Phoebe. He's there when we stumble around—like I did."

"Like I did too."

"I still am. I haven't handled everything well, especially between us."

Her blue eyes gleamed. "You've handled things just fine, Jalon."

A lump came to his throat. "I knew from the first letter you sent that you were special."

"I only wrote a few words."

"It wasn't the words." He didn't know how to explain it, how to tell her that he sensed a connection between them and that's why he'd written her back. "There was just something there . . ."

"Between us?"

He nodded.

"I felt it too." She glanced down, then looked up at him shyly. "I thought I was reading into things, though. Wishing for something that wasn't there."

"It's definitely there." He straightened, feeling a confidence he hadn't felt for a long time, maybe not ever before. "I don't think I'd suddenly out of the blue want to farm after years of avoiding it unless God was at work. And I don't think"—he touched her cheek—"you and I would be here if he didn't want us to be together."

"What are you saying?"

Jalon paused. What was he saying? "I—"

She put her finger to his lips. "Never mind."

He moved her hand away. "Never mind?"

"Jalon, I don't want to rush into anything. You're important to me. Important enough that I want both of us to be sure about this."

She was right. Now wasn't the time for either of them to make any rash decisions. He'd made enough of those lately. He moved away from her, not wanting to, but knowing it was the right thing to do.

"What are you going to do about Adam?" she asked.

He stared at the ground and kicked away a piece of stray straw. "I'll have to talk to him again. I can't leave things between us like this." He looked up. "He says he forgives me."

"You don't believe him?"

"I do. But it seems too easy. He's paralyzed, Phoebe."

"He doesn't strike me as the kind of person to brood over the past and hold grudges."

"He's not. He's definitely not like that."

"It's time to let *geh* of the past, Jalon."

He turned to her. "It's time for you to let *geh* too. You don't have to be ashamed of what happened with Brody. Not anymore. You've been forgiven."

"Just like you have."

He nodded, the words finally, *finally* sinking in.

She touched his arm. "Now, *geh* talk to Adam. Set things right between you." Then she stood up and left.

He rose from the hay bale and glanced at the wall. The beer was drying, the smell dissipating. He swept up the shards and threw them away. He'd made it past a huge hurdle tonight . . . but he hadn't done it on his own. He had God in his corner. He had Phoebe. And now he knew he had Adam too.

. . .

Adam sat at the base of the tree, frustration welling up inside him. He was used to this type of frustration, the kind that started in his gut. He clenched his hands, his well-worn leather gloves crackling with the movement. This frustration wasn't only about Jalon, although giving his cousin over to God made it lessen. It was over losing his ability to walk—all because he had chosen to climb up a tree.

He'd told Jalon the truth about accepting his disability. But there were times when it hit him square on that he'd lost the use of his legs forever. Now, looking at this tree—a beautiful, grand oak that stood majestically on the Chupp property—he fought anger and resentment. Maybe he hadn't completely come to terms with it after all.

Memories flooded over him as he remembered that day when he and Jalon had challenged each other to climb it. Jalon was almost halfway up by the time Adam reached the base. Jalon was always faster and stronger, but Adam tried to keep up.

"Slowpoke," Jalon called out to him as he shimmied up a couple more branches. He was right by a thick one and sat on the edge of it. Jalon was fearless.

Adam knew he was teasing him, but it still rankled. He was on the short side and had legs like thick tree trunks. Still, he was determined to climb as far and as high as Jalon. He started to climb up the tree. His foot slipped on the trunk.

"You're going to give up now like a little *boppli*?" Jalon taunted. His legs hung in the air and swayed back and forth, as casually as if he were sitting on a chair in the kitchen.

"I'll never give up!" Adam resumed his footing and got a grip on the branches. He hauled himself up one branch, then another, the whole time Jalon calling him names. Nothing cruel, just ribbing like young boys did, but it was enough to spur Adam on. He put his foot on what he thought was a strong branch. It gave way, knocking him off balance and making him let go of the tree. He felt himself falling... falling... as if the ground had disappeared beneath him. Then he slammed into the hard earth and felt the base of his spine crack.

"Adam?"

He turned to see Karen walking toward him, the dusky purple sky behind her. He wiped his eyes, forcing a smile. "Hey, Karen."

"Are you okay?" she asked, stopping short in front of him.

So much for hiding his tears. He looked away. "Yeah. Just a little dust in *mei* eyes, that's all."

She nodded, even though there wasn't any dust at all.

He saw she was carrying a small case. "Going somewhere?" he asked.

"Home, remember? Now that you and Leanna are here, I'm not needed."

Disappointment threaded through him. He'd enjoyed listening to her talk over supper. He also had hidden the fact that he'd plain enjoyed watching her, taking in her slender hands and animated eyes. She was also a good cook, which was an added bonus in his book.

"I remember you," he said. What was with him blurting out things around her?

Her pale red eyebrows lifted. "You do?"

"I remember you and *yer* sister coming over here when *mei familye* would visit. There was that one time we played volleyball. Leanna accidentally hit you in the head with the ball and you started to cry."

"I was only eight," she said, sounding a little indignant. "Besides, those balls are hard and you know how Leanna can punch a ball." She rubbed the side of her head as if reliving the memory. "It hurt."

"I'm sure it did. But after you cried you went back in the game and started playing again like *nix* happened." He grinned. "That was kind of a cool thing for a twelve-year-old *bu* to see."

"A tough girl?" Her lips quirked into a smirk.

He couldn't stop himself from looking her up and down. "You don't look so tough anymore."

She tilted her head, her expression inscrutable. "I don't know if I should take that as an insult or a compliment."

"A compliment," he said, throwing caution out the door. No reason not to be plain spoken with her. If that put her off, it wasn't his fault. "Definitely a compliment."

She stilled and looked down at him, her face still blank.

He shifted, his bluster disappearing. This was one of the things he hated about being in a wheelchair. People looked down at him. They had no choice, of course.

But sometimes there was a sense of superiority in their eyes too. Or worse, pity. Women were even more difficult. Many of them thought he was either helpless or invisible. He didn't want Karen to see him that way. If he could, he'd stand up right now. Show her he was more than useless legs and a wheelchair. That he was a man.

She took a step forward and put down her case. She crouched down in front of him, her face close to his. "I remember you too," she said, her voice soft and lilting. "Not just because of the accident." She met his gaze straight on. "I had a crush on you. A huge crush."

His eyes widened, and for a split moment he believed her. Then he came back to reality. She was being nice. Plus, a childhood crush didn't equal adult attraction.

"You were the most handsome *bu* I'd ever seen."

"At ten?" He couldn't help but roll his eyes.

"*Ya*. More handsome than any of the others here in Birch Creek."

"Now you're making things up."

"Why would I do that? Here I am revealing the deepest feelings of *mei* youth and you're dismissing them." He thought he detected an edge of annoyance in her voice.

"I'm sorry," he said seriously. "I thought we were just talking about the past. Silly childhood stuff."

"It wasn't silly to me." She leaned forward and rested her hands lightly on his knees. "And I'm not so sure it's just a childhood crush anymore."

He inhaled a sharp breath as she stood up, picked up her case, and left as if she hadn't just turned his world upside down.

His heart thrummed as he turned and faced the tree

again. This time it didn't loom so large. Didn't feel so threatening. And the memories stayed at bay, replaced with thoughts of a pretty red-haired woman who had definitely made him feel like a man.

. . .

It was dark by the time Jalon approached Adam, and the moonlight illumined the tree, casting it in eerie shadow. Adam didn't turn around, but kept facing the tree. Jalon stood by Adam's wheelchair. The two men didn't say anything for a long time.

"You were right," Jalon finally said.

"I know." Adam glanced up at him. "But tell me anyway."

Jalon shook his head, smiling a bit. "It was easier to wallow in guilt than forgive myself for what happened." He paused. "I've been carrying it around for so long. It's not going to be easy to let *geh*." He put his hand on Adam's shoulder. "I can't promise that I won't be a moody jerk sometimes."

"And I can't promise that I won't point it out." Adam looked at the tree again. "Nice hatchet job."

"Yeah. Tried to take it out on *mei* own. Didn't realize what a bad idea it was until it was too late."

"If you leave it like this, it's going to die."

"I thought about finishing the job—with help, of course—and using the wood to add onto the barn."

"So you're really doing it. You're going to be a farmer. Leanna told me your plans."

"*Ya*. Although I've got to say, the odds are stacked

against me right now." He explained his financial situation. "But even if all I can manage is a small garden, it will be a start."

Adam didn't say anything right away. Jalon was about to tell him good night when Adam reached into his pants pocket. "Here," he said, handing a small, folded piece of paper to Jalon.

Jalon opened it, held it up to the moonlight, and grimaced. A check. He didn't bother to note the amount. "I'm not taking *yer* money," he said, shoving it back at Adam.

Adam ignored him. "It's not *mei* money. It's *yers*."

"I sent it to help you. I see now that you don't need *mei* help, but I still want you to have it."

"Even if you're the one who needs it now?"

Jalon stilled. *A foolish man . . .* That's what he was being right now, turning down the check. Foolish. Yet he couldn't bring himself to accept it. He had given the money to Adam to assuage his guilt, but that wasn't the only reason. He'd wanted to help his cousin. He'd wanted Adam to have the best life he could. That motivation hadn't changed.

"Think of it as an investment," Adam said.

"In what?"

"The farm."

Jalon opened the check again. His jaw dropped at the amount. "This can't be right."

"I saved every single penny you sent me, plus I invested some of it."

"But this is—"

"Plenty to get the farm going."

"You want to invest in the farm." Jalon was still reeling from the tens of thousands of dollars in his hand and the fact that his cousin wanted it to go toward his farm.

"*Ya*, but under one condition." Adam grinned, his teeth flashing white in the silvery moonlight. "I want to be an onsite investor. Which means I would move here to Birch Creek." He held up his hand. "Before you say anything, I think I can be a valuable addition to *yer* enterprise."

Jalon laughed at the fancy words. Adam was very smart, and when they were kids, when he wasn't playing outside or climbing trees, he had his nose in a book. "How so?" he said.

"I can definitely handle the business aspect of it. I may not be able to guide the plow but I can handle money."

He'd already proven that. "Are you sure you want to move here?"

Adam nodded. "There's not much for me in Mespo. I like working for *mei onkel*, but you're right, it's not what I want to do. I like the challenge of trying to make this farm into something. I have some ideas too."

Jalon listened as Adam explained about his plans and sketches. His cousin had been studying farming without knowing the opportunity to help run a farm would arise. And now he was here, providing the money Jalon needed, money that had been Jalon's to begin with, but was now Adam's. *God is faithful.* He absolutely was.

Adam reached out his hand. Jalon grabbed it, marveling at the strong grip. His palm rested against the leather palm of Adam's fingerless glove as they shook and sealed the deal. This felt right, and he couldn't wait to start working alongside his cousin . . . his friend.

"Tomorrow over breakfast we can discuss the particulars." Adam yawned. "I'm too tired tonight." He glanced at the tree. "It's a shame it's coming down. It was a beautiful tree."

"It's going to be part of a fresh start." Jalon nodded at the tree. "For both of us."

CHAPTER 18

That night as Phoebe settled Malachi in bed, Leanna opened the bedroom door. She was holding a book. "This was *mei* favorite growing up."

Phoebe straightened and took the huge children's book from her. "*The Very Hungry Caterpillar*?"

"The colors are gorgeous and the story is cute. I thought Malachi would enjoy listening to it."

"I'm sure he will." She glanced over her shoulder, but he was fast asleep. "Another night, though," she whispered. Blue was curled around him. "I'm sorry Malachi's taken over Blue."

"It's okay. That cat needed to socialize more anyway." When Phoebe tried to hand back the book, Leanna shook her head. "Keep it in here. For tomorrow night."

Nodding, Phoebe put the book on Jalon's dresser, then left the room and quietly shut the door. Leanna had already gone downstairs. She was almost as swift as Malachi, and like Phoebe's son, she never seemed to be still for long. Phoebe went into the kitchen, wondering where Jalon and Adam were. Leanna was standing at the back door in the mudroom, looking out the window.

"Those *buwe* are finally talking," she said. She turned around, looking satisfied. "Jalon calls me bossy, and I know he thinks I cross the line sometimes, but sometimes you have to take matters into *yer* own hands. Adam and Jalon were best friends when they were *kinner*. It's past time to renew that friendship."

"I have a feeling they will. Jalon is ready to put the past behind him." *So am I.*

"Do you want some tea?" Leanna asked.

"I'd love a cup." She sat down and waited while Leanna ran water from the tap into the kettle.

After Leanna set the kettle on the stove and lit the burner, she turned to Phoebe. "So exactly what are *yer* intentions toward *mei* brother?"

Phoebe laughed, glad she could find the humor in such a straightforward question. "We're taking things slow."

"Oh." Leanna frowned slightly. "I thought you two might be getting married by fall."

"Are you in that big of a hurry to marry him off?"

Leanna nodded. "I love Jalon, but he's twenty-five now. Past time to get married."

"How old are you?"

"Twenty-four, but that's not the point. Now that Jalon has bought this house and farm, he needs to make something of them." She smiled, and it softened her angular features somewhat. "Jalon changed when he started writing to you. He was happy, something I hadn't seen in him for a long time. Of course, that didn't keep me from teasing him mercilessly." At Phoebe's questioning look, she said, "Don't worry. We didn't talk about you at all. Jalon's very private. I think he wanted to keep you to himself."

Phoebe understood. She had kept Jalon to herself, partly because of Aunt Bertha's reaction to everything she did, but mostly because Jalon was special. He was hers, and she knew that deep in her heart. Yes, they planned to build their relationship slowly, but she didn't see her feelings for him changing anytime soon.

"Malachi's adorable, by the way." Leanna pulled two mugs out of a cabinet. "Blue clearly has good taste." She set the mugs on the table. "Karen said you're going to *geh* to *yer* cousin's in Ashtabula."

"That's . . . the plan," she said, barely getting out the words.

"I don't see a reason why you can't stay. Jalon's out in the *dawdi haus*, I'm here, Adam's here . . . I think between the two of us we can make sure you two don't get into any trouble." She waggled her eyebrows and winked. "Although *mei* brother could use a little trouble every once in a while."

Phoebe didn't laugh. "I . . . I'm not like that." Not anymore.

"Oh, that's not what I meant." Leanna hurried to her. "I was making a joke. A very bad one, apparently. What I mean is, Jalon needs to loosen up. He's spent years beating himself up over what happened to Adam. He was . . . he got involved in something he shouldn't. But he's turned that around, and he deserves to be happy." She put her hand on Phoebe's shoulder. "I think you'll be a big part in that happiness."

Blushing, Phoebe said, "I hope so." She thought about how she'd felt when she and Malachi first arrived in Birch Creek. She'd been here because she had no place else to go. Now she was staying here because she wanted to. She was falling in love with Jalon, and it was deeper and more intense than any fantasy she'd had of the two of them together. But she had also fallen in love with the people of Birch Creek, and the idea of moving somewhere else didn't appeal. "Malachi and I want to stay."

"Exactly what I wanted to hear." She smiled, then put tea bags in the mugs. She brought the hot tea kettle and poured the water. Steam curled into the air. "If Jalon's going to make a *geh* of the farm—and I hope he does—it's going to take a group effort. Between you and me, I'm hoping to convince Adam to stay too." She glanced at the window. "I wonder what they're talking about out there. Not that it's any of *mei* business. Wait. It actually is *mei* business since I'm the one who got Adam here."

Phoebe chuckled. She couldn't help it. Leanna was the most unusual Amish woman she'd ever met. She was also easy to like and feel comfortable around.

Her decision was made. Tomorrow she would write to her cousin and thank her for the invitation to stay at her home, then let her know that she and Malachi would stay in Birch Creek. She'd write to her parents and assure them she was all right and that she would be here indefinitely.

And maybe, hopefully, Leanna would be right . . . and one day her brother would be a married man.

$$\cdot \ \cdot \ \cdot$$

"But I don't like broccoli."

Phoebe sighed. Nearly a week had passed since she

had decided to stay at Jalon's. He'd suspended his job search, and he and Adam had explained how the two of them were going to be business partners. Leanna had been thrilled and had taken partial credit. "I knew this was going to work out," she'd said, giving her brother a kiss on the cheek and Adam a hug around the shoulders. Jalon wiped off the kiss, but Phoebe had seen his small smile.

Jalon had spent the rest of his time finishing up the *dawdi haus*. He planned to add an extra bedroom, and when it was finished, he and Adam would live there. Phoebe thought if he was half as good a farmer as he was in construction and carpentry, the farm would be a huge success. He worked with singular focus from dawn until dusk. She hadn't seen much of him, but she also understood. There was work to do, lots of it, before the warm weather arrived.

Jalon and Adam were also making plans for spring planting, while she and Leanna were put in charge of the garden.

Now they were discussing the planting in the kitchen, and of course Malachi overheard them and had to give his opinion. "Broccoli is *gut* for you, Malachi," she said. Not only was it nutritious, but Jalon loved it, so it was definitely going in the garden.

He wrinkled his nose while Blue did figure eights between Malachi's short legs.

Phoebe put down her pencil, glancing at Leanna, who didn't even bother stifling a smile. She'd gone back to work at the Rabers' earlier in the week, but was off today. "I'll probably get more work soon," she'd said, "now that

Daniel's brother Roman has left." When Phoebe asked her why, she shrugged. "Don't know. Don't care. More work for me, and that's what matters."

Turning to Malachi, Phoebe asked, "What else should we plant in the garden?"

"Marshmallows."

Leanna laughed. "Sounds good to me."

"And pizza." When that got another laugh from Leanna, Malachi laughed with her. "And cookies! And pie! And brownies—"

"Now you're just being silly." But Phoebe was smiling, and it felt so good to be here in the warm kitchen, fresh bread baking in the oven, making plans for the future.

A knock sounded on the back door. "I'll get it," Malachi said as he ran through the mudroom to the door. She could hear him fling it open.

"Good morning." Karen walked inside, holding a cake carrier. This wasn't the first time she'd brought by a dessert since moving back home. "I brought a little something for—"

"Adam?" Leanna arched a knowing brow.

Karen's cheeks pinked, but no one would miss the sparkle in her eyes which had coincidentally appeared the same time Adam showed up in Birch Creek.

"He's at a livestock auction with Jalon," Phoebe said.

"The cake isn't just for Adam. I baked it for everyone."

"Orange Bliss?" Malachi said hopefully.

"That's right." Karen smiled at him. "You remembered."

"Jalon likes it a lot."

"So do I," Leanna said, eyeing the cake.

Phoebe reminded herself to get the recipe from Karen.

"I'll set this on the counter," she said.

"*Danki*." Leanna took the paper and pencil from Phoebe. "Here, Malachi. We're going to plant a row of bects just for you."

"Beets? Yuck."

"We can pretend they're marshmallows."

Malachi frowned, deep in thought. "Okay, but I still won't eat them."

That brought a laugh from everyone. Malachi grinned, but by the confusion in his eyes he wasn't sure what everyone thought was so funny.

"Phoebe," Karen said when they regained their composure, "I saw the mailman on *mei* way here." She held out a letter to her. "The return address is Fredericktown. I thought you'd want to read it right away."

Phoebe stood and took the envelope from Karen. She recognized her father's handwriting. Quickly she opened it.

Dear Phoebe,

Your mother is real sick. The doctor says she has Lyme disease. She's on medicine, but the symptoms aren't getting better. She's too tired and sick to take care of the little ones. We need you here. Whatever made you leave, we can work it out. Right now we all want you to come home.

Dad

Her heart felt as though it had stopped in her chest. The letter was just like her father's speech—brief and to the point.

"Phoebe, what's wrong?" Karen asked.

Tears formed in her eyes. Her mother had to be extremely ill for her father to write and ask for help. She said a quick, silent prayer for her mother, then went to Malachi. Without hesitation she said, "We have to *geh*." Her voice sounded sharper than she intended.

"Where?"

"Home."

"But we are home."

His simple statement gave her pause. She'd been thinking of this place as home too. But now cold reality had hit. She had to set her fear of Bishop Weaver aside. She would face whatever she had to if it meant helping her family. "Don't argue, Malachi."

"Phoebe," Leanna said. "Tell us what's going on."

But she didn't answer. Hot tears ran down her face.

"Let me call the taxi," Karen said softly.

Phoebe nodded her thanks, turned away from Karen, and rushed upstairs to pack.

• • •

"Think we made a good buy?" Jalon asked Adam as they neared the house.

"An excellent buy. Those are two of the finest drafts I've ever seen. We got them for a *gut* price too."

Jalon leaned back in the front seat of the van, relieved. It wasn't that he didn't know horses. He did. He'd gone to the auctions with his father, who always ended up getting the cheapest horse, not the best. As he and Adam had made plans for the farm, he realized how many times his father had sabotaged himself, whether by being miserly when purchasing animals and seed or by planting too late or harvesting too early. Adam had gleaned a lot of good knowledge about farming—and other topics—through reading and observing.

"Sometimes that's all you can do from the chair," he'd said one night when they'd been talking about how to divide the land and what crops to plant. "It made me feel a part of things, though. And who knew all this would come in handy one day?"

God knew. If Jalon hadn't been convinced before that God's hand was guiding him, then he had the proof now. His father giving up the land, Jalon having just enough savings to make the back payments and take over the mortgage, Adam arriving here after Jalon had lost his job with enough money to get things started, and now Adam having as much of an interest in the farm as Jalon did, even though neither of them had ever considered becoming farmers.

Then there were Phoebe and Malachi. He wished he'd been able to spend more time with Phoebe lately, but so much had to be done. She seemed to understand, and he did try to carve out time with Malachi, who wasn't starving for companionship anymore. Between Adam teaching him how to whittle a bar of soap and Leanna telling him wild tales and promising to take him fishing as soon as it was warm enough, Malachi was happy. He was also Blue's preferred companion, which Leanna didn't seem to mind. Jalon continued to teach him yo-yo tricks when he could, which delighted them both. Once things settled down, he and Phoebe would be able to spend time together. She wasn't going anywhere.

"Jalon?" Adam said from the backseat. "We're home."

He blinked. Home. It wasn't the home he'd expected to have—a farm, a sister who drove him crazy more often than not, his cousin and best friend back, and the woman he loved and her son. Their son, which was how he thought of Malachi sometimes, especially when Malachi wanted both him and Phoebe to tuck him in bed at night and read *The Very Hungry Caterpillar*. Jalon could recite the book in his sleep now, but Malachi couldn't get enough of it. Yes, this was his home. His family. And when the time was right, he planned to make it official.

The van pulled into the driveway. Jalon got out and went to the back, then pulled out Adam's wheelchair. He unfolded it and pushed it over the gravel to the side of the van where Adam was already at the edge of the seat. He hurled himself into the chair seamlessly.

"I already paid the driver," Adam said, wheeling himself away from the van.

Jalon nodded and slid the door shut. This taxi driver wasn't as friendly as Max, but he had a large van that could accommodate Adam's chair. He waved to the driver, then started for the house just as Phoebe and Malachi came rushing out the front door. Phoebe was carrying a suitcase.

"I don't wanna *geh*!" Malachi cried, skidding to a stop

on the porch. He plopped down on it, crossed his arms, and wailed.

"Malachi, stop it!"

Jalon flinched, not just at Malachi's distress but at Phoebe's tone. Even in her most exasperated moments he'd never heard her snap at Malachi like that.

"What's going on?" Adam asked.

"I don't know." Jalon rushed to the porch. "Phoebe?"

Malachi got up and ran to him, arms outstretched. He scooped up the boy and held him tight. "Malachi, what's wrong?"

"*Mamm* says we have to leave." His grip tightened around Jalon's neck. "I don't wanna *geh*."

Pain stabbed through him. "Leave?" He looked at Phoebe. There was a haunted look to her eyes, and he could tell she'd been crying too. What on earth had happened while he was gone?

"Malachi, please." Her voice choked as she set down the heavy suitcase.

Jalon, still holding Malachi, went to her. He put his arm around her, glad that at least she wasn't shrugging him off. Just the opposite. She turned and buried her face in his chest. They stayed like that for a brief moment, and Jalon decided no matter what had happened he wasn't going to let her go.

Then she pulled away from him. Looked up into his eyes . . . and he realized the choice wasn't his to make.

"*Mamm*'s sick," she said. She explained what her father said in his letter. "I have to help take care of *mei familye*."

"I . . ." The lump in his throat felt like the size of a boulder. "I understand." What else could he say? He couldn't beg her to stay, although he wasn't above doing that if the circumstances were different. This was her family. If his mother were sick, he would do the same thing. It didn't make the twist of the knife in his heart any less painful.

"I don't wanna *geh*."

Jalon leaned down and whispered in Phoebe's ear, not wanting Malachi to hear. "You could leave him here with me while you're gone. You know we'll take *gut* care of him."

Phoebe looked at him. Touched his cheek with her hand, then let it fall. "I don't know how long I'll be gone."

"It doesn't matter," Jalon whispered. "He can stay with us as long as you need him to."

"But he belongs with me. He's *mei* responsibility."

The words dug deep into him, because he knew they were true. Malachi wasn't his son. It didn't matter if Jalon wanted him to be. Phoebe was his mother, and she would make the final decision.

"*Danki*," she said, tears dripping down her cheeks. "For being willing to."

"I'd do anything for both of you."

"I know." She reached up and took Malachi from Jalon. But Malachi wasn't going without a fight. He clung to Jalon as Phoebe tried to pull his arms from around Jalon's neck. He cried, his wails directly in Jalon's ear and going straight to his heart. Finally, Jalon couldn't let it go on. He walked away from Phoebe, took Malachi's arm from around his neck, then sat the boy on the porch railing. "You have to *geh* with *yer mamm*," he said, strengthening his resolve.

"I don't wanna."

"I don't want you to *geh* either. But it will only be for a short time." Jalon shouldn't have said it, but he hoped hearing the words out loud would make it true. He glanced at Phoebe, who was standing there with her arms wrapped around her waist. Then he turned back to Malachi. "Do you have *yer* yo-yo?"

Malachi nodded and pulled it out of his pants pocket.

"Then here's what I want you to do." He covered the yo-yo and Malachi's hand with his. "Anytime you get lonely or upset, look at this yo-yo. Remember that you've got a part of me with you all the time . . . until you and *yer mamm* come back to me." He could feel Malachi's hand tightening around the toy. "Make sure you practice all the tricks I showed you. When you come back, I'll show you even more."

Malachi nodded. Then he threw his arms around Jalon, and after a tight hug, he let go.

Jalon set him down on the porch. The taxi pulled into the driveway. Jalon carried the suitcase to the car, then after the driver put it into the trunk, he stepped back and didn't move. He watched Malachi and Phoebe get into the car and drive away. *They will come back.*

"They have to."

CHAPTER 19

March 6

Dear Phoebe,

You left your father's letter here. I hope you don't mind that I read it. I don't know anything about Lyme disease, but if your mom is on medicine, she should be getting better soon. I understand why you had to leave, and I'm not surprised you rushed back to take care of your family. I would have done the same thing.

I miss you so much, Phoebe. I'll pray for your mother and your family every day. If you need me, all you have to do is ask. I'll be there as fast as I can.

Jalon

March 8

Dear Jalon,

I don't mind that you read my letter. My mother is still weak, and she's had bouts of nausea and vomiting that are worrisome. One of the ladies in our church dropped by some special herbs that are supposed to help her stomach. Hopefully they'll work. Until she's better, I need to be here for my family.

Malachi carries your yo-yo everywhere with him. He misses you. So do I. I don't want to take you away from the farm. We'll be all right. Don't worry about us.

Phoebe

March 10

Dear Phoebe,

Don't worry about taking me away from the farm. Adam and Leanna can handle things while I'm gone. Karen's been coming over most evenings to drop off dessert, although I suspect she's doing it more for Adam's benefit than mine and Leanna's.

Phoebe, I miss you and Malachi so much. I want to see you. I need to see you. The minute I can come visit, tell me. I'll drop everything. There's an empty space in my heart right now, and it won't be filled until we're back together. I know that sounds corny, but it's how I feel.

I love you, Phoebe. I want to be able to tell you that in person. I should have told you long before now, because it's how I felt even before you left your aunt's. I love you, and I always will.

Jalon

March 26

Dear Jalon,

My mother is doing a bit better, but I don't think it would be a good time for you to visit right now.

Phoebe

March 28

Dear Phoebe,

It was so long since your last letter, I almost went to visit you, but I don't want to cause you any more stress. I want to help you, Phoebe. It's hard for me to stay here when I could be there supporting you while you go through this.

We purchased a few chickens last week. Adam helped me build a chicken coop—he's a pretty good carpenter, considering he doesn't have much experience.

If I can't visit you, can I call? I want to hear your voice. Letters aren't enough. I love you, Phoebe, even though we're apart right now. Nothing will change how I feel about you.

Jalon

April 7

Dear Phoebe,

I thought I would hear from you by now. Is everything okay?

Love,
Jalon

April 11

Dear Jalon,

I can't call because I don't have access to a phone. My mother is doing about the same. The rest of us are fine here. Please don't worry.

Phoebe

April 14

Dear Phoebe,

   Your letters are short and too far between, which makes me think something else is going on. Please let me come see you. I won't stay long. I learned some new yo-yo tricks to show Malachi. I've been practicing while you both have been away. Don't shut me out, Phoebe. I love you.

                    Jalon

April 30

Dear Phoebe,

   It's been over two weeks since your last letter. Please write to me as soon as you can. I miss you. I love you.

                    Jalon

May 11

Dear Phoebe,

   You won't let me call or visit. You've stopped writing me.

   Is it over between us?

                    Jalon

May 24

Phoebe,

   I got the message. You won't be hearing from me anymore.

                    Jalon

• • •

Phoebe read the letter through blurred eyes. She'd hurt him, his terse words stabbing her as if they were knives. He was angry and he had the right to be. She'd purposely stopped writing to him, and the few letters she had written were short and didn't acknowledge what her heart felt. Writing to him now was different than when she was at Aunt Bertha's. Back then his letters had been a beacon during a dark, oppressive time. Now they reminded her of what she'd lost. The pain of their separation was always with her. But her duty was to her family. They had stood by her when she needed them. She wouldn't turn her back on them when they needed her, not even for Jalon.

She pressed his letter against her heart, as she had every letter he'd sent. He loved her. The first time she read those words, she had surprised herself by not being surprised. Hadn't he shown her how he felt? The words were nice, but she had felt his love. Had seen it in action. That meant more than words.

But the time away from him had revealed something else—he didn't need her. Not really. He had his sister, his farm, his cousin, good friends, and a warm community. What could she offer him? She felt so empty, so alone, despite being surrounded by family—a family that was barely surviving. That was why she hadn't wanted him to visit. He would take on that burden, too, and she couldn't allow that. He had his own life to lead, his own dreams to fulfill. He'd been chained by his past for so long, and now that he was finally free, she wasn't going to put more obstacles in his way. She loved him enough to let him go.

She folded the letter and put it between the pages of a book she'd tried to read but had given up on weeks ago. She sat up on the couch and stretched, her back aching from sleeping on the lumpy furniture for more than two months. Pale light streamed through the front window, signaling the sunrise. There were no curtains over the window anymore. Now that Bishop Weaver was in charge, he'd enforced the rule in the *Ordnung* about window treatments. Their previous bishop's view had been "as long as they aren't fancy." But Bishop Weaver had a different view. Phoebe had learned quickly that the man had different views on a lot of things.

But at least one fear hadn't been realized since her return to Fredericktown—Bishop Weaver seemed to have dropped the threat of marrying Phoebe off. He hadn't talked to her at church, and he hadn't stopped by for a visit. Neither of her parents had brought it up, which meant they didn't know about the bishop's previous threat. He must have changed his mind, which was a relief. It was also a slight reprieve from the oppression hanging over her family.

As quietly as she could, she rose from the couch, folded the faded quilt that had belonged to generations of her mother's family, then crept over to the crib against the wall near her parents' bedroom. Elam was eight months old and didn't always sleep through the night.

When Elam wanted his *mamm*, Phoebe knew it tore at *Mamm*'s heart that she couldn't take care of him. It had been Phoebe's idea to move the crib out of her parents' bedroom and into the living room so she could be there when Elam awakened. She'd do anything to help her mother recover and let her father get a decent night's sleep.

She walked over to Elam's crib and smiled when she saw he was still fast asleep. She kissed the tip of her finger and pressed it lightly on his head, which was already covered in dark, fine curls. Malachi had been nearly bald at the same age, and he'd looked as sweet as Elam when he was sleeping. He was now sharing a small bedroom with four of her brothers, the ones who were nearest to his age. Since they'd arrived, he seemed to have succumbed to the gray mood of the rest of the family. He'd long since stopped asking when they would return to Birch Creek, as if he knew they couldn't leave anytime soon. Yet he carried Jalon's yo-yo with him everywhere, not playing with it, but just holding it tightly. *Remember that you've got a part of me with you all the time.*

Shoving Jalon's words out of her mind, she went into the kitchen, picked up a basket, and went to the chicken coop to gather eggs for breakfast. When she went inside, she checked the first laying box. The hen tilted her head as Phoebe searched for an egg. "Didn't feel like laying this morning, girl?" She moved her hand to the next box. The hen pecked at her when she removed her hand. "Ouch!" Not only was the hen ornery, but she hadn't laid either.

Phoebe checked each box, and while she wasn't pecked again, she also didn't find any eggs. This wasn't good. They didn't have much food in the pantry, and breakfast would have been thin even with the eggs. She frowned, hoping this was a one-time thing. It would be disastrous if their hens stopped laying. They relied on those eggs, not just for breakfast but for other meals.

As she went back to the house, she reevaluated her menu for the day. She'd planned to prepare a ham steak for supper, the last one they had. Instead she'd cook it for breakfast. Her dad and brothers couldn't have just bread and butter for breakfast and put in a full day of farmwork. She'd have to figure out something else for supper.

When she went inside, she checked on Elam again. He was stirring but still asleep. Quickly, she prepared breakfast, finishing just as her brothers and son came downstairs and bustled into the kitchen. Malachi tugged on the skirt of her dress. "Elam's crying," he said.

She touched his cheek. "*Danki* for letting me know. I'll get him in a minute."

"I've got him." Her father walked in, carrying Elam. "I changed him too."

Phoebe set down the plate of sliced bread, then took Elam from her father. She fixed a bottle while everyone settled at the table, several of them two in a chair. "I'm sorry for the skimpy breakfast," she said as she leaned against the counter and fed her youngest brother.

Her other brothers ignored her as they inhaled the food. They didn't seem to care what they ate, as long as it was edible. Boys. Then again, she was thankful for their lack of pickiness. Even Malachi had stopped complaining about eating.

When they were finished, *Daed* said, "You *buwe geh* outside."

"You want me to let the cows in the pasture?" Devon asked.

"*Ya*. Then you can all play for a little while."

"Really?" several of them said in unison.

"Yep. I want you all to have some fun for a change. *Geh* on, before I change *mei* mind and put you back to work."

The boys nodded, a few of them grinning as they left the kitchen. Devon and Zeb gave *Daed* a puzzled look. He didn't return it as he sipped his coffee, staring straight ahead. They shrugged and disappeared after their brothers.

Phoebe didn't bother to call them back to clear the table, something she insisted on after they finished a meal. She sat down next to her father and sat the bottle on the table. Elam was finished eating, and she sat him on her knee as she patted his back to help him burp. Her father's gaze remained unmoving, and she saw the multiple creases on his forehead and at the sides of his eyes. His beard seemed to grow grayer by the day. "*Daed?*" She didn't have to ask if something was wrong. She knew there was.

"Chickens didn't lay this morning, did they?" *Daed* asked.

She shook her head. "I'm sure they'll have eggs for us tomorrow."

"Cows are drying up too." He sighed and finally looked at her. "A huge thundercloud is hanging over us, Phoebe, and I don't know why. Bishop Weaver says I need more faith—"

"I don't know why you listen to him." The words shot

out of her mouth and she clamped her lips together. Saying anything ill against the bishop had always been met with unyielding eyes from *Daed* and a strict and unpleasant reprimand. She steeled herself for his chastising, but she wouldn't take back the words. Not when they were the truth.

To her surprise, her *daed* didn't admonish her. Instead, his shoulders slumped a little bit. "I'm worried about *yer mamm*. Real worried. She's not getting any better."

"I know," Phoebe whispered.

"Doc said the antibiotics would work."

"He also said it could take awhile for her to feel better." How long, no one knew. Lyme disease was unpredictable. *Mamm* could feel better tomorrow . . . or she could continue to decline for months. Phoebe held Elam close.

"If she doesn't get better . . ." He wiped at his eye with his thumb. "She's the one who holds this *familye* together. You've done a fine job since you've come back—"

"But I'm not *Mamm*." She mustered an encouraging smile. He seemed to desperately need it. "She'll be right as rain before we know it, *Daed*. Like you've always said, God is faithful." She waited for him to agree, as he always did.

He didn't say anything, his gray-blue eyes still wet with unshed tears. "*Danki* for the reminder." His throat bobbed. "There was a time when *yer mamm* and I thought we lost you to the world. We spent so many nights on our knees, hoping you'd come back to God and to *yer familye*. He answered our prayer. You're loyal to God and *yer familye*, and you're a *gut mamm* to Malachi. I know I'm not supposed to say this, Phoebe, but you've done both *yer mamm* and me proud."

Phoebe kept her head down as a lump formed in her throat. For so long she believed she had shamed her family. The bishop had said it. Her aunt Bertha had said it. And she had said it a million times to herself ever since she'd gotten pregnant. Now her father was telling her the words she longed to hear. Not about pride, but about God answering prayer. He had saved her from herself.

"I better check on the *buwe*. Got lots of work to do today." His chair scraped against the floor as he pushed back. "Hopefully we'll get some rain. We sure do need it."

Phoebe returned Elam to his crib with a few toys, then cleared the table, put the dishes in the sink, and made some tea and toast. She took the food to her mother's bedroom. *Mamm* hadn't had much of an appetite. She was lying on her bed, her face and lips pale, two quilts on top of her even though it was the middle of summer. "*Mamm*?" she said softly.

Her mother opened her eyes. Her thin lips formed a small smile. "Phoebe."

She flinched at her mother's weak voice, then hid her despair and went to the side of the bed. "I brought you some breakfast."

"*Danki*, but I'm not hungry."

"At least drink some tea." Her mother had to at least stay hydrated if she wasn't going to eat. Phoebe set the tea and plate of toast on the dresser.

Mamm pushed herself to a partial sitting position

and Phoebe arranged the two bed pillows behind her. Then she handed her the mug of tea. It shook so much in *Mamm*'s hand that Phoebe had to help hold it while she sipped.

"I'm glad you're here," *Mamm* said, not for the first time as she let Phoebe take the mug from her unsteady hands. She leaned back against the pillows. "I missed you while you were gone."

"I missed you too." She put the mug on the dresser, then sat down on the edge of her parents' bed.

Mamm's eyes closed, and Phoebe thought her mother had drifted off to sleep again. Suddenly *Mamm* said, "Why did you leave us?"

Phoebe stilled, meeting her mother's half-open eyes. "I told you I didn't want to be a burden, remember?"

Mamm nodded. "You and Malachi were never a burden. I remember telling you that too."

"You and *Daed* didn't need more mouths to feed, especially after Elam was born." She looked away.

"That's not the complete truth, is it?"

It wasn't. Yet she couldn't tell them about what Bishop Weaver had demanded. Since he seemed to have decided to drop the idea of forcing her to marry, it didn't matter anyway. "It's the main reason." A half lie, but the only reason her mother needed to know.

Mamm held her gaze for a long moment, and Phoebe thought she might question her further. Instead she relaxed against the pillows again. "Have you heard from Jalon since you left?"

"A few times." She couldn't lie to her mother again. "He's busy with his farm."

Her eyes fluttered closed. "Maybe we'll get to meet him someday."

More than anything Phoebe wished that could be true. "Maybe." The word came out in a thick whisper. When *Mamm* felt better, she would explain that she and Jalon were no longer together. She didn't want to give her mother anything else to worry about.

Mamm's eyes fully closed, and Phoebe tucked the quilt around her slim body. She'd lost weight, and if she didn't get her appetite back soon, she would have a harder time healing.

Picking up the nearly full mug of tea and the uneaten toast, Phoebe glanced at her mother again, then went back to the kitchen. Her throat tightened as she filled the sink with soap and water. Her heart hurt—for her mother, her father and brothers, her son, herself . . . and for Jalon.

CHAPTER 20

So how long are you going to wait before you *geh* after her?"

Jalon looked at Adam in disgust. "When are you going to mind *yer* own business?"

"If you weren't a gloomy jerk twenty-four hours a day, I would."

Wiping the sweat off his face, Jalon stood. A week ago he and Sol Troyer, Sol's brother Aden, and Aden's brother-in-law Andrew had cut down the tree in the backyard. The wood had come back from the mill, and he and Adam were adding slats to the wooden fence around the pasture. Adam held up the wood slats while Jalon nailed them in place. The only ones he couldn't do were the ones on the bottom of the fence. Jalon would hammer those later. "Are you going to run *yer* mouth or hold up that slat?"

"Point proven." Adam angled his chair and faced him. "Answer *mei* question first."

Jalon wasn't a violent man, but he was tempted to throw his hammer at his cousin. "Again, none of *yer* business."

"Jalon, you're being ridiculous. And an idiot. *Geh* see Phoebe."

Gritting his teeth, Jalon knelt back down, even though

there wasn't a board in place for him to nail. "She made her feelings clear." Or rather her lack of feelings. For whatever reason, she'd cut him off. Maybe she'd found someone else back home. The thought made him want to punch a wall. Or a fence slat.

"And you're going to give up without a fight? Without talking to her face-to-face?"

Jalon hung his head. It was the warmest day of the year so far, and his hat provided little relief. The cows and horses were standing under several shade trees in the small pasture, swinging their tails to beat away the flies that relentlessly pestered them. "You're the last person to give me romantic advice. What about you and Karen?"

That shut him up for a minute. "If Karen ever leaves, I'll *geh* after her."

Jalon dropped the subject. That was the closest Adam had come to admitting he had a real interest in Karen.

"We're talking about you and Phoebe," Adam said. "Stop changing the subject."

He turned to Adam. "Phoebe and I are over. End of subject. Now, pick up that board and hold it up."

"*Nee.*" Adam crossed his arms over his broad chest. "Not until you admit you need Phoebe."

"Are you serious?" Adam was acting like a child. Like a girl, actually. He expected Leanna to pull something like this, not his cousin.

"Absolutely serious. You haven't been the same since she and Malachi left, and to be honest, you've been a bear to be around. Besides, we all miss her. Things aren't the same around here without her and Malachi."

Adam was right, but that didn't change anything. It didn't make Phoebe want to be with him. It didn't bring her home. His home, which he wanted to be their home more than he wanted to draw breath. "I don't need her," he muttered. He hammered a nail on one of the lower planks and barely missed hitting his thumb. *She clearly doesn't need me.*

"Are you afraid of what you'll find out if you *geh* see her?" Adam said.

That was exactly what he was afraid of. If he found out she'd fallen in love with someone else, his heart couldn't take it. "Like I said, she made her feelings clear. Me chasing after her isn't going to make a difference." He stood. "If you're not going to help me with the fence, I've got a dozen other jobs to do." There were plenty of them to tackle. Working the land, training the horses, raising the livestock . . . But he had a sense of accomplishment when he saw the crops he'd spent so much time planting starting to push through the soil and grow. Adam worked just as hard, and even Leanna had a renewed attitude about the farm than she'd had growing up. At the end of the day he fell into bed knowing he'd put in a full, satisfying day's work.

Yet at night, when he was alone with his sore muscles and racing mind, all he could think about were Phoebe and Malachi. The void they'd left in his life was almost unbearable. But what could he do about it? He wasn't going to beg. He'd put his heart on the line and she'd stepped all over it. He'd offered to help her, to stand by her. She refused him.

Fine. He was done.

"Suit *yerself.*" Adam spun his chair to face the house and started to roll away.

"Hold up," Jalon said. "We're nearly finished. We need to get this fence done."

"We will," Adam said over his shoulder. "After you get *yer* head on straight."

Jalon put his hands on his hips, sweat dripping down the sides of his face. As far as blackmail went, Adam's attempt fell far short. He could fix the fence by himself. It would be difficult, but he could do it. He could do all of this on his own. He didn't need Adam or Leanna . . . and he definitely didn't need Phoebe.

He spent the rest of the afternoon proving that point, trying to fix the fence alone. He was managing it, but he'd only been able to add three of the slats without Adam's help. At this rate it would take an extra day to finish the fence. A wasted day. But he wasn't about to give in to Adam—or anyone else.

"Need a hand?"

He stilled at the familiar voice behind him. Slowly he rose to his feet and turned around. His father stood there, his thumbs tugging on his black suspenders, his hat pushed back from his forehead. "*Daed,*" Jalon said, his guard going up. "I didn't know you were here."

"Just arrived. *Yer mamm* was missing you *kinner,* so she wanted to come for a visit. She's inside with Leanna and Adam."

"How long are you staying?"

"Just for the day. We've got to get back." He moved closer to the repaired part of the fence, then draped his forearms over the top. "Things are looking *gut* around here," he said after a long pause.

"We're all working hard." Jalon didn't move to stand next to him.

"I can see that." Another pause. "Adam seems happy."

"He is."

"Never thought he'd be a farmer." He turned to Jalon. "Never thought you'd be one, either."

Jalon ground his teeth, measuring his next words. He didn't want to get into a fight with his father, not since he had been able to empathize with him about the farm. Neither of them won when they fought. "I'm suited for it . . . regardless of what you think." Then again, maybe he was itching for an argument.

Daed turned and faced him fully. "You don't know what I'm thinking, Jalon."

Jalon gripped the hammer in his hand, about to say something else sarcastic. His father's next words stopped him.

"You don't know, because I never told you." He sighed. "I didn't tell you the whole truth a minute ago. It wasn't just *yer mamm* who wanted to come here. I wanted to. Scratch that. I needed to. It's been long overdue for me to set things straight between us. I'll start with saying I'm sorry." He swallowed. "I was a lousy father to you."

"*Nee*—"

"Don't lie for the both of us. I was. I took out *mei* frustration and anger about *mei* failures on you. Worse than that, I knew you felt guilty about what happened to Adam. It was what led you to drink. I should know. *Mei* own guilt and failure are what drove me to it."

Jalon didn't know what to say. He had never expected this much openness from his father.

His father turned back and faced the field. "I didn't realize how much I'd been drinking until I went back to Mespo. I also didn't know how much *mei* drinking affected everyone. I thought I hid it. I thought I was handling it, and everything."

This time Jalon did move to stand by him. He put the hammer on the ground and looked at the field. "I know exactly what you mean."

"You helped me," *Daed* said.

Lifting his brow, Jalon said, "What?"

"When you quit, I saw how you were turning your life around. I knew then that you were ready to do what you truly loved—farm. If I hadn't totally killed that desire in you. I'm glad to see I didn't. *Yer* farm will be a success. Much more than mine ever could have been."

"Why?" It was the question Jalon had always wanted to ask. "Why couldn't you make a *geh* of this place?"

"Because I didn't believe in myself. I guess I didn't have enough faith in God, either. I tried to force things, tried to take the easy way. I needed to trust, and I couldn't." He clapped Jalon on the shoulders and moved away, bonding moment over. "I better say hi to Leanna before she gives me an earful for not paying attention to her." He started to move away, then paused. "Looks like everything is going *yer* way. You deserve it, *sohn*. That, and so much more."

Jalon waited for his father to leave, then leaned forward against the fence, his head down, trying to figure out what had just happened. His father had faith in him. A wound he didn't know was still bleeding had suddenly closed.

Yet he couldn't shake something his father said. Everything wasn't going Jalon's way. He needed Phoebe and he needed Malachi. All the grouchy protesting in the world wasn't going to change that.

Go to her.

Lifting his head up, he looked at the sky. This wasn't the first time he'd heard that still, small voice in his heart, the one that didn't sound remotely like Adam, despite echoing his cousin's words. He'd dismissed it, like he'd dismissed Adam. "What if she doesn't want me?" he choked out.

Go to her.

That wasn't the answer he wanted. He needed a sure thing, not more uncertainty. He'd had enough of that in his life, despite always seeking for consistency that seemed out of reach.

He looked out into the expanse of farmland, then over to the small pasture. Right now things with the farm were going fine, but even with his father's confidence in him, the bottom could drop out. Lack of rain, hail, sickness—he'd seen all of it happen over the years to his father. Yet Jalon had taken the risk with this farm, both he and Adam. They had believed in it enough to try to make something of it. They believed God would be faithful.

I am faithful.

He stilled. God's faithfulness was the only sure thing in his life. There was only one—no, two things missing. Phoebe and Malachi. Could he risk his pride and his heart for the woman he loved? What did it say about him if he was unwilling to take that risk?

. . .

Near the end of May, Phoebe's mother started showing slight improvement. It helped when the boys visited her, even if all they did was play cards at the end of her bed. The nausea had gone away so she was finally able to eat, but the illness had left her too thin. She was also still tired. Everything that had happened had taken its toll on Phoebe's father too. His appetite was down and he'd lost weight. He was also working hard, harder than she'd ever seen.

But despite the hard work, and even with the boys' help and the community bringing food, helping with the washing, and visiting, an oppressive cloud still hovered over them. For whatever reason, God wasn't lifting it. The chickens still weren't laying, and the garden had produced only half of what they'd planted in the early spring.

Then, soon after Phoebe received her last letter from Jalon, Malachi and her youngest brothers, including baby Elam, had come down with a terrible stomach flu that had kept her up for almost a week taking care of them and *Mamm*. She was exhausted. Still, she reminded herself that God was faithful. Even her father believed that, and had said as much when *Mamm* started to show slight improvement. "We'll get a break soon, Phoebe. I'm sure of it."

On a sultry morning, she was sitting on an old rocker

on the front porch, snapping the few green beans the garden had yielded. Her father and three of her oldest brothers were repairing yet another hole in the roof of the barn. The rest of the boys, including Malachi, were visiting their neighbors down the road. Although worry and strain were always present, right now she was able to appreciate her quiet surroundings, the soft, warm breeze that rippled through the leafy maples and oaks, and the birds twittering, fluttering, and chasing each other as they soaked in the morning sunshine. Her gaze followed them for a few moments, realizing she hadn't thought about her sketches since she'd arrived. Even if she had, she wouldn't be in the mood for drawing. She didn't have the time, either. Sketching seemed like a frivolous and childish pursuit now, and they didn't have the money to spare for her to buy drawing paper or a sketchbook. She shook her head. She'd never thought she'd find herself agreeing with Aunt Bertha.

Halfway through snapping the beans, a buggy pulled into the driveway. She quickly snapped a couple more, then stopped when she saw the man exiting the buggy. Bishop Weaver. A knot formed in her stomach, only to unwind a bit as she realized he was probably here to visit *Mamm*. During the past week alone the bishop's wife and three other women had brought casseroles, loaves of fresh bread, vegetable salads, and a couple dozen cookies, all of which she appreciated. But with so many mouths to feed, the food hadn't stretched far, and she knew her father didn't like taking so many handouts, even though he didn't have a choice. Sure enough, the bishop was carrying a foil-covered dish.

Phoebe set down the bowl of green beans, then met Bishop Weaver at the bottom of the porch steps.

"Hello, Phoebe." He handed her the dish. "Chicken and noodles. Julia made them."

"Please thank her for us." The casserole dish was still slightly warm. They would have it for supper tonight. "*Mamm*'s resting right now. I'm not sure she's up for company. *Daed* is working on the barn roof with some of *mei* brothers, but I could *geh* get him if you'd like."

"Another repair? Isn't that the third one this month?"

"The roof is old." Her stomach twisted again. "*Daed* says it's time to replace it."

"So that's what he's doing right now? Replacing it?"

"*Nee.*" She gripped the dish. "Just patching it."

"Why not replace it?"

Why was he drilling her with all these questions? "He's been busy with the crops. There hasn't been time to replace the roof."

"But he has all these sons. Many hands make light work."

Was he trying to get her to admit they didn't have the money? That wasn't going to happen. For some reason her father hadn't gone to the bishop and asked for help from the community fund. Phoebe didn't blame him. "Would you like some cold tea?" She'd offer him coffee, but her parents hadn't been able to afford it in months.

"Tea would be nice on such a warm day."

Phoebe went up the steps and held the screen door open for the bishop. Once inside, they went into the kitchen and, after inviting him to sit down at the table, she poured tea into glasses. They didn't have any ice. That was a luxury. But she wasn't going to apologize to Bishop Weaver for it. She pulled out a few spice cookies from the container on top of the fridge. Despite being short on food, she always made sure to have some kind of sweet in the house for her *daed* and brothers and Malachi as a treat. She'd even figured out how to make eggless ones. She arranged the cookies on a plate, then set them on the table. "I'll *geh* see if *Mamm*'s up," she said.

The bishop raised his hand. "There's *nee* need. I didn't come to see *yer* parents."

The knot strangled her stomach.

"We've been long overdue for a talk, Phoebe. I'd been waiting for *yer mamm*'s health to improve, but . . ." He clasped his hands together and laid them on the tabletop, then gestured with his head to the chair across from him. "Please. Have a seat."

She slowly lowered herself onto the chair. Unlike their former bishop, who had been old even when Phoebe was born, Bishop Weaver was in his thirties. He and his wife had two children who were a little older than Malachi. Yet despite his youth, he had the command of an older man, one who was sure of himself and his purpose.

He picked up a cookie and took a bite. "I understand you went to stay at *yer aenti* Bertha's after our last talk," he said when he finally finished chewing and swallowed.

She nodded but didn't say anything.

"I'm assuming you didn't mention our conversation to *yer* parents, since they didn't bring up the topic with me after you left."

"I didn't see any reason for them to know, since I'm

not getting married." Oh, saying the words were like a dagger to her soul. But they were the truth. She wouldn't marry, not when her heart belonged to Jalon. She would never, ever get over him.

"Do you think something has changed since you've been gone? That living in our community as an unwed *mamm* is acceptable?"

"Bishop Kline thought so."

"Bishop Kline was lax with the rules. Rules are important, Phoebe. Keeping the *Ordnung* is how we become closer to God. How we maintain our faith. And how we keep our community together."

"I thought prayer and worship are how we grow closer to the Lord."

"Which is part of the *Ordnung*." His eyes narrowed, showing her that her words had ruffled him. *Good*. "Believing we are outside the *Ordnung* is prideful, Phoebe. Add that to *yer* list of sins, and you'll be lucky if any man will have you."

Tears pricked her eyes, the shame she thought she'd left behind slamming into her with full force. Still, she lifted her chin. She wouldn't let him get to her, and she wasn't going to be coerced. A very special man did love her—*did* being the operative word—and that was enough.

"I've spent the time since *yer* return finding someone willing to marry you." The bishop took another bite of the cookie, again chewing slowly. "Someone finally agreed."

Phoebe didn't let her gaze leave his. "Who is it?" she asked weakly.

"Atlee Shetler."

Phoebe flinched. She'd known Atlee her entire life because he was close to her father's age. He'd lost his wife ten years ago, and had remained single—and nearly hermit-like—ever since. "I'm not marrying Atlee."

Bishop Weaver's eyes softened, which surprised her. "Malachi needs a father. You need a husband."

"I have *mei familye*. They love and support me. They also love Malachi. There isn't a better place for us." Except with Jalon, but she couldn't allow herself to think about that possibility anymore.

"*Yer familye* is struggling, Phoebe." His voice lowered. "Did you ever stop to think that it's *yer* fault?"

She froze at his accusation. "*Mei* fault?"

"You slept with a man outside of marriage. You conceived a child. You refuse to marry and submit to authority." He paused. "How old is Malachi?"

"Four."

"And when did the farm start failing?"

"Four years ago." Her throat closed.

"And now on top of everything else, *yer mamm* has a strange illness. Can't you see the connection? Are you so filled with pride and stubbornness that you'll continue to allow *yer familye* to suffer?"

"*Nee*," she said, choking out the word. "I'm not." This wasn't her fault. Or was it? Could the bishop be right, that God was punishing her family because of her sins?

"Phoebe." For once his voice was gentle. "You know in *yer* heart I'm right. You also know what you need to do. Repent. Marry Atlee. Be the respectable, obedient wife *yer* faith requires."

She clenched her hands together until her fingers cramped. "If I don't?"

He let out a sigh, his head dipping as if he didn't want to say his next words. "Then it's clear where *yer* heart and loyalties lie. Not with *yer* faith or *yer familye* . . . and not with God."

No. That wasn't true. She loved her family, and would do anything for them. She was also dedicated to her faith. *God, it's not true.*

"That's enough."

Phoebe looked up to see her father walk into the kitchen, his expression stormy. "You will not bully *mei* daughter," he said in a tight voice.

Bishop Weaver stood. He was a few inches taller than *Daed*, which allowed him to look down on him. "I'm not bullying her, Jesse. I'm trying to help her. And you." He glanced at Phoebe before looking back at *Daed*. "Phoebe needs to make things right with God. *Yer* continual support of her rebellion is why he is displeased with you."

Daed crossed his arms over his chest. "You told me it was because I lacked faith. Which is it?"

The bishop's face reddened, seemingly caught off guard by the question. He tugged on the bottom of one suspender. "Perhaps it's both. Either way, I've found a suitable husband for *yer* daughter—"

"I heard. Atlee isn't suitable to be anyone's husband. The poor man has been mourning his wife for over a decade."

"Which is why he needs a new *frau*."

"Then let God lead him to a woman who will love

him. Both he and Phoebe deserve better than marriage by default."

Phoebe was shocked. She'd never seen her father stand up to any bishop like this.

"I love *mei* daughter," *Daed* continued. "She made a choice, and she's handling the consequences. She's given me and *mei* wife a wonderful grandson. She's a good *mamm*, and she's been holding this *familye* together since *mei* wife took sick." His expression switched from heated to regretful. "If you're counting sins and laying blame, don't leave me out. I should be a better husband to *mei* wife. A better father to *mei kinner*."

Phoebe stood and went to him. He shouldn't berate himself like this. He had no reason to. "*Daed*," she said, "you're a wonderful husband and father."

"But I can do better. We all can do better." He took a step toward the bishop. "Even you."

The bishop's jaw visibly clenched. His gaze flicked to the right before meeting *Daed*'s square on with new determination. "Are you saying you haven't followed the rules of the *Ordnung*? Because if you haven't, then that will need to be dealt with. You will need to confess in front of the church. That and obedience are the only way to receive God's favor."

The man was missing the point. He was so stuck on rules and appearances he couldn't see grace. Not just God's grace, but the grace her parents had extended to her after she'd hurt them by making so many bad decisions.

"I think we're done here," *Daed* said. "Phoebe gave you her answer."

But Bishop Weaver didn't move. "Jesse, listen to

reason. You and *yer familye* have fallen under some demonic power, that much is true. If you can't see the error of *yer* ways, there will be *nee* choice but to excommunicate you and *yer* entire *familye*." He glanced at Phoebe again. "I now see where you get *yer* prideful nature."

Daed blew out a furious breath. "Get out before I throw you out."

The bishop opened his mouth as if to say something, then clamped it shut. He shook his head. Straightening his shoulders, he turned and walked out the back door.

Phoebe couldn't move. She could barely breathe. She'd never seen her father so incensed. He'd never lashed out like that at anyone.

As if the impact of threatening the bishop hit him, he collapsed into a chair. Yet when he looked up at Phoebe, she could still see the steel in his eyes. "I don't regret saying that to him. I do regret you had to witness it."

She knelt in front of him. "*Daed*, I'm sorry."

"For what?" He lifted her chin with a thick, work-roughened finger. "This isn't *yer* fault."

"But maybe the bishop is right. I've disappointed God and he's taking it out on you. If I get married—"

"He's not right and you're not marrying Atlee. That's final."

Putting her hand over her father's, she asked, "What are we going to do?"

He sighed, squeezed her hand, and leaned back in the chair. "I don't rightly know at the moment. I could use some of Eli's wisdom right now," he said, referring to Bishop Kline. "I've known Samuel Weaver for a long time. He never used to be like this."

"Like what?"

"Judgmental. As if his word was law, not God's. He's always been a stick in the mud, though. Becoming bishop hasn't helped that, obviously." Then he touched the side of her head lightly, making sure not to dislodge her *kapp*. "Don't worry, Phoebe. We'll sort this out. Just don't let what he said get to you. We're going through hard times. I can't deny that. But I believe we're going through all this to strengthen our faith. Not as punishment."

He rose from the chair, giving her a weary smile. "Gotta get back to work. But first I have to get a drink. That was the reason I came inside in the first place." He gave her another encouraging smile. "I'm glad I did."

She went through the motions of making lunch, trying to follow her father's advice and not dwell on the bishop's visit. One of her mother's friends had brought over turkey and cheese sandwiches, and Phoebe would add potato salad with mustard only and carrot sticks. A meager meal but it would have to do.

Despite her focus on preparing the meal, her mind continued to war with itself. *Daed* had given her an escape from Atlee, but that didn't change anything. They were still struggling. *Mamm* was still sick. Now they were on the wrong side of Bishop Weaver, and nothing good could come of that. And she still couldn't get the thought out of her mind that she was responsible for all this. If only she hadn't rebelled. If only she hadn't slept with Brody. If only she hadn't become pregnant.

But then she wouldn't have Malachi, and she couldn't imagine her life without him.

She stopped peeling the carrots and closed her eyes.

Lord, thank you for mercy and forgiveness. Daed's right.
*I need to be faithful, and I promise that no matter what
happens to our* familye, *I will always put my trust and
love in you. Even if I can't see a way out of our situation,
I know you're here, loving all of us. And that's more than
enough . . . more than I deserve.*

When she opened her eyes, tears stung. Yet she felt
peace wrapping itself around her heart, cloaking and
soothing her soul. Everything would be okay. She knew
that now, despite the bishop, the failing farm, her mother's
sickness . . . and despite her own heartbreak over Jalon.
God would see them all through the pain and hardship.
She believed it with all her heart.

A knock sounded at the front door. Her body tensed.
Was the bishop back? Had he brought reinforcements
to convince her and *Daed* to comply with his demands?
They didn't have a deacon or minister in the district.
Several of the men were her father's friends, but they
were also close to the bishop. What if they were here to
gang up on her and her family? To convince them to repent and force her to marry Atlee?

Faithful . . . God is faithful. She repeated the words as
she went to see who it was. When she looked through
the door's window, she stilled. Jalon stood on the other
side.

CHAPTER 21

Jalon's heart wrenched when the door opened and he saw Phoebe. She looked pale, thinner than she'd been when she left Birch Creek, and her eyes were red-rimmed. "Have you been crying?" he asked, then wanted to kick himself. That wasn't how he wanted to open this conversation. Actually, he didn't want to say anything at all, only to take her in his arms and never let her go.

She stepped back and wiped her eyes, shaking her head. The combination of movements threw her off balance and he reached for her. And just like that, she was in his arms.

"Jalon," she said, crying against his shirt. "I can't believe you're here."

He couldn't believe it either, and had fought with himself the entire trip about whether he was doing the right thing. Now he knew he was.

She lifted her head and tried to pull away from him. "I'm sorry," she whispered thickly.

"I'm the one who's sorry. I should have been here sooner."

She shook her head. "*Nee*. There's *nix* here for you,

Jalon. And I can't leave *mei familye*." She tilted up her chin. "I won't leave them."

"Phoebe?"

At the sound of the weak female voice they both looked up. The woman standing in the living room looked just as weak and thin, thinner than Phoebe. Yet her *kapp* was perfectly placed, and her dress, which was a bit loose on her, looked freshly pressed. She walked toward them, her gait a little wobbly, but a smile on her face. "You must be Jalon. I'm Phoebe's mother, Miriam."

Realizing he was still holding Phoebe, he released her. "Yes, I'm Jalon Chupp. Nice to meet you."

"It's nice to meet you too. I didn't realize you were coming for a visit." She looked at her daughter. "Phoebe didn't mention it."

"Because she didn't know. I wanted to surprise her." He looked at Phoebe, seeing the bewilderment in her eyes. "But if this is a bad time—"

"Not at all. Why don't you two sit while I bring tea?"

The woman didn't look strong enough to carry one cup of tea, never mind two. Phoebe evidently didn't think so either. "*Mamm*, you sit down. I'll get the tea."

She shook her head. "You've done plenty for me. Let me do this for you."

Phoebe hesitated, then sat down. Jalon joined her, making sure to leave plenty of space between them on the couch. He had to tread carefully here. He had to make sure she understood how much she meant to him without scaring her off or overwhelming her. She seemed like the same woman he'd met at her aunt Bertha's, though possibly a little more shell-shocked. Which made him even more angry with himself that he hadn't come sooner. Adam had been right. He had been an idiot. And a coward. Had Phoebe paid the price?

She looked down at her lap. "You shouldn't have come."

"I should have come sooner. Phoebe, why didn't you write me back?"

"I . . ." Her gaze met his. "I didn't want you to feel obligated."

"Obligated?" She could be so frustrating, but even that came from a tender heart. "Phoebe, I love you. I told you that in *mei* letters. It wasn't the best way to do it, but that doesn't change how I feel." He couldn't hold back the words. "You're not an obligation. You're the woman I love. The one I need and can't live without. Whatever happens with you, Malachi, or *yer familye*, I want to help. I want to be here for you."

"You have *yer* own life. The farm . . . We would be holding you back."

Not able to take the separation anymore, he moved closer to her. "I don't care about the farm. Not when you're away from me. Not when you're struggling. I thought you knew me better than that."

"Jalon." Her eyes filled as she looked at him. "I do know you. That's why I stopped writing. I knew you'd come here and try to fix things." Then she looked at her lap. "But it's unfixable."

"Listen to me." He peered around to catch her gaze. "*Nix* is impossible, especially when we face it together. Now, tell me what's really going on here. I can see *yer mamm* is still sick."

"She's actually doing a little bit better," Phoebe said.

Relieved, he let out a tense breath. "Then you'll be able to come back home soon?"

"*This* is *mei* home." Her tone was firm. "I won't abandon *mei familye*."

"I saw some cookies on the table." Phoebe's *mamm* entered the room, carrying a plate with three small cookies on it and a mug of tea. There wasn't a coffee table in the room, so she handed the mug to Jalon and the cookies to Phoebe. "I'll be back with *yers* in a minute," she said to her daughter.

"*Danki, Mamm.*" Phoebe set the plate on the couch between her and Jalon.

He stretched to put the tea on an end table, ignoring it. "There's something you're not telling me," he said. "I'm not leaving until you do."

"You'll have to *geh* eventually. You have *yer* farm to take care of."

"Forget the farm. I'll give it to Adam and Leanna if I have to."

Her eyes widened. "You can't do that."

"I can and I will, if it means being with you. Don't you understand, Phoebe? I'm willing to risk everything for you. I'm willing to say good-bye to Birch Creek if it means I can be with you and Malachi. I don't care where we live or what I end up doing. Without you," he said, lightly touching her hand, "I'm empty."

The front door opened and her younger brothers and Malachi burst into the room. They all stopped when they saw Jalon. Malachi's eyes grew round, then he launched himself into Jalon's arms. Jalon hugged him so tight he thought he might crush the child.

"I missed you," Malachi said, nearly choking the air out of Jalon.

"I missed you too." He closed his eyes, breathed in the sweat and dirt of a boy who lived life to the fullest, and felt a part of his heart heal. He sat Malachi on his lap.

"Look," Malachi said, pulling away from Jalon but still with his arms wrapped around his neck. "Jalon's here."

"Who's that?" a young boy with blue eyes the same color as Malachi's said.

"*Buwe*, *geh* wash up," Phoebe told them. "We'll be having lunch soon. And before any of you ask, it's not pizza."

They all grumbled and went upstairs to where Jalon presumed the bathroom was. Malachi stayed put, sitting on Jalon's lap, leaning against him as he pulled something out of his pocket. The yo-yo.

"He keeps it with him always."

Jalon peered over Malachi's head at Phoebe's watery smile.

"I've been practicing *mei* tricks." Malachi gripped the yo-yo. "Do you wanna see?"

"I do, but I have to talk to *yer mamm* for a little while longer. After we're done, then you can show me everything you can do."

Malachi nodded, gave Jalon another quick hug, then scrambled down off his lap and ran upstairs, tripping on the way up. Jalon couldn't help but smile. How he loved that kid.

Then he shifted his gaze to the woman he loved. "Tell me what I have to do to be with you and Malachi."

• • •

Jalon was relentless, and that made Phoebe feel more loved and cherished than she ever had. Seeing Malachi's reaction had made her heart swell. He belonged with Jalon. They both did. Yet she couldn't leave her family, not now. She didn't know when she could. Was that fair to Jalon, to make him wait?

And she would never ask him to leave Birch Creek and give up his life there.

"Phoebe." At some point he'd removed the cookie plate and moved even closer to her, and her heartbeat raced. He looked like he wanted to kiss her. She wanted him to. Not in her parents' living room, of course. Not with her younger brothers and son ready to bound down-stairs at any minute. But someplace private, with the two of them alone. Where they could hold each other and never let go.

She forced herself to focus on his request. "I won't ask you to give up anything for me, Jalon. And I don't know when we can ever go back to Birch Creek."

"You keep saying that, but I don't believe it."

He was forcing her hand. "Bishop Weaver was here."

"The one who wanted you to agree to an arranged marriage?"

"*Ya.* I thought he'd changed his mind, but he was only biding his time. And he's no longer singling out only me. He's singling out my whole family." She explained what the bishop said, and as she talked, she saw Jalon's jaw clench. Then she told him about her father taking a stand, which caused him to relax.

"I'm glad he did that," Jalon said. "I just wish I'd been here to set the bishop straight."

She frowned. "How would you do that?"

He took her hand. "I'd tell him you were already getting married. To me."

She nearly choked. "Is that a proposal?"

"Absolutely yes."

Her body warmed all the way through, but she kept her composure. "It's not that simple."

He let out a bitter chuckle. "It never is."

"*Daed* taking a stand, that caused a problem with the bishop. He might be disciplined in front of the congregation."

"For standing up for his daughter?"

"For going against the head of the community. That's not done here, Jalon. And then there're the problems with the farm."

"What problems?"

She ended up telling him everything, from the dry cows to her mother's slow recovery. "*Mei daed*'s got so much on his shoulders, and he's trying to be strong for everyone. I can't leave him to bear all this alone." She lifted her chin. "I won't leave him."

Jalon didn't say anything for a long moment, which scared her a little. His face was unreadable. She expected him to be upset with her. She was choosing her family over him, and that had to hurt. It would hurt if the situation were reversed.

"Where's *yer daed*?" he asked, finally speaking.

"Outside. He and some of *mei* brothers are working on the barn roof. Part of it caved in last night."

"The animals?" Jalon asked.

"All okay, thank goodness."

Jalon rose. Without saying another word he walked out the front door.

Phoebe popped up from the couch. What was he doing? She peeked through the front window, but didn't see him. Had he been so angry he was leaving her? But he wouldn't do that to Malachi, not without telling him good-bye. That gave her a small measure of comfort, which quickly disappeared when she realized she would eventually have to tell Jalon good-bye. For good. And not through a letter, but to his face, where she would see the pain she'd feel reflected in his eyes. Her decision would hurt both of them. Still, she couldn't change her mind.

"Phoebe."

She turned, surprised at the strength in her mother's voice. Only then did she realize her mother hadn't brought in the other drink. "*Mamm*, you should lie down and rest," Phoebe said, going to her.

"Later. We need to talk."

Her mother almost sounded like her old self, and she walked into the living room and sat down on the couch with purpose. Phoebe followed her. Then she knew. *Mamm* had heard the whole thing.

"You have to *geh* with Jalon. That man loves you, and you love him." *Mamm* smiled. "He also loves Malachi, and he'd be a terrific father."

"*Mamm*, I can't. I won't leave you and *Daed* and *mei* brothers."

Mamm took her hand. "Phoebe, we'll be fine. I'm

getting better, and the older *buwe* can pitch in and do some of *mei* chores."

"Which one of them is going to cook?"

Mamm laughed. "They can learn. The point is, we'll be fine. I don't want to hold you back from *yer* life, Phoebe. You deserve to be happy."

"I'm as happy as I deserve to be."

Mamm's eyes softened. "You don't believe you can have more?"

Phoebe knew what her mother was doing. "I do, but I can be content helping *mei familye*." There was a time she didn't think so, when she was more concerned with her own selfish, foolish desires than her family. But she'd grown up since then. She was a mother now, and she understood the importance of taking care of her own. Jalon had shown her as much too. He was willing to sacrifice everything for her, but she couldn't allow him to do that. It wasn't fair to him.

"Phoebe, did you *geh* to *yer aenti* Bertha's because of the bishop?"

Malachi and the other boys galloped down the stairs. "In the kitchen with you," *Mamm* said. "Don't forget to say *yer* prayers before you eat."

"Where's Jalon?" Malachi asked.

"He'll be back soon," *Mamm* said before Phoebe could answer.

After the boys left, Phoebe looked at *Mamm*. "How did you know about the bishop?"

"It's hard to keep secrets around here, you know. Sarah's *mamm* asked me if there was a wedding in the future. When I told her I didn't know of one, she said maybe the bishop's wife had been mistaken. I started putting two and two together, but *mei* suspicions weren't confirmed until I overheard *yer daed*."

"You've been eavesdropping a lot today," Phoebe said.

"How else do I find out anything? I wish you would have come to us."

"I didn't want to be the cause of strife between you and Bishop Weaver."

"If he was planning to do something so awful as marry you off? We should have known about it." She softened a bit. "Even before I got sick, *yer* father and I had been talking about the future. It hasn't felt right being here since Bishop Kline died. Bit by bit we've felt as though we've been slipping away from the community, especially spiritually. We believe God is confirming that by what's happening here—*mei* illness, the problems with the farm. The challenge is finding another place we can afford. We need farmland and it's expensive. We need a large *haus*, and that costs money too. But as soon as I'm back on *mei* feet, we're going to figure things out. If *yer* father has to give up farming, so be it. God has another plan in mind for us, then. In a couple of years some of *yer* brothers will be old enough to work jobs year-round, which will help."

Mamm put her hand over Phoebe's. "What I'm trying to tell you is that we'll be okay. We always are. God has us in the palm of his hand. Never doubt that for a second."

"Phoebe!"

Both women jumped at the sound of her father's raised voice. *Daed* walked into the living room from the kitchen, Jalon right behind him. While *Daed* looked furious, Jalon looked complacent. Calm, even, which confused Phoebe even more.

"You need to talk sense into this man." *Daed* pointed at Jalon, who put his hands on his waist.

"Jesse, settle down." *Mamm* got up and went to him. When *Daed* steadied himself, *Mamm* said, "Now, what in the world is going on here?"

"I simply told Jesse that you all could live with Phoebe and me. After we're married, obviously. Of course, she still has to say yes."

"Jalon." Phoebe went to him. "Do you realize what you're saying?"

"I do."

"Have you counted all *mei* brothers?"

He chuckled. "I have. Phoebe, we can add on to the *haus*. There's a parcel of land next door, and I was finally able to track down the guy who owns it. He says he's willing to sell, for the right price. We can purchase that and build a new *haus* for *yer* parents and siblings. We'll all be a *familye*."

Phoebe couldn't believe what she was hearing, and her heart soared with hope, only to come crashing down when reality hit. "All that costs money."

"Have faith, Phoebe." He moved closer to her. "Isn't love worth taking a risk?"

"*Daed*." She turned to her father, who had his arm around *Mamm*. She was leaning into him, and they were both smiling. "You're agreeing to this?"

"I wasn't going to a minute ago." He tugged on his beard. "But I see he's serious. Generous and maybe a little foolish, but serious."

"Like I told you, he loves you," *Mamm* said.

"I've told her that." Jalon gently turned Phoebe to face him. "We can make this work, Phoebe. Together, we can do anything. Marry me . . . please."

Now all her brothers and Malachi piled into the room, filling it to the brim.

"Ugh, mushy stuff," said Ezra.

"Does this mean we're moving?" said Nelson.

"Malachi ate the last cookie," said Perry.

"Did not," said Malachi, crumbs circling his mouth.

Without a word, Phoebe took Jalon's hand and led him upstairs and down the hallway so they could be as far from her family as possible. "Are you sure?" she asked him.

He put his arms around her waist. "I've never been more sure of anything in *mei* life. *Yer familye* is mine. Malachi, *yer* brothers, *yer* parents."

"What about Leanna and Adam? Will they be okay with this?"

"Leanna practically shoved me out the door when I said I was going to see you. She also said I couldn't come back without being engaged. Adam agreed." He tilted Phoebe's chin upward. "There's *nix* standing between us anymore, Phoebe. Not the past, and not the future." He bent down and kissed her so sweetly and gently that tears welled in her eyes. "Do I have to beg?" he whispered. "When it comes to you, I'm not above begging—"

She shut him up with a kiss, then said, "I love you. And I can't wait to marry you."

EPILOGUE

Phoebe added a plate of Hunan beef to the last of the three tables spread across the backyard of their house. An odd choice for outdoor fare, but Jalon had mentioned last week that he had a hankering for it, and that her Hunan beef was better than the restaurant's in Barton. She liked nothing better than pleasing her husband, especially when it came to food. Plus, he always showed his appreciation in the best ways.

She rang the cowbell that signaled mealtime, and everyone headed for a place to sit. Her brothers got there first, sunburned and sweaty from harvesting the crops. Adam had been in the barn, and he wheeled himself across the grass, kept especially short and trim for easy wheelchair access. *Mamm* and Leanna came out of the house. They'd spent the morning shucking corn on the front porch, which Phoebe would help them put up this afternoon.

Then Jalon and her *daed* arrived. Jalon grinned, and his smile widened when he caught sight of the Hunan beef. There was plenty of other food for the kids—and any adults who had delicate palates. *Daed* sat down next to Jalon and across from Adam, and soon the three of them had their heads together as they normally did, discussing plans for the house Jalon was building on the land he'd purchased next door. That house would be theirs, and a welcome reprieve from the cramped quarters of the current house.

Once their house was built, Jalon would sell the original house to *Daed*, who had gotten a job working for the construction company that had previously employed Jalon. Money was tight and space was tighter, but they were all together now because she and Jalon had made the untraditional choice of marrying at the end of July, and she wouldn't have it any other way. Even Leanna, who often went and stayed at the Yoders'"so I can have some breathing room" didn't complain. Considering she spent plenty of time playing volleyball with Phoebe's brothers, she seemed fine with the arrangements.

"Hi, everyone." Karen approached the group, holding her usual cake carrier, which held not an Orange Bliss cake but a triple fudge cake. Phoebe knew this because she had invited Karen for lunch and had requested she bring it. It had become one of Adam's favorites. She stopped to smile at Adam, who nodded to her. By the blush on his cheeks, it was clear to everyone he was smitten. She knew Karen was.

After putting the cake on one of the tables, Karen sat down next to Adam. Phoebe sat down next to Jalon. Leanna, in her own original way, had decided to sit with Malachi and the youngest boys. Everyone bowed their heads, and after prayer they enjoyed a delicious lunch, a warm fall day, and the best company around.

Later that night, after everyone else had gone to bed, Jalon took Phoebe's hand and led her outside. He was holding something behind his back as she went with him to the field next door. Then he sat down on the ground and pulled her into his lap.

"What are we doing out here?" she asked him.

"I need to give you this." He handed her a birdhouse.

Under the moonlit sky she could see it was brightly painted, although she couldn't tell exactly what the colors were. It looked beautiful, though. "You're giving this to me now?"

"Everything has been so busy I kept forgetting. I had it made for you months ago, after you wrote me about wanting birdhouses in *yer aenti*'s yard."

Those letters seemed like they were written years ago, but she had saved every one. She still wished she could have read the letter her aunt cruelly tore up. Jalon told her what he had written, saying what he'd felt that night didn't compare to how much he loved her now. Still, it would have been special to read it. "This is lovely. *Danki*."

"I've got something else." He handed her a sketch book. "To replace the one you left at *yer aenti*'s. I know you've missed drawing."

"I really haven't had the time, with everything going on."

"You should make time. It's something you enjoy, and it's important to you. Besides, I can't wait to see *yer* first drawing." He kissed her, then looked up at the clear sky, which revealed thousands of twinkling stars. "You can make a wish," he said. "You've got *yer* pick of stars."

She leaned her head on his shoulder. "I don't have to. *Mei* wish has already come true."

ACKNOWLEDGMENTS

As always, a big thank you to my editors Becky Monds and Jean Bloom for their encouragement and impressive ability to keep me on track (especially timelines!). Thank you to Jodi Hughes and Karli Jackson, who keep me on track during the last stages of the publication process. I appreciate you both. As always, thank you readers for joining me for a new series set in Birch Creek. I hope you enjoyed reading Jalon and Phoebe's story as much as I enjoyed writing it.

Discussion Questions

1. Jalon has difficulty taking risks and chances. Has God ever led you to take a risk? Was it an easy thing to do, or did you find it difficult?

2. Both Phoebe and Jalon are ashamed of choices they made in the past. How has God helped you deal with pain from your past?

3. Did you agree with Phoebe's choice not to tell Jalon about Malachi? What would you have done if you were in her shoes?

4. Jalon used money and alcohol to assuage his guilt over Adam's accident. How could he have handled things differently after Adam was paralyzed?

5. What challenges do you think Karen and Adam will face if they decide to start dating?

6. Do you think Phoebe was right to stay with her family after her mother was sick? Why or why not?

7. Jalon bonded with Malachi over a toy yo-yo. What was your favorite childhood toy?

8. Who was your favorite character in *Written in Love*, and why?

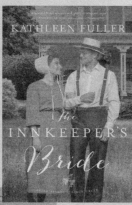

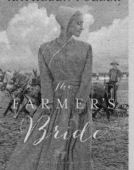

Read more from Kathleen Fuller
in her Amish Letters series!

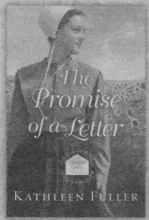

ABOUT THE AUTHOR

With over a million copies sold, Kathleen Fuller is the author of several bestselling novels, including the Hearts of Middlefield novels, the Middlefield Family novels, the Amish of Birch Creek series, and the Amish Letters series as well as a middle-grade Amish series, the Mysteries of Middlefield.

Visit her online at KathleenFuller.com
Instagram: kf_booksandhooks
Facebook: WriterKathleenFuller
Twitter: @TheKatJam